Other books by Fred Patten

Best in Show: Fifteen Years of Outstanding Furry Fiction (2003)
Reprinted as:
Furry! The World's Best Anthropomorphic Fiction! (2006)

Watching Anime, Reading Manga:
25 Years of Essays and Reviews (2004)

Already Among Us; An Anthropomorphic Anthology (2012)

The Ursa Major Awards Anthology:
A Tenth Anniversary Celebration (2012)

What Happens Next: An Anthology of Sequels (2013)

Five Fortunes (2014)

Funny Animals and More: From Anime to Zoomorphics (2014)

Anthropomorphic Aliens: An Interstellar Anthology (2014)

The Furry Future : 19 Possible Prognostications (2015)

An Anthropomorphic Century: Stories from 1909 to 2008 (2015)

Cats and More Cats

Feline Fantasy Fiction

Edited by Fred Patten

Cats and More Cats
Feline Fantasy Fiction

Production copyright FurPlanet Productions © 2016
Cover artwork copyright © 2016 by Donryu

Published by FurPlanet Productions
Dallas, Texas
www.FurPlanet.com

ISBN 978-1-61450-297-5

Printed in the United States of America
First Edition Trade Paperback January 2016

This book is dedicated to

Wanda Gág (1893-1946)

whose children's picture book

Millions of Cats (Coward-McCann, September 9, 1928)

was one of the first picture books that I read.

"Hundreds of cats; Thousands of cats; Millions and billions and trillions of cats..."

Wikipedia says, "*Millions of Cats* is the oldest American picture book still in print." It was a finalist for the Newbery Medal in 1929. Most reviewers credit it as the first American picture book for children; earlier books were English imports.

Table of Contents

Introduction

by Fred Patten

Cats.

More cats.

Still more cats!

Cats have been popular in fantasy fiction for a very long time. "The Cat and the Mice", about a cat trying to trick mice or rats, was a well-known fable by Aesop in about the sixth century B.C. or earlier; or, if he was just retelling it, from well before his time. It shows that farmers and peasants kept domesticated cats to prey on vermin at least 2,500 years ago. But we already knew that this goes back to ancient Egyptian times. "Belling the Cat", despite being included in most popular collections of Aesop's Fables today, only goes back to the Middle Ages—the earliest written version dates from about 1200 A.D.—showing that people tied bells around their cats' necks that long ago. Dick Whittington had his legendary cat; he was a teenager in London around the 1370s. (Lord Mayor of London in 1397.)

What was the earliest fantasy cat? Probably Lewis Carroll's Cheshire Cat, who talked to Alice and could disappear into thin air. Carroll's, or Charles Lutwidge Dodgson's invention of the Cheshire Cat dates from between July 4, 1862 when he told the story that later became *Alice's Adventures in Wonderland* to the little Liddell sisters during a boat outing, to July 4, 1865 when his book with John Tenniel's famous illustrations was first published. When did fantasy cats become popular in literature? The earliest novel that I know of is *The Professor On Paws* by A. B. Cox (W. Collins & Sons, July 1926; vii + 306 pages). The intelligence and speech centers of the dying Prof. Ridgeley's brain are transplanted surgically into his pet cat by his lab assistant, Prof. Cantrell, resulting in a talking cat. A three-way squabble results between the cat, who feels that he/she (it was a female cat) should remain in charge; Prof. Cantrell who wants to use the cat for his own scientific prestige; and Prof. Ridgeley's daughter and son-in-law who want the talking cat to make them a fortune as a music-hall "marvel cat". (All the characters are unlikably selfish, resulting in a very unfunny comedy. You aren't missing a thing by not reading it. Anthony Berkeley Cox later became a popular British author of mystery/detective novels, many of which feature cynical humor.)

During the 1930s and 1940s onward, short-story authors like Stephen Vincent Benét and John Collier made fantasy cats popular. S-f/fantasy writers like Fredric Brown, Henry Kuttner, Fritz Leiber, and James White used them frequently. The earliest reprint anthology of s-f/fantasy stories devoted to cats was *Supernatural Cats: An Anthology* edited by Claire Necker (Doubleday, November 1972; xiv + 439 pages; 45 stories and poems by Edgar Allan Poe, Bram Stoker, H. P. Lovecraft, L. Ron Hubbard, Cleve Cartmill, Cordwainer Smith, and others). *Catfantastic: Nine Lives and Fifteen Tales* edited by Andre Norton & Martin H. Greenberg (DAW Books, July 1989; 320 pages) launched a flood of anthologies of original short stories featuring s-f and fantasy cats that went on for over two decades.

In 2006, I was invited by that year's World Science Fiction Convention, L.A.con IV in Los Angeles, to join a panel titled "Are There Too Many Cats in Science Fiction?", moderated by Jody Lynn Nye and with Nicki Lynch, Lisanne Norman, and Connie Willis as fellow panelists. The program synopsis was: "Cats seem to be everywhere. Science Fiction. Fantasy. There are entire anthologies of cat stories. And not just in our genre. Romances and Mysteries have more than their share of cat tales as well. Are dogs anywhere to be seen? Why is literature so catty?" We decided that, no, it was impossible to have too many cats in s-f.

In the decade since then, cat-themed fantasy and s-f anthologies have slowed down but continue to appear. Yes, there have been a few dog-themed anthologies, as well as one or two horse- and bird-themed anthologies, but they are definitely in the minority. In addition to books of short stories featuring cats, there have been novels starring cats using computers, cat detectives who actually investigate crimes (as opposed to the more prolific "cat cozies" about pet cats who tag along with their human amateur detectives), and more. Practically every urban fantasy starring a modern wizard or witch also gives him or her a sarcastic talking cat familiar.

Among the more interesting are *Sue Slate, Private Eye* by Lee Lynch, starring a tough lesbian feline private investigator in a feminist anthropomorphic cat novel; *The Great Catsby* by Linda Stewart, a pastiche of *The Great Gatsby* by F. Scott Fitzgerald with a feline cast; and the self-evident *Twists of the Tale: An Anthology of Cat Horror* edited by Ellen Datlow. *Watership Down* by Richard Adams features rabbits, but it started the trend of dramatic adult fantasy novels about an animal species with its own language and religion. Cat fantasies soon followed: *Tailchaser's Song* by Tad Williams, *Solo's Journey* by Joy Smith Aiken, *In the Long Dark* by Brian Carter, *Stray* by A. N. Wilson, and others; notably the Warriors series of Young Adult books by "Erin Hunter" (HarperCollins), now up to over four dozen novels.

What really caught my attention was all of the anthologies of original cat-themed fantasy and s-f short stories that began with *Catfantastic* in 1989. There were seemingly dozens of these, each with a dozen or more stories. They added up to… well, a *lot* of stories. Most of these were written for paperback anthologies that stayed in print for a year or two, and then were forgotten. Of course, most of these stories were eminently forgettable—you know Sturgeon's dictum: 90% of *everything* is crud—but what about the few that didn't deserve to be forgotten?

Here is yet another anthology of fantasy and s-f stories featuring cats. The difference is that these are not original for this book. They are selected from other cat anthologies, and a few other places. These are the best of the best! If you read *Cats and More Cats*, you won't need to read any of the other books. (Most of them are long out of print, anyway).

For the record, a title suggested for this anthology was *A Clowder of Cats*, using the little-known collective name for a group of cats. But that has already been used numerous times for nonfiction books about cats; at least by W. S. Scott in 1946, by John Merrett in 1957, by H. C. Barnard in 1978, by Brian Holme in 1985, and by Graham & Sylvana Nown in 1989. There is also a 2004 murder mystery by Warren Freeman with that title. The world doesn't need another book with the same title.

Fantasy cats commonly are either the companions of wizards, or they rescue children from danger. Trouble the cat does both. But his story is more complex than you may guess.

Trouble

by P. M. Griffin

Trouble purred loudly to tell Dory that he was content and to let her know that she was doing well.

She deserved the praise. She also needed it. These humans were sad creatures. They seemed to have so little innate belief in themselves, the most of them, even those of high inner quality and real, strong talent like this kitten of their kind.

Well, that could hardly be counted a fault in his Dory. Those around her had either actively striven to strip her of confidence and stunt her rightful development or else had lacked the courage to do anything very positive in her cause. Her strength of soul had sustained her thus far, keeping her spirit unbroken and her basic fineness intact, but even that would not suffice forever.

The purring stopped. He had realized for some time that this abuse must cease. It was fortunate all this had occurred, disruptive as it was. She had been forced to act at once, without the agonizing and indecision which would have preceded a planned move. That was another area in which humans differed from felines. They did not seem to know their own minds, and even when the correct, the only reasonable, course was plain before them, they had great difficulty in acting upon it if it involved any degree of significant change whatsoever.

Once more, Trouble began to purr, more loudly this time as affection swelled within him. That was not fair to Dory. No kitten left his home readily, however wretched it was. Cat and human alike, all youngsters, needed the care and instruction provided by the adults of their species.

For an instant so fleeting as almost not to have been, he growled. It was little of either that she had enjoyed in her life! Even her body was ignored, and the neglect of such a mind, such a gift, was worse than that which kept her so wan and thin.

The wind whipped up, and the big cat allowed Dory to press him closer to her. He did not require the additional warmth she was striving to give him. It was she who was cold in her threadbare jacket; his thick coat gave no passage at all to the brisk autumn breeze. No matter. She was offering love and care, which were not to be rejected, and, in truth, it felt good to have her arms around him in the midst of all the uncertainty and confusion surrounding their lives at present.

Shouts, the bellowing of many voices sounding together, shattered the early morning stillness.

Trouble yawned and, wriggling free of the girl's hold, stretched himself. Stupid human herd! Did they imagine she would come to them when they summoned and threatened in the same breath?

The girl, however, was terrified. She leaped to her feet. "Oh, Trouble! They're sure to find us! They're on the street, and there's no other way out of this alley!"

"*The fence, foolish one. They is why I brought you to sleep here in the first place.*"

She could not hear him, of course. That would not come for another few months, not until the attaining of her physical womanhood opened her inner ears and voice, but for the moment, that was just as well. Humans were trying, all of them, and he sometimes found it difficult to restrain his sarcasm when dealing with them. She did not need that right now, poor kitten.

Dory looked about her in despair. Three-story buildings towered on either side, and a fifteen-foot brick fence walling off some comfortably fixed person's courtyard was in front of her. Behind was the only exit, and that was blocked by the presence of Jocko and his cronies.

She had to do something! The communal voice of the mob was getting distinctly louder, and those comprising it were indeed searching every possible hiding place for her.

The fence had to be it. Trouble was already sitting upon it, patiently waiting for her.

It was too high for her to reach its top unaided, but there was plenty of debris scattered about including a number of big wooden crates, empty, fortunately, but sturdy enough to support her not terribly crushing weight.

With fear to drive her, she soon had the biggest of them, that in which she had slept, dragged over to the fence and a second, smaller one placed on that. By standing on them and stretching herself to the full, she was able to get her hands over the top.

Voices! Those hunting her would be on her in a moment! She half scrambled, half hauled herself up the rough-set bricks and hoisted herself over the narrow top. Without pausing even to look, she dropped down the other side, first lowering herself on her arms as far as she could to make the actual fall as short as possible.

* * *

Dory sat up. Her hand flew to her mouth in horror. She had escaped one firepot, temporarily at least, but it was only to leap headfirst into a second. She had landed in a garden, in a bed of alternating yellow and white flowering shrubs, and the gardener was standing not twenty feet from her.

Trouble was sitting regally at the edge of the flower bed, watching her in that silent amusement which only a cat can experience or display. Before his charge could either ruin everything by screaming or trying to flee, he got up and casually walked over to the man, rubbed against his leg, and raised his head, demanding to have it scratched.

The human complied, but his amazement at having a scrawny girl-child and a superb black-and-white tomcat suddenly and quite literally drop into his sanctuary did not lessen.

It was a measure of the man that he saw with very nearly the first glance that the child was terrified and, submerging his astonishment, gave her a friendly, natural smile.

"Are you all right?" he asked with unmistakably real concern.

"I-I think so," she stammered.

"Stay where you are, then, and I'll lift you out. You've created enough havoc with your surroundings."

"I am sorry about that, sir," Dory told him earnestly.

"Doubtless. You don't look particularly malicious. Actually, you were quite considerate in your choice of a landing place. Mums are hardy enough to take some abuse. My roses over there would be in a lot sorrier state had you come down on them even though they're done flowering." He smiled again. "So would you. I seem to prefer varieties blessed with strong and plentiful thorns to match the quantity and color of their blooms."

He took one long, carefully placed step into the bed. It brought him close enough to reach his unexpected visitor whom he picked up without apparent effort and carried out onto the walk where he set her on her feet once more.

"There, that's better. Now, I believe an explanation is rather in order."

"Over a meal, donkey tail. She is hungry. So am I."

That was a demand. Trouble knew from Jasmine that this man's inner ears and voice were both fully open. That fact and the tabby's other reports had induced him to bring Dory here in her need. He should have done it sooner, but, of course, he was a very young cat himself…

"In good time. Kindness coming too fast can frighten as much as brutality," the human answered in kind, giving no outward indication that anything had passed between them.

He held out his hand to the girl. "I'm Martin."

She took it gingerly. "Dory." Bending, she brushed her friend's head with her fingers. "This is Trouble."

Martin's gray eyes sparkled as they rested on the cat. "*That, I can well believe.*"

Trouble did not reply. It was beneath his dignity to do so. Besides, it was a merited revenge after his donkey tail remark of a few moments before.

"And is he?" the man asked smoothly.

"Oh, no! No cat could be more wonderful! It's just that he was in a lot of it when we first met."

All the while, Martin had been studying Dory. Her age was hard to judge. She was painfully thin, and she had a very young-looking little face, now remarkably smudged, but he imagined she would be about twelve. She was pale complexioned, too pale at the moment, with stringy light auburn hair which should have been attractive had it been styled at all. Her eyes were truly lovely, blue-green in color, large, and fringed with long, thick lashes the same color as her hair.

Her clothes were unremarkable, well-faded blue trousers, check shirt, also faded, and a jacket that was nearing the end of its useful life. The nearly universal brógs of the region covered what appeared to be quite small feet.

She looked to be what he expected she was, a badly used little apprentice or servant. The like were common enough, too common, even in this none-too-affluent neighborhood. He normally paid small heed to any of them, but this one he did know, if only by sight.

"I've seen you before," he remarked. "You're always talking to Jasmine when she's out in the foregarden." As he spoke, he pointed to a delicately boned tabby who had glided into the yard and was sniffing curiously and without fear at Trouble, who was not slow to return her attentions.

"Whenever I see her. She's such a friendly little thing.—I think she's prettier than any flower there!"

The girl stopped herself, embarrassed.

Martin sighed. She had probably learned early in her life not to reveal too much enthusiasm for anything.

"It's good to meet another full-blown cat lover," he said casually, then inclined his head toward the big house forming the opposite boundary of the well-planted courtyard. "Why don't we go inside? It's just about time for breakfast. You can tell me about yourselves while we're attending to that." There was no mistaking her look of interest. Trouble was right. The child was hungry. "Good. I'll make a quick run in to arrange everything and then come back to show you the way."

He would arrange things, all right, Trouble thought. A lot of people would be astonished at the means by which the promised meal was produced, but he did not object. Cats are practical beings, not narrow-minded fools. The food would be good to taste, wholesome, and quite real. What more could one ask? *"Excellent thought. Do not take too long."*

"I won't, Sir Trouble. As my little lady has probably already told you, I don't mistreat my guests."

* * *

As promised, Martin returned quickly, and soon all four of them, humans and felines alike were sitting comfortably in a small, sunlit eating room.

There was no talk during the meal. Dory's attention was fully centered on her plate. Her host watched in good-natured amazement at the speed with which she put its contents away. She might not have eaten for a month the way she was going at it.

"A day! That is long enough."

"Too long. Someone should have a bit of a talk with her master."

"More than that. You will hear."

The girl handled her cutlery well for all her eagerness, and when she at last finished eating, she set the ware aside in the correct manner and politely thanked him.

Trouble, too, did full justice to his meal. After clearing his well-filled dish, he carefully washed himself and rubbed against Martin's leg, purring loudly. Manners were not demeaning, and good service such as this deserved a reward.

"Well, Dory," the man said as he settled back in his chair, "tell me about yourself."

"What would you like to know, sir?"

"Everything. Where you live would be a good start, I suppose."

"I don't live anywhere now," she responded frankly. "I used to stay at Jocko the Farrier's three squares north of here. Imelde, his wife, is my mother's cousin. That makes her mine, too, I suppose."

"Your parents?"

"They died when I was three. Quick plague. It missed me somehow."

"And that was the last kindness you knew," he muttered.

"I don't know," she replied seriously. "Imelde made a fuss over Trouble and claimed she loved him even though she really didn't, just so I could keep him. That was a kindness, wasn't it?"

"It was," he agreed slowly.

"Also," Dory added, trying to be fair—and not wanting to entirely blacken her kin before this stranger, "I may not be fat, but I get enough to eat that I'm never sick. And I've always had a good dress for church even though I do have to work like this."

Work hard, he thought, to judge by the state of her hands. That was not right for a child

Trouble sighed. These humans! They seemed to have no instinct whatsoever for digging out a story properly. Now Martin was going to ask why she left, and by the time she answered and went back to explain how the situation had come about in the first place, they would have spent triple the time needed to tell a simple tale.

"*Ask how she met me,* he instructed patiently. *That is the beginning of it.*"

"*Very well, Sir Trouble. Thank you for the hint.*"—"At least, you were able to bring Trouble away with you when you did go," he remarked. "When did you two get together?"

"About a year ago." She smiled again and began to caress the cat. "He's the best thing that's ever happened to me."

Her expression clouded. "There's a well in back of Jocko's house. He won't cover it even though there are some big families in our square. Says it's up to the parents to watch their brats, and he doesn't want any of them on his place anyway. He doesn't worry about garbage falling in since it's my job to fish it out. It was my job, that is. He'll have to do it himself now."

"A considerate neighbor as well as kindly kin, I see," he muttered dryly. "Your mother's cousin showed poor taste in her choice of a husband, girl, or her father chose badly for her. But please continue. Trouble managed to get into the well?"

She nodded. "He did. I don't know where he came from, since he was too tiny to have been away from his mother for long, but there are a lot of dogs around. One of them must've scared him into bolting down there.

"Anyway, I was going for water when I heard him crying. I couldn't see anything at first when I looked in, but then I spotted the white stripe on his nose. He was clinging to this ledge that goes most of the way around the well down almost as far as the water. It used to snag the bucket on me if I wasn't careful.

"I couldn't think of any other way to get him up, so I took the bucket off and tied the rope around myself."

Martin frowned. "You lowered yourself down that hole?"

"*She hardly flew!—Do you doubt that my kitten has spirit?*"

"*Your kitten should have had help,*" he said sharply. "*That was an adult's job.*"

Dory's eyes darkened. She took his seeming silence for disapproval, and her chin lifted. "What else could I have done? I couldn't very well have left him down there."

"No, not and remained human yourself. I was just wishing someone like me had been there to give you a bit of a hand, that's all."

"Oh, I mostly have to do everything myself. I'm used to that."

Martin sighed. "I know. You're to be admired, but I can't say I like the idea all the same."

Dory saw the speculative look her host was bending on her, and her eyes fell. She had done it again, she thought miserably, but she really could not help that she sometimes sounded more forty than twelve as Imelde put it, and like a schooled forty at that. She certainly could not help her thoughts. She had learned to read before that accursed plague had taken her parents, and she had continued to read, everything she could lay her hands on that was worth the effort, thereby rendering her life at least bearable. Unfortunately, she had somehow modeled her speech more after those formal writings than after the example of those around her. Jocko hated that—how he hated it!—and his friends hated it, and she had learned to say very little around any of them, but her tale was long, and already, even before it had rightly begun, she had given herself away.

The hard, sick knot of fear and unhappiness loosened in her stomach when she raised her eyes again. Martin was a different man entirely. She saw no resentment, no rejection, in him, only mild surprise, guarded interest, and, she thought, excitement.

The man's pulse had quickened, though reason insisted that he check his hope for the moment. A highly intelligent, sensitive child like this could be expected to lose her loneliness in books, assuming she possessed the basic skill to read them, and it certainly was not unknown for some in that situation to develop an astonishingly mature manner of thought and the vocabulary to express it. Dory could be no more than an example of that.

It was also just possible that she was many times more. Verbal and mental precocity almost inevitably accompanied strong talent, and he thrilled with anticipation at the thought of watching and helping such a gift develop again. It had been so long since he had last been privileged to share in that blossoming.

For a moment, he put that dream out of his thoughts. This storm-tossed pebble might indeed be a true diamond, but they did not have the leisure to explore that possibility now. Besides, he believed she had detected his awareness and was frightened, a natural enough reaction in the face of the upbringing she had received. Bullies like this Jocko the Farrier rarely cared for any sign of superiority in the weak little things they terrorized.

He smiled encouragingly. "Go on, Child. I want to hear the rest of this tale. Did you have any problem getting him out?"

"Not from Trouble. He let me pick him up and just snuggled close to me, like I was the only safety in all the world."

Anger flashed suddenly into her eyes, making her appear both older and stronger. "That was when the rope dropped. Jocko was above and had loosed it. He shouted that he'd lower another but that he wasn't going to lift two loads and that I'd have to leave the cat behind."

"He what?" Martin hissed.

Both the girl and Trouble looked swiftly at him, startled by the cold, controlled fury in this seemingly mild man.

"It was a false threat," she told him quickly, not wanting to provoke an outburst of anger, even one not directed at her. She was trying to escape such storms. "It's a busy square like I said and someone would've hauled us out in no time. Jocko knew that, too, and anyway, he didn't want me dead. I did too much work for him. He just thought I'd panic and not figure all that out."

Her hands clenched. "I wasn't scared. I was furious. I'd never been angry like that before in my whole life. He actually tried to make me leave that poor, terrified, trusting little creature to die alone and cold and wet, to make me choose to do it."

She gripped herself before she could either fly into a rage herself or burst into tears. "I don't know what came over me, except that I was so mad and couldn't do anything else, but I glared at the rope, which was still sort of floating in the water below us, and I shouted at it to go back up, tie itself again, and pull us out." She swallowed hard. "It did. It did just that."

The man drew a long, sharp breath. He glanced at the cat, who was purring softly, seemingly unmoved by his human's emotion, then his eyes returned to the girl.

"Had anything like that ever happened to you before?"

"No, of course not! I didn't even know such things were possible except in books."

"*Trouble, was it you?*"

"*It was not,*" the cat replied half contemptuously. "*It was the kitten. Listen to her.*"

"A great many things stranger than that are possible, child," he said softly. "What was Jocko's reaction?"

"Oh, believe that he was mad, but that came later. Right then, he was raw scared that someone might have seen what had happened."

"Did anyone?"

She shook her head.

"Not as far as I know. He was lucky there. He'd have been in big trouble if they had. He's in the Antimagic League, you see. President of the local cell, in fact—"

"That bunch! Well, from the sound of it, he fits right in with the rest of them."

"They're hard cases, the most of them," she agreed. "Anyway, he dragged me into the house and started whaling me. I think he'd have half killed me, but Imelde told him to let me be, that I'd had a fright enough and that I'd brought her the kitten, which she was going to keep." Her voice softened. "She'd seen, from the way I had been holding him, I suppose, that I loved him. She was sorry for him, too. She said later that he and I were both orphans and should stick together, but we'd have to keep him out of Jocko's way, which we did between us.

"After that, things sort of went back to normal, except that Jocko started asking me questions. I was always good at guessing things like what the weather would be or that someone would be coming to the house and maybe even why. Now Jocko wanted to know who'd win a race or fight or something like that, and he'd bet on the name I'd pick. Never much, mind you – I'd often be wrong – but there'd be peace around the house when he did win. I'd get a knock when he lost, of course, but not too hard as such go. He did know I couldn't control that part of it."

She rubbed her ear, and her eyes brightened momentarily. "He might even have done me some good. I don't make nearly as many mistakes now as I did at first."

"The practice did you the good. Knocks do nothing, or they hinder. Talent can't be forced by abuse."

"Talent? It's not much of one, sir."

He smiled. "Big things often start out small." Martin's expression darkened again. "You didn't have ideal living conditions, but it was nothing worse than you'd always known. What caused the break?"

"Imelde, I guess, though she didn't mean to," the girl answered promptly. "You see, she's the one with the money. Her father thought he had done well in binding her to a tradesman, but when he saw what he'd really gotten for a son-in-law, fair enough to him, he moved to protect her since she didn't want to leave Jocko."

"Some people don't, no matter how bad their partners are," he explained in response to the lack of comprehension in her tone. "What did he do for her?"

"He set up something called a trust. She gets money out of it every three months, but no one can touch the whole lot as long as she's alive. Jocko's the laziest man you could meet, sir. He's a farrier like I said, but he'd much rather sit in the local and talk bull with his friends than work at it. That's why she's always been able to keep some control over what goes on in the house provided she doesn't try to push him too far. He knows full well that she can manage very nicely without him and that he'd lose a comfortable lifeway if she upped and left.

"He's always had his fancy ladies, though," she continued contemptuously, "either stupid little things he can brag to until they see through him or else those who put up with him for pay, but his latest's something different. She's young and pretty and too smart not to know she could do a lot better than Jocko. He knows that as well, and he does want to hold onto her. He's not so young anymore, and he's not going to attract anyone like her again. Sure, he never could before.

"Well, Imelde's no fool, either. She saw what was going on – the whole square did – and she belted off to her father. Imelde told him her story and said that she didn't want to be worth more dead than alive to anyone. By the time she got back two days later, she had it arranged that the money would all go back to her father if she died without a babe, as seems likely now, or be handled by him or her older brother if she went after having a child. Jocko'd have no part of it at all without her."

She shivered. "I thought he'd gone stark mad when he heard. That's how bad his rage was. He shouted and cursed and slammed his fist against the wall so hard that I hoped he had busted his knuckles, but Imelde didn't blanch or blink. I've never seen her face him better. She just let him rave on, always keeping out of reach, of course. When he'd tired himself out with yelling, before he could start with his fists, she calmly told him that they could either go on as in the past, or she could return to her father. The choice was his. If he kept on cheating, that was her answer right there. She was still packed and would just turn around and leave again, and this time, she would not be coming back." Dory grinned. "He just shut his mouth like it was a trap, and out he went. That was the night before last."

She shuddered, and her whole body tensed as if in anticipation of a death blow.

Trouble left off grooming Jasmine and leaped onto the girl's lap. He licked her hand and looked up into her face. As he had known she would, she smiled tremulously at the rasping caress and almost unconsciously began stroking him.

"He didn't come back until morning," she continued in a small voice. "He was drunk. Jocko always gets mean when he drinks, and this was about the worst he ever was.

"I spotted him coming in, and you can lay money down that I stayed up in the attic where I sleep until I thought he'd either gone to bed or dropped off in the kitchen." Her hand trembled on the black fur. "I guessed wrong. He was waiting for me."

Jasmine picked up her horror and responded with a soft, inquisitive meow, but the male cat only gave a loud, rumbling purr.

"*Go on, Kitten,*" he encouraged, although she could not hear him. "*You are doing well.*"

Martin, too, read her terror. He reached over and covered her bony hand with his. His grasp was firm, reassuring. Only Trouble, whose back the long fingers also touched, was aware of the strength in them, a power surprising in a scholar who spent his life amongst books, as this human represented himself to be. That could even be true – his mind was that of a seeker – but it was obvious he respected his body as well and knew enough to keep it sound.

"It's all right, Little One," the man said gently. "Take your time and tell it in your own way."

He felt sick inside. Was this Jocko the Farrier monster enough to brutalize her sexually as well as with his hands?

"*No. Soon, perhaps, but not yet.*"

His head bowed in relief. "*Praise the Most High for that.*"

Dory had used the brief silence to collect her thoughts. "He wanted revenge, but he's a coward. He didn't dare take it directly. He thought Imelde loved Trouble, and he'd often heard her say how beautiful and dignified he is, so he ordered me to-to put a pair of donkey's ears on him. I told him I couldn't, that I didn't know what had happened with the rope and that I didn't know how to do such things, but he wouldn't listen. He said that if I refused, he'd beat me until I did do it or until I was a pulp, and he meant it, sir. He meant every word of it."

"Imelde—"

She shook her head. "She knows better than to come near Jocko when he's drunk. So does everyone else, and it's well known that he'd never done permanent hurt before. By the time anyone'd realized this was different and could interfere, it would've been too late for me."

"One thing I don't understand. If he believed you could do that to Trouble, where did he get the nerve to tangle with you himself? You've said the man's a coward."

"I don't know. Maybe he was too potted to think of it."

Trouble growled low in his throat and yawned. Humans! Who cared what moved the beast, anyway?

"Bullies never think that what they dish out can happen to them."

"That's just as well in this case. He'd have killed her after that rope business if he felt anyway threatened."

Once more, he squeezed the girl's hand. "No matter now. What did you do? Run or stall?"

"I couldn't do much of either. I didn't have time. The door was shut, and he was between me and the window, so escape was out unless I could get him to move, or forget how fast I could run. I planned to say I'd try and then start jumping around and saying strange things and maybe distracting him enough for me to be able to make a dash for the window, but straight away I knew it wouldn't work. Trouble was still somewhere inside, you see, and I couldn't leave him. Jocko'd be sure to kill him outright or do something even worse if I did.

"I was scared, shaking scared, but I was angry, too, when I thought of him. – Look at Trouble, sir. He's a prince, more a prince than any human man wearing a crown, and he'd never done Jocko or anyone else harm. All he did was love me and trust me, and I was supposed to do something like that to him in return!"

"He'd still have been a prince, Dory," Martin told her. "Nothing can take that from him."

"I know, but I wasn't going to hurt him. I wouldn't even pretend to agree to hurt him. I-I just hoped it wouldn't hurt for too long, that I'd pass out or something."

Tears sprang to her eyes, but she blinked them back. Her voice changed as confusion melded with her former fear and anger.

"All of a sudden, I started thinking about those ears, big, hairy, floppy ears. I could really see them there in my mind. I could almost reach out and scratch them. The next thing I knew—"

She began to sob for a fact, and this time, she was powerless to check herself.

Even before the cat could do anything, Martin had her in his arms. "Easy, Child. Take it easy, Dory. It was only an illusion. Talent can't be forced to work against the real will of its wielder. Look at Trouble. He's fine, and he certainly puts no blame on you."

The tomcat's green eyes fixed on him. *"The ears were real. She did not set them on me."*

Martin's lips parted. They curved into the beginnings of a smile.

He released the girl. "Dory, just where did you put those ears?" he asked, already knowing what she would say but waiting with delicious pleasure to hear her confirm it.

"On-on Jocko," she whispered.

The man laughed. He laughed until he fell back in his chair and his cheeks were wet with tears. When he finally regained control over himself again, he caught her hand and kissed it in delight. "Well done, Little Sorceress! That was the finest and most fitting bit of magic I've heard about in a long, long time!"

"So you will help her?"

A frown touched the human's thoughts. *"I'd have helped her without this. You knew that, or you wouldn't have brought her here."*

"Calm down! She is laughing. Do not spoil it."

Martin's merriment was contagious, and Dory did laugh as memory of that moment of realization returned to her.

"They aren't proper donkey ears. They're floppy, just like I pictured them." She giggled. "They bent down over his eyes. You should've seen his face when he saw them hanging there. He gave them a tug, then another, real hard one.—What a yowl he let out! He sure as anything knew they were real after that!"

Her host shared her laughter, but then they both sobered.

"That was when you made your break?" he asked.

"Seconds later. Trouble appeared at that point. It was like he was watching the whole thing and knew just when to show up. He jumped onto Jocko's back and really gave him reason to scream. He caught hold of those ears and went to work on them with his claws. Trouble kept at it, whatever Jocko did to try to catch hold of him.— Even sober, he's not as good as my cat. Drunk, and with Trouble on his shoulders, he had no chance at all!

"Only when I made it through the window did Trouble let go. He sprang out after me, and the two of us took to our heels.

"We knew we'd be done if we went back, so we just kept going." She sighed. "I was lucky I'd been going out for water, or I wouldn't even have this jacket."

"You didn't get far."

"I-I needed time to think, to figure out somewhere to go, or even just a direction, and I was hoping to pick up a little food after the market today. There're usually a lot of leavings when the farmers go home if one's not too fussy.

"I came this far to put some distance between me and my old haunts, figuring Jocko'd probably know those and search them out after he bound up his ears. He had to do that first; they were dropping blood all over the place.

"It took time to get here. Everyone knows us, and we didn't want to be seen, so we had to sneak from spot to spot. Then it was threatening to rain, and I was tired. I wanted to find a place to hole up. Trouble led me to your alley. There was this nice, dry box just big enough for both of us, and we spent the night in it.—See, not a drop touched us, though it poured the whole time."

She bit her lip. "Everything was fine, apart from being hungry, until we heard the mob a little while ago and knew we were trapped.

We had no choice then but to go over the fence.—We wouldn't have done it otherwise, sir."

"Forget that, Child. It was fate and the will of the Most High that sent you to me." And Trouble's plotting, he added mentally, to the cat's satisfaction. When credit or partial credit was due him, Trouble liked, and expected, to receive it.

The girl's fingers twisted together. "I thought we had the time. I truly didn't believe he'd call in the League, not—" Her voice trailed off.

"He has no choice but to hunt you down and try to force you to undo your magic. Failing that, he'll at least want the satisfaction of killing you."

"He'll kill me anyway now," she said dully.

"Probably. If he takes you.—Cheer up, Little Sorceress. That's not going to happen, and you've had some payment for all he's put you through. He'll be a laughingstock from now on, whether he regains his old form or not."

"That'll just make it the worse for us," she said glumly.

Dory took a deep breath. This was the hardest thing she had ever been forced to do, but she could not fail Trouble.

"You like cats, sir. Please keep Trouble with you. I-I'll be happy just knowing he's safe and well fed."

Martin stared at her. Most High, but she had courage! That tomcat was her only friend, the only one who had loved her since the day her parents had died, and yet she was willing to part with him in order to spare him the perils and hardships she knew she faced. But, then, her entire tale was testimony to that strength.

"Of course the kitten has courage."

The man looked at him. A prince, Dory had called him, and a prince he was, a fitting companion for such a queen.

"Do not worry on that score, Dory," he said with frigid certainty. "No one in that mob will do a thing to any of us or to my property that I do not choose to permit."

Her head cocked to one side. "There are so many of them. How—"

Martin raised his hand to silence her. "How old do you think I am?" he asked.

She shook her head. She was still young enough that all adults seemed old to her, but she knew enough and was sensitive enough of others' feelings not to say that.

Trouble, too, looked at him curiously. His body's appearance and smell were that of a man in his prime years, but his inner scent did not reflect that, and Jasmine could give him no information or explanation. She was a young cat herself, only a little older than him, and she was timid by nature. She had not learned as much as she might about her companion, as much as he, Trouble, would assuredly have uncovered.

"I don't know, sir," Dory responded.

"I was already old, ancient even, when the Antimagic League was first formed."

She looked at him as if he were mad. "That was over five hundred years ago!"

"There are some benefits in possessing talent and knowing how to use it," he replied mildly, his gray eyes turning almost silver with amusement.

"Then you are—"

"A sorcerer? Oh yes. I'm head of our Great Circle, as a matter of fact. Have been since my youth."

"So the League didn't get you all like they claim," she mused. "I'm so glad!" She had little sympathy with any of the organization's aims considering what she knew of its members.

Martin laughed without humor. "Those curs couldn't get their great-grandmothers if the old ladies set their backs against them! They eliminated a lot of charlatans, true, and they made life pretty miserable for minor, unschooled talents until we quietly stepped in and took the pressure off them, but face down a sorcerer of the first water? Hardly! Look what happened when one of them clashed with you, and you've had no training at all.

"We eliminated our own evil members. The League did accomplish that much good. It forced us to police ourselves. Before that, we were lax, lazy and cowardly both, I suppose. An adept can always recognize a fellow sorcerer who walks the dark path, and so we were never threatened. As a result, we contented ourselves with keeping an eye on those of our number who did turn sour, making sure none of them made a grab for too much control over the untalented and did not go too far in other ways, but that was all. The formation of the League pushed us into action. It was a vigilante organization, and we dearly wanted to keep it that, to remove its cause before it could have real laws pushed through against us. We reasoned, rightly as it turned out, that if we did, the movement would soon stagnate into a social organization for bully boys. We succeeded so well that most of its members don't even believe that magic really exists now." He smiled faintly. "Except your friend Jocko, of course."

He was silent a moment as his thoughts drifted back through time. "It was not an easy fight we waged. A number of us died, and some of us still bear scars. Painful scars—"

The sorcerer recalled himself to the present. "That's neither here nor there at the moment."

Dory shook her head. "I'm glad you all survived." She paused. "There must be hundreds, thousands, of you if you all live for centuries."

"On the contrary. We are very few. Major talent is rare, and many a century passes without giving us even a single recruit.

"Of those who are born with the gift, some fall victim to accident or illness or violence, and there are always the few who turn to the dark and so are lost to us."

The gray eyes met hers. "That's why you're so precious, Dory, and also so dangerous."

She stared at him a moment, uncomprehending, then her eyes widened. "You think *I* have talent?" she gasped half in protest.

"I believe you are a major talent, possibly one of the strongest I have ever encountered," he replied seriously.

"And I'm...dangerous?"

He nodded. "Yes, unfortunately. Your power is just stirring in you now. It will awaken fully when your body settles down to assume its biological adult role. You will not be able to suppress its manifestations entirely unless you are properly trained to handle it, and the outcome of uncontrolled displays may not always be beneficial to yourself or those around you. What has happened already is proof enough of that."

"Where can I get that training?" she demanded. "Who can teach such things? I can't stay here with you, even if you'd want me. I'm too well known in this area. Someone'd be sure to see me, and Jocko'd get me thrown in jail or something, and maybe you with me."

He leaned forward. "I'd be proud to have such an apprentice, and I can protect you so that no one would recognize you, but the price of working with me would be very high. I'll fully understand if you choose not to pay it and will arrange to send you to another very nearly as knowledgeable as I who will be equally delighted to have both you and Trouble."

Dory stiffened. Price? Imelde had warned her that some men... And there were the old stories, too, those about the payment anyone trafficking in sorcery was supposed to have to pay.

Martin read both thoughts easily enough without recourse to any special abilities of his calling. "Your virtue's safe enough, girl. I like women as well as any man, but they do have to be adults and neither victims nor purchases. Your soul's equally secure. That can be won or lost only by your own choices, not by a mere commercial transaction."

"What, then?" she asked, puzzled. Surely he realized she had no fortune, nothing valuable to give. If not, she did not want him for a teacher anyway!

"*Patience, Kitten,*" Trouble thought wearily. Why must her species always leap to ridiculous conclusions, and in matters of such importance, too? It would be a tragedy if she reared up and ruined her chances with the sorcerer before they had even begun to work together.

Martin sighed. "Your youth, Little One. What's left of your childhood and your adolescence. No one will take a grown woman for a twelve-year-old girl."

Dory started to ask if he could really do that but bit the question back in time. If he was what he said and proposed this, then he could accomplish it.

"My childhood hasn't been very happy," she said after several minutes' deep thought.

"No, but the rest would be. Consider this carefully. I would teach you well and treat you well, but the step's irrevocable once taken. You will appreciate the loss as an adult, Dory, and regret it. That's why I'm not pressuring you now, much as I want to have you with me."

"What about Trouble?" she asked slowly after a moment. "You can't make him old, too."

"No. He'll have to spend the next two or three years as an all black cat. After that, we'll be moving anyway. Those of us who don't age must change our base periodically to avoid arousing comment. Once we do, it'll be safe for him to resume his natural coat again. I, for one, will welcome that. He's beautifully marked.—Do you agree to that course, Trouble?" he concluded in both verbal and inner speech.

The cat slowly inclined his head. "I prefer my true coloring, but this is necessary."

Dory's eyes widened. "It's like he really understood and answered you!"

"For shame, Child! These animals comprehend a great deal. You'll soon realize how much, whether you accept my offer or not."

His offer. Her mouth felt dry. She had to give Martin his answer and give it soon. As matters now stood, she was a danger to all of them. One way or another, she had to escape her enemies and learn how to manage this unwanted but apparently unavoidable power of hers.

Indecision tore her. Stay, and she must trust herself to this stranger's magic. Flee… She would have to trust him still, him and some other as well, maybe someone who would use her as hard as Jocko had or harder.

The girl looked frantically to Trouble, but the cat sat motionless and unblinking on her lap, more warm statue than living being for all the response he gave her. Never had he been so cold to her need…

"He won't tell you what to do," the sorcerer said gently. "He can't. He knows that only you can make a decision this important to you."

There was no contradiction or comment from the cat, just understanding, respect, and the hope that his comrade would choose well.

"*Thank you, friend,*" Martin whispered.

Dory's head raised. Both courses seemed equal in their potential for good and for ill. Her heart and instinct had to be the deciding factors.

"I've never had a chance at real schooling," she said "If I'm going to start now, it might as well be with the best. That seems to be you."

"Are you certain, Child?" he asked with a strangely sharp pang of regret. He would not be calling her that again.

"I am," she responded with surprisingly mature firmness. Now that her decision was made, she found she had no qualm about standing by it.

Trouble gave a half purr, half meow of delight. He rasped his tongue once along her cheek to emphasize his happiness and approval.

She held him close to her. "I'm not wrong about this. Trouble wants it, too, and he likes you. That's all I need to tell me it's right, really right, for all of us."

Wikipedia says that humanity domesticated the cat 9,500 years ago, and that the first ship's cats are almost that old. Cats were taken aboard boats for the same reason they were domesticated in the first place—to hunt and kill the mice, rats, and other vermin that have followed men to eat their food. Over the centuries the ship's cat has become a symbol of good luck. Don't go to sea without one, or you'll suffer bad luck.

In the pens of fantasy writers, the ship's cat has become more than just a good luck charm. The opening of World War II brought traumatic losses to the Royal Navy from the guns of the German battleship Bismarck. Clare Bell presents Bomber, the cat mascot of one of the most famous ships that the Bismarck sunk. He wants vengeance...

Bomber and the *Bismarck*

by Clare Bell

Bomber and Feathers, all met on May 23, 1941 aboard the British aircraft carrier H.M.S. *Ark Royal*. The meeting didn't change Bomber much, for he was a cat. It left a more indelible impression on Lieutenant "Feathers" Geoffrey-Faucett.

H.M.S. *Ark Royal* was part of Force H, a fleet of battleships and destroyers sent out from Gibraltar to protect British convoys in the Atlantic. One of the newer British aircraft carriers, she was equipped with an aircraft control tower to monitor the takeoffs and landings of the antiquated Fairey Swordfish torpedo-biplanes aboard her. If she'd been a carrier of the old "flat-iron" design, her decks all runway and all operations controlled from below, no one would have ever spotted the half-drowned animal struggling in the seas alongside.

Geoffrey-Faucett was sharing a cup of tea and a rare idle minute up in the tower with the air controller while the "airedales" in the deck crew brought his Swordfish biplane up from below decks on the lift. He had straight sandy hair and aristocratic features except for a slightly snub nose. He also had a reputation for sending his torpedoes into the aft end of a target ship, "right up the bastard's tailfeathers," as he often put it. That led to the nickname of "Tailfeathers," which was quickly shortened to "Feathers."

Jack Shepherd, the air controller, put his cup down so hard that spoon and saucer clattered. He pointed through the tower window to the heaving swell just off the starboard quarter and said, "What the devil is that?" Shepherd took his field glasses, squinted through once, scratched his black curly hair and squinted again. "Eyes must be playing me false. Here, you have a look." He handed the field glasses to the pilot.

Feathers focused the binoculars, scanning the whitecaps that splashed along *Ark Royal's* sides as she kept her station several hundred miles off the Spanish coast. He frowned. Was that dark spot just a bit of flotsam caught in the chop? It moved in a funny way. And did he see the outline of a head and ears and, God bless, even the end of a tail sticking up from the gray-green Atlantic?

"It's a cat. It really is a cat," he said, slinging the field glasses back to Shepherd. "Must have fallen off some passenger transport. Look, see if you can get the helm to hold off on the upwind run."

"What are you up to now, Feathers?" Shepherd glanced down at a Swordfish biplane rising up through the lift hatch. "The airedales will have your plane ready."

"Bugger the old Stringbag," Feathers threw back over his shoulder as he clattered down the iron spiral of steps. "She'll keep. I'm going to fish that cat out. Can't let the thing drown."

He drew his sheepskin jacket collar tight about his neck as he butted his way into the wind sweeping across the flight deck. The *Ark Royal* was giving short hard bounces in the chop, which made it hard for the pilot to keep his footing. Ignoring the waves of the flight deck crew who were prepping his aircraft, Feathers ran to the bow, threw open a locker, grabbed a life ring and hurled it out in the direction where he had last seen the cat. Behind him he heard footsteps, the unmistakable gimpyleg gait of Patterson, his gunner.

"Who's gone in the drink?" the gunner asked in a voice made raspy from scotch and tobacco. "I didn't hear no man overboard alarm."

"Nobody. It's a cat." Feathers frowned, shading his eyes against the hazy sun. "Can you spot him, Pat?"

"Go on, you're daft, Feathers. The old man will have your nuts for a necktie if you hold up the reconnaissance flight."

Geoffrey-Faucett scanned the seas, feeling a bit foolish. All this fuss about an animal, especially during wartime, when human lives were being lost. And had he really seen a cat?

The white ring bobbed up and down in the troughs. The dark spot began to move toward the ring. Its progress was terribly slow, but Feathers felt a sudden surge of unmilitary delight. The animal was still alive, a miracle in the freezing North Atlantic. It fought its way to the ring and Feathers saw it scramble on.

Carefully he drew in the line attached to the ring, fearful that the rough seas might sweep the cat away before he got it aboard. But at last the ring hung from its line over the *Ark Royal's* bow rail. On the life ring, spreadeagled with its claws driven deep into the white-painted cork, was the castaway.

Feathers reached down with both hands, grabbed the outside of the ring, and brought it aboard. Yellow-gold eyes the color of sovereigns glared at Feathers as he tried to pry the cat's paws from the ring. The brine-drenched animal held on tenaciously, growling deep in its throat.

"Grateful one, he is," said Patterson. "Take your face off if you're not careful."

"You take a swipe at me and I'll chuck you back," said Feathers to the cat. With a clasp knife from his pocket, he cut the line from the life ring, then carried the ring like a platter with the cat sprawled out across the top.

"What are you going to do with him?" Patterson asked, trotting after.

"Give him to old Shepherd in the tower. He won't have anything to do once the squadron takes off. I'll let him coax our friend here off the life ring and nurse him with some tea and biscuits."

The crackle of the *Ark Royal's* public address system sounded on the flight deck, breaking through the shouts of the airedales and the sound of Swordfish engines warming up. "Attention, air and deck crews. All scheduled air operations are canceled. Repeat, all scheduled air operations are canceled on orders from the War Office. Stand by for further announcements."

As the system shut off with a sharp crack, Airedales and pilots alike stared at each other, dumbfounded.

"Operations canceled?" squeaked Patterson incredulously. "What's happened? The bloody war's over?"

"Might be worse." Matthews, a grubby airedale with carroty hair and freckles came up beside the pilot and gunner. "The Nazis might have invaded. U-boats in the Thames and the swastika flying from the House of Parliament, I shouldn't doubt."

"Don't think so," said Feathers. "More likely this has something to do with that new German battleship we've been hearing about over the wireless."

"The one named after that Prussian. Otto von something-or-other."

"*Bismarck*," Patterson supplied in his smoky rasp. "Ah, she's no threat. Remember, lads. We've got the *Hood*."

A cluster of men had come up behind Feathers for a look at the cat. They all broke into shouts when they heard the flagship's name. "The *Hood*, the *Hood*, the mighty *Hood*. Three cheers for the *Hood*!"

Fists lifted in the air and voices bellowed out. Feathers, still encumbered with the life ring and its occupant, couldn't lift his hand, but he shouted along with the rest. For twenty years the battleship H.M.S. *Hood* had been the staunch symbol of British sea power. With her 42,000-ton displacement and her fifteen-inch guns, she was the most powerful battleship in the world.

The cheering faded as the *Ark Royal's* loudspeaker crackled to life again. "This is the Captain speaking. The War Office and the Prime Minister have requested that the following information be announced to all members of the British Armed forces. This morning, at six hundred hours, the H.M.S. *Hood* blew up and sank during an engagement off the coast of Iceland with the enemy battleship *Bismarck* and the heavy cruiser, *Prinz Eugen*. Three survivors were taken aboard H.M.S. *Repulse*. Their names are..."

Feathers stood, stunned. The *Hood* gone? Bang, just like that? And three survivors out of how many? The *Hood* had carried a crew of more than fourteen hundred. He felt a burning lump in his throat. Three survivors out of fourteen hundred! And he had been messing about with a bloody cat after the pride of the British Empire had gone down beneath the waves.

The "bloody cat" gave a sharp meow. Feathers meant to answer its imperious glare with an indignant one of his own, but he noticed something about the animal's neck. It was a brown leather collar with a buckle and bronze nameplate. As Feathers turned the collar, letters in a flourished engraved script came into view. They read, "H.M.S. *Hood.*"

At the sight, the pilot felt his face flush, then pale. He stared at the half-drowned shivering cat, then at the collar. The words didn't change, as he half-expected them to.

"It can't be," he muttered.

In principle there was no reason why the animal couldn't have been the *Hood*'s ship's cat. Many British vessels had cats aboard, whether officially or otherwise. The stores of food aboard were too tempting to the rats that infested the most well-run ships. Therefore a cat, or perhaps a pair were an essential part of a warship's crew.

Feathers was still baffled. According to the announcement the *Hood* had gone down in the Denmark Strait, between Iceland and Greenland. The *Ark Royal* was, at this moment, only a few hundred miles off the coast of Spain.

How could this cat have gotten here, more than three thousand miles from the *Hood*'s last known position. No. This had to have another explanation. Perhaps the cat had been on another ship, being brought to or from the *Hood*. Maybe it had fallen ill or grown too old and had to be retired. The *Hood*'s crew might have let it keep the collar and nameplate as an honor for years of service.

Feathers admitted his reasoning was pretty flimsy, but it was the only explanation that made sense.

And then be noticed something else about the cat. In the light gray fur on its left haunch, the pilot saw a sooty mark. When Feathers touched it, the cat flinched and stiffened. Even though the fur was soaked, the hairs looked black and brittle. Burned. And in the cat's fur was the lingering smell of cordite.

Suddenly an image came into his mind. A small four-footed figure darting across the tilting deckplates while guns roared and fire licked out from the superstructure of a doomed battleship.

The *Hood* had blown up. A tower of fire amidships. Fire and smoke and scorched fur. And the collar.

"Well, some cook could have thrown a hot kettle at you in the galley," muttered Feathers, looking down at the cat, but suddenly all his contrived explanations fell apart.

As he backed through the hatchway with cat and ring still held out in front of him like a tea tray, Feathers Geoffrey-Faucett could not help wondering if he held a fourth, if unrecognized, survivor from the H.M.S. *Hood*.

Since the orders had been changed and the Swordfish biplanes were again being stowed below decks, Feathers Geoffrey-Faucett decided that he could spare a moment to look after the cat. The animal was shivering after its drenching in the sea, though it clung as stubbornly as ever to the life ring.

As the pilot carried the cat between decks to his cramped cabin, he felt the deck vibrate as a roar shook the carrier, then subsided into a rumble. The *Ark Royal's* engines were coming up to full throttle; she was no longer at station but bound for some destination. Feathers guessed that they were heading for the North Atlantic, where the battleship *Bismarck* must be lurking.

As he was tilting the cat and life ring against his chest to squeeze them and himself through the narrow cabin hatchway, he heard Jack Shepherd's voice. The air controller stopped, stared, then broke into a grin beneath his neatly clipped mustache.

"So there really was a cat out there. You weren't just ragging me, Feathers."

"Get some rum from your kit, would you, Jack? This little perisher needs it and I could use a nip as well."

Feathers spread a slicker on his bunk, laid cat and ring down, then grabbed a terrycloth and toweled the animal until its fur stood up in spikes. When Shepherd came in with the bottle, Feathers laid a gentle hand over the top of the cat's head and slipped his fingers into the corner of its mouth, prying its jaws apart. Shepherd filled the bottle cap with a small dose. Feathers deftly poured it down the animal's throat, then followed with a second.

"My, you know how to handle it," said Shepherd admiringly.

"My mum kept moggies and vetted them herself. Always had a soft spot for the creatures. All right," Feathers said to the cat. "Sit up and let's have a look at you."

By now the cat had released its grip on the life ring. Feathers gently lifted the ring off over the cat's head. The castaway shook itself, grimaced, and raised its flattened ears. It was a compact little animal with the short thick fur and the rounded head characteristic of the sturdy British shorthair. A few more rubs with the towel and the fur was soft and fluffy, if still a little damp. The cat opened its gold eyes and stared Feathers full in the face.

Now that the beast was halfway clean and dry, Feathers could see its markings. All along the back, sides, chest, and down the front legs on both outside and inside, the animal's fur was a rich leathery brown. The brown ended in a border just behind the animal's middle and its flanks, hind legs and tail were gray. Two white wristlets encircled the forelegs just above the paws. The paws themselves were black.

"Well, aren't we the natty little gentleman," said Feathers, leaning over with his hands on his knees. "Look, Jack. He looks like he's got on a bomber jacket."

The cat arched its back and rubbed against Feathers' hand, then butted his palm with its nose. Its head and neck were tan, with a slightly darker color on the ears. And the ears themselves were a bit odd. They stood up like normal cat's ears, but the outside edge of each one curled outward and the tips pointed together like little horns.

"Poor beggar. The wind's blown his lugs inside out," said Shepherd.

Feathers guffawed. "No Jack. That's just the way he is. Looks a bit jaunty with those ears, doesn't he? Doesn't need an R.A.F. cap to match the rest of him."

Feathers' fingers touched the collar as he stroked the cat. He remembered the nameplate and its upsetting message. He didn't want anyone else in the crew to see that. Quickly he slipped it round and started to undo the buckle, but the cat raised a paw to stop him. No claws, just a firm press of one black foot and a gaze into the eyes.

Luckily Jack Shepherd was occupied at the other end, doing a quick inspection to be sure they were using the correct gender when referring the animal.

"Definitely a little tom, all right," he announced, proud of his first venture into the veterinary field. "Got all the equipment intact, far as I can see."

Feathers, who had kept his hand on the collar, made a decision. "Jack, what do you make of this?" He showed Shepherd the bronze nameplate and the scorched spot on the cat's side. He saw the air controller flush, then go pale, just as he himself had done.

"H.M.S. *Hood*. Well, of all the queer happenings..." Shepherd sat down beside Feathers on the bunk. The cat walked onto the air controller's lap, stood on his thighs and tilted its head back, watching him expectantly.

"He doesn't want me to take his collar off. Pushes my hand away."

"If the sinking hadn't just been announced, I would have said that the collar was a prank," said Shepherd.

"Jack, no one's been at him since I hauled him over the rail, I swear. The only thing I can think of is that he belongs to the wife or child of someone on the *Hood* and he fell off a transport in rough weather." He looked at the cat. "But it just doesn't seem to fit."

Shepherd agreed. "They don't have room for pets on the transports. Look," he said, switching the subject. "Why don't you nip down to the galley and coax some tinned mackerel out of the cook while I look after Bomber?"

"What? You're already given him a name?"

"Well, we don't know what he was called aboard the *Hood*. There was no name on the tag and his markings do look like a bomber jacket."

Feathers grinned as he walked down the hallway on his errand. Bomber. It wasn't a bad name. And it was certainly appropriate for a cat aboard an aircraft carrier. When he returned to his cabin with the fish on a saucer, he heard Shepherd's voice querulously scolding the cat.

"That's the property of the Royal Navy, you ungrateful animal!"

Feathers stepped through, mackerel in hand. Bomber spotted it and made a dive for the plate as Feathers laid it on the floor. The pilot stared at the air controller, who rolled his eyes at the cat.

"What's the matter?"

"I shouldn't have given him that name," Shepherd said. "I bet he thinks he's got to live up to it. He's perfumed your cabin like a bloody bug bomb."

Feathers took a sniff. The smell was redolent and well remembered from his childhood among his mother's feline household. "He's just staking out his territory. Obviously knows his way about a ship."

"Well, I think I'll be getting along," said Shepherd, making a hasty exit. "I'd keep the cabin door shut until he… ah, makes himself at home. Cheerio."

While Bomber was still preoccupied with the mackerel, Feathers made one more foray into the galley for an old baking tin and some newspapers. He fled under assault from the cook, who had grown indignant at such raids upon his territory. A ladle clanged against the wall behind Feathers as he made a quick exit, bearing pan and papers. Once he had regained his cabin, he shredded the papers, stuffed them in the pan, took the cat by the scruff and pointed his nose at the makeshift sandbox.

"You'd bloody well better use that, or you'll find yourself right back in the Atlantic," he growled, then pulled the slicker from his bunk and stretched out on top of the blanket. He noticed that Shepherd had, in his haste, forgotten his bottle of rum. He uncapped it, took a pull and lay back for some quiet thoughts.

After scruffling about in the shredded papers for a while, Bomber came over, leapt onto Feathers' chest and settled there, kneading with his paws and exhaling a faint odor of mackerel.

Feathers put one hand behind his head and dabbled in the cat's fur with the fingers of the other. "Where did you come from, eh? Are you really the *Hood*'s ship's cat? If you are, I'll wager you'd like to be in on a scrap with the *Bismarck*."

Bomber's ears twitched back and his tail wagged briefly while his eyes slitted. In them, Feathers thought he saw the unmistakable glint of anger. He sighed, laid his head back, wondering if his imagination was getting the best of him.

The captain called the ship's company out on the flight deck for an announcement that Feathers expected. Force H was being sent north to join in the hunt for the German wolves that had destroyed the *Hood*. The two enemy ships now lay poised to prey on the transatlantic convoys that were the only resource keeping England in the war.

"Though what good we'll do is beyond me," whispered Shepherd, who had come up behind Feathers. "Flying outmoded Swordfish chicken coops with only one torpedo each. If we had some decent carrier-based aircraft…"

"Don't you count out the Stringbags yet," snapped the gunner Patterson, standing nearby. "Remember the ships we sunk at Taranto Harbor? Knocked out half the Italian fleet."

Feathers said nothing. Though he felt a fierce loyalty to his airplane, he knew Shepherd was right. The Fairey Swordfish torpedo biplane, while reliable, maneuverable and easy to fly, was no match for the guns and armor of enemy ships and aircraft. If any of the Swordfish saw service in the coming fight, it would be as a last-ditch attempt after all else had failed. And it would likely end in disaster.

There was nothing they could do about it in any case. Pilots and crew would have to sit out the hours drinking coffee, studying maps, and listening to reports on the wireless while *Ark Royal* and the rest of Force H churned their way north to join the hunt.

Feathers returned to his cabin. When he stepped in, he saw Bomber nosing about the corners of the cabin. The little cat stopped, turned his gray hindquarters to the wall, and began a meaningful quivering of his tail.

"Oh, hell," growled Feathers, lunging forward to grab the offender, but he was too late. A misty aerosol formed in a cloud behind the cat's tail, Bomber's benediction to the wall. "One stinker on this ocean is enough, but I'm blessed with two. You and the bloody *Bismarck*."

But even as Feathers was drawing back his open hand for a slap at the cat, Bomber spun around, pointing his head at the wall. His fur bristled and rippled as if some unseen hand were stroking it backward. His head ducked, pointing his ears toward the bulkhead.

Undulations swept through Bomber's jacket, up his neck to his ears. The air around the cat grew electric with static. With a crackle, a hot white spark leaped from each eartip to the damp spot on the bulkhead.

Feathers jumped back so fast he nearly fell on his rump. "I've heard of a cathode," he muttered to himself. "But I never thought it would be attached to a cat!"

And then he stared even harder, for Bomber's show wasn't over yet. The spot on the whitewashed cabin wall started to smoke and glow, making Feathers wonder if it would ignite like petrol and burst into flame. But instead the bulkhead started to ripple, just as Bomber's fur had done. Rainbow-colored rings bloomed in the center, spreading outward. And the once-substantial metal bulkhead was somehow becoming hazy, transparent.

Feathers quickly snuck a glance at Shepherd's rum bottle to see how much he had actually consumed before falling asleep. It did not reassure him to see that the level had only dropped by a half-inch. So it wasn't spirits that were causing this. Not alcoholic ones, at any rate. The wall continued its alarming transformation until it contained a medium-sized hole. Bomber turned to Feathers and crooked the tip to his tail.

The pilot dropped down on his knees and peered through the hole. It did not lead into the next cabin, as he had assumed. It seemed to go somewhere... else. Feathers quickly got up and locked his cabin hatch from the inside. He returned to cat and wall, finding both as he had left them. The hole, if anything, was a little larger.

Tentatively, Feathers put his fingertips to the edge of the opening. They tingled strangely. He peered through. The somewhere else definitely resembled the inside of another ship. But not the *Ark Royal*. He was looking at walls and decking that had a different color and texture from the ones on the carrier or any other Royal Navy ship he'd ever been on. They were a heavy blue-gray and the air had the factory smell of newly manufactured metal. The rumble of engines sounded though the opening, but their sound was foreign.

The click of footsteps sounded on the other ship, making Feathers draw back from the gap. They grew louder. Feathers felt himself break into a sweat. Whoever was coming could hardly fail to notice a three-foot hole that hadn't been there a minute before. He waited, expecting the steady click of the footsteps to cease and exclamations of astonishment and dismay to break through from the other side.

The steps did stop. But the expected outcry didn't come. Unable to stand the tension, Feathers knelt and peered through the gap. He saw the hem of a double-breasted navy blue coat with two rows of buttons. The cuff bore a single stripe and a gold star on the sleeve, the insignia of a lieutenant in the German navy. The man had stopped right opposite the hole! But he wasn't doing or saying anything. Perhaps he was simply struck dumb. Feathers waited for all hell to break loose.

The pilot shifted so that he could gaze slightly upward. Yes, a young German naval officer. He could see the Reich eagle on the cap. The man didn't look as if he'd seen anything unusual. He was leaning slightly against the bulkhead on the opposite side of the corridor, finishing a cigarette. He took a last draw, tossed the butt down, and strode off.

Feathers wiped his sweaty hands on his trousers, scarcely able to believe that the officer hadn't seen anything. Apart from the hole itself, the noise coming through from the *Ark Royal* should have drawn the man's attention. Unless…

Unless the gap only worked in one direction, like a one-way mirror. Perhaps the officer had glanced down and seen only the unbroken expanse of metal.

Bomber came up and butted Feathers impatiently, as if urging him to go through the opening. Feathers took a pen from his pocket and edged it into the gap, half expecting the pen to be chopped off by the sudden reappearance of the bulkhead. There was something on the other side, on the metal floor. The officer's discarded cigarette end. Feathers snatched it up and whipped his hand back through the hole.

He stood up, staring at his prize. It still smoked between his fingers. It was crushed and dingy, nevertheless, he could still read what remained of the tobacconist's imprint. Three Castles. A German brand, popular with naval officers. He had stuck his hand through the hole and brought back the end of an enemy fag. That clinched it. That ship on the other side. It must be one of those that sank the *Hood*. *Prinz Eugen*. Or *Bismarck* herself.

His brain suddenly came alive with crazy plans. With this entryway to the German ship, men from the *Ark Royal* could slip aboard the *Bismarck* and cause all kinds of havoc. A charge could be planted in her engine room. Her captain and high officers could be picked off. The ship itself could be taken from within! What a triumph for the Royal Navy if the mighty *Bismarck* could be seized and turned against the Axis nations who built her.

But even as dreams piled atop each other in the pilot's head, the hole trembled, shrank and popped shut. Shaking a little, Feathers touched the bulkhead. It was as solid as ever. Bomber gave Feathers a look halfway between resignation and disgust.

Feathers sat back on his bunk. He was tempted to take a large gulp of rum and dismiss the entire thing as a feverish hallucination. Until he looked at the German cigarette butt in his hand. There was no way to explain that.

He scratched his head. Apparently the effect was transitory, perhaps lasting only as long as the concentrated essence that created it. But if that was true, why hadn't Shepherd noticed anything when Bomber first began to display his proclivities? Feathers hadn't remembered any unexplained dimensional apertures in his cabin when he'd returned from the galley with a plate of fish.

Feathers sighed. Even if he could get the cat to perform again, no one in his right mind would believe him or be ready to duck through the interstice before it closed. And how would they get back? Could Bomber reverse the route from the German ship back to the *Ark Royal?*

The pilot flung himself back on his bunk, his arm across his eyes. Anyone in his right mind? Was he even in his right mmd or was he going completely round the bend? He felt a heavy warm weight on his chest and saw the cat once more curled up on top of him.

"I don't know what the hell you are, but as a secret weapon, you leave something to be desired," he growled.

Bomber, however, didn't answer.

The carrier *Ark Royal* plowed ahead on a northwest course along with the other craft of Force H who were hoping to intercept the *Bismarck* and *Prinz Eugen*. The men aboard cheered at reports over the Wireless that the *Bismarck* appeared to have taken a hit on the bow during the final engagement with the Home Fleet. The radar-equipped heavy cruiser H.M.S. *Sheffield*, which had been shadowing the German battleship, reported that *Bismarck* was leaving a wide swath of oil in her wake. But the excitement slowly died down when further reports indicated that the warship was not losing any speed and appeared essentially undamaged.

And then came the news that *Bismarck* had given her pursuers the slip and vanished into the fogs and rain squalls of the North Atlantic. Now all that the British forces could do was to wait and hope that air reconnaissance would spot her.

Force H kept steaming north, hoping the intercept *Bismarck* if she made a run for ports in Spain or France. But no one knew where the great ship had gone. It was as if she had vanished from the sea.

During the run north, Feathers had more free time than he wanted. He spent it drinking more than he should from Jack Shepherd's rum bottle and pursuing Bomber about the cabin, trying to persuade the cat to repeat his extraordinary performance. But Bomber, perhaps in disgust at having to deal with creatures of such low sagacity and perception, was behaving in a maddeningly normal manner. He even used the baking tin and its nest of paper for its intended purpose without creating the tiniest of interspatial holes.

Feathers braved the cook's wrath to abscond with more tinned mackerel, hoping that something in the fish had contributed to the cat's display. But even though Bomber consumed every morsel with relish, nothing happened.

At last Feathers decided that the whole thing must have been a total fantasy or a dream. He could not bring himself, however, to toss out the German cigarette butt. The pilot resigned himself to the fact that if the *Bismarck* was to be taken, it would be done without any feline assistance, fantastic or otherwise.

May 26 dawned with gray heaving seas underneath the *Ark Royal* and an even grayer mood among her crew. *Bismarck* had been sighted again by a Catalina flying boat off the coast of Ireland, but the ensuing attacks against her were ineffective.

The battleships H.M.S. *Prince of Wales* and *King George V* plus the cruiser *Suffolk* had tangled with her briefly, only to be driven off by the German ship's deadly and accurate shelling. And a flight of Swordfish from *Ark Royal's* sister carrier, H.M.S. *Victorious*, had loosed nine torpedoes at *Bismarck* with only one hit. It hadn't fazed her in the least. She was still running at 20 knots, well ahead of the pursuing Home Fleet and likely to escape. The only way to slow her down lay in the *Ark Royal* and her aircraft.

The *Ark Royal* had already sent two Swordfish equipped with long-range tanks to shadow the *Bismarck* and make sure she did not slip from sight again. These relays of shadowers were continually replaced during the day. Then came the announcement that the fifteen Swordfish not engaged in shadowing operations would mount an afternoon torpedo attack on the *Bismarck*.

Feathers ate his lunch, then he and Crockett, his observer, went up to the briefing office with the other aircrews to plan the attack. When he went down to his cabin to collect some last-minute gear, Bomber tried to follow him out.

"Look, sport," said Feathers, pushing him firmly back inside. "You had your chance to put some holes in that bloody battleship. Now I'm getting mine," With that, he locked the cat inside the cabin, although he wondered whether Bomber might use his unusual talents to make an escape.

He didn't have time to think about Bomber once he reached the flight deck. At two-thirty, the airedales had his Swordfish prepped and ready, torpedo slung underneath. Despite the tossing seas and rolling deck, he, Crockett, and Patterson made it off and buzzed away with the rest of their squadron, all hungry for a shot at the *Bismarck*.

About two hours later, a chagrined crew of Swordfish were circling about *Ark Royal* while the carrier headed upwind for their fly-on. The whole attack had been a fiasco from start to finish. Emerging from heavy cloud cover in an attack formation, the Swordfish had dived at a lone ship, thinking it was their sought-for target. But it wasn't. Confused by the weather and over-eager for combat, they mistook the cruiser *Sheffield* for the *Bismarck*.

"God, what a bloody-balls-up," groaned Feathers as he scrambled out of his cockpit onto the rain-swept deck. Patterson followed quickly so that the airedales could hustle the plane onto the lift and below decks before the next Swordfish made its approach. "They send us out and what do we do? Nearly sink one of our own ships!"

"I don't know what those other blokes were about," said Patterson. "We've used the *Sheffield* for all our dummy practice runs. As soon as I saw that superstructure, I knew it was the old *Sheff* and I told you to hold the torpedo. Was right, wasn't I?"

"I imagine the War Office has lost all faith in the Stringbags and they won't give us a second chance," said Feathers gloomily.

"Boyo, they don't have a choice. We don't have anything else to throw at the bugger." With that cheerful observation, Patterson shoved open the tower hatchway and held it for Feathers. "You'll feel better when you've got some grub in you. I have an itch that the old man is going to give us a chance to redeem ourselves."

"If the *Sheffield* isn't sunk," said Feathers. He trooped along with the others into the canteen and ate as much as he could hold, though the food might have been sawdust for all he cared. He was slightly cheered when news came that *Sheffield* had managed to maneuver so deftly that none of the torpedoes had hit her; He perked up even more when the captain announced that a second wave of Swordfish would depart the *Ark Royal* at 6:30 P.M. for one more crack at the *Bismarck*.

After the meal, Feathers was tempted to go immediately to the briefing room and then down to the hangar below to check his plane. But he remembered Bomber, still locked in his cabin. He hadn't left the cat any water. Feeling guilty, he made his way down to his quarters and opened the door. Bomber was still there, nosing about the corners of the room. Feathers patted him roughly, then fetched him water in the empty mackerel tin. As he did so, he talked to the cat, telling him what a mess the attack had been.

"If you could just do your trick again and let me get aboard *Bismarck*, I'd have a better chance of wrecking her than I have flying that firecracker-carrying chicken coop."

Bomber drew back his ears and narrowed his eyes. For an instant Feathers hoped that he had understood after all. The pilot was ready to grab his sidearm and dive through the moment that Bomber created a passageway between the *Ark Royal* and the *Bismarck*. But instead, the cat sprang away from Feathers, out the cabin door, and down the hallway.

"Where the devil are you going," Feathers shouted out the door as a gray tail disappeared around a corner. "I don't have time to chase a cat about. Dammit, come back!"

But Bomber was gone.

Perhaps he had decided to tackle the *Bismarck* on his own. Feathers could just imagine Bomber waging his own sort of guerrilla war with the enemy. He could , almost hear the harsh Prussian voices scream in bad World War One movie dialogue about "eine verdammt geschpritzen-katzen!"

Feathers Geoffrey-Faucett shrugged. Bomber had gone off on some mission, now Feathers had to attend to his own. He jammed his cap back on his head and made his way to the briefing room, where the aircrews were already assembling.

The plan was essentially the same as before, except this time, presumably, they would attack the right ship. A subflight of three Swordfish would approach in a steep dive behind the quarry. As the planes pulled out of the dive, they would fan out and approach the enemy in line abreast. At ninety feet, flying a flat course, they would drop their torpedoes into the sea and sheer away from the barrage of flak from enemy anti-aircraft guns.

The trick was getting close enough before dropping the torpedo. The optimum distance was 900 yards, but Feathers doubted that *Bismarck* would let anything get within that range before blowing it out of the air. He felt his hands begin to sweat. *Sheffield* had held her fire from the attacking planes. *Bismarck* would give it all she had.

They would have to fly low and hope for luck.

Bad weather had dogged the first attempt and threatened to scuttle the second. The rain squalls that gusted fitfully around the carrier became a full gale. Feathers pulled his leather flying cap down over his head, pulled his jacket collar up around his neck and braved the pelting rain. The sky, already dimmed by twilight, was darkened almost to blackness by the storm. The deck crews could only work by floodlights.

As he approached his Swordfish, a sweating crewman in a grime-streaked slicker was rolling a torpedo on a dolly toward the plane's undercarriage. Between the rain the glaring lights and the seesawing deck, the airedale was having a struggle to get the torpedo in place. Feathers hastened his steps to help the airedale, fearing that man, dolly, and torpedo might be swept over the side by the rush of white water spilling over the carrier's bow and sluicing down the deck.

Before he could reach the dolly, he saw a little four-footed shape gallop from the shadows toward the torpedo. With a yell, the airedale shouted and flailed, driving the animal off. What the hell was Bomber doing out on the flight deck, Feathers wondered, but he had no time to go after the cat. He overtook both airedale and dolly adding his strength to the crewman's. Together they wrestled the torpedo back toward the airplane, raised it and secured it in the rack between the Swordfish's wheels.

"Thanks, sir," panted the crewman. "Might have lost 'er over the side if you 'adn't 'elped. Rum thing, that cat running out from nowheres. Gave me a start, it did."

Feathers squinted against the rain and the glaring floodlights but saw no sign of Bomber. He spotted the shapes of Patterson, his gunner, and Crockett, his forward observer. With a few last words to the two about the attack plans, he boosted them into their cockpits, then took one futile look about for Bomber.

Before he knew it, a lithe shape launched itself from somewhere behind the Swordfish's tail, bounded across a stream of seawater, scrambled up his trousers, and tunneled beneath his jacket. Feathers swore in a mixture of delight and annoyance. He was glad the cat hadn't been swept overboard, but what the hell was he going to do with him? There wasn't time. The other Swordfish crews were in their planes and one was starting the tracking run down the deck line. As the biplane skittered and wobbled, Feathers wondered how it would ever make it through the curtain of heavy spray and crashing waves from the ship's bow.

Somehow the carrier's deck lifted at the critical moment, giving the plane an additional boost into the air. Feathers saw it wallow unsteadily, on the edge of a stall, then gathered speed, circling away from the carrier. He prayed that he would be that lucky. Bomber, tucked away beneath the pilot's jacket, had sunk his claws into Feathers' shirt in a way that suggested it would be difficult and time-consuming to remove him. And even if he did pry the cat loose, the airedales had their hands too full to bother with a cat.

"All right, you're going," said Feathers to the furry lump underneath his jacket. "I just hope you know what you're letting yourself in for."

"What are you standing there talkin' to yourself for?" yelled Patterson. "Sayin' your prayers?"

"Might need 'em," said Feathers as he swung into the center cockpit behind the pilot's windscreen.

Now, you blessed old Stringbag, he thought to his airplane, as he revved the engine and the airedales took away the chocks, *let's not decide to go for a swim.*

Just as he began the takeoff run, *Ark Royal* hit a deep trough that tilted her bow down until her deck was like the steep side of a hill. Feathers could see whitecaps on the sea below as he hurtled right downhill toward it. It took all his willpower not to pull back on the stick before the plane had attained flying speed. At the last instant, when he was sure he was going in the drink, the bow started to lift, tossing him in the air.

Bathed in sweat, he pushed the throttle to full power, feeling the plane begin to mush at the edge of a stall. A short dive let the Swordfish pick up speed and stability. With a surge of excitement, Feathers pulled back on the stick, starting a slow climb to attack altitude. The Stringbag might be old, slow and outmoded, but by God there was no other plane that could have gotten off a carrier in weather like this.

As he circled, climbing, he saw the rest of the torpedoladen Swordfish leave the deck of the carrier. All fifteen made it safely.

Bomber squirmed inside Feathers' jacket. With the plane trimmed for a climb, he could spare a moment for the cat. He let the stowaway slide out from the bottom of the jacket and stuffed the cat between his knees and the edge of the seat.

"Now stay there and don't get tangled up in the control cables. And if you get airsick, it's your own fault. I don't know what made you decide to come along, but there's no turning back now."

Bomber seemed to understand. He wedged himself into the small space, keeping out of the way. He didn't seem to be frightened by the vibration or the hiss of the wind past the open cockpit. He also, Feathers noted thankfully, had shown no indications of airsickness.

Catching sight of another plane in Subflight Two, Feathers joined it and soon both were twining about each other's paths as they climbed to an altitude just below cloud level. Once aloft, the full squadron assembled in formation and flew over the *Sheffield*. The cruiser gave them a somewhat wary welcome and directions to the *Bismarck*. When the flight was past *Sheffield*, they climbed to attack altitude of nine thousand feet. Crockett, Feathers' forward observer, reported a blip on the radar that couldn't be anything but the *Bismarck*.

After a short cruise, word came back from the squadron leader that he had sighted their quarry through a hole in the clouds. Most of the Swordfish would come in on the *Bismarck*'s port side, but Subflight Two was to attack from the starboard.

"Let's go get her, lads," came the voice of the squadron leader over the wireless and the fifteen Swordfish started the hunt.

Rain pelted against the Swordfish's windscreen and Feathers' goggles as he dived the torpedo plane from nine thousand feet. Between the rain squalls, the low clouds and gusty winds, Feathers could hardly keep track of the dark gray silhouette of the enemy ship. She was moving fast, crashing through the force eight gale that blew about her and sending up fountains of spray from her bows.

"What's her heading?" the pilot shouted to the observer in the forward cockpit. The lash of rain and wind coupled with the wavering drone of the Swordfish's engines drowned out Crockett's reply, but the discomfited look on his face told Feathers that the weather was making it impossible to do more than guess the warship's heading. And the radar set aboard the Swordfish was too crude to show anything but the ship's approximate location. He couldn't tell if the battleship was in a turn or running a straight course. God, what he'd give for a look at the *Bismarck's* compass.

And then something stirred beneath his feet, reminding him that the Swordfish was carrying an extra crew member, whose usefulness was doubtful. As if Bomber had caught the gist of that thought, he crouched on the cockpit floor in the cramped space underneath the pilot's knees. His tail began to shiver in an unmistakable manner.

"Not here! Not in the bloody aircraft!" Feathers yelled, but an appallingly familiar pungency rising from the cat showed that Bomber had already begun his performance.

With both hands on the stick and feet on the rudder pedals, Feathers could only curse impotently. Then the cat wriggled to one side beneath Feathers' right thigh, pointed its ears, rippled its fur, and let loose a crack of miniature lightning from eartips into the center of the damped spot.

Wrestling the Swordfish's control stick with one hand, Feathers caught Bomber by the scruff. He was considering a quick toss over the side, but he realized that he was far too late. Rainbow rings were already blooming in the center of the cockpit floor as they had on the cabin wall.

In fright the pilot pushed back against his seat as a circular gap appeared in the floor and enlarged. Would it spread underneath his seat, dropping him through to God knows where? He began to wish he had been a little more diplomatic toward the cat. And if he disappeared right out of the plane, that would leave the observer and gunner still barreling along in a pilotless craft. Surely Bomber didn't have it in for them, too?

The thoughts sped through his mind as the Swordfish continued in its hurtling dive through the clouds. And then he suddenly noticed that Bomber's hole wasn't getting any bigger, but the haze inside it was clearing. He could see through. And what he could see was the top of a military cap, a pair of uniformed shoulders and two arms whose gloved hands rested on the huge upright steering wheel of a ship. A huge glass-faced compass before the wheel read one hundred and six degrees. East-south-east. Roughly the same direction that the *Bismarck* was heading.

In a rush Feathers realized that Bomber had provided him with exactly what he needed; a view right into the *Bismarck's* helm control room. He was looking right down on top of the helmsman's head and the ship's great main compass. Abruptly the needle began to slide toward one-twenty as the helmsman's hand bore down on the right side of the wheel. The *Bismarck* was starting a turn to starboard, zigzagging to avoid torpedoes tracking in on her from other Swordfish.

If she'll stay in that turn, thought Feathers, *I can send that torpedo to hit her aft, in the rudder or screws.*

A banging on the fuselage behind him made the pilot jump. "What the hell are you playing at!" the gunner bellowed into the slipstream. "Do you want to send us into the sea?"

Feathers stared at the onrushing waves below. Too many seconds of inattention had sent the Swordfish into too deep a dive. A surge of adrenaline made him pull back the stick barely in time. He swore that spray from a high-breaking wave splashed the torpedo-plane's undercarriage as the Swordfish pulled out of her dive and roared along at wave-top height. Ack-ack fire spat uselessly over the top wing, for the Swordfish was so low that she was beneath the firing range of the *Bismarck's* anti-aircraft turrets.

He glanced between his knees at Bomber's viewhole down onto the enemy's helm station. The compass was still swinging steadily as the great warship kept to her same rate of turn. In his head the pilot estimated the trajectory needed to hit the *Bismarck* astern. Keeping his course dead level and his airspeed at 75 knots, he bored in toward the rain-shrouded shape of the German warship. He wanted nine hundred yards, but he knew he couldn't make it. The anti-aircraft fire was missing, but the big ship had taken to shelling the sea around itself, the explosions causing eruptions of water like geysers that could swallow a light aircraft and drag it down into the sea. At twelve hundred yards, Feathers pushed the torpedo release.

The bronze cylinder plummeted from the plane. Stay in that turn, you bastard. Stay in that turn, Feathers prayed as he veered away and caught sight of the torpedo's wake making a white trail directly toward the *Bismarck's* stern.

One quick glance down between his knees through Bomber's viewport onto the enemy helmsman told him the warship had spotted the attack. He heard orders in German barked down the speaking tube to the wheelman. The officer leaned to one side, gathering the momentum needed to bring the great wheel hard to port.

Instantly Feathers knew that if the warship swung her stern aside, the tracking torpedo would miss. He'd launched it from too great a distance. *Bismarck* had already shown amazing maneuverability for so long a ship and great adeptness at dodging torpedoes.

With a yowl, Bomber, who had been poised on the edge of the hole, launched himself right through it. Feathers had the most amazing bird's eye view of the cat tumbling straight down onto the head of the *Bismarck's* wheelman.

The officer threw both hands up in the air with a hoarse yell as a ten-pound bundle equipped with raking claws, teeth, and its own peculiar brand of chemical weaponry descended upon him. Bomber knocked the man's hat off and delivered a flurry of scratches to the hapless victim's head and shoulders. As a parting shot, the cat gave the flailing officer a final blast in the face as he sprang at the ship's wheel.

He landed, caught and held, his weight dragging the wheel back over and ending the change of course the helmsman was about to make. The *Bismarck* continued her sweeping turn to starboard.

Feathers strained his head over the side. Through the driving wind and rain, he saw the wake of his torpedo driving straight and true for the *Bismarck's* stern. Water fountained up, mixed with smoke. The aft end lifted for an instant, then slammed back into the sea.

From the rear of the Swordfish came more pounding and a roaring cheer from Patterson. "Hoorah! We got her right in the arse!"

From the gap in the plane's floor that miraculously looked onto the helm of the enemy came an unholy racket. Feathers glanced down at the scene happening between his knees. Bomber was still fighting the helmsman, screeching and spitting while the officer fended off the attack. From the voicetube connected to the *Bismarck's* bridge came frenzied shouts for the helm to obey. The uproar grew, Prussian bellowing mixed with British caterwauling, until the officer lunged, seized Bomber by the scruff, and hurled him against the wall.

Wild-eyed, the embattled wheelman seized control once again, hauling the wheel sharply to port as his captain had ordered, but it suddenly jammed at a rudder position of twelve degrees and wouldn't budge. The torpedo had done its work.

But what about Bomber? Ignoring Patterson's banging on the fuselage and demands to fly the bloody plane straight, Feathers stared down at the scene below him searching for the cat. He spotted Bomber on the floor looking up at him with something near desperation in the gold eyes. But Feathers himself couldn't fit through the gap. It was too small. He grabbed wildly at a coil of rope m the cockpit, hoping to throw a line down for the cat to snag. But before he could even find the rope end the interstice shivered and popped shut.

For a second, Feathers could only stare numbly at the now-solid floor of the cockpit. There was nothing he could do to rescue Bomber short of trying to land his Swordfish on the *Bismarck's* decks. And that would be sheer suicide.

"Would you tell me what is so interesting between your bloody knees?" Patterson roared again. "Get your head up and this crate home!"

Feathers pulled himself together. Bomber would have to rescue himself as best he could.

The Swordfish's forward observer, who had been completely forgotten during the wild ride, turned a pale but smiling face to the pilot and handed him a slip of paper. It read "Hit confirmed. *Bismarck* circling to port. Rudder looks stuck."

Feathers gave him a thumbs up and headed the plane for home. As soon as he was beyond range of the warship's anti-aircraft fire, he started a climb to cruise altitude. Again he looked down over the side and was heartened by the sight of the *Bismarck* making a wide confused circle in the rough sea.

All the way back to the *Ark Royal*, the Swordfish rang with cheers and snatches of song. Feathers joined in, but his enthusiasm was tempered by the thought of Bomber lying on the deck of the enemy ship. The helmsman had thrown the cat hard enough to break his back, Feathers thought. But there wasn't anything he could do about it. And he had to get his plane and crew back to *Ark Royal*.

The carrier's stem was still bucking in fifty-foot heaves when the Swordfish began their fly-on. Feathers concentrated everything he had on getting down in one piece. He was given additional motivation when the plane ahead of him touched the deck during the upward surge, smashing the craft's undercarriage and sending it skidding along on its belly, shedding pieces. The crew scrambled out and the airedales pushed the wreck over the side before it could burst into flame.

When Feathers' turn came, the deck dropped away just as he was starting to settle and he had to make another go-round. But on the second try he landed.

He heaved himself out of the cockpit as the airedales rolled his Swordfish toward the lift.

"That was some of the damned craziest flying I've ever been through in my life," said Patterson to him. "I was beginning to wonder if you'd forgot how to pilot."

Feathers just ducked his head and walked through the driving rain. He knew there was no way he could explain to Patterson what had happened there up in the sky. The gunner hadn't even known that Bomber was aboard.

Shepherd was among those down below, welcoming the aircrews aboard. The news had spread quickly throughout the ship that two Swordfish of the second subflight, coming in on the *Bismarck's* starboard quarter had got in one torpedo hit amidships and one aft. And the aft strike might have crippled her.

"That was your flight," Shepherd said excitedly to Feathers, amidst the general hubbub. "Which was your shot?"

"He kicked her right in the bum!" howled Patterson over his shoulder. "You should have seen it!"

"How the hell did you do it? And where's Bomber got to? I haven't seen him since you took off."

Feathers took Shepherd aside from the throng of rejoicing men. "Jack, he went with me. And he didn't come back. Come on. I'll tell you the whole story, if you'll believe it."

In Feathers' cabin, he and Shepherd shared what was left of the rum while the pilot told his friend the entire tale.

"You must think I've gone crackers. But I swear, that's the way it happened." Feathers ran his hand through his sandy hair. "Jack, you've read more scientific stuff than I have. Do you think it's possible to make a 'hole' between two different places the way Bomber did?"

Shepherd rubbed the stubble on his chin. "I don't know," he said thoughtfully. "The fellows at Farnborough play around with all sorts of queer ideas. But one thing I do know, Feathers. You're not given to fantasies. If it happened the way you said, I believe you."

"I feel terrible about leaving the little chap behind. But there was just nothing I could do."

"Well, look at it this way. You saved his life when you pulled him in from the sea. I think he just wanted to square the deal."

Feathers sighed, then looked at Shepherd with a wan smile. "Thanks. That helps a bit." He hung his head, his hands between his knees. "You know, I'm really beginning to miss him. I wonder if he really was just a cat. Seemed more like a guardian angel. Aah, I'm going all soppy on you, Jack."

"Well he definitely was a cat as far as one thing was concerned." Shepherd said, with a grin.

"I wish I had him back again," said Feathers.

"Even if he were to… ah… continue asserting himself?"

"Even if he did," said Feathers.

"Well, if it helps any, I'd suggest we give him an award, in memory of services rendered to king and country and all that," said Shepherd. "I'll get the tin snips from the repair shop. We can cut out a little Victoria Cross from the bottom of that mackerel tin and we'll have a proper posthumous presentation ceremony. How's that?"

Feathers agreed that such an award would be the best thing. He and Shepherd embarked on its construction, during the intervals when he wasn't being debriefed about the mission. In the confusion of the attack, no one could definitely assign which torpedo hit to which pilot. Only Patterson stoutly insisted that the aft hit was theirs, but the other aircrew also claimed it. Feathers took no part in the argument, since he had decided not to reveal Bomber's story to anyone except Shepherd.

Several hours into the evening, new reports came over the wireless. The torpedo hit had indeed done critical damage. After making two aimless circles in the North Atlantic, *Bismarck* was now heading northwest, in a wobbling course that indicated that she no longer had rudder control. She was backtracking helplessly, right into the guns of the oncoming Home Fleet.

Both Swordfish aircrews were decorated by the ship's captain and praised for their part in the battle. After the presentation, Feathers took his ribbon below, put it in a drawer and went back to Bomber's Victoria Cross. Ignoring the cuts on his hands from the jagged metal of the mackerel tin, he worked determinedly.

Shepherd came in just as Feathers was laying the finished piece in a little leather case that had once held someone's cufflinks. He pronounced it a beautiful piece of work given the contrariness of the mackerel can and the awkwardness of making fine cuts with tin snips.

"I think Bomber would approve," Shepherd said softly, laying a hand on the pilot's shoulder. "The news of that hit has gone right up to the Admiralty, to Sir John himself. They're all saying that it was a miracle, a hundred-thousand- to-one chance. It proves to me that your story must be true." He paused. "*Bismarck* is surrounded now. She hasn't got a prayer. And the Germans will fly their colors to the end, so we have to sink her. They're so sure of the end now that some bloke on the BBC has gone and written a bloody song about it."

Feathers looked down at the homemade Victoria Cross. "I'd give him the proper words to write, I would," he growled.

"If Bomber's alive and still on board," Shepherd said, "he hasn't got much time. Maybe we'd better think about holding that ceremony."

"Just hold off another few hours, Jack. Maybe the little beggar can somehow piss his way home."

Shepherd gave the pilot a light pat on the shoulder and started to leave the cabin.

Abruptly an unholy racket broke forth from the direction of the galley. It sounded like a war was being fought with pots and pans. And then came the indignant tramp of feet along the deckway. Shephard backed inside again, clearing room for the red-faced, indignant cook, who held out a large, meaty fist clenched about the scruff of a very wet, oil-stained, and generally bedraggled cat.

"If this animal is yours, keep it out of the galley or Oi'll complain to the captain, Oi will," the cook bellowed, brandishing a ladle over his captive's head. "Oi don't know 'ow 'e got in, but 'e's made a perfect shambles."

"I think we can cope with him," said Shepherd, smoothly taking the cat from the cook and gently escorting the indignant individual out before pushing the cabin door closed behind him.

Feathers had risen from his bunk, his eyes wide. "Bomber!" He took the cat from Shepherd, held him up and looked at him in disbelief and delight. "It really is him, Jack!" Quickly he sat down with the cat on his lap and gently felt along the little body. "I think he may have a few bruised ribs from the smash against the wall, but he seems pretty fit otherwise. Wait till I dry him off a bit!"

"Wonder what he was doing in the galley?" Shepherd asked.

"I imagine he was making for my cabin and missed. Must have been in a bit of a hurry. And that's why he fell in the sea instead of the *Ark Royal*. He must have had to pop off the *Hood* pretty fast, too." Carefully Feathers cleaned and dried the cat. He grinned as he scratched Bomber's head between the ears. "He certainly got his revenge."

"The Nazis should know better than to get a British ship's cat… ah, a bit niggled at them."

Feathers broke into chuckles, then laughed until he had to hold his sides. "I wonder if they have any idea what happened?"

"I suggest we have the presentation ceremony right here and now," said Shepherd. "Uh, what title were you planning to give him?"

"Why, there can only be one. To Bomber, ship's cat of the late H.M.S. *Hood*, I proudly bestow this Victoria Cross and name you mascot of Swordfish Sub-flight Two and," Feathers drew breath and presented the cufflink box with its tin medallion, "Bombardier, First Class!"

When is a cat not a cat? When it's a human in a cat's body. Tom Mackintosh isn't a traditional werecat, but every time that there's a full moon, his mind is transferred into the body of a nearby large yellow tomcat. He enjoys a night out on the town every month, until a larger, cat-eating coyote moves into the neighborhood.

Tom can always climb a tree or to a rooftop, but his curse requires that to turn back, his cat body has to be in physical contact with his human body when the full moon sets. Otherwise he'll remain a cat forever. Tom doesn't have the time to stay aloft until the coyote goes away.

... But a Glove

by John E. Johnston III

"Tom, this is our anniversary! What do you mean we can't be together tonight?"

Anniversary? How can people have an anniversary when they're not married? "Excuse me, Lori?"

"You don't even remember that we met a year ago today, do you, Tom Mackintosh?"

Uh-oh. Tom suddenly had a sinking feeling in the pit of his stomach. "We did?"

"Yes, we did. And you've been gone for two whole weeks, and now you're trying to tell me that you're just too busy tonight to spend any time with me." Lori put one hand on her hip and started tapping a foot on the sidewalk.

Tom sighed. "That's not how it is, Lori. I just have something that I have to do the next few nights. I don't have any choice in the matter, so I thought I'd ask you to an early dinner this afternoon because I was going to be so busy for a while."

"Early dinner! Hah! I get a quick meal and then get sent home before sundown, while you spend the night with someone else!"

"Lori, there isn't anyone else."

"Oh, yeah? Well, let's see: every once in a while you're just not available for a few nights. You don't answer your phone or your door, and your car sits there in back of your house." *Uh-oh. She's been checking on me.* "Do you think that I'm stupid? There's another woman."

"No, there isn't."

"Then give me another explanation."

Tom thought for a few seconds. "I can't, Lori."

"Ah-hah! I knew it!"

Tom hated scenes like this, but they just seemed to happen to him over and over again. *Well, I can't very well tell her the truth.*

Lori glared at Tom. "I knew that you wouldn't have an explanation!" She spun on her heel and stormed off across the street, throwing a parting message over her shoulder. "Good-bye forever, Tom. Don't call me, don't write me, and don't even think about me!"

Tom sighed again. He would miss Lori. She was more than a little temperamental, but for all her faults she was bright, well-read, well-educated, stylish, and pretty. She also loved animals.

Even more than she ever knew, as a matter of fact.

Tom watched her walk out of sight and then spoke to the empty street. "Want the explanation, Lori? It's real simple: every time there's a full moon I become a cat. A big, fluffy, yellow tomcat, in fact." Frustrated, Tom kicked a mailbox so hard that it hurt his foot, and then walked the long block to his car. *I hate this. I'm never going to be able to have any kind of long-term relationship with a woman.*

Tom drove home, angry at himself the entire way. Tom's house, in the expensive Kentwood subdivision, was one that his real estate friends called "a classic two-story." Kentwood was one of the older neighborhoods in town, and it was known for expensive homes that were spaced fairly close together on well-landscaped lots. Tom couldn't have afforded the house himself; his father had left it to him. *Along with a few other things. Thanks again, Dad.*

Tom parked his car in the driveway off the alley behind his house and heard a familiar friendly canine whine as he got out. His next-door-neighbor, Bob Hammond, had a big red Doberman pinscher named Beauregard who only liked three people in the world: Bob, Bob's wife, and Tom. "Hello, Beau," said Tom, walking over to Bob's back gate. "How are you? Better than me, I'd bet." Tom reached his hand over the gate, and Beau raised up on his hind legs and put his front paws up against the gate so that Tom could scratch his ears. "Catch any squirrels today, Beau? Guard the yard well?" Beau, a dog of good heart but very simple mind, didn't mind anything that went on outside his yard but tolerated nothing within it with the exception of the three people he approved of. *Heck, Beau probably only puts up with me in the yard because I feed him when the Hammonds are out of town.*

"Bye, Beau. Have a good day." The sun was setting as Tom went in his back door. He checked his watch. Got a few hours left until the full moon. He walked upstairs and into his bedroom and stared at part of his legacy: an elaborate family coat of arms, mounted on the wall over the head of the bed. It showed a cat, raised up on its hind legs to strike, and bore the motto: "Touch not the cat, but a glove." At the bottom was the clan name: Mackintosh, part of a confederation of Scots clans known as Clan Chattan. *Why couldn't I have been a Campbell? They have no strange hereditary problems and have a great tartan to boot.*

Tom propped open his bedroom window with an odd-looking H-shaped metal device, and then bolted and locked the device into the window frame. *I won't ever make same mistake Dad did. I'll always get back here in time.*

Becoming a cat every full moon was bad enough, but the complications that went with it made it even worse. First off, Tom just didn't turn into a cat; when the moon became full, his consciousness was mysteriously transferred into a large, yellow cat that suddenly materialized from who-knows- where and appeared on his abdomen. *Wasn't that fun the first time that happened? Well, at least I learned right off not to wear clothes that my cat form might get trapped in. And I also learned not to use claws on my human form when I was a cat.* Second, to return to human form, Tom had to have his cat body in physical contact with his temporarily-unused human body when the full moon set, or suffer some major—but still unknown—consequences. Tom had been able to figure that last one out by himself from what had happened to his father.

Once Tom had begun making the transition and understood a little about it, it was easy to look back and see that his father showed all of the signs of a man who went through the same changes himself. His father was noted for sleeping alone next to an open window, regardless of the weather, and had been known as a very private, reclusive, and secretive man. His father had ended up paying a steep price for having the condition; his mother-in-law, who stayed with Tom's family after her own husband died, had unexpectedly strolled into this very room one night, seen Tom's father calmly asleep on the bed with the window propped open and, as an enemy of fresh air, had closed the window. Early the next morning, a large cat had awakened every member of the household—except Tom's father— by screeching and throwing itself over and over again at that very window from the tree limb right outside. Tom and his mother and grandmother had watched the cat trying desperately to get through the window, and tried fruitlessly to wake Tom's father up to ask his advice. After about an hour of this, the cat had given up and vanished, shortly after which Tom's father had stopped breathing.

Tom knew now that the cat had been his father, trying to get back to his body before the moon went down. *I wonder if he lived on as a cat.* He hadn't understood the incident at the time; Tom was only thirteen when it occurred and hadn't begun going through the changes himself until he was eighteen, when the meaning of what Tom had seen became clear to him. *What happened to Dad will never happen to me. Never.* Tom had added the bolts and locks to his father's old metal window prop after he had begun making the transition himself. *It'd take Harry Houdini to get this prop out of the window now.* Tom now left the house every night secure in the knowledge that the window would be open when he returned, and he was also smart enough to make sure that he knew how long each full moon would last and when he had to be home. The memory of his father made Tom play things very safely.

Tom read a book and tried to relax until it was time to get ready, at which point he took off his clothes and lay down on his bed. *This is ridiculous.* Tom was, as far as he knew, the only living person in the world who went through this. Among the things left to Tom by his father was a note that read "Things to tell Tom" with two cryptic entries: "Not all are" and "Others." Tom thought he'd figured out the first part of the note. Through espionage in feline form on other people who were descended from the families of Clan Chattan, starting with his own cousins, Tom had established to his own satisfaction that his relatives—or at least all of the ones that he could find— did not turn into any type of animal under the influence of the full moon. The latter part of the note was even more cryptic than the former. "Others"? Could "Others" and "Not all are" mean that there were, indeed, others like Tom out there somewhere? Tom desperately wanted there to be others like him, but outside of that cryptic note, Tom had never seen or heard even a hint of such a thing, and Tom had made a point of studying everything that he had been able to find out about the subject in great detail.

It was easy for Tom to be angry at his father. Not only had his father's genes placed him in this situation, his father had vanished without leaving Tom any kind of decent written explanation or any help whatsoever. On top of that, he'd given Tom a joke name: Thomas Catlett Mackintosh. The whole name said "tomcat" in big letters. *Great joke, Dad. Thanks a bunch.* Tom suddenly got a wry smile on his face. *Well, at least you didn't name me Felix.*

Tom's emotions vanished as he felt the familiar tingles of the transition begin. They started off faintly, gradually grew in intensity, and finally peaked… and Tom found himself once again to be a large, yellow cat, one that had suddenly materialized on the abdomen of the human body Tom had been occupying a few seconds earlier. *Off we go.* Tom took control of his cat body, gently stepped off his now-unused human body, and hopped from the bed to the window sill. With a quick jump he was in the orange tree outside and headed off.

Being a cat was always a pleasure for Tom; he enjoyed the smells his cat senses could detect and he really liked the lithe feel of his cat body. Tom jumped from the tree to the top of the fence separating his property from Bob Hammond's and watched Beauregard raise his head up and track him. While Beau would go after any cat that actually dared to enter his yard, cats on the fences were something that Beau never really cared about. *See you later, Beau.* Tom hopped down to the alley and took off south toward Third Street at a lope.

He made it the entire long block to Third Street before he realized what was missing tonight: Tom hadn't seen or smelled another cat the entire way. That was unusual; normally the alley had at least two or three other cats in it. *Oh, well, maybe they're all across Third Street.* Tom looked both ways across Third Street, found a traffic-free moment, and trotted across. *Well, there'll be cats here.*

Only there weren't.

Tom started looking and smelling for cats, but there was nothing to be seen and little to be smelled. Finally, Tom found a track that he recognized in an alley: that of a female he called Rose, who'd had a fresh litter of kittens the last time Tom had seen her. Tom tracked her to where she normally stayed, and found a scent track that indicated she and the kittens had left there and gone elsewhere in a hurry. Overlaying the scent of Rose and the kittens was a strong and obnoxious scent that Tom couldn't identify. Whatever it was, it made Tom's fur want to stand on end.

Tom followed Rose's and the kittens' scent around a corner, to a quiet cul-de-sac off of Third Street near the Third Street Veterinary Clinic. There, at a storm drain, he smelled something the smell of which he had grown to hate: death. *Oh, no, Rose. Not you.* The kitten smell went into the storm drain. The obnoxious smell didn't. Tom was too big a cat to fit into the storm drain entrance to see where the kitten smell went. *Maybe the kittens got away.* Rose hadn't. *Good-bye, Rose.*

Very upset now, Tom started checking for cats. He went to an area off of Third Street that was almost always patrolled at night by an angry yellow tomcat that Tom called Jeremiah, who was probably one of Tom's own offspring. There was no Jeremiah to be found. Tom went to the one place he knew he could always find a cat, the backyard that was the regular court of the languid Persian female that Tom called Lady Kay. There was no sign of Lady Kay either.

There was, however, a lot of the strong and obnoxious smell all over, and here and there was the horrible odor of death. Something was very, very wrong. There was something hunting cats... and, unless Tom's nose was mistaken, some dogs, too. *It's not a dog, it's not a big cat, and it's not human. Smells closer to a dog than anything else, though.*

The rest of Tom's evening was spent in cautious patrol work. He skulked, he scouted, and he slithered, but he turned up no more clues about what was going on, and didn't see another cat the entire time. The sky finally told Tom that it was time to head home. *Don't have much longer. These short full moons in the late summer sure don't leave you with much time to prowl.* Tom trotted over to where the alley that went by his house continued on past Third Street and turned north toward Third Street and home. He was almost to Third Street when he stopped cold. That obnoxious smell was suddenly very, very strong.

Tom froze. Turning to his left, he looked into the corridor between two garages where there was a small stand of shrub. Tom looked closely into the shrub, and he could see that there was something large and blurry in there. Suddenly, whatever it was raised up, and Tom was looking into what he knew instinctively were the yellow eyes of Death. The human part of his mind stopped and said, "Coyote," but his feline reactions had him in full flight toward Third Street and home before the coyote had time to react any further. Tom was a very fast cat and he took full advantage of that speed as he headed for Third Street at a pace few cats could match. He heard the coyote chasing after him and Tom ran as he had never run before. *Coyotes are faster than cats, aren't they? Or are they?* Tom reached Third Street, hearing the sounds of the coyote behind him as he ran. As Tom closed on Third Street, he looked at the cars on the street, timed their speeds in his mind, and adjusted his direction slightly: he hit Third Street at full speed and virtually flew straight across it into the alley on the other side without having even to slow down a step. Shrieking brakes and honking horns told him that the coyote had not been able to do the same thing. *Hah. Got you there.*

Tom had reached very familiar territory now. There should be an orange tree just down the alley—right there—that was not only on the same side of the alley as Tom's house, but was also one that he should have enough lead time to climb. Tom heard the coyote coming up behind him, smelled the orange tree, got within jumping range of it, jumped as high as he could up its trunk, and scrabbled up the trunk of the tree by his claws for his life. He heard and felt the coyote behind him leap and hit the tree underneath him. *Hah. Too late.* Tom reached a horizontal limb and flattened on top of it, swiveling his head down to look at his pursuer. What he saw was frightening: the largest coyote that Tom had ever seen or heard of was sitting patiently at the base of the tree, looking up at Tom with an evil malevolence that Tom found chilling. *So you're the killer. Whatever are you doing in my neighborhood? Why aren't you chasing rabbits up in the hills where you belong?*

Well, there's nothing more that I can do here. Good-bye, Killer. I'll see you again. Tom went higher up the tree, crossed to a long limb, jumped from it onto the roof of the corner home's garage, and began roof-, fence-, and tree-walking home. The coyote paralleled him on the ground, obviously waiting for Tom to have to take to the ground again. Tom, however, knew something the coyote didn't: the combination of the number of large trees in the neighborhood and the proximity of the neighborhood houses to one another gave Tom a convoluted but safe high road home to his own window via limbs, fences, and roofs once he had made it back to his own block.

Tom made it back to his window with some time to spare before the change and looked back to see the coyote sitting in the alley behind his house, calmly staring at him. *Good night, Killer.* Tom jumped through his window. *Until we meet again.*

Tom didn't feel all that well the next morning. His arms and legs hurt, and he was even more tired than he usually was after one of his cat nights. A shower and breakfast made him feel somewhat better, but he still wanted to go back to bed. He didn't, though; instead, he called the city's Animal Control office to see what he could find out about the coyote running loose in his neighborhood.

"Animal Control. Jordan speaking."

"Yes, ma'am, my name is Mackintosh. I live in Kentwood, and last night I saw a coyote in the alley behind my house. Do you know anything about that?"

"Mr. Mackintosh, I'm going to let you talk to Mr. Gage. Hold on."

A pause of a few seconds, and then, "Gage here. Jordan says that you saw a coyote over in Kentwood last night."

"Yes, I did. A very large coyote, in fact. Can you explain that to me?"

"Sure. Remember the brush fires in the hills the last couple of weeks?"

Tom didn't. He'd been out of town. "No, I was gone. What happened?"

"Well, about half of the natural coyote habitat around here was destroyed. The survivors are hungry, and a lot of them have moved into town to try and find food."

"This one's after the cats in my neighborhood."

"That's not news, they're after cats all over town. Want to know what else they've done? They've eaten all of the ducks in Monroe Park and some of the smaller animals at the zoo. Heck, one of them even got the mayor's wife's poodle the night before last. Boy, is she upset."

Uh-oh. "Mr. Gage, that's all bad news, but can you do anything about the coyote in my neighborhood?"

"Sure, we'll get him for you. Give me your address."

Tom gave it to him. "It's going to be a while before we can get to him, though."

"What exactly does 'a while' mean, Mr. Gage?"

"Well, the mayor, the City Zoo, the Parks Commission, and a couple of other neighborhoods are in line ahead of you, and we only have so many traps and so many officers. We'll get all the coyotes, though, and we'll get to yours when we can."

"And just how long might that be?"

"Well, Mr. Mackintosh, that depends on how fast we take care of the other problems."

"But just how long could that be? Give me the worst case, would you?"

There was a pause. "Don't quote me on this, Mr. Mackintosh, but it'll probably be weeks. Maybe a month. Maybe longer. If you have a cat, I'd advise you to keep it indoors."

Tom's shoulders sagged. "Thank you, Mr. Gage. Can I get you to call me so I know when you're going to be in this neighborhood?"

"Sure. Leave your number with Ms. Jordan."

Tom did, and then hung up the phone and sat lost in thought. *Well, there's no help coming any time soon, the odds on me finding that coyote while I'm in human form are minuscule, and I can't do anything much to him but provide him with a meal if I do find him again while I'm in cat form. And every day—or night—that I do nothing about him will probably cost lives.* Tom walked to the window and looked out into Bob Hammond's yard. Beauregard sat under the big tree in the middle of the yard, calmly scratching himself. *Hmm, I wonder just what you'd make of that coyote, Beau?*

And then the idea hit him.

The setup work in human form that night was easy; Tom slipped over to Hammond's alley gate just after sunset, reached over the fence and unlatched the gate so that it was just slightly open: open enough that it could be forced open from the outside, but not enough for Beau to get out. Beau walked over to the gate while Tom was there and made friendly noises. "Good Beau. Down, boy. Don't lean on the gate, okay? Good Beau." Beau sat down with his head cocked at an angle and looked at Tom. "Get some sleep, Beau. Big night tonight." Tom went back up to his room, propped and locked the window open, checked the time, and got ready for the change.

When it came, Tom was out the window and headed for the alley in a flash. *Third Street, here I come.* He made it across easily, and worked up and down the streets and alleys around Third Street, concentrating on the area around the Third Street Veterinary Clinic, carefully checking for the coyote, and carefully avoiding positions where he might be jumped or ambushed. There wasn't a sign of the coyote—not a scent since last night, not a sign of a struggle, not a track. After a long and hard search, with time starting to become an issue, Tom gave up. *Another night.* Tom headed back to Third Street, figuring to lope across it and make his way home quickly and to try again tomorrow night.

Tom waited until there were no cars coming, and made it across Third Street at a brisk walk. He was just starting down the alley leading home when he smelled it: coyote. Suddenly, out of the cluster of trash cans in the back of the house on the left corner, a gray streak flashed, leaping straight and true for right where Tom was. Tom ducked underneath the leaping coyote and, doing the unexpected, ran for his life straight toward the trash cans. He could hear the coyote hit the ground hard and try desperately to reverse direction. *Hah. Too late. You overcommitted.* Tom leapt over the now-scattered trash cans his foe had concealed himself in and headed straight for the low storage shed he knew was at the back of the house. *This is the Maguire place. Storage shed, plum trees, three-story house. Fairly safe.* Tom jumped, caught the wooden edge of the shed in his claws, clawed and swung up to the top of it, and then leapt from the shed to a large horizontal branch of the Maguire's prize plum tree. From fifteen feet up, Tom looked directly down onto the coyote, who had followed him on the ground as soon as he had been able to. *Well, you missed again. You ought to bathe more often, your smell gives you away. I got away from you again. You're not that good.*

Then it dawned on Tom: he was on the other side of the alley from his house.

There was no safe way home from this side of the alley.

And if Tom didn't get home within about twenty minutes he'd be a cat forever… or maybe worse.

And sitting down below him was a large, deadly, probably very hungry coyote patiently waiting for his chance to make Tom into a late dinner.

Well, Killer, you didn't miss after all. You got me, even if you'll never understand how.

Tom calmed his initial panic. *I have to think. There has to be a way out. There is always a way out.* Tom turned ideas over in his mind and finally concluded that his only real hope was to head for home and make a break when his best chance came. *Maybe a car will come down the alley and create an opportunity for me to get across. Maybe the coyote will get bored and leave. Maybe he'll fall asleep.* The coyote carefully paced Tom as he headed from tree to roof and back to tree again on his way up the alley toward his house. *And, then again, maybe he won't.*

It took Tom about ten minutes of roof and tree work to make it to the house directly across the alley from his own. He sat on the flat roof of his neighbor's garage, staring across the alley at his own house, fence, and trees. *Thirty feet. I could make it in a flash. I could jump to the top of my fence, or I could go through Hammond's gate and get Beau. It would just take a few seconds.* Then pessimism set in. *Thirty feet? It might as well be thirty miles. I'd never make four of those feet before that coyote would be on me.*

The coyote sat patiently in the alley, watching Tom and waiting. *You've done a lot of damage, you lousy coyote. One day you'll pay for that.*

Tom checked the sky. He was running out of time. *Well, maybe I can make a break for Hammond's gate, and maybe I can hit it hard enough to attract Beau's attention, and maybe, even if I can't get through it, just maybe I can knock it open far enough for Beau to work his way out, and maybe Beau will get this killer after he gets me. Looks like my best shot.* Tom raised up and stretched, trying to look bored. The coyote snapped to attention. *Crap.*

And then, unexpectedly, sauntering toward the two of them from the Third Street side of the alley was the last thing Tom expected to see—another cat. It was a young reddish-orange female, and she looked as though she was paying no attention at all to her surroundings. Cats don't normally act like that. *If she doesn't see that coyote and she gets any closer…*

She did get closer. The coyote patiently looked at her, checked Tom, weighed his choices and chances, spun, and then everything seemed to happen at once. The coyote turned and ran full speed at the reddish-orange cat, and the reddish-orange cat did the fastest pivot Tom had ever seen—*she's faster than I am*—and headed full speed for the nearest tree. Tom immediately jumped off of the garage roof and broke for Bob Hammond's alley gate as fast as he could run. Tom glanced back—*I shouldn't be turning my head to look like this*—as he ran and saw the female reach the tree and leap upward to try to escape the coyote's fangs. The female cat wasn't as big as Tom and couldn't jump as high, though, and the coyote was blindingly fast; he jumped and was able to catch her in his jaws by her lower right leg. Tom thought she was done for, but she planted her left rear claws in the coyote's nose, twisted them, pulled free of the coyote's jaws when they popped open in shock, and scrambled up the tree to safety. Without a second's pause or thought, the coyote did an immediate full pivot and made straight for Tom.

Too late, Killer. I'm too close to the gate. Tom straightened himself up, jumped for the gate, balled and buttoned himself up in midair as best he could, and then hit Hammond's back gate with all the force that a large cat at a dead run could bring to bear. The gate popped open just far enough for Tom to scramble through. Right behind him Tom heard the coyote hit the gate hard, bounce back, and then start forcing the gate open far enough to admit his larger body. Tom didn't turn around but raced full speed for the Hammond's orange tree. He leapt, hit the tree, dug his claws in, and was ready to climb to safety when he suddenly felt an excruciating pain: the coyote had him by the tail. *Well, this is it. I didn't make it after all.*

Only it wasn't it. Suddenly, there was a noise.

A growl.

A very deep growl.

Beau's growl.

The coyote obviously had heard it, too; he let go of Tom's tail, and Tom scrambled straight up to the nearest safe branch and looked down. What he saw made him a very happy cat: Beauregard was standing between the coyote and the gate with a look of pure territoriality in his eyes. *Here it comes. Get him, Beau!*

And then Tom looked up at the sky. *Uh, oh. The moon is almost gone!* Tom wanted to stay and watch what happened, but he had no time: he streaked along the branches, jumped to the roof of his house, dove through the window, and barely made it back to his human body just as he felt the change starting. *Never cut it this close before. Never will again.* And then he was gone.

Tom awakened in human form. It was early morning, and Tom didn't want to get out of bed; he was a little groggy and more than a little sore. Then Tom remembered the night before and tried to get up all at once. He had a problem doing that, though; there was an excruciating pain in his behind. Tom did a half roll in the bed, looked at his backside and made a face: it was obvious that any sitting down that he was going to do for the next few days was going to be extremely painful. Tom carefully swung his legs over the side of the bed and headed gingerly for the window. *Beauregard, how did you make out?*

Looking out the window, Tom could see the aftermath of what must have been the canine battle to end all canine battles in Hammond's yard below. It was a battle that the coyote had obviously lost: the yard was torn up, there were patches of fur everywhere, and there was what was obviously a dead coyote over by the gate. Lying next to the coyote's supine form, though, was Beauregard, and from where Tom was he didn't look all that much better off.

Damn. Tom threw clothes on as quickly as he could, given his painful posterior, grabbed a blanket, and ran downstairs and over to Bob Hammond's front door as fast as he could, trying to ignore the pain in his rear the whole time. *A shame that I can't use the tree route in this form.* Hammond answered Tom's repeated loud knocking on his front door wearing a bathrobe and a puzzled look. "Tom, what are you doing over here at this hour of the morning?"

"Bob, Beau's been badly hurt! I saw him from my window!"

"What? How?"

"Looks like a dogfight of some kind. Come on!" Tom, still uninvited, slipped past Bob Hammond and ran through his house into Bob's backyard. Beau looked even worse up close than he had at a distance; when he saw Tom coming, though, he lifted his head up a little and tried to wag his tail. *Stay alive, Beau. Stay with me.*

Tom started slipping the blanket under Beau. "Bob, we need to get Beau to the vet right now. Get your car, and I'll get Beau." Tom was grunting as he picked Beau and the blanket up gently—*Beau, you are one heavy dog*—even before Bob answered him.

"Can't, Tom," said Bob. "My wife took the car about a half hour ago. Can we take yours? I'll be dressed in a minute." He looked around. "That's a dead coyote! What in the dickens happened here? How did a coyote get in my yard?"

Tom didn't answer Bob's last two questions. "Bob, we can take my car. And I can wait for you to get dressed, but I'm not sure Beau can." Tom staggered under his load toward Hammond's partially open alley gate, beyond which Tom's own car sat parked in his own alley driveway just a few feet away.

"You go on without me, then," said Hammond. "You know where the Third Street Veterinary Clinic is? Take him there. There's a new vet there, but they still know him and me there. Leave Beau there, tell them to put it on my bill, and come back and get me."

Well, I ought to know where the Third Street Clinic is, given that I patrolled around it half of last night. Tom didn't know who the vet was, though. *Funny, I'm a part-time cat, and I don't know any veterinar-*

ians... *heck, I've never even been to a veterinarian.* Tom gently maneu-
vered the blanket and a softly moaning Beau over the dead coyote—
got you, you killer—through the gate, and into the passenger seat of
his car. Tom got in the car, backed it out, and then drove far faster
than he normally would have toward the clinic, all the while trying
very hard not to sit down. *Here I am, driving like a teenager and sitting
on half of my rear end. What a life.* Then the real absurdity of the situation hit Tom, and he started laughing out loud. *This is great. This is
probably the only time in the history of the world that a dog has ever been
driven to a veterinarian by a cat.*

Tom was still laughing when he reached the clinic. Disregarding
the signs, he parked the car in the red zone right out in front, got out
painfully, and limped around to the passenger side. Tom reached in
and picked Beau and the blanket up as gently as he could and staggered under the load—*what do you weigh, Beau? Feels like a hundred
pounds*—toward the clinic door. A young woman wearing surgical scrubs and a startled expression opened the door for him, and
he found himself in a reception area. "Emergency," he said. "Badly
injured dog. Where do I take him?"

"Straight to the vet. Follow me," said the girl. Tom did, and carried Beau down a hallway and around a comer into what was obviously an examination room. The room wasn't empty; there was
a redheaded woman in surgical scrubs in there lecturing a seated
woman who was clutching a lapdog. *Sheesh, lady, that's one ugly little
dog.* Tom ignored them, walked right past the woman in scrubs, and
set Beau and his blanket down as gently as he could on the large
metal examination table in the middle of the room.

The redheaded woman suddenly stopped her lecture, went
right to the table, and began looking Beau over quickly. *Are you the
veterinarian?* She looked at Tom suspiciously. "This is Beau, Mr.
Hammond's dog. Who are you? I've met Mr. Hammond, and you're
not him. Where's Mr. Hammond? Just what happened to Beau?"

And hello to you, too, lady. "I'm the next-door neighbor. Bob told me to bring Beau to you. Beau got into a fight with a coyote. By the way, are you the veterinarian?"

The redheaded woman started, and turned way from Beau and looked Tom square in the eyes. *Green eyes. A redhead with green eyes. Freckles, too. Lovely, but bad news, I bet.* "A coyote?" she asked, in a softer voice. "What happened to the coyote?"

"Dead as a post," said Tom.

"Good," said the woman. "Make sure that you bring the body in later. I'll need it." She turned her back on Tom and started working on Beau. Over her shoulder she said, "And, yes, I am the veterinarian. Would you mind waiting in the reception area? I have a lot of work to do here." The fat woman with the lapdog had vanished. *Ran her off for good, I'll bet.*

Tom walked into the hallway while the veterinarian began yelling at her assistants to bring her various things. Tom was tired and his rear end hurt. *Well, I'm not going to go sit in the reception area in this condition. I'll walk around a while instead and wait and see if Beau's okay. Then I'll go get Bob once I know for sure what's going to happen. Don't want to drive any more than I have to in this condition.* Tom turned in the opposite direction from the reception area. The clinic was oddly shaped; it was built in a sort of a deformed U shape, and when Tom walked toward the other arm of the U, the sounds of barking dogs and angry cats made it clear that there must be kennels in the back. *Wonder if any of the missing cats might be injured and in the kennels here? Can't hurt to look.*

Tom passed a series of what looked like empty examination rooms and the veterinarian's private office on the back way to the kennels but didn't stop to look in. When he walked past the dog kennels to the cat area, he smiled. Sitting in the second row of kennels, his muzzle and side stitched up and with one leg in a cast but still looking like a defiant yellow feline pirate for all that, was Jeremiah. Two cages over and one up was Lady Kay, stitched here and there, a little the worse for wear but still looking smug. On the bottom row, in a cage with a bottle feed attachment, was Rose's litter of kittens. *Looks like Rose held that coyote off long enough to see you kittens safely into the storm drain where he couldn't get you. I'll bet somebody heard you crying in there later and got you out and brought you here.* Tom smiled again. *Things are looking up. I wonder how many more made it?*

Better go check on Beau. Tom walked back down the hallway and looked into the veterinarian's office as he walked by. There were a lot of framed diplomas and certificates mounted on her office wall. *Wonder where she went to school? Ah, there's the vet school diploma. UC Davis, eh? Not a bad school.* And then Tom saw what was also mounted on the wall besides the diplomas and certificates and froze on the spot.

Mounted on the wall, behind the veterinarian's desk, was a familiar coat of arms—a Clan Chattan coat of arms, angry cat and all. The cat was a little different in this coat of arms, and Tom didn't recognize which branch of the clan it was from, but Clan Chattan was Clan Chattan. *Well, well, well. Hello, cousin.* And then Tom had a thought that almost staggered him.

Tom was still standing in the hallway facing the office door some time later when the veterinarian finally appeared in the hallway.

"There you are! What are you doing here? Why aren't you in the reception area? Where's Mr. Hammond?"

Hello again to you, too, ma'am. Smiling, Tom motioned to her. "You need to come here to find out. How's Beau?"

He wasn't surprised to see the redheaded vet limping slightly as she walked up the hallway. The bandage on her lower right leg, even though pretty well hidden by the surgical scrubs, was visible when you knew to look for it. Her anger, on the other hand, was far easier to see. "Beau's badly hurt, but he's going to be okay. What are you doing back here? What do you think gives you the right to…"

"That does," said Tom, pointing into her office at the coat of arms. "And full moons. And that doesn't even mention the fact that I'd bet everything that I own that you were the one who distracted that big coyote last night long enough for me to get through that gate!"

The woman was looking at him with those same green eyes, but this time they looked as large as saucers. She didn't say anything, and her face remained impassive.

Uh-oh. Maybe she's afraid to admit what she is. Maybe I just stepped in it. Well, here I go down the drain again. "I think that you and I kind of belong together, and you probably know as well as I do that there's a full moon tonight. Would you like to meet somewhere tonight and do a little, well, shall we say, howling at the moon together?"

The woman just looked at him for a moment. Finally, she spoke. "What's your name?" she asked in a very quiet voice.

"Tom. Thomas Catlett Mackintosh." Tom saw the corners of her mouth turn up in a slight grin when she heard the name.

"Doctor Melanie Farquharson."

"Charmed."

"About tonight?"

"Yes?" *Here it comes.*

"I'd like you to know that I have never once in my life agreed to go out with a man that I just met, but I wouldn't miss being with you tonight for the world."

"You wouldn't?"

"No, I wouldn't. You see," she said, smiling and reaching forward to take Tom's arm gently, "I've been waiting for a man like you all of my life."

There are many stories of reincarnation, of a deceased human being reborn as a cat. A deceased cat being reborn as another cat doesn't seem to offer much difference. But "Born Again" has Mu Mao the Magnificent as a supporting character. Elizabeth Ann Scarborough created Mu Mao in her novel Last Refuge (Bantam Spectra, September 1992) as a human bodhisattva who chose to be reincarnated as a cat, to help other cat spirits find their new lives. The protagonist in "Born Again" is Peaches, who was a timid cat in life. After Peaches' death and still in the spirit world, he asks Mu Mao to help him find his former human friend. What the two cats find shocks him, but he's not about to abandon his human, especially with Mu Mao's help.

See also Scarborough's "The Cat Quest of Mu Mao the Magnificent" in Catfantastic III, and "Mu Mao and the Court Oracle" in A Constellation of Cats. They are all in her e-book collection 9 Tales o' Cats (Amazon Digital Services, October 2011).

Born Again

by Elizabeth Ann Scarborough

He had never been the kind of cat to have adventures. Timid, he had spent much of his early life hiding under couches and beds and behind bookshelves when company called. Peaceful by nature, he did not hunt and thought the dry food his friend placed in the communal dish the best of all possible foods. Contemplative and spiritual, he was relieved to take his surgical vows and live the life of a brother, son, and companion.

The wilder pleasures he had always found frightening. Lying under the garden bench on a sunny day, or beside the heater in the office while his friend worked, indulging himself with a bit of catnip on occasion; these were his quiet enjoyments.

Some might have found it dull; indeed, the other cats in the household chided him that he had always been an old man, but he found his life deeply fulfilling, and had mourned to leave it almost as much as he was mourned.

He had outlived all of the cats with whom he was once young, and was nearly twenty when the illness fell upon him. He had thought that after all those years of friendship he would have to die alone, but in the end he was in her arms and she was weeping into his grizzled fur, singing him lullabies and crooning the words that baffled him now. Even though there were no fleas on this plane, he sat down and had a scratch, as was his habit when he was troubled, and considered his options.

All around him different colored lights zoomed in and out, but it was just light, nothing to worry about. Strange-looking figures would hiss at him, and he'd hiss back. Kindly, beautiful figures would offer him tasty looking dishes, but the delicacies had no smell, and besides, he wasn't hungry. He just sat there, wondering how he was supposed to find his way home.

After a while, he expressed his displeasure. To his surprise, his voice was strong and plaintive, not the whiney, old man's meow it had been during the last few months of his life. If help for a stranded cat was available in this neighborhood, that mew ought to bring it running.

Running was not all it did. It pounced, rolled him over three times and gave his tail a swat before he squared off with it. "It" was another cat, a long-haired type with a gray face, paws, and tail. Probably thought he was hot stuff because his tail was high and plumey, and a golden glow shone all around him. Golden glows were all right, but some cats, superior cats, were already golden enough and always had been, so what was so wonderful about a little yellow light?

"What in the name of the Buddha are you doing here?" the long-haired newcomer demanded.

"I'd like to know that myself. Who're you?"

"I'm Mu Mao the Magnificent, of course, formerly the Last Cat in the World—well, almost, and Decanter of the Damned. But that's another story. I know what you are. Obviously, from your aura, you're a bodhisattva such as myself, though not as highly evolved, of course. But who are you and what are you doing in the Bardo?"

"The what?"

"The Bardo. The Isles of the Dead."

"Is that so? What kinds of dead things are there?" he asked with interest. Some of them might be tasty.

"You, for one. But you're in the wrong place. Someone with your aura should be in Nirvana. I haven't had to come here for generations, myself, but I couldn't help hearing you yowling, and you spoiled my nap. I'm between lives at present and thought I'd see what the fuss was about. So I repeat, who are you? I know all of the cats still existing. I'm the father of most of them."

"You're not my father. And I am Peaches, Mr. Peaches to you."

"Peaches? As in canned peaches? What a curious name."

"It's an excellent name. My friend gave it to me when I was a kitten and she observed that the peach ice cream she was eating when she first saw me in my incarcerated state matched the color of my baby fur. She claimed me and we were inseparable until recently. Now I can't find my way back to her."

"You're not supposed to go back, my friend. You're dead."

"That has nothing to do with anything. She's my friend, and she said I could go back if I wanted. And I want."

The other cat licked his long chest fur contemplatively, "Just—er—how long have you been here, entertaining this desire, Peaches, my friend?"

"I've no idea. I hadn't been well, you see, and things have all been a little muddled."

"This may come as a shock to you, but it's been longer than you think. A lot longer. A lot has happened in the world in the meantime. It has, I'm sorry to tell you, ceased to be as you once knew it. I hope this friend you're looking for was a very good woman."

"We suited each other," Peaches replied with a lick to his tail tip.

"That means little," Mu Mao said. "Sometimes one chooses a companion because of the needs they can fill rather than for virtue. If your friend was of your caliber, she should be in Nirvana. Otherwise, she's no doubt wandering the Bardo, as you so mistakenly do now, looking for some life form to become."

"You mean she's dead?" Peaches cried. That had never occurred to him. Companions usually outlived cats, even very old cats, by many years. And she had been a fairly young woman when he saw her last.

"Most people are," Mu Mao said, giving his right front paw a discreet swipe. "As I mentioned, the world as you knew it ended some time ago."

"So you think she's in this Nirvana place?"

"Perhaps. It's certainly where you belong. You've lived nine lives of devotion to imparting the wisdoms of calm, patience, detachment and humor. You belong in the highest place now."

"Is that the place where you become an angel, with wings and a halo?" Peaches asked. "My friend and I watched some vids about those, but I thought they only concerned humans."

Mu Mao sat down and folded his paws and explained with only slightly exasperated patience, "Angels are just the way one religion interpreted auras and the gift of astral travel. All beings are one in a sense, and all achieve enlightenment according to their merits. You've been a very meritorious kitty indeed, Mr. Peaches. Now let's scat out of here and achieve Nirvana, shall we, hmm?"

"Not without my friend," Peaches said, planting his paws as firmly as they'd plant in relative nothingness.

"She's probably waiting for you there," Mu Mao wheedled. "It's the best place she could be."

"Not unless Nirvana is our office, with my cushion by the heater," Peaches grumbled, or tried to. Lights and clouds swirled around him and nothing was familiar except the mocking, knowing eyes of Mu Mao. He was very glad when everything settled down again. The whole experience made him feel like he wanted to toss a hairball.

Nirvana was nice enough. There were fluttering things and dangling things, things to chase and places to lie high up and warm. All the people seemed to like cats. But none of them was his particular friend.

It didn't take him very long to start meowing and clawing at insubstantial things until they kicked him out, along with Mu Mao for bringing him.

"Now look what you've done," Mao said.

Peaches groomed himself with a certain grim self-satisfaction. "I know perfectly well what I've done. I meant to do that. She wasn't there and I had no intention of staying. I told you I wouldn't. Where else can we look?"

Mu Mao meditated on the matter for a moment. He looked very wise but Peaches felt that wise was as wise did and he wanted no cheap philosophy. He wanted to be back with his friend, period. He switched his tail impatiently while the other cat seemed to be dozing with his eyes open.

"If she's not here," Mu Mao said finally, "and she's not in the Bardo, then she may have reincarnated already. Do you still want her if she's a gecko lizard, say, or a mouse?"

Peaches had to give that some thought but he finally concluded, "I'd want to be with her if she was a junkyard dog. She won't hurt me. She'll know me. She said she would."

"No wonder you're a bodhisattva," Mu Mao said. "That's what I call faith."

"But she won't be a dog," Peaches continued, "and she won't be a gecko or a mouse either. She's too big. She'll be herself, a human being, as sure as I'm a cat."

Mu Mao did not appear as enlightened by this statement as Peaches had expected. "The life you lived with this—friend—was your ninth life, right?"

"It was my life," Peaches replied simply.

"You do know there were others?"

"I'm not much for theology," Peaches replied, "but the place I was at first—the Bardo, you called it?—seemed familiar, as if I'd dreamed about it."

"And you only remember being a cat, then."

"What else should I remember?"

Mu Mao blinked at him, the wide blue-gray eyes closing and opening as if to pull him in. "How one with such an enlightened aura can be so ignorant and steeped in samsara—"

"What's that?" Peaches demanded, pouncing on the term. "Could my friend be there?"

"Samsara is the painful cycle of life and rebirth from which most of us escape when we attain enlightenment but which you seem determined to cling to with tooth and claw."

"You bet your tail I do," Peaches said grimly. "And you didn't answer my question. Could she be there? My friend?"

"She could be anywhere, but it's unlikely she survived. Few did. Where did you last live? Do you know when?"

"We lived first in a very cold place called Alaska, where I was born, and then my friend put me and the other cats of the house onto a big thing that smells horrible and makes your ears hurt. I thought it was the end of us all, but then after a while she was there and found us a Home where it was never too cold and we could go in and out as we pleased. The others hunted a great deal, but I was needed to help her with her writing and so I remained inside, of course."

"That's all very well, but where was it?"

Peaches tried to help but he had limited himself somewhat with his indoor duties and had not really been aware of his environment. "You could smell fish and salt there all the time, and the air felt like water."

"So, on the coast of the United States."

All of a sudden the voice of Peaches' friend sprang into his head so clearly he cried out, missing her. "Box 11111, Port Chetzemoka, Washington," he said.

"What?" Mu Mao asked.

"That's what she told people on the telephone who wanted to send us nice things. She'd tell the telephone that, and things would be left at the door. The brown people always knew how to find her again from us from there. Can you find her again from that?"

Mu Mao blinked and settled down to clean between the pink pads of his gray paws, taking particular care with each scimitar-shaped claw. "Peaches. Friend. I don't like to tell you this, but I've seen what became of Washington in America. Much of what was near the water is now under the water. Your friend must surely have died."

Peaches hunkered down until his eyes, one brown and one green, were level with the blue eyes of Mu Mao, and their whiskers almost touching. He laid his ears back and hissed. "Ssso" and spat, "what?"

"No need to be rude, I'm sure," Mu Mao said.

"No need to be stupid. I'm dead, you're dead, what should it matter if she's dead? We could still find her, but she's not in that Bardo place nor in your Nirvana.

So she must be living, mustn't she?"

"There's a bad place she might go," Mu Mao said.

"She wouldn't go to a bad place. She was good. She was my friend," Peaches said.

"You mustn't rule out any possibility."

"Fine, but you said you know where Washington is. Let's look first for Port Chetzemoka and try to find her among the living." He gave his tail three quick flicks, then conceded, "And if we don't find her anywhere among the living, then we'll look in the bad place."

"You look. I'm a very enlightened being. I spend all my energy trying to keep myself and others out of that place. But we can go to Washington if you like."

"How?"

"On the astral plane, we can travel very quickly. You have only to envision your home…"

"I can't think of anyplace else…"

"And we can go there. I'll do the navigating."

"Should I hold onto your tail or anything?" Peaches asked, suddenly feeling timid again, now that he seemed close to getting what he sought.

"No. Just think of your home."

Peaches thought hard. The house with the logs inside, the heavy oak office furniture with the glass fronted bookcase and the computer and printer and all the special awards and knickknacks only he, of all the cats, was permitted near. And of course, his special cushion by the heater.

"I need more to go on than one room," Mu Mao said.

So Peaches visualized the yard, the open spaces filled with dandelions and tall grass, the bushes where you could hide and wait for birds, the trees, and all the saltwater and fish smell.

He thought very hard, his eyes closed to shut out the nothingness around him and invoke only home.

"You can look now," Mu Mao said in a discouraged voice.

Peaches opened his eyes eagerly nonetheless, thinking to see at least the yard, maybe the house, maybe his friend herself calling him from the front door.

But when he looked, he could only wail, "You did something wrong. It's nothing but water!" And indeed, there was nothing but gray smoking skies with dirty rain falling into a gray turgid sea stretching so wide that surely nothing had ever lived there.

"I told you," Mu Mao said. "A lot of the coastal places were drowned under tidal waves or split off and washed out to sea."

But Peaches hardly heard him. He could do nothing but cry, mourning his home and his office and his cushion by the heater. "It's all gone."

"Sorry, friend. I did try to warn you. You have no home to go to. Now will you come to your reward?"

"I suppose I—no," Peaches said. "Just because our home is gone doesn't mean my friend is gone. Of course, she won't be here, but perhaps she's nearby? She'll be looking for me, I tell you."

"Peaches. Friend. It isn't pretty, the things humans are doing to others now. The only place your friend would be safe is in Shambala."

"Why didn't you say so?" Peaches asked. "Probably she's there already, waiting for me."

"I can promise you that she is not. I brought all who are there since the end of the world to Shambala myself and no one there was looking for a stubborn orange cat. Besides, it's half a world away from here."

"Can you not simply think of it and take us there?"

"You. Now. Yes. Not a living being. That mode of travel is for astral beings only. There are the tunnels, of course, but they can be negotiated only by such as myself."

"What tunnels?"

"All over the world is a network of tunnels connected to Shambala. Once in them, time is altered. But they are secret, known only to Shambala beings such as myself and the yetis." Mu Mao changed the subject abruptly. "You know, now that we're where you used to live, we could try homing in on your friend instead of her house. Think of her very clearly and try to see where she is. I'll help you."

Peaches closed his eyes and saw his friend clearly, her large comforting form, her eyes as green as his green one, her head fur brown and somewhat white now, her hands and voice soft and loving with him mostly, though sometimes stern when he wet inappropriately.

"I don't know why you're so intent on this one human. They leave cats all the time, you know," Mu Mao said irritably.

"I know," Peaches said. "But my friend always returned to me. She had to leave us to work in another country and was gone for months, kind with us, and when I became very ill and she wasn't expected to return for weeks, all of a sudden she was there. I was so happy I felt almost normal for two days and she was happy, too. But when we both knew I had to go away, she said, "If you come back as a cat and want to come home, find me or let me know where you are and I'll find you." Thinking of his death again, and especially of her sorrow, made him sad and he began crying, her face still clear in his mind behind the weepiness at the corners of his eyes as he yowled.

"But humans move on and forget about us. You can have the highest reward in Nirvana or, if you like, come with me to Shambala to live once more in comfort and happiness."

"How can I be happy somewhere she's not? After I left my body, I hovered in the corner of the room and saw that she held me until she was sure I was gone, then she took a basket so good that she once chased us out of it and put me in it, along with some of the weaving we did together, some catnip and some seeds, and called her friends to help bury my earthly remains. She was very sad. Now our home is gone—what's become of her? I have to know and go to her again."

"That is," Mu Mao said, "Unless she's moved some place where they don't allow cats."

Peaches laid back his ears, narrowed his eyes and lifted a leg to wash beneath his tail in response to that remark, but just then Mu Mao asked, "There. Is that her?"

Peaches wasn't sure at first. She wasn't large anymore, but thin, and her hair was in patches as was her clothing. She was among about twenty other people and was busy with a pointed thing, breaking up soil and rocks. All around were mountains and she stood on a rocky path leading into one.

"That's a funny way to garden," Peaches said. "My friend has never been fond of yard work actually. She's a scholar and a thinker, as I am."

"She's not gardening, Mr. Peaches," Mu Mao said his name derisively. He might as well have come right out and called him "kitty-cat." "See the men with the guns? She's a prisoner. It's forced labor."

Peaches wanted a closer look and without trying to he found himself staring up into his friend's sweating, sunburned face. He wished he could smell her, but just by looking, he could tell that she didn't feel at all well and needed to spend a long time curled up in bed with him purring beside her. He twined around her ankles, filthy and spread far apart to brace her for the impact of the blows she dealt the ground with the heavy implement she wielded. Peaches cried to see her like that and for a moment she stopped and listened.

The nearest man with a gun hit her with it and knocked her down. "Get up, lazybones. That'll teach you to stop work." He also said some other things Peaches didn't understand except that his tone was so mean, it made the cat want to hide at first, and then it made him so mad that all of his fur stood on end, his tail lashed and he wanted to fly claws first into the man's sneering face and rip him a new one. Instead, he took his usual revenge and peed on the man's boot but since he was not yet living, the boot didn't get wet.

Peaches rejoined Mu Mao, who was curled on a rocky ledge high above the workers.

"Still want to go back to your comfy home, eh?" Mu Mao asked.

"What's become of her that she's forced to do this?" Peaches asked, looking down at his friend's prostrate form, as the other people worked around her. "She's not bad. Why did that man hit her?"

"You are one sheltered pussycat," Mu Mao told him. "As I mentioned before, the world ended, more or less, a few years ago. What's left has in most places allowed the worst element to gain control. Eventually, this may be a good thing and order may be reestablished, then civilization will have a chance to build again. But in the meanwhile, those who are not strong and ferocious are dominated by those who are. In this case it seems to me your friend is part of a chain gang, rebuilding the road that goes into this mountain." Mu Mao looked down, a model of detachment. "You won't have long to wait, I'd say, before she joins you and then you can see if she's eligible for Nirvana."

"It's not the same," Peaches said. "And if you mean she's to die, I don't want her to die. I want us to be together again."

"That's no place for cats. But if you insist, we'll have to go back into the Bardo and wait for a portal near here."

"Portal?"

"A womb into which you can be born. It won't be easy to find, though with your spiritual status, you do have a certain preferential…"

Peaches would have run ahead of Mu Mao had he known where to go. Mu Mao presented several possibilities but none of them were right. He needed something special, something absolutely right if he was to be reunited with his friend and make his home with her again. As Mu Mao pointed out, such people as the man with the gun had only one use for cats and it wasn't to catch mice.

It was the unearthly, echoing cry that alerted them to the possibility, and Mu Mao quickly said the words that guided Peaches back into the Bardo, where, Mu Mao told him, he must grapple with the first demon he encountered, for that would be the aspect of himself he must embrace with this rebirth.

Mu Mao didn't mention, though Peaches knew, there would also be other souls to grapple with.

There were. For the first time he could remember, Peaches felt no wish to hide under the couch. "I'm sorry, my friends," he said resolutely to the two dogs, six salamanders, three former soldiers, and one ex-President who were also thronging toward the unusual new portal.

"I have special need of this one. You'll have to wait for the next one." What really surprised him was that he was fully prepared to back it up with fang and claw. The others knew this. They felt his desperation and they backed off, not all the way, but a little way, in case something went wrong and they could overpower him and gain the advantage.

Then the demon arose, blocking the greenish light emitting from the opening in the haze. It had claws like butcher knives, just one of which could rip a cat in half. It had slavering, slobbering fangs dripping blood and the skulls of many past opponents strung around its powerful neck. Its tail lashed and its jaws gnashed. Its ears were laid back and its blood-red eyes glared down at Peaches.

Every orange hair on his incorporeal body was standing up, every nerve was screaming to run away, but Peaches was mindful of what he had seen and heard in the company of Mu Mao. At first he slunk, then walked, one paw at a time, then ran forward under the waving claws of the demon to twine himself around its feet.

He even tried to purr, which was mad. Mad. The thing was going to destroy him.

But then, he heard Mu Mao's voice saying in the back of his mind, he was already dead. So what was he worried about?

He twined some more while the demon loomed and glared and waved its claws and ground its fangs.

Then suddenly the great clawed paws descended upon him, scooping under his belly and lifted him high, toward the gaping maw of the demon, through which the green light of the portal shone, strong and bright. Peaches remembered Mu Mao's counsel and leapt from the demon's grasp, into its mouth and straight through it and...

He sat up, blinking, smelling the fresh scent of rain and earth all around him. His head hurt a little, and the broken branch was under him, where he had dropped before, in that other life, the one that had departed this body just before Peaches gained admittance.

He ignored the pain and lifted his nose, sniffing. The man scent was near. Already many memories of the Bardo were fading, memories of his former life, but his compulsion was so strong. He knew he was looking for someone among the men.

He also knew it was sheerest idiocy to go among those men. But, keeping to the cover of rocks and what was left of the forest, he stalked through the brush as the rain began to fall and the fog rose. The rain washed away much of the man scent. All but a single scent that was like catnip to his nostrils.

He leaped onto a rock and looked below him and saw the pitiful, crumpled form below, and his purpose flooded back into him. There she was. His friend.

They had left her lying there as if she were nothing but bird's feathers or mouse fur and they had already eaten the useful bits.

The cat who had been Peaches jumped down and padded over to the form, sniffing her, prodding her with his paw. Breath still moved her torso, shallow and faint though it was, but her body was losing its warmth. He knew somehow that her skin was too tender for him to take her neck in his jaws, as he would a kitten's, but he grabbed a hunk of the false coat humans called clothing and tugged. The going was so slow. She was floppy, and he didn't want to break any of her parts or damage her further and yet he knew neither of them must be there by dawn, when the men with the guns would return. He pulled first one piece, then another, nudging the stray parts back toward her body so they didn't twist out of shape while he pulled. He was at the mouth of the mountain, the sun just sending a warning hint of blue into the blackness of the night, when he heard a voice behind him.

"Well, well, kittycat. I didn't think you had it in you."

The cat who had been Peaches growled, a sound so ferociously it startled even him. The small fluffball taunting him was asking to be eaten.

"Calm down, kittycat," it said. "It's me, Mu Mao the Magnificent. I'm here to help you. I didn't point out this cave by accident, you know. There's an entrance to the Shambala tunnel here. Follow me, bring your friend and you'll both be safe inside while I reincarnate and go for help."

The cat who had been Peaches looked down at his friend. Dragging her all night had not improved her health or appearance. He licked her face with his great tongue and made a noise that sounded something like the mew he would have made as Peaches.

"Don't worry. Once inside the cave, she will not deteriorate further. We haven't got all day, you know. Move your tail."

The cat who had been Peaches dragged and nudged and hauled and nudged some more, following after the taunting plumey tail of Mu Mao until the small cat suddenly walked into what had appeared a solid wall. Since it was not, the cat who had been Peaches went through it, too, bringing his friend and nudging her here and there until at last, as her foot joined the rest of her, the wall that it had held ajar closed as if it had never existed.

Mu Mao had gone by then, a flickering light in the darkness of the tunnel. The cat who had been Peaches lay panting beside his unconscious friend. Outside the tunnel, he could hear the voices of men and the heavy implements striking the ground. His friend's skin was very cold; he wrapped as much of him around her as he could to warm her and tried to remember how to purr.

He was used to his new form now, and his own memories returned to him, and he was very sad, thinking of all his friend had lost, all that was now lost to him as well. He thought it would be a very long, time before Mu Mao returned, for Shambala was on the other side of the world.

He forgot that Mu Mao had told him that the tunnels contained bends in time and that vast spaces, even those with oceans in them, could be traveled very quickly. In the meantime he nursed his friend, licking and rubbing against her, keeping her warm, singing to her softly, and also, knowing his strength would be needed, he slept.

In a shorter time than he would have believed possible, he awoke to behold a white object suspended in the darkness, approaching through the tunnel. At first he thought it was Mu Mao, but then it grew larger and he saw it walked upright, like a man, but was covered in white fur. He didn't know what it was, and he growled at its approach.

From behind its head peeked a silver face, and a familiar, impertinent voice said, "Ooh, down, kittycat. Not so fierce. This is a friend of mine. He's a yeti. He can carry your friend the rest of the way to Shambala. You may follow."

After rubbing his face all over his friend's head and body to mark her firmly as his own, he allowed the yeti to lift her in its massive arms and trot away with her.

He followed as best he could, weary from his labors of the night.

The tunnel was more disconcerting than the Bardo, for the sensations of missing a step between one reality and the next beset him while within a physical body. Its very skin and fur rebelled at the dissonance that his ghost form had not noticed. But he followed the distant hairy form of the yeti and the mocking plumed tail of Mu Mao up out of the tunnel and into an underground house.

Food smells filled his nostrils, mingling with the scents of flowers and snow, sweating people and new babies.

Sounds of laughter and chimes and happy conversation sang in his ears.

The yeti laid his friend down just inside the door of the underground dwelling and then ran away. Mu Mao scampered out through a flap left in the door, returning with several people.

"My word, what kind of animal is that?" a woman's voice asked.

"One of the other species of big cat. A mountain lion perhaps," her companion answered.

"Mu Mao, please tell this beast we need to move the woman to assist her."

But the cat who had been Peaches understood perfectly well and with a final lick and rub to his friend, stepped back two paces and sat down to groom while they lifted her.

He followed them when they carried her, however, and lay beside the mat they gave her on the floor. He watched all that they did, though he never lifted a paw to stop them. Her breathing grew more normal as the doctors palpated her and rubbed smelly things into her skin and even poked little needles into her.

And finally she began to move, and whimper and cry out in her sleep. The cat who had been Peaches gave her a reassuring lick when she cried and wrapped himself close when she shivered.

They had been there hours, and he had to go outside to relieve himself, though as he was now, nobody would have dared shoo him away.

Mu Mao was out there. "Well, kittycat. What now?" the little cat asked.

"What do you mean?"

"You were right about her. She's not a junk yard dog or a mouse or a bird. She's still human, though just barely. But you're the one who's changed. You're a wild animal now. She might be afraid of you."

That had never occurred to him. The others weren't afraid of him, but he'd hardly fit on her lap anymore, come to think of it. He favored Mu Mao with a glare and peered back into the room, through the door that had been left ajar. She was sitting up eating!

She looked up, cringing as he could only guess had been her habit for all the long days and nights she'd been under the rule of the men with guns. He waited, to avoid startling her, and she stared at him, the folds of her sagging flesh making her eyes seem somewhat smaller but not dimming their brightness.

Those eyes he knew so well looked straight into his, and the mouth that must not have smiled in a very long time curved up and she said, "Peaches! You did come back!" And he ran to her and fitted as much of himself as he could into her lap after all while she stroked his nose and scratched behind his ears and under his chin and kissed his fur and told him how she'd missed him, just as he'd known she would.

The snow lions called to him to come and mate, to come and play, and sometimes he did briefly, but mostly he stayed on the padded pallet she made for him near her fire, where she sat and wrote of all that had happened to her while he had been between lives. And the puma called Peaches purred a purr that shook the compound with the vibrations of his contentment.

Author's note—
This story is dedicated to the late Peaches, who was my office cat and best friend for twenty years. It first appeared in Catfantastic IV edited by Andre Norton and Martin H. Greenberg, with a book cover by Mark Hess showing a post-reincarnation Peaches as the feline nobleman Valar Silversmoke.

Editor's Note—
The cover of this book was desinged to represent Peaches' reincarnation as a puma, and so was inspired by the Catfantastic IV cover.

Cats have been the well-known magical companions of wizards and witches for centuries. (They have also often been considered Satan's demonic agents who bring a witch her evil powers. But let's not get into that.)

But how does a magic-user choose his or her feline familiar? And what if the cat has an excellent reason to not want to be a familiar? Bryan Derksen's "Masters and Students" features not only a cat who doesn't want to be a companion, but a man who doesn't want to be a cat.

"Masters and Students" was previously only posted as an online short story, almost twenty years ago. This is its first appearance in print form.

Masters and Students

by Bryan Derksen

It had been another one of those days, the sort that slowly but surely crushes your head in a vice of tension and conflict. A headache was pounding in my temples by the time I left the office and headed home, desperate for a Tylenol and a rest on the sofa. The management back at the office had once again managed to remain oblivious to my common sense. Ah, the joys of self-delusion. They would come around eventually, I was an expert at dealing with people like that by now, but it was still a long and frustrating process sometimes…

Then it finally happened, with absolutely no warning. One minute I was driving along, the throbbing in my temples merely a dull background ache, when suddenly the pain erupted and stabbed through my brain like an icepick. Brilliant lights flared in my vision, a roaring filled my head, and I saw the steering wheel rushing up towards my face. I didn't feel it hit.

The next instant, everything was different. I screamed, thrashing wildly in a total panic with my eyes screwed tightly shut. I've never been so terrified or confused in all my life; everything felt *wrong*. *I finally had a stroke*, I thought frantically as I tried to make sense of what my body was telling me. *The stress finally did me in. Blew a brain artery wide open.* And I had been in a speeding car, too. Now I was probably in an intensive care ward. But stroke or no, that just didn't seem correct…

I wound up lying curled on my side, huddled against some sort of rough wall and frozen with fear. I seemed to be in a small cage of some sort rather than a conventional bed, made of wicker and sitting on the floor of a huge open room. There was the smell of burnt… *something* in the air, very thick but not too unpleasant. A bit like incense, though not as nice.

Something huge moved out there, and I was instantly drawn to its motion before I had a chance to think further. The shape took a moment to resolve itself in my addled brain, however; my eyes were still blurry and unfocused. It was a giant humanoid, perhaps five times my height, raising itself to its hands and knees with a deep groan and clutching its head feebly. It, or rather he from its appearance, was obviously in pain. "Gods," he mumbled, "that was terrible." I would have agreed if I could think at all; I was still too stunned for that.

Then he crawled over and looked down at me through the cage, towering twice as tall as it, and said. "Hello? Did… did it work?" **How the hell should *I* know?** I thought numbly. But at my thought, a wide smile broke over the giant's face. "It *did* work!" he exclaimed. "The spell still worked!"

I was starting to regain my equilibrium, and though this situation was clearly beyond my experience I decided that I should try to gain some measure of control over it. "What spell?" I tried to ask, but my throat must have been paralysed; all I could force out was a strange high-pitched moan. I reached out to grab the wicker-like bars of my cage.

The hand I reached out with wasn't a hand. It was a fur-covered paw with stumpy digits that barely separated as I splayed them, claws curving out from their tips. Breathing faster as panic again started to swell, I looked down at myself; more fur, more unfamiliar body shapes. I didn't look at all human, and it sure didn't feel like something I was wearing. So I did a most understandable thing, considering the circumstances; I screamed my head off. So much for regaining my equilibrium.

"Hey, hey! What's wrong!?" The giant man exclaimed.

I crouched on the cage floor, clawed fingers and toes clutching the wicker tightly as I looked up at him. **What's wrong?** I thought wildly, stifling my high-pitched yowling. **Are you blind? What the hell's happened to me!?**

"You don't know?" he asked in surprise.

I, too, was surprised; **Geeze, can you read my thoughts or something?** I wondered.

"Yes," the man responded. "That's the way it's supposed to work."

I closed my eyes and forced my breathing to slow. **Okay,** I tried to take stock. **So you can read my thoughts.**

"Yes, I can," the man confirmed, as gently as someone fifty feet tall could make himself sound.

Alright. I took a deep mental breath. **Then who are you, and what the hell have you done to me!?**

"Something… something's gone wrong after all, hasn't it?" The man asked cautiously. "You really don't know what happened, do you?" I snorted derisively, and he got the picture. "Okay, uh, then where are you from? What are you?"

What am I? I have no idea, you idiot! I looked down at myself and pawed at my body with my "hands". **I look like an animal or something!**

"No, I mean *before* you answered my summons." The man seemed genuinely concerned, though at this point I was too upset to let that affect my mood.

I was human, I thought. **My name is Jeffery Gilbert. I was driving home from work, when bang! My head felt like it exploded. And here I was. Now, where is here? What happened?**

"I think…" the man paused, uncertain. "I think I screwed up the spell after all. I don't suppose you know what plane of existence you come from?"

Uhhh… no. The planet's called Earth, though. Are you trying to tell me I'm on some sort of alternate plane of existence? At this point, I was willing to believe almost anything.

The man sighed and put his head in his hands. "You're *not* a spirit, then, from the ethereal plane?" I shook my head. "Hoo, boy." I waited for him to continue, and eventually he did. "Okay, then. You're an alternate material plane denizen, I guess, right?" I tried to shrug, but my narrow shoulders apparently didn't work that way. He seemed to get the message, thought. "All right. I owe you a big explanation, then."

"I'm Kellor Gazin, a magic-user." He began. "I just finished an apprenticeship, in fact. And I was trying to summon a familiar spirit. But something went wrong, it all blew up in my face just as I was casting the spell. It looks like the spell worked, but snagged the wrong spirit. Oh gods, what will I do now?"

How about sending me back, for starters?

Kellor looked up. "I have no idea how," he said quietly.

Swell. Then let me out of this cage, and start telling me exactly what you did to me. What *am* I? I had developed a pretty good idea just from looking down at myself, but I wanted confirmation. I'd never had to determine my species from the *inside* before.

"You're a cat," Kellor said. "A nice big tabby, the best I could buy. I had originally thought maybe a raven, but…" I stopped paying attention to him as I crawled out of the cage. I was walking on all fours, and it felt natural; I could tell it would be a struggle to stand on only two. I looked back at myself, noting my fur and flicking my tail experimentally. My god, I really was a cat! No wonder everything looked huge. I tried to speak out loud, but all I could produce was a sort of mumbled meow.

This is no good, I thought at Kellor accusingly. **Look at this! I can't be more than a foot or so tall down here!**

"I, uh… I'm sorry," Kellor apologized. "It's traditional to use small host forms for familiars, I guess it's supposed to be more convenient…"

I sat down and sighed, shaking my head and trying to rub the bridge of my nose with a forepaw. Assuming I wasn't simply having a coma-induced nightmare I had just been thrust into an alien universe and an alien body, and yet I could *still* tell right off the bat that this supposed "wizard" knew less about what was going on than I did. At least my headache was gone and I could think straight, ignoring the rest of my senses for the moment.

Start at the beginning, I told him patiently. **Tell me exactly what you were *trying* to do, and where you think you went wrong.** Perhaps even without personal knowledge of magic I could help him get me back in my proper body...

"Familiar spirits are summoned from the ethereal plane," Kellor explained carefully, as if reciting a lesson memorized from a book. "The spell should have presented a request for service; familiar spirits usually *want* to visit the material plane. I don't know why it was different in your case, just like everything else it must have gone wrong. Anyway, the familiar enters the shell of a small animal prepared by the summoner, and is bound to the summoner. We're linked; that's why I can understand your thoughts. Normally, the familiar boosts my spellcasting power through the link, and comes with arcane knowledge and experience to teach its master, but..."

Yeah, I'm substandard in the arcane knowledge department. And can the 'master' bit, too; I'm not here for that.

"Sorry, Jeffery. Standard terminology." Kellor stroked his chin, thinking. "Let's see, now. There're other aspects of the spell beyond those, but they're sort of secondary; I'm supposed to get boosted special abilities from you, and you get boosted special abilities from me. The link shares our health; we're each harder to hurt than average because of that. But if you get killed I take a blow, and if I get killed, you die too."

Woah, waitaminute! That's not fair.

"What?"

You don't die if I get killed, but it doesn't work the other way around?

"I don't know, I think it must be because ethereal spirits just return to their home plane instead of discorporating... hey, now there's an idea!"

It took a moment for me to realize what that idea was, and quite reflexively my back arched and my fur stood on end. An odd sensation, that. **No. You are *not* going to kill me in an attempt to send me home,** I told him, punctuated with a very feline hiss. Kellor actually took a step back, to my gratification.

"Sorry," he apologized again. "But wait a minute. I know you're not the right type of spirit, but the spell might bounce you back anyways if our link gets severed. You could plop straight back into your original body, or something."

Even if Kellor's wild guessing hadn't been enough to put me off of his plan, a fact occurred to me that would seem to kill the idea once and for all. My ears flattened against my skull as I realized it, another new sensation I didn't have time to pay much attention to at the moment. **Kellor... when I left it, my original body was doing fifty miles an hour down the expressway. Nobody's been piloting it since I got here. Does time run at the same rates in other dimensions?**

"Um..."

Right. It looks like I might not have a usable body back home to plop back into.

Kellor looked down at his feet and scuffed them guiltily. "I'm sorry I killed you, Jeffery. I didn't mean to, I did everything by the book..."

I sighed and rubbed the back of my paw over my face. It seemed that even in other dimensions the irresponsible and ignorant were always the ones to wind up with the most power. Now it looked like I might be stuck in the role of this idiot wizard's familiar for the foreseeable future...

I grinned, an expression my pointed teeth were well suited for. Not necessarily an idiot, perhaps, just young... **Okay Kellor,** I began after a long pause to collect my thoughts, **it looks like you'll have a familiar for a while after all. Yeah, I've got sod-all arcane knowledge, but you've apparently leapt ahead with too much of that** already right now. But I *do* have a little life experience, something you seem to be lacking. Fresh out of apprenticeship, you say?

Kellor nodded unhappily. "Yeah."

Then you must have been apprenticed *to* someone, someone who I assume knows more about how to fix this mess we're in than you do...

* * *

Nichodemus, Kellor's old master, answered the door promptly when Kellor knocked. Unfortunately, just as promptly, he began to snicker. "Ah, Kellor. Back already for help with your exercises? I thought you'd finally decided to strike out on your own."

From my inconspicuous location at Kellor's heels I couldn't see his expression—frankly, trying to look people in the eye from ground level still gave me vertigo—but I could have felt him tense up with resentment and shame from a mile away. **Actually, my new familiar wants to talk with you,** I mentally prompted him, and Kellor snapped out of it to repeat my words.

"Your familiar, eh?" the elderly man said with some surprise, glancing around suspiciously. I stepped out from behind Kellor's legs, returning his stare self-consciously. I don't think I'd ever get used to being this small, though hopefully I wouldn't have to...

Nichodemus took one look at me and then scowled fiercely. "You tried to summon a familiar? That spell was too advanced for you, boy! Why do you think I forbade it while you were still my apprentice?"

"I know, I know," Kellor interrupted meekly. "I screwed it up. My familiar spirit didn't come from the etheric, it came from someplace called Earth. He didn't want to come, he wants to go home. Can you help him?"

"Bah!" Nichodemus waved his hand dismissively. "You screwed it up, you fix it. I'm not your keeper any more." He closed the door on us again, and I emitted a small yowl of dismay.

"Wait! I'm not asking this for me! It's for him!" Kellor cried. "I'll do whatever it takes to set things right!" There was no answer, and after a minute's silence stretched out Kellor sagged slightly in defeat. "I'm sorry, Jeffery. If only he hadn't had to save my own hide so many times, maybe he'd have been willing to help you..." He was interrupted when the door opened again, just a crack.

"Oh, come on in," Nichodemus snapped testily. "Let's talk with this cat of yours."

Kellor immediately swelled with gratitude, but I managed to interject my thoughts before he made a fool of himself; **Just go inside and save the thanks for later, Kellor. You want him to respect you, right?** Kellor nodded and managed to rein himself in before he went overboard. I followed him inside, paying close attention to my tail so that it wouldn't get caught in the door. Very painful, as I had so recently learned on the way out of Kellor's small apartment.

The room through Nichodemus' front door was a densely cluttered magic shop, its walls covered with shelves filled with jars packed with herbs. Nichodemus sat down at a small round table off to one side, motioning for Kellor to sit across from him. After taking a moment to gather my nerve, I leapt up onto Kellor's lap and peered out over the tabletop as well. It wasn't a particularly spectacular jump for a cat, but I was still new to this...

"So you scooped the wrong dimension," Nichodemus began. "Why am I not surprised. Are you from a prime material plane?"

The last was directed at me, and my ears flicked back for a moment as I struggled to think of a reply. **I am, right?** I asked Kellor. He nodded, and I gave Nichodemus a satisfied look. He harrumphed.

"Well, assuming he has a body to return to, it should be fairly easy to send him back. I'm surprised even you didn't figure it out, Kellor."

"Uh... Jeffery tells me he left his body on the verge of certain death, sir."

"Ah." Nichodemus again glanced in my direction, and I nodded in solemn confirmation. "Well, that's a fine mess you've sucked him into, then. Prime material spirits need a physical host, and all he's got now is a cat!"

A quick prick of my claws in his thigh to nudge him on, and Kellor continued with his request for help. "I know, sir. I was wondering if you had any ideas where I could get him a new one."

"And well you should," Nichodemus replied. "You owe him." He sat back in his chair for a moment, lost in thought. "I *could* just swap the two of you, you know," Nichodemus mused at last. "Give Jeffery here your body, and you his. The summoning spell has safeguards against just that sort of thing happening, but I'm sure you messed those up with the rest of it."

Kellor winced and glanced at the door for an instant, reflexively thinking of escape. Then a defeated expression came over him. "I suppose it'd be fair justice," he sighed. "I'd probably make a more successful cat than I do a wizard anyways..."

"I'll need leola root. Wait here, I've got some in back." Nichodemus stood up, a hint of concealed sadness showing through his crotchety exterior.

I was stunned for a moment, not quite believing that they were serious about giving me Kellor's body. Then, once I had recovered, I leapt onto the table with a sharp meow to catch everybody's attention again. It worked, Nichodemus hesitated and Kellor literally jumped in surprise. Though my accidentally unsheathed claws may have also played some role in the latter reaction...

"What is it, Jeffery?" Kellor asked nervously.

I don't want your body, I told him, slightly embarrassed by the turn of phrase.

Any possible insult Kellor might have perceived from my refusal was indistinguishable under the immense wave of relief that almost made his knees buckle. "He says he doesn't want my body," he told Nichodemus.

Nichodemus looked at me, puzzled. "Why not? It could be said you have a right to it, since Kellor here lost you your old one. And since *I'm* the one saying it, that's the way it goes."

Kellor, you took me away from my entire life. But I don't want it back at the expense of yours. I glanced at Nichodemus. **That old wizard may have taught you a few magic tricks, but he apparently missed the reality training for when you had to go out on your own. Or something, I don't know much about your apprenticeship system here. Whatever the case, tell him that if he can't send me back outright right now, I'm willing to stay for a while. And to keep an eye on you, give you a voice of experience next time you think of pulling something like this.**

Kellor repeated my words, and Nichodemus frowned at me. "You want to be his mentor? Do you know anything about magic?"

I shook my head. **No idea. But I *do* know how to deal with power in the hands of the inexperienced. I lived with it all the time, back where I came from.**

"You'd be my familiar after all?" Kellor asked, astonished.

Yeah, I guess I will I thought, as much to myself as to Kellor. **But none of that 'master' stuff, though,** I addressed him directly. **I'm not going to be a talking *pet*.**

Kellor was shaking his head earnestly. "Oh, of course not, I wouldn't dream of it. We'll be partners, fifty-fifty."

"I take it you've reached an accommodation," Nichodemus observed dryly. Then he again addressed me directly. "You realize, of course, that I'm not going to be able to 'magic up' a new human body for you any time soon. If ever. And even if I did, sending you home would be an awesome challenge. You're willing to stick with Kellor in the long term?"

I nodded solemnly. Kellor seemed like a decent sort, and not terribly assertive; I was sure I'd be able to keep him in line. And as for remaining in this world, in the body of a cat... well, I could think of *far* worse extended vacations. In my brief time like this so far, I had found that felines were amazingly competent at *relaxing*...

Nichodemus smiled. "Then perhaps there's hope for you yet, boy," he told Kellor. "And I can finally be rid of you without *worrying* about you so much. Listen to your familiar; even though he doesn't know any arcane secrets I'm sure he'll guide you well. Now shoo! Didn't you want to strike out on your own to make a name for yourself or something? I've got a shop to tend!"

Kellor grinned and turned to leave, and I jumped off the table to follow.

Cats are famously the companions of lonely women. But in folklore, they aren't the only companions that a lonely woman can have.

When ninety-four-year-old Sally Schultz dies, her cat Trixie—who is her only companion that anyone knows about—is taken to a new home. Trixie wants to bring Sally's other companions along with her.

Trixie

by Lawrence Watt-Evans

The black kitten swivelled her head back and forth, her golden eyes wide, wary, and staring, as she was carried down the block and up the front walk of No. 1224. When Annie raised her arm to ring the doorbell the kitten panicked and tried to scramble up her blouse to her shoulder, only to be grabbed firmly and held where she was on Annie's chest.

"There, there, sweetie," Annie said soothingly, as she petted the frightened creature. "You'll be fine."

The door opened and the kitten turned her head to stare at an unfamiliar face, a round but heavily lined face beneath fine, frizzy white hair.

"Hello, Sally," Annie said. "May we come in?"

"Of course!" Sally said. "You'll have to introduce me to your friend."

Annie stepped into a living room that smelled of lavender and chicken soup. "She doesn't have a name yet," she explained, setting the kitten on the sofa. "I brought her for you – I thought you could use some company, living here alone."

"For me?" Sally looked down at the kitten. "Oh, you shouldn't have! I'm not so alone as all that – I have help. And, well, I'm not a young woman. I'm ninety-two… bending down to clean a box…"

"Oh, I'll do that," Annie interrupted. "I'd be glad to. I'll come over every Sunday to take care of it – more often, if you like. It must be so hard for you to take care of this place! And you do it so well – it's spotless! I wish *my* house were half so tidy."

"Oh, really, it's not hard to keep up; you'd be surprised who helps out."

"That nephew of yours?"

Sally snorted. "Albert? Not likely! No, I have other friends who take care of some of the housework."

"I'd love to meet them."

Sally frowned. "Well, maybe someday."

"But they're not here all the time – couldn't you use some company?"

Sally looked at the kitten. "I'm not sure how my helpers would like it."

"Are they allergic to cats?"

"They might be; I'm really not sure."

The kitten ignored the human conversation; she had gotten over her fright sufficiently to take a look around. She crept forward and peered over the edge of the cushion at the floor, thought about jumping, then reconsidered. Instead she turned and ran to one end, bounced off the arm of the couch, then scampered to the back of the cushion and thrust a paw into the opening there.

"She *is* an adorable little thing, though, isn't she?" Sally said, as she watched her feline guest's actions.

"I knew you'd like her. If she ever gets to be too much trouble I'll take her back, but really, I'd feel better if I knew you weren't completely alone here."

Sally gave in. "All right," she said. She reached out to pet the kitten.

The kitten allowed a few quick strokes, then decided she'd had enough and rolled over, out from beneath Sally's unsteady hand, down behind the couch cushion.

That was not quite what she had intended; she scrabbled along, then burst up into the open air a foot or so away from where she had disappeared.

"Oh, she's a tricksy little thing!" Sally exclaimed.

And from then on the kitten's name was Trixie.

Annie brought over Trixie's litterbox and a supply of cat food, and the matter was settled – Trixie would live with Sally Schultz henceforth.

Trixie spent the rest of the afternoon happily exploring her new home, discovering which furniture she could fit under and which she could not, finding the kitchen with its wonderful smells and her litterbox's new location in the laundry room, and running wildly back and forth for no reason other than kittenhood.

When she had had enough running she discovered Sally's lap and settled there for a time, purring as Sally gently petted her. When Sally's hand grew tired, Trixie bounded off to explore behind the sofa.

Supper was followed by another session on Sally's lap, this time with the TV on; the supper dishes were left, unwashed, in the sink.

And then, finally, Sally stood and announced, "I'm going to bed, Trixie; you'll have the house to yourself for awhile. Take good care of it for me!"

She turned off the TV and the light and shuffled into her bedroom, but this time, when Trixie tried to follow, Sally closed the door, shutting her out.

"I'm sorry," she said through the closed door, "but I'm not up to having a kitten bouncing on me while I'm trying to sleep. Maybe when you're a bit older, and we know each other better."

Trixie didn't understand a word, but she heard and accepted the apologetic tone. She didn't meow at the door or otherwise protest; instead she rambled off around the house, looking for prey.

She stalked down the darkened hallway, smelling the air and watching the shadows. A faint whiff of something caught her attention – not a mouse or bird, something sweet. She made her way silently to the kitchen doorway – even kittens can be silent when they want to.

Something was moving in the kitchen – she could hear rattling and thumping. It wasn't loud enough for humans, but it wasn't cat-like, either. She crept in and looked around.

There was something moving on the kitchen table, and something on the counter; water was running and the dishes were rattling in the sink. Everywhere was a gingery, unfamiliar scent.

Trixie leapt to the seat of a chair, and then onto the table, and found herself face to face with something she had never seen before.

It was roughly her own size, but shaped like a human. Its skin and clothing were entirely gingerbread-brown, from the tip of its pointed hat to its curly-toed shoes; its face was long and narrow, with a pointed chin, and pointed ears thrust up on either side of its cap. It held a great wad of cloth in one hand, and had evidently been polishing the table when it heard Trixie's approach.

It squeaked at the sight of her, and the rattling from the sink ceased abruptly. From the corner of her eye Trixie could see more of these creatures on the counter and the edge of the sink, all of them turning to stare at her.

Trixie considered the situation for a moment.

One of the creatures would be a little large for prey to begin with; half a dozen of them were definitely more than any sensible kitten would tackle. The fact that they weren't running away made it plain that *they* didn't consider themselves prey, either.

They were too small to be considered humans, and therefore she could not expect food, petting, or pampering from them. She didn't think they could even open the bedroom door for her, so she could crawl into bed with Sally.

They might be playmates; Trixie had had playmates when she was younger, before being separated from her two littermates. She meowed questioningly.

The creature before her squeaked again, then shrugged, made a shooing gesture, knelt down, and began polishing the table.

That wasn't any fun. Trixie ambled over and batted at the polishing cloth with one paw, claws sheathed.

The creature chittered angrily and snatched the cloth away. Trixie leapt after it.

The creature dropped the cloth and glared angrily at Trixie, then whistled.

Trixie paid no attention at first as she batted the oily cloth around the slippery tabletop; then she felt a sudden grip on her tail and looked up to find herself surrounded by the little brown people.

One of them snatched away the cloth, and when she tried to pursue it another yanked at her tail. She turned, spitting, and swiped, claws out.

The brown things didn't back down or give back the cloth; instead they moved in in a coordinated effort. One grabbed each of her four legs, one ducked under her chin and lifted her head, and one kept a grip on her tail. Then, together, they carried her to the edge of the table and dropped her, no more roughly than necessary given her squirming, to the floor.

She angrily jumped back to the chair and prepared to jump back on the table, only to find herself confronted by a solid barrier of the creatures.

Trixie knew the proper cat thing to do in a case like this; she sat down and began washing herself, pretending she had never had any intention of jumping onto the table.

After that she generally ignored the brown creatures. She watched them occasionally as they washed and dried and put away the dishes, dusted the furniture, and swept the floor, but did not interfere with them.

And at the first light of dawn they all scurried away and vanished – Trixie didn't see where they went, which annoyed her, and she resolved to do better next time.

An hour or so later Sally emerged from her room, and a new day began with a generous breakfast, followed by curling up on Sally's lap in front of the TV.

The days thereafter followed a similar pattern – by day Sally and Trixie kept one another company, and at night while Sally slept Trixie and the little brown creatures ignored each other while the creatures cleaned the house. Over time Trixie grew from a kitten into a cat; Sally slept longer and moved about less. Annie visited often, remarking sometimes on how tidy Trixie was in using her box – which wasn't really true; the brown creatures cleaned up spills, though they didn't change the litter. Sally's nephew Albert stopped by occasionally, and tried to talk Sally into moving into a nursing home. There were phone calls and other visitors, as well, and the comforting flicker and mumble of the TV.

One day each year Annie brought over a little cake for Sally's birthday. Trixie was there for the ninety-third and ninety-fourth.

And then one morning Sally didn't come out of her bedroom to give Trixie breakfast. Trixie waited and waited, but Sally never emerged. Trixie began meowing, and when that didn't work and the hunger became serious she began yowling. She reached up and batted at the bedroom doorknob, but couldn't budge it.

The phone rang, interrupting a yowl, and Trixie ran to the device, ready to demand attention when Sally came to pick up the receiver, but even then, Sally didn't appear. The phone rang and rang, but finally stopped.

A few minutes later it rang again, and was again ignored.

And then, perhaps half an hour later, the doorbell rang – again, without effect.

Albert's voice called, "Aunt Sally? Are you all right?"

Trixie meowed loudly.

A key rattled in the lock, and Albert stepped in. Trixie meowed anxiously and ran beside and around him as he called, "Aunt Sally?" and made his way to the bedroom door. His big human hand easily turned the knob Trixie had been unable to move. The instant the opening was wide enough Trixie dashed inside and jumped on the bed.

Sally was still there – but cold and lifeless.

"Oh, hell," Albert said. He turned and hurried to the phone in the living room.

Trixie meowed at Sally for a moment, then gave up and went out to the living room to meow at Albert.

No one paid any attention. No one fed her or petted her.

And then strangers came, and talked to Albert, and looked at Sally, and took her away, and still no one paid any attention to Trixie, until at last Albert and Trixie were alone in the house, and Trixie meowed so insistently for attention, practically climbing his leg, that Albert finally noticed her.

"What am I going to do with *you?*" he asked.

Trixie meowed once more and led the way to the kitchen, to her bowl.

Albert sighed and got out food, and sat at the table watching as Trixie ate.

"I suppose it's off to the pound for you," he muttered. "I don't want a cat, certainly!" He looked idly around the kitchen. "At least you haven't made a mess of the place the way I thought you would. It's amazing that Aunt Sally kept this house up so well at her age."

Trixie was too busy eating to pay much attention.

She was just finishing, licking her paws, and Albert was sitting at Sally's desk looking through the drawers, when the doorbell rang. Albert closed the drawers and rose, and Trixie trotted out to see who had come.

It was Annie, her expression worried. "Albert?" she said. "What happened? I just got home from work, and Ms. Rose next door told me there was something going on here..."

Albert stood silently, helpless to answer; Annie saw his face and asked, "Where's Sally?"

"She's gone," Albert said.

Annie sat down heavily on the sofa. "*Gone* gone?"

"She was ninety-four," Albert said.

"I know, but..."

Trixie had long ago given up on Albert, but Annie knew how to pet a cat, and right now Trixie desperately wanted some proper attention. She jumped into Annie's lap, interrupting whatever Annie had been saying.

Annie's breath came out in a startled rush, but she recovered quickly and began stroking Trixie, scratching behind her ears and smoothing her fur.

Trixie settled down and began purring.

For a moment no one spoke; Albert settled uneasily onto a chair and sat facing Annie with his hands on his knees.

"What's going to happen to Trixie?" Annie asked at last.

Albert hesitated. "Well, I don't know," he said. "If I don't find someone who wants her I guess she'll go to the pound..."

"No!" Annie said, startling Trixie out of purring. "No, I'll take her. I don't have a cat right now; I'd be glad to keep her."

"I hoped you would," Albert said, relieved.

And that was settled. Twenty minutes later Trixie found herself being carried up the street to No. 1216, reversing the trip she had taken two years earlier.

Once she was delivered Annie returned to the other house to fetch Trixie's food and litterbox, while Trixie began to find her way around her new home.

Annie's house was both familiar and different. The rooms were in the same places and the same sizes as in Sally's house, but the furniture was entirely different – and it wasn't anywhere near as clean. Trixie wrinkled her nose in disgust as she explored her new home. Where Sally's house had smelled of fresh food and flowers, Annie's smelled of mildew and neglect.

This, Trixie thought, would never do. She looked up at Annie as the human passed by with the litterbox and meowed reproachfully.

"What is it, Trixie?" Annie asked. "Do you miss Sally?" She knelt, put the box aside, and petted Trixie. "So do I. But she's gone, and we'll just have to get used to it."

Trixie meowed again, but Annie did not respond properly by getting out a broom or duster; instead she just went on stroking Trixie's fur and talking about Sally.

After awhile Trixie noticed with distaste that Annie had stopped talking, and water was dripping from her eyes. She pulled free of Annie's petting hand and went to wash herself in private – and to think.

Annie was all very well; Trixie had liked Sally, after a cat's fashion, but she understood that Sally was gone, and while that was unfortunate there wasn't much she could do about it, and Annie was an acceptable substitute.

This new house, though, was so dusty Trixie found herself sneezing every time she poked her head under the furniture, and it simply didn't smell right at all. It wouldn't do. Any cat who stayed here would have to spend all her time just licking dust from her fur.

Annie didn't seem to understand that, and presumably, since she had lived here for some time, she didn't care.

Trixie couldn't very well clean the house herself; even if she had hands, it would be beneath her dignity as a cat. But *somebody* had to clean the place.

Of course, Sally hadn't cleaned her own house; she had had the brown creatures to do it. Why didn't Annie have any?

Trixie looked around and decided that Annie *needed* some brown creatures – and after all, with Sally gone, they wouldn't have anything to do at the other house any more.

The question was, how could she get them from *there* to *here*?

The direct approach seemed in order; Trixie went to the back door and meowed.

Annie emerged from the laundry room and saw her.

"Oh, no, Trixie," she said. "You live *here* now. And I'm not going to let you outside – it's too dangerous. You could catch something; I don't know if Sally ever got you all your shots."

Trixie meowed.

"No," Annie said emphatically.

Trixie knew what "no" meant. It meant that the human saying it was not going to cooperate.

Well, she thought, we'll just *see* about that. Then she sat down and began grooming herself, to lull any suspicions Annie might have.

Just then the doorbell rang; Annie hurried to answer it, and found Albert standing on the stoop. Trixie followed at Annie's heel, watching and awaiting her moment, and when Albert started to step inside she dashed for the opening.

Before anyone could stop her she was outside. Annie shrieked, but couldn't push her way past the startled Albert quickly enough to grab Trixie before the fleeing cat ducked behind a bush, out of sight.

A moment later Annie and Albert were standing on the front lawn, looking up the street toward Sally's house, calling, "Here, Trixie!"

"I don't see it anywhere," Albert said.

"Well, but she *must* have wanted to go back home," Annie said. "Where *else* would she go?" She looked about, mystified.

Behind the bush Trixie crouched down, her black fur invisible in the shadows. There wasn't any point in going back down the street yet; the brown creatures wouldn't come out until the middle of the night.

Annie and Albert walked down the street, calling and searching; Trixie watched them go.

Some time later they came wandering slowly back. Albert said, "I'm sure the cat will turn up again. When it gets hungry it'll find you. Or maybe it'll be waiting on Aunt Sally's steps tomorrow when I go back."

"I hope so," Annie said, unconvinced. She climbed the two steps to her front door and stood there, arms crossed over her chest, as she looked around the neighborhood for some sign of Trixie's whereabouts.

Albert waved goodbye and left, and at last Annie shrugged, shivered in the cooling evening air, and went back inside.

Trixie snoozed cheerfully behind the bush.

Hours later she awoke, yawned, stretched, and ambled out of concealment.

The street was dark and deserted. No cars rumbled on the pavement; most of the windows were unlit. This was just what Trixie wanted; the brown things would probably be hard at work. She strolled easily down the block.

In front of Sally's house she paused, considering.

She was outside. The brown creatures were inside. This could be a problem. Cats couldn't open doors.

She had seen the brown things open cabinet doors often enough, though, and sometimes the pantry or the laundry room door – they had never opened the bedroom door, but Trixie thought they *could* have, if they wanted. If they could do all that, they could presumably let Trixie into the house.

The question was, would they?

Trixie thought they would. After all, they liked everything to be in its proper place, and Trixie's proper place had always been inside that house. If she could just get their attention…

She ambled around the side of the house, and bounded up to the kitchen windowsill – fortunately, the screen was not in place. There she peered in through the glass.

The brown creatures were there – and apparently puzzled by the lack of dirty dishes, as two of them were sitting on the edge of the sink, looking about unhappily.

Trixie meowed, loudly, and thumped her tail against the glass.

The brown creatures started and looked up at her. Then they began to make their odd little noises at each other.

Trixie meowed again, and patted the glass with one paw.

One of the brown creatures climbed up on the sash and pried at the latch, while no fewer than four of the others gathered on the inside sill, staring out at Trixie.

That was perfect. Trixie had thought out exactly what she had to do, and it appeared she would have her chance.

The latch snapped open, and the brown creature jumped down from the sash; then all five bent down and began heaving. The window slid open slowly; Trixie waited. Then, when the opening was wide enough, she pounced.

The brown creatures scattered, squealing, but not quickly enough. She had caught one of them in her forepaws. Now she snatched at it with her mouth, and got her jaws around its neck.

Then, as gently as she could, as gently as if she were handling her own kitten, she picked the shrieking creature up, turned around, and leaped back out the window to the ground.

There she began trotting up the block toward Annie's house, holding her head up as high as she could, with the brown thing squirming in her hold.

Behind her the other creatures chattered and squealed, then followed her, one by one, leaping out the window and chasing her across the close-trimmed lawns.

At last she reached Annie's house, climbed awkwardly up the two steps to the front door, and waited, still securely holding her captive.

The brown creatures gathered around her, chattering. Trixie waited, making it as obvious as she could that she expected them to open the door for her.

Eventually, as Trixie's jaws began to tire, two of the creatures stepped forward. One hoisted the other up onto his shoulders, and the top creature stretched up until he could reach the doorknob. He grabbed it and pulled himself up, then climbed on top and seated himself on the knob, where he looked thoughtfully at the lock in front of him. He pulled a tool from his pocket, squinted into the keyhole, and set to work.

A moment later he squealed in triumph and pocketed the tool. Then he stood up, braced his feet against the knob and his hands against the doorjamb, and pushed.

The knob turned, and a moment later the door was open.

Trixie trotted inside, into the center of the living room. There she sat down and waited until all the brown creatures had collected around her.

Then she released her captive. It fell to the floor and moaned quietly, then sat up, dazed but unhurt, as Trixie jumped aside.

The others surged forward and hugged their freed companion, squeaking at one another. Then they stopped and looked around.

They looked at dust bunnies and cobwebs and cookie crumbs, at forgotten saucers and used tissues and lost coins, and in unison they said, long and low, "Oooooh!"

And then they set to work, as Trixie curled up, purring, on the couch.

The next morning Annie found Trixie asleep on the living room sofa. She stopped dead in her tracks and stared at the cat.

"How'd you get in?" she demanded. She crossed to the front door and found it closed, but unlocked. She frowned, and turned back to Trixie.

"See how upset I was about you?" she said. "I forgot to lock this last night! A burglar could have come in and killed us both."

Then she stopped and looked at the door again. It was quite solidly closed – but Trixie was inside.

Had a burglar gotten in, and let Trixie in by accident? Annie looked around to see if anything was missing.

The TV was where it should be, and the stereo… but *something* didn't look right. She stared for a moment, trying to see what it was.

Then, finally, it struck her. Everything was *clean*.

Annie had never heard of burglars who dusted.

"Did *you* do that?" she asked Trixie. Then she shook her head. That was silly. Cats couldn't clean house.

"It must've been elves," she said. "Or brownies."

Trixie began purring. Annie understood, and she didn't seem to mind. Living here would be all right, then. She hopped off the couch and rubbed against Annie's leg.

"You want breakfast?" Annie asked. "Is that it?"

Trixie had just been expressing her pleasure at how things were working out, but food was always welcome; she ran ahead, and met Annie at the kitchen door, meowing for her food.

Annie took a single step into the kitchen and stopped dead. In the living room the cleaning had been fairly subtle; here it was staggeringly obvious. Dishes had been washed, dried, and put away; years of soap-scum had been cleaned from the sink and faucets, and the old chrome gleamed brightly.

"It *is* brownies," she said, and this time she meant it. She looked down at Trixie. "Or Albert – did he find you somewhere, and bring you back, and clean everything to surprise me?"

Trixie looked up at her in utter disgust at such an absurd suggestion, then meowed.

"Oh, you want your food," Annie said. She filled Trixie's bowl quickly, and set it down. Then she looked around again.

"It's as clean as Sally's," she said. "I never understood how she kept it…"

She stopped dead in mid-sentence. Her hand flew to her open mouth.

"Sally's helpers," she said. "*She* had brownies helping her!" Her eyes widened. She looked down at Trixie again. "*That's* why you ran off! You were bringing them here!" She stared at the shining-clean sink. "Are they going to stay?"

Trixie began purring again. Annie smiled.

"Trixie," she said, "you *are* a tricksy one!"

It can be argued that Solanda isn't really a cat; she's a Shapeshifter of the Fey. But if it looks like a cat, and it meows like a cat... Solanda will need all of her experience, both as a Shapeshifter and as a cat, to maneuver through the politics of the Black King's court and the social customs of newly-conquered Nye.

Solanda also appears in Kristine Kathryn Rusch's seven novels of the Fey's warfare: Sacrifice *(Millennium, August 1995),* Changeling *(Millennium, March 1996),* Rival *(Millennium, April 1997),* The Resistance *(Bantam Spectra, June 1998),* Victory *(Bantam Spectra, November 1998),* The Black Queen *(Bantam Spectra, August 1999), and* The Black King *(Bantam Spectra, August 2000).*

Destiny

by Kristine Kathryn Rusch

Solanda walked the cobblestone streets of Nir, the capital city of Nye, her tail up. She had a meeting with Rugar, the son of the Black King. He had sent a Wisp to find her, and it had taken the little creature nearly a day to do so.

Solanda was in her cat form, as she had been since the Fey captured this repressed country—and thus very difficult to find. The Nyeians had many faults—they were prissy, overdressed, and pasty faced, not to mention abominably poor soldiers—but they did treat their animals well. She had found a family who fed her to excess, allowed her to roam outside, and pampered her as no cat should be pampered.

How appalled they would be if they ever discovered the golden cat their daughter had adopted was really a Fey Shapeshifter.

Solanda's tail twitched once in amusement. Every day she imagined eating her lovely tuna dinner in the glass plate that the family gave her, and then Shifting into her Fey form just to say thank you.

She didn't know what would appall the Nyeians the most: the fact that she was Fey, or the fact that she would be naked. She doubted any of them had seen a naked woman before: the wife managed to change her clothing one piece at a time, without ever taking it all off at once, and the husband didn't seem to think this unusual. He would probably be more shocked than his wife at the appearance of a naked Fey woman in his house. He would probably fall over in a dead faint.

Only the daughter, a girl of five, was redeemable. Esmerelda was a good child. She had to be. She was raised Nyeian. Her mother trussed her in layers upon frothy layers of clothing, making movement nearly impossible, and then yelled at the poor child whenever she did something natural, like running.

Sometimes Solanda thought she went back to that household at night because she felt sorry for the child. But in truth, she stayed there because they gave her fish properly deboned and they brushed her, and they put a warm cedar bed in Esmerelda's room. Esmerelda, good child that she was, never confessed to her parents that she often picked up the cat and carried her to bed, cuddling with her long into the night.

And Solanda would never tell anyone—Fey or Nyeian—that sometimes she purred when she slept, pressed against the little girl's back.

Shifters were supposed to be the coldest of the Fey, the most fickle members of a warrior people, incapable of real emotion, flighty, restless and completely self-absorbed. They also were supposed to take on the characteristics of the animal they had chosen to Shift into, so Solanda's fickleness—theoretically—was doubly-compounded by the fact that she had chosen the cat as her alternate Shape.

Of course, it didn't matter how many times she had proven herself trustworthy. In the war against Nye, such as it was, she had done intelligence for the Black King. She had worn her cat form and slinked into Nyeian villages, soldiers' camps, and mess halls, keeping her ears open, and learning more than she should have.

Most countries that the Fey had fought had banned strange animals from military compounds. Solanda had heard that the Co had gone so far as to slaughter any strays, thinking they might be Fey reconnaissance. But the Nyeians had a fondness for cats, and while they kept stray dogs out of their camps, they fed cats on the side.

Solanda had spent most of the war the pampered resident of a Nyeian general's tent. He used to feed her bits of meat off his own plate while telling his staff his battle plans for the next day.

And then when he fell into his snoring sleep, she would go to the nearest Shadowlands and inform the Fey general of all she had heard. Toward the end of the war, she reported directly to the Black King, who shook his head at the stupidity of the Nyeians.

Conquering Nye was the first step toward world dominion. The Black King didn't say that, but Solanda knew that was his goal. The Fey were a great warrior people, but they only owned half the world right now. The Black King—and the Black Throne—wanted all of it.

Solanda entered the merchant sector of Nir, and silently cursed to herself. The merchants often shooed cats out of this area. Her presence here was suddenly noticeable, and she didn't dare Shift. She'd shock an entire community of Nyeians—which would probably be good for them.

Scents from the nearby vendor stalls caught her nose. Fried beef, more fish, some sort of vegetable; something which turned her feline stomach. The fish was enticing. It almost made her forget that she was here because she had been summoned by the Black King's son.

Rugar had been her commander for part of the Nye campaign. He was an able warrior, frustrated under his father's tight leash. The problem with Rugar was that he believed himself to be the equal of his father, and he was not.

Solanda would rather work with the Black King, ruthless as he was, than with his less-talented son.

The tall stone buildings prevented the sun from getting to the cobblestone. The stone was wet beneath her paws from the morning rain. The air was thick and muggy, making the six layers of clothes the Nyeians wore look even more uncomfortable.

The handful of Fey who were on the street wore their traditional uniform—a leather jerkin and pants. The Fey were so much taller than the Nyeians that even if they didn't dress differently, they would be noticeable.

She ducked under some clothing stalls, past the buildings that housed the year-round indoor merchants, and turned on the street that led to the Bank of Nye. The Black King had taken over the building. It was four stories of gray stone, towering over the buildings around it—as close to a palace as there was in Nye.

She sighed heavily and crossed the street, climbing up the stone steps and staring at the large stone door. She'd have to Shift just to get into the place.

Then she saw a nearby window ledge. The window was open. She leaped onto the ledge and jumped to the stone floor inside. She thought this building unusually cold for a Nyeian structure. The house where she was pampered was made of wood, and had thick rugs on its floors. Every surface was soft, and the air perfumed.

Here the air smelled like chalk and the stone was chilly despite the heat. There were no guards in this room, although there should have been. It looked like it was someone's office—a desk in the center, chairs on the side for supplicants.

The door was open and led into a cavernous hallway. She heard voices and followed them. Several Fey guards huddled in an alcove. They were Infantry and young, tall even though they hadn't come into their magic yet. Their dark skin and black hair was a welcome sight. She'd gotten tired of looking at the pasty-faced Nyeians, and hadn't realized how much she missed her own kind.

"…fool's errand, don't you think?" One of the young men said.

"If it's so important, why doesn't the Black King go?" another asked.

"Blue Isle is important," said a young woman. "It's the only stop between here and Leut."

Leut was the continent on the other side of the Infrin Sea. The Black King wanted to go there more than anything. He wanted to conquer as much of the world as he could before he died.

"If we are going to conquer the world," the girl was saying, "we have to go through Blue Isle first."

"Then it doesn't make sense," the first man said. "Why send Rugar? He's not as good a commander as his father."

"Maybe," Solanda said in her most authoritative voice, "the best commander in the world has a plan that's too sophisticated for you to understand."

They all turned. They had similar upswept features, narrow faces, and pointed ears. Solanda had often thought that her people looked like foxes—most of them, anyway. Shifters, like her, often took some of the characteristics of their animals. Her hair and skin were more golden than dark, and she had the Shifter's mark on her chin—a birthmark that established who and what she was when she was in her Fey form.

But they couldn't tell now. All they could do was tell that a cat had spoken to them.

"Well," she said, sitting on her haunches and wrapping her tail around her paws. "Where do I start? Do I reprimand you for gossiping in the middle of the day? Do I tell you that I got into the building through a window that some careless fool left open and, if I had been some young Nyeian bent on assassination, I could have walked right past you and you wouldn't have noticed? Or do I ask that one of you poor, magickless fools get me a robe so that I can have my meeting with Rugar?"

They didn't answer her. She raised her chin slightly. Amazing how she could intimidate them, even though she was so very small.

"By the Powers," she snapped. "Get me a robe. And put a guard on the window."

She nodded over her head toward the room she had just come out of.

Two of the young men ran off toward the room. The third young man hurried off, presumably to get her a robe. That left the young woman.

"I really should report this," Solanda said. "Technically, you put the Black King's life in danger."

"From the Nyeians?" the young woman snorted. "You snarl at them and they run. They couldn't fight us in the war, and once they found out that they'd remain in charge of their businesses, they really didn't care that we took them over. Why would one of them try to get in here?"

"Revenge?" Solanda said. "We did, after all, slaughter half their army. Those young men were related to someone."

"Then that should take away half the threat, shouldn't it?" the young woman said. "After all, the Nyeians believe that only men are capable of fighting."

Solanda felt amused. "I have a hunch that belief has changed since they were defeated by us. What's your name?"

"Licia," the girl said.

"You haven't come into your magic yet, have you?"

The girl straightened her shoulder. Magic was always a touchy subject with Infantry. They were tall enough to show that they would get magic, but chances were if they neared adulthood and still hadn't come into their magic, their abilities would be slight.

"No," she said.

"You showed a tactician's mind. Why do you waste it gossiping with people who aren't worthy of you?"

The girl straightened her shoulders. "I don't normally guard. I am usually in the field."

"But there's no field at the moment, is there?" Solanda said. "What are you doing here?"

"Rugar asked me to come. He says his daughter needs more swordfighting training."

Solanda narrowed her eyes. Jewel, Rugar's middle child, was the most promising of all his raggedy off-spring. She hadn't come into her magic yet either, but her height and her heritage suggested when her magic came it would be powerful. She was a good swordswoman now—Solanda had seen her fight in the last of the Nye campaign.

"Why would she need more training?"

Licia shrugged. "I suspect it has something to do with the fight Rugar had with his father this morning."

Solanda tilted her head to show her interest.

"They just left that room you came through. They were screaming at each other all morning long."

"About what?" Solanda asked, realizing that she was now gossiping. But she didn't want to go into a meeting with Rugar with less knowledge than he had.

"About going to Blue Isle. Rugar says he won't go without his daughter."

"Not his other children?"

"He didn't mention them." Then Licia smiled. "At least not at the top of his voice."

Solanda suppressed a sigh. The Black King favored Jewel. He felt that her brothers were idiots—and he was right. Their magic was slight, like their mother's had been. Rugar's entire life had been about defying his father. Rugar should have married a woman who had great magic. Instead, he had chosen someone he could control.

The young man returned with a flowing golden robe that was clearly of Nyeian origin. Solanda didn't ask where he had gotten it. She didn't thank him. Instead, she said, "Place it over me."

He did, blotting out the light. The robe smelled faintly of perfume and perspiration, but it clearly hadn't been worn in some time. The fabric was heavy satin—too heavy for a humid day like this—but she wasn't in the position to be choosy. If Rugar was planning something stupid, she wanted to meet him Fey to Fey. Psychologically, it gave her an advantage.

She Shifted, feeling her body slide into its familiar Fey form. Her body stretched and grew. Her tail and whiskers slid into her skin, her hair flowed down her back, her front paws became hands. She ended up in a sitting position, her knees drawn to her chest, the robe draped over her like a tent. Inwardly she sighed, and wished that there were a more dignified way of Shifting into clothes.

Then she slid her arms through the sleeves, and her head through the neck hole, letting the stiff fabric flow around her. It was a woman's garment, although she had no idea why someone would store one in a bank—or perhaps she did, and didn't want to think about illicit affairs among Nyeian bankers.

She lifted her long hair out of the garment's neck, and let it fall down her back. Licia bit her lower lip, and the other Fey looked down. They hadn't realized they were talking to the best Shifter in the Black King's army—at least, not until now.

Fools. Shifters were rare. How many of them would come into the Black King's dwelling and order Infantry around?

"Licia," she said, "announce me to Rugar."

The girl's skin colored slightly, but she moved in front of Solanda and led her down the hall. It got stuffier the farther in they went. Solanda was grateful that her feet were bare. The cool stone was going to keep her from melting in this robe.

Licia led her up a flight of stairs into a rabbit's warren of what had once been offices. Solanda smiled. Rugar was hidden here, in an obviously less desirable area of the building. The Black King had a thousand ways of showing his displeasure with everyone around him.

Licia knocked on a door at the end of the hall. Solanda stood far enough back that she wasn't visible from inside. She heard Rugar's gruff voice, and then Licia's response, announcing Solanda.

The door opened, and Licia stepped aside.

"I guess that means you're supposed to go in," she said.

Solanda stopped and put a hand on the girl's shoulder. She spoke softly so that Rugar couldn't hear. "If Rugar and his father are fighting," she said, "side with the old man. Rugar is not the future of this race. You're better off remaining in Nye with the Black King than going to Blue Isle with Rugar."

Licia nodded, then glanced over her shoulder as if she were afraid of Rugar. Solanda walked past her and through the open door.

Rugar stood in the center of the small room. He was of medium height for a Fey, and his features had a predatory, hawklike look to them. His almond-shaped eyes were the deep black that Solanda associated with the Black Family. It was as if the Throne echoed in their very essence. He had thin cruel lips, and an expression of permanent unhappiness.

For a man in his fifties with grown children, he looked startlingly like a petulant child.

"You sent for me," she said, not disguising her lack of respect for him.

He clasped his hands behind his back, his father's favorite stance. "I'm taking an army to Blue Isle. You will be part of it."

She snorted. "I serve your father, not you."

Rugar glared at her. "He gave me permission to chose whomever I wanted from the standing armies in Nye."

"You have no need for a Shifter," she said. "Blue Isle is a tiny place, filled with religious fanatics who have never seen war. You'll sail in with your troops, wave a few swords, and be able to claim victory over an entire country in the space of a day. I'll be useless to you."

He shook his head. "I'm taking you, and a lot of Spies and Doppelgängers. I am to be military governor of Blue Isle. My father will launch an attack from there onto Leut."

Solanda narrowed her eyes and was glad she wasn't in cat form. She probably would have found an excuse to scratch Rugar, and that wouldn't have been good for either of them.

"Spies, Doppelgängers, and a Shifter," she said. "It sounds like an intelligence force. You won't need it if you conquer the country as quickly as you believe you will."

His gaze went flat. "I will need it."

She stared at him for a moment. He knew something and he wasn't going to share it with her. Spies made sense, even in an easily conquered country. They would find the pockets of resistance. But Doppelgängers had no place there. They killed their hosts and then took over the body, including the memories. Except for the gold flecks in the eyes, no one could tell them from their victims. Doppelgängers had a sophisticated magic—one that the best commanders used sparingly. And certainly didn't waste them on an already conquered country.

"You have no need for me," she repeated. "I stay with the Black King."

"You'll come with me."

"Your father said so?"

"No, but he will."

"Because he already acquiesced on Jewel?"

Rugar started. He hadn't expected her to know that.

Solanda raised her eyebrows and allowed herself a small smile. "I am good at gathering intelligence."

"And," he said, "as you pointed out, there's no need for intelligence gathering in a conquered country."

She nodded. "I'll go to Leut with your father, when he's ready. Until then, I'll relax here."

"Solanda—"

"Rugar," she said, holding up a hand. "You and I have no great liking for each other. I have a hunch your father is sending you to Blue Isle to get you out of his sight. I'd rather not be associated with you in any way. Right now, I hold your father's respect. I'd rather not change that."

Rugar took a step toward her. She could feel the violence shimmering in him.

She grabbed the door knob. "Touch me," she said, "and I'll scratch out your eyes."

"You can't touch me. I'm a member of the Black Family."

She smiled. "I'm a Shifter. Unpredictable, irresponsible, flighty—remember? I'm sure the Powers would let this slide."

"But my father would not," Rugar said.

"Oh," Solanda said softly, "but I think he would."

* * *

She tried to see the Black King before she left the building, but he was nowhere to be found. His personal guards were gone as well. She decided she would find him in the morning, and went back to her life as a pampered Nyeian cat.

The home that she had chosen was a large one on the outskirts of Nir. It had two stories filled with more clutter than any home she had ever seen. Books of poetry, musical instruments, incredibly ugly paintings, and furniture everywhere. The only saving grace was that the furniture was comfortable and the kitchen had a cat door that she could escape through when the wife decided it was time for music.

Solanda slipped through the cat door, past the kitchen hearth. One of the three Nyeian servants was cleaning the pots from the evening meal. The air smelled faintly of roast beef, and Solanda's stomach rumbled.

Still, she didn't beg from the servant. She knew better. The idiot had kicked her "accidentally" once, and had the scars to prove it. But Solanda knew if she attacked anyone in the house too many times, she would be thrown out, and she wasn't willing to lose her rich dinners and soft bed just yet.

She blended into the hideous yellow wallpaper as she hurried up the stairs to Esmerelda's room.

Esmerelda sat on the edge of the bed, fingering a rip in her dress. She had a forlorn expression on her small face. Her brown hair hung limply around her cheeks, and a streak of dirt covered the pantaloons beneath the skirt.

Solanda had never seen Esmerelda look dirty before, nor had she seen the girl's hair loose at any time except bedtime.

"Oh, Goldie!" Esmerelda raised her voice in relief. She was speaking Nye, which was a language that Solanda hadn't known well when she moved into this house. Here her Nye had improved greatly, but she wanted to be fluent in it by the time she left.

The little girl launched herself off the bed and grabbed Solanda before Solanda could jump out of the way. Esmerelda wrapped her arms around Solanda and held tightly. Esmerelda had never done that before. If she had been a grabby little girl, Solanda would have been gone a long time ago.

So this meant, quite simply, that something was wrong.

Solanda let herself be held for a moment, then she turned her head toward the door and flattened her ears. Esmerelda, smart child that she was, understood both signals. She pushed the door closed, and then let Solanda go.

Solanda jumped on the windowsill. Esmerelda followed her, but didn't open the window like she usually did.

The room was hot and sticky. Solanda wouldn't be able to stay here too long if that window wasn't opened.

"I don't dare," Esmerelda said softly. "Mommy's really mad at me. She didn't even let me have dinner."

Now Solanda was interested, but she didn't want the story, not yet. She bumped her head against the window's bubbled glass.

Esmerelda bit her lower lip and shook her head.

Solanda placed a paw on the glass and meowed softly.

"Okay," Esmerelda whispered. "But if anyone comes, I'll have to close it."

Solanda almost nodded, then caught herself. When Esmerelda came close, Solanda bumped her affectionately with her head, and then watched as the little girl pulled the window open.

A cool breeze made its way inside. That was the other nice thing about this house. Esmerelda's room opened onto a large undeveloped area, so the smells of the outdoors came in strong. Breezes were unencumbered. Esmerelda's mother hated this, and often wished for close neighbors, but Solanda saw it for the blessing it was.

Esmerelda knelt down beside the window and put her elbows on the sill. She didn't touch Solanda, but she was still a bit too close. Her body heat was ruining the breeze.

"I've been so bad," she said, "I won't get to go outside ever again."

Solanda watched her. The little girl had never been able to resist a cat's gaze. Solanda had never seen a child who was so very lonely. Esmerelda wasn't allowed to play—except with dolls with clothing as frilly as the stuff she was trussed in—nor was she allowed to associate with the neighboring children who were, in her parents' mind, beneath her. She had lessons in poetry and music, art and dancing, but she liked none of it. What she really wanted to do was run as far as she could, and climb trees and learn how to swim.

She'd probably never get to achieve those goals.

"I was running this afternoon," Esmerelda said. Her face was wistful. She leaned her forehead against the glass. "Mommy was looking at fruit and I thought I could just go around the block, but she saw me. I guess she followed me."

Esmerelda had done this before, and it hadn't gotten her sent to bed with no supper. Solanda suspected the problem had something to do with the rip in the dress. Clothing was sacred, at least to this family. Solanda wanted to tear every piece so that this little girl could be free.

"She saw me fall." Esmerelda said, fingering her skirt. "She saw me hit a Fey."

Solanda stiffened. She almost asked who, and caught herself. Two near lapses in one conversation. She was getting much too relaxed with this child.

Esmerelda ran a soft hand over Solanda's head. Her touch was gentle again, as it had always been before.

"She said she was the Black King's granddaughter, and she yelled at Mommy for dressing me the way she did. And Mom yelled back. The lady said yelling at her was like yelling at all the Fey all at once."

Only one Fey woman could make that claim. Jewel. No wonder Esmerelda's mother was upset.

"And then Mommy told Daddy and he said that the Fey might hurt us. Because I ran." A tear coursed down Esmerelda's cheek.

And those fools were blaming the child for being a child. Solanda pushed against the girl's hand, and Esmerelda sniffled.

"I didn't mean to run. I just can't stay still sometimes."

Solanda understood that. She could never stay still. It was a curse of being a Shifter. It was the reason Fey wisdom said that Shifters were the most heartless of the Fey. Most Shifters did not have children, and most rarely stayed anywhere long enough to form a real relationship.

Esmerelda sighed. "I wish I was like you. I could do what I want. Or like that Fey lady. She was nice to me. She didn't like Mommy though."

Neither did Solanda.

"She said children shouldn't be dressed like me. She said I ran into her because my clothing didn't let me run properly."

Probably true, Solanda thought.

"And that made Mommy really mad."

Esmerelda let her hand slide off Solanda's neck. She bunched her hands into fists and rested her chin on them, looking fierce and strong. Solanda felt her whiskers twitch in amusement. One day, Esmerelda's parents would no longer be able to control this child. If she was this strong, articulate, and intelligent at five, she would be impossible to control at fifteen.

Especially with all of the Fey influence around her.

"I wish I had magic," the little girl said. "Just a little bit. Then I could run and no one would know. I'd make myself invisible and no one would see me."

Solanda looked out the window, knowing her expression was too sympathetic for a cat. There was a ring of oaks at the edge of the lawn. They were blowing in the breeze. Maybe there would be another storm. Maybe this storm would finally cool the place off, although she doubted it. Nye's hot season was the worst she had encountered in any country she had ever been in.

"Esmerelda!" her mother's voice echoed from the hallway. "Why is your door closed?"

Esmerelda gasped and pulled down the window so quickly she almost caught Solanda's tail in it. Then she leaped onto the bed, stretching out. Solanda jumped beside her and curled up at her feet just as Esmerelda's mother opened the door.

The woman's face was flushed. She looked like a tomato about to burst. She was so tightly corseted that her body looked flat, and Solanda wondered how the woman could even breathe. She wore an evening dress of white satin that accented the redness of her face. The sides were lined with sweat.

"What are you doing?" she asked. Then she frowned. "How did that mangy cat get in here?"

Solanda growled softly in the back of her throat. She was not mangy. And the woman had never called her that before.

"I told you that you were supposed to be in here by yourself to think about what you did today. Things could have been much worse. Fortunately, she was in good mood. You know what those people can do? Why it's said they can cut the skin off a person with the flick of—"

Solanda yowled, and the woman stepped back, a hand over her heart. Esmerelda sat up, worry on her small face.

"Are you okay, Goldie?"

Solanda licked her right paw as if she had twisted it. She was not going to let that woman tell this little girl about Fey atrocities—even if they were true.

"Come on, Goldie," Esmerelda's mother said. "There's some beef for you in the kitchen."

Usually that would have gotten Solanda off the bed. But she could sneak down after everyone was asleep and take what she needed. Right now, she wanted to stay beside Esmerelda.

"Goldie," the woman said.

Esmerelda, good child that she was, bit her lower lip and said nothing. She didn't beg for the company that she obviously wanted.

"Goldie!" her mother sounded exasperated now. Then she shook her head. "Why do we put up with this animal?"

Neither Solanda nor Esmerelda answered.

Finally Esmerelda's mother sighed. "All right, she can stay. But I do expect you to sleep in that dress tonight and to think about how you could have hurt us all. That rip should be a reminder of the danger your misbehavior put us in. Nye isn't the place it used to be, child. Do something wrong, and those Fey will harm all of us."

Then she pulled the door closed, and Solanda heard the boards creak as she made her way down the stairs.

Esmerelda's fingers played with the rip. Solanda looked at it, then crossed the bed, took the skirt in her teeth and pulled. The rip grew. Esmerelda giggled, then covered her mouth. Solanda pulled harder. If the little girl had to sleep in these clothes, she might as well be comfortable.

Esmerelda ripped the pantaloons too, along the dirt line, giggling as she did so. "Mommy will think I did it when I was running," she said. "You're so smart, Goldie."

Of course she was. Solanda preened and allowed herself to be petted one more time.

Then Esmerelda looked at the door, her smile fading. "Sometimes I think Mommy doesn't want me. She wants somebody else. Somebody perfect."

Too bad she didn't realize that the child she had was better than perfect. Solanda sighed softly. Some people had more than they deserved.

* * *

The idea came to her in the middle of the night, in that hot and stuffy room. She could take Esmerelda away, and Esmerelda's parents wouldn't even know it had happened. But it would take the cooperation of the Fey Domestics.

Fey magic was divided into two parts: warrior and domestic. Warrior magic was designed for warfare. Some Fey magic turned its practitioner into a weapon, like the Foot Soldiers who had fingernails that could slice better than a blade. Domestic magic could not be used to fight any war. Domestics lost their magic if they killed. Their magics were healing magics or home-bound magics, such as spells that made chairs more inviting or fires warmer.

The next morning, after making certain that Esmerelda got breakfast, Solanda slipped out the cat door. She went to the Domicile that the Fey Domestics had set up just outside of town. The Domicile had been built especially for the Domestics, and covered with various protection and healing spells. It was a traditional U shaped building—with hearth and home magics in one length of the U, the healing wards in the other, and the middle section as a meeting place in between.

Solanda usually didn't seek out the Domestics. They always wanted to experiment with her—have her try on a new cloak covered with some sort of rain protection or have her taste a new food to see if it had an effect on her Shifting. The last time she had been in a Domicile had been when she had broken a paw jumping from a tree in one of the last Nye battles. The Domestics had mended the bone, and had given her a smelly ointment she had to apply in cat form. She had thought the stench alone would kill her.

As she mounted the steps to the center part of the building, she shook off her paws. Here she would not Shift to Fey form. The Domestics weren't as obsessed with power as Rugar was, so she didn't have to use her height as a reminder of the strength of her magic.

She pushed open the door and stepped inside.

The air was cool and welcoming. It smelled of a sea breeze. Bits of magic floated in the air. Spinner's magic. They were working on their looms. She could hear the hum just down the corridor.

A Baker entered, his fingers dusted with flour. They glowed. And she knew he had spelled the bread he'd been baking to remain fresh for as long as possible. It was a traveling spell, one most often used when troops were heading off to battle. She wondered if someone had requested it.

"I'm here to see Chadn."

The Baker nodded, then slipped through a door that led to the Healing part of the Domicile. Solanda hopped onto a chair. Her mood rose and she cursed, jumping down. She didn't need to be spelled, to wait, happy and contented, on a chair dusted with Domestic magic. Instead she paced the cool floor and wondered why she couldn't smell the baking bread.

Finally Chadn entered the room. She was a young Shaman, although the toll of her power had already turned her hair white. Her face was wizened, her mouth a small oval amid wrinkles. Only her eyes were bright—sparkling black circles of light in a ruined face.

She had been assigned to stay with Rugar during the war and she was happy to be free of him. Shaman were the most independent Fey: their Vision as strong as those of the Leaders, but their magic Domestic so they could not rule a warrior people. They were the wise ones, the advisors, supposedly the strength behind the Black Throne. The Black King required a Shaman of his son, but did not use one himself. He had dismissed his own, years ago, for disobeying him. It was one of many areas where the Black King broke with tradition.

"Solanda," Chadn said. "I had hoped to see you."

Solanda jumped on an end table and was relieved that her mood did not change. She sat on her haunches and looked into Chadn's face.

"I have a request," she said. "It's for a Nyeian child."

"A child?" Chadn sounded surprised. "Not a Fey child?"

Solanda shook her head.

"I had Seen you with a Fey child."

The Shaman's Visions—and the Vision that leaders like the Black King had—allowed them glimpses into the future. Some said that the glimpses allowed the Visionary to change the future. Others believed that the glimpses led the Visionary to that future.

Solanda's eyes narrowed. "I have not been with a Fey child."

Chadn nodded. "It was on Blue Isle. The child was a Shifter, and you kept her from death."

Solanda's whiskers twitched. "I told Rugar I would not go to Blue Isle with him."

"The future of our people lies with you, Solanda."

"And a child?" Solanda raised her chin. "Are you sure it was a Fey child?"

"Not entirely," Chadn said. "The child had blue eyes."

Solanda gave a soft grunt of surprise. She had heard of blue-eyed people, but she had never seen one. "The child couldn't be Nyeian?"

"She was Fey, and newborn. She had a birthmark on her chin. Only her eyes were strange, and perhaps that was because of the Shifting. I Saw you put your hands on her lips, and swear to protect her, raise her, and make her strong. Then I Saw her full grown, saying you had been the closest thing she had to a mother."

Solanda laughed, although inside she felt cold. A Shifter only swore to protect a child who held the future of the Empire. A blue-eyed child that Shifted? The center of the Empire?

"Visions can be altered," Solanda said. "I am not leaving Nye."

"You may have no choice."

"I'll always have a choice," Solanda said.

Chadn inclined her head toward Solanda as if giving in on that point. "What does the Nyeian child need?"

Solanda took a deep breath. "She is different from any other Nyeian I've seen. Strong, independent. She met Jewel yesterday and is being punished for it. I would like to remove the child from her family and bring her here, to be raised among us. She will be useful when she's grown. She will be part of the second-generation, the Nyeians that rule Nye for the Fey."

Chadn stared at her for a moment. "So take her. Shifters steal children."

"This one's mother will raise a fuss if she's gone."

"What mother wouldn't?"

"She'll come to us."

"And you can't prove to the Black King that we must keep the child."

"Not yet, anyway," Solanda said.

Chadn folded her hands over her stomach. "You want a Changeling."

"Yes," Solanda said.

"How old is the child?"

"Five."

Chadn sighed. "Have you asked the child if she's willing to leave?"

"Not yet. I wanted to know if I have help first."

"You will keep the child at your side?"

Solanda frowned. That wasn't a normal request. Shifters rarely kept children. They usually brought them to Domestics to raise. "Must I?"

"At five, it will be you she trusts."

Solanda shrugged. "Then she shall stay with me."

"And you will stay away from Blue Isle." Chadn said that not as a question, but as a statement.

"Rugar will not let a Nyeian child in his war party."

"So the child serves two purposes." Chadn's eyes narrowed. "Has she magic?"

"Of course not." Solanda laughed. "There is not magic outside the Fey."

Chadn frowned. "I am no longer certain of that."

"Because you Saw a blue-eyed Shifter?"

"Because I Saw a great war, coming when we least expect it."

"War is part of Fey life." Solanda jumped off the table and headed for the door. "I'll bring you news of the child tomorrow."

"I'll have a Changeling stone ready," Chadn said. "But realize before you act, that this is for life."

"I already know that," Solanda said. "I have chosen well."

"I hope so," Chadn said.

* * *

Solanda went to the docks and sat on a fence. She loved it here. The Infrin Sea formed the most natural harbor on Galinas, and there was always some sort of activity. Toward the north end of the harbor, the Nyeian builders made the great ships. Those ships traveled all over the known world, and now Fey Domestics helped unload cargo that would go all over the Empire.

Ships from Blue Isle had stopped coming to Nye when news reached them of the Fey takeover. She would never see an Islander, never learn more about them than she already had.

And that would be all right.

For there were some things she couldn't discuss with Rugar's Shaman. Like the prophecies that had been made by another Shaman at Solanda's birth, prophecies that claimed her legacy would be in the children she saved.

Children—not child, like Chadn had seen. Solanda would influence the life of more than one.

The breeze was cooler here, carrying with it the smell of salt and a tinge of dead fish. That smell made her stomach rumble. She tried not to think of the things she ate in her cat form, things she would find disgusting when she was in Fey form. Right now, raw dead fish sounded extremely appetizing.

But she didn't go in search of the source of the smell. She had some thinking to do. Prophecies and Visions made her nervous. She had no idea what to do with the information Chadn had given her. Because, at various points in her life, Solanda had been told by Visionaries that her future held contradictory things.

One Shaman had told her she had to avoid the Black Family for she would kill a Black Heir. Another Shaman had told her she would raise a Black Hair. And now Chadn had Seen her swear to protect a blue-eyed Shifter, a newborn who couldn't survive on her own.

Solanda bowed her head. The prophecy she never mentioned, the one her parents had kept silent, had come the day of her birth and she had never forgotten it. The prophecy was a cold one: she would die before her time, far from home, for a crime she did not regret.

The Fey did not believe in crime. They were constantly at war, so the crimes that plagued other races—murder, theft—were absorbed into the wars themselves. The Fey only punished two crimes: treason and failure. Both of those crimes were considered crimes against the Empire. Failure was a large crime, encompassing the failure to follow an order, or the failure to defeat an enemy in a prolonged battle.

Treason was any crime against the Black Family and was such a heresy, that it wasn't even discussed among rational Fey.

Both crimes bore the penalty of death.

It seemed to her that she would never commit crimes like that, that the prophecies had come because she was a Shifter, not because of her character. She wasn't as flighty or as difficult as anyone said she was.

And besides, she had to take care of Esmerelda.

She wished she could be there the morning that Esmerelda's parents discovered the Changeling. It would look like Esmerelda, even act like her—if stone could act like a living breathing creature. But it would only last a few days, and then it would cease to exist. They would think Esmerelda dead, when, in actuality, she was only gone.

Then, perhaps, that wretch of a mother would regret how she treated her daughter.

Esmerelda would live a life she couldn't even imagine now. She wouldn't have to wear six layers of clothes on the hottest day of the year, and she would learn how to live life to its fullest instead of remaining indoors and studying all the time.

Esmerelda would be the closest thing to Fey that a Nyeian could be—and for the first time in her young life, she would be happy. Solanda would see to that.

They would both be very happy.

* * *

Solanda returned to the house after dinner. Ultimately, she found she couldn't resist the dead fish that were piled near one of the docks. She had eaten herself sick, and then had to clean every inch of her fur before she even attempted the walk home.

Not that the house was home. In some ways, Esmerelda was.

Solanda used the cat door. Esmerelda's parents were talking softly in the parlor.

"Perhaps boarding school," the mother was saying. "If she is this incorrigible now, imagine what she'll be like when she gets older."

"Give it time, darling," the husband said. "She's still a child. She will learn, as we all did."

"It's just I despair of ever teaching her manners. You didn't see her with that Fey..."

Solanda had heard enough. She hurried up the stairs. She would talk to Esmerelda tonight. Tomorrow the Wisps would come, carrying a bit of stone in their tiny fingers. They'd fly in the open window, leave the stone on the bed and it would mold itself into a replica of Esmerelda while Solanda was leading the real Esmerelda out of the house.

Quick, neat, and completely perfect. The parents wouldn't have to worry about manners or boarding school. Esmerelda would get her heart's desire. And Solanda would have her reason for staying in Nye.

The door to Esmerelda's room was open. Esmerelda sat beneath a lamp, a long skirt over her lap. The air was stuffier than usual, and Solanda saw that the window was closed.

It had probably been closed all day. Sunlight had poured in, and the poor child had had to sit in the heat, working on some task her mother assigned her.

When Solanda got close, she saw what it was. The child was attempting to mend her own ripped dress.

The stitches were uneven, and Esmerelda had stitched the bottom layer of fabric onto the top. That would make her mother even angrier. Esmerelda's eyelashes were stuck together, her nose was red, and there were tearstains along her cheeks.

"Goldie!" she said, and let the dress topple to the floor. She was wearing another dress, equally inappropriate to the hot weather. She reached for Solanda, but Solanda jumped onto the window sill.

She was not going to be hugged by a hot sweaty child—not, at least, until the window was open and the fresh air came inside.

Esmerelda glanced toward the door. She put a finger to her lips, as if she thought Solanda were going to give her away, and then called, "Mommy! Can I go to sleep now?"

Solanda froze in her spot. She didn't want to be seen in here, not tonight. She wanted to have her conversation with Esmerelda in private.

"Are you done with your dress, darling?"

"Yes."

Solanda looked at it. The dress was ruined. The poor girl would have an even more difficult day than usual tomorrow.

"Then blow out the lamp. Good night."

"Good night." Esmerelda pushed the door closed. Then she went over to the window and opened it.

A strong breeze came in, and on it, Solanda smelled rain. Maybe, after she spoke to Esmerelda, she would go outside. By then it would be raining, and she would be able to cool down.

Esmerelda put her hand over the lamp's chimney and blew. The flame inside the glass went out. Solanda blinked in the darkness, letting her eyes adjust. It only took a moment. There were clouds over the moon this night, and it was very dark.

Esmerelda went back to her chair. "I wish you knew how to sew, Goldie."

"I don't," Solanda said. "But I know someone who does."

Esmerelda let out a small yelp, and put her hands over her mouth. She peered around the room as if looking for the source of the voice.

Solanda had to go slowly with this. The child wasn't used to magic, not like Fey children were.

"I could take the dress to her tonight," Solanda said, "and by morning, you wouldn't even know there had been a rip in it."

Esmerelda's eyes were wide. She finally turned in Solanda's direction. "You can talk, Goldie?"

"As well as I can listen." Solanda jumped from the windowsill to the bed. The room had cooled down. The fresh air felt marvelous. "What would you think, Esmerelda, if I took you to a place where you could wear comfortable clothes, play with children your own age, run and jump and swim to your heart's content? What if I told you that you would never have to sew another stitch, have another music lesson, or sit in a corner when you've done something that your mother didn't like."

Esmerelda looked for her, but clearly didn't see her. Cat's eyes were far superior in the dark. Solanda watched the child lick her lips, rub her hand over her knees, and then sigh.

"How long would I stay?" Esmerelda asked.

"Forever," Solanda said.

"Would I have to be a cat?"

Solanda laughed. For all her verbal sophistication, Esmerelda was still a child at heart. "No," Solanda said. "You'll stay just as you are."

"Would Mommy come?"

"No."

"Daddy?"

"No."

Esmerelda's shoulders stiffened. Her little body looked rigid. "Who would love me then?"

Solanda started. She hadn't expected that question. "I would be with you," she said.

Esmerelda was silent, as if she were thinking this over. "Where would you take me?"

"To my people," Solanda said.

"I'd live with cats?"

"No," she said gently. "With the Fey."

Esmerelda gasped. She held onto her chair as if she expected to be dragged from it.

Solanda wondered if she should have said that, but she had never taken a child before. Certainly she knew of no one who had ever taken a child of this age.

But Chadn had said she had had to speak with the child, and the choice to come had to be the child's. There was sense in that. Esmerelda, at age five, would always have a memory of living with her parents. She needed a memory of her choice to leave them.

"Esmerelda," Solanda said. "I—"

"No!" Esmerelda screamed. "No!"

She launched herself out of her chair as if her voice had given the ability to move again.

"Help! Mommy! Help!"

Solanda's ears went back. She hadn't expected this from Esmerelda, not her sane, different child.

"Esmerelda, I only want to give you a better life—"

"Mommy! Daddy! Help!"

Finally Esmerelda pulled the door open and blundered into the hallway. Solanda followed, tail between her legs, ears still back. The little girl's screams echoed down the stairs. Her parents had reached her, and they both put their arms around her. Esmerelda was too terrified to be coherent.

Then the mother looked up the stairs. She saw Solanda, her gaze flat.

And Solanda realized she had no choice.

She Shifted, her body lengthening, her tail disappearing, her fur becoming skin.

Then she walked, naked, to the floor below.

Esmerelda's mother gathered her child in her arms and backed away. The father placed himself in front of his small family, arms out.

"You came from the Black King, didn't you?" the woman said. "To punish us by stealing our child."

"It's not about you," Solanda said.

Esmerelda peeked around her father, eyes wide. Solanda had never, in her entire life, been so conscious of her nakedness.

"Wh-what do you want?" the father asked. He was trying to sound brave. Like most Nyeians, he was failing.

"I had hoped to take your daughter, but it seems that she prefers this place, even though you treat her as less than a housepet. It seems, for reasons I cannot understand, that she loves you."

"Of course she does," the woman said. "We're her parents."

"As if that's a divine right." Solanda stopped on the middle stair.

The family cringed below her as if they expected her to strike them with a lightning bolt. She didn't have that kind of magic. They had seen the extent of her powers, but apparently they didn't know that.

"She is a child," Solanda said. "She is to run and play. She is to have friends of her own age. She is to have comfortable clothing so that she can move without tripping. She is supposed to get dirty, to rip her skirts, and fall on her behind. She is to have some joy in her life. Do you understand?"

"I thought you Fey were supposed to leave us alone," the mother said. "I thought—"

"Be quiet," the father said.

Esmerelda clung to her father, her curiosity moving her closer.

"You will give her those things," Solanda said, "or I will take her from you. Do you understand?"

"Yes," the father said.

"You can't do this," the mother said. "You can't change our customs. The Black King promised you wouldn't."

"A promise made to a conquered people is worth nothing," Solanda snapped. "You will do what I say, or the child is mine."

"Mommy." Esmerelda reached for her mother. Solanda's eyes narrowed. Couldn't she see that her mother saw her only as a thing to be trained, to be forced into the right and proper life?

Probably not. It was too sophisticated a concept for her. The same innocence that allowed Esmerelda to accept a cat's speech, allowed her to believe that she was loved.

"Do I take her now?" Solanda asked.

"No," the father said. "We'll do as you say."

"But our friends—"

"Shut up," the father snapped. "Do you want to lose her?"

For a moment, the mother's gaze met Solanda's and in it, Solanda saw something she recognized, a coolness perhaps, a calculation. How would that woman have answered if she had been asked who would love me then? Would she have dodged the answer like Solanda had? Or would she have heard it at all?

"She will stay with us," the woman said. She sounded resigned.

Solanda felt a hope she hadn't even known she had die inside her. "Then I'll watch. You will treat that child as if she is more precious than gold. And if you fail, even once, she's mine. Is that clear?"

"Yes," the father said.

But Solanda did not take her gaze from the mother.

"Yes," the woman said.

Esmerelda had stepped to her father's side. She was still holding his leg. "Are you Goldie?" she asked.

Solanda gave her a small, private smile. "Only for you."

The little girl slipped behind her father again. Her answer was clear, too. She would stay, no matter what. And Solanda had done all she could.

So she Shifted back to her cat form. For a moment, she watched them all, tail twitching, then she ran up the stairs and into Esmerelda's room. She stopped for only a moment, knowing she would never return.

She leapt onto the window sill, and sighed. She had just lost her excuse for staying on Nye. She was bound to the Black Family. She had to do as they wished.

Rugar wanted her to go to Blue Isle.

Where a Shifter awaited her care. A newborn child, with blue eyes. A child who would think her the closest thing she'd ever had to a mother.

Solanda looked over her shoulder. She heard Esmerelda's voice, high, piping, excited; the soft answers of her parents. Solanda had lied to them. She would not be able to watch.

She hoped they would take good care of her little girl.

Then she jumped out the window, and climbed along a tree branch. Maybe her future had been preordained. Maybe she had no choice. She would raise a Black Heir, maybe kill one, and influence children.

How different would tonight have been if she had told the child that she would love her?

She would never know. Perhaps that was the moment in which everything could have changed. Maybe she had just missed her only chance to save herself.

Martin Grospar, a human space merchant in the interstellar future, has the black cat Raven to keep the Horus, his Free Trader ship, free of vermin—until the Horus picks up a new kind of space vermin that is particularly poisonous to humans. Soon Raven is the ship's only hope of survival.

"Three-Inch Trouble" is both a representative of the ship's-cat-in-interstellar-space story, and a standalone short story set in Andre Norton's galactic Solar Queen *series (the first three as by Andrew North):* Sargasso of Space *(Gnome Press, May 1955),* Plague Ship *(Gnome Press, April 1956),* Voodoo Planet *(Ace Books, February 1959),* Postmarked the Stars *(Harcourt, Brace & World, October 1969),* Redline the Stars *[with P. M. Griffin] (Tor, April 1993), and others. The* Solar Queen *series was one of my adolescent favorites; I wrote my M.L.S. thesis (UCLA School of Library Service, May 1963) on the works of Andre Norton.*

Three-Inch Trouble

by Andre Norton

Tailed banners, bearing the codes of many trading companies, snapped in a brisk wind over the booths jammed together. A constant din of voices, raised in argument or in praise of this or that ware, assaulted the ears.

Raven tightened his claw-hold on the perch where he rode with the ease of long practice. As a crew member of the Free Trader *Horus*, he had experienced such gatherings before. Cargo Master Grospar was in no hurry. Once the main cargo was aboard, the star-sailors combed these fairs for personal gambles of their own, a tradition going far back to a time when ships were borne on planet-bound seas and men never dreamed that the next port could be another world. Fortunes had been gained from more than one lucky private deal.

"You choose, Raven. Or are you more eager for offerings to satisfy the innards?"

Raven butted his black-furred head against that of the man on whose shoulder he rode. Such a crude suggestion! He'd provide an answer to fit. Languidly, he drooped his tail to one side.

"Ros-rats? You're losing it, mate!" Grospar sneered, but, disdain notwithstanding, he pushed through the crowd in the direction the cat indicated.

Ros-rats were nasty vermin, but even they had value: they could clear alien wildlife out of a cargo hold in a very short time. As a result, every warehouse had cages of the creatures.

However, a booth to one side displayed distractingly exotic offerings. A pile of furs lay heaped there, with two other spacers arguing over prices. Cages of brilliant-hued flying things hung on display chains. Raven spat at a hand-sized dragon from Kartum as it flickered a forked tongue at him. Transporting live cargo was twice as hard as hauling nonliving wares, and only a few large ships could do it successfully; but even reduced to bundles of bright plumes, lengths of scaled skin, mounds of sensuous fur, outworld creatures would attract buyers.

A woman squeezed around a booth and stepped directly into Grospar's path. "Moon be clear for you, Cargo Master."

Martin Grospar laughed. "You here, Lasseea? I hope fortune favors you, as well, and I trust your moons are clear indeed."

The tall, thin female was not in space uniform but rather wore a colorful flowing robe. Her hair was hidden by a glitter-sewn scarf, and the breeze played with the fringes of twin shawls about her shoulders. Lasseea was a star-reader, and justly famous: several of her important predictions had been accurate.

The seeress leaned forward and tapped Raven between his golden eyes.

"Greeting to you, brother-in-fur." Feline eyes and green human ones locked in a deep gaze. "Sooo—" Now she spoke directly to Grospar again. "There will be work for this little one soon, and then he will prove the worth of all the cargo you have checked into your ship."

The cargo master's smile faded. Lasseea may have insisted, planet-years ago, that Raven shared an important birth star with her and was a bringer of good fortune, but Grospar prided himself on being free of the superstitions that spacefarers could collect. Star-voyaging brought much that was difficult to believe when experienced, and the unusual—even more so than for other adventurers was the usual for Free Traders.

"He's already earned his rations several times over," the man answered gruffly. "What will we have to thank him for now?"

"One sees ahead but little." The star-reader pulled her top shawl closer about her. "Watch and wait."

Then she was gone.

Grospar and Raven continued on to the booth that had attracted the cargo master. As they arrived, the dealer was occupied with a sale, bargaining with two spacers who wanted the shining furs of Arcalic Night-Bats. The *Horus'* officer took advantage of the chance to survey the wares. He was attracted first by a string of small bone carvings hanging against a display rack. Then his eyes shifted to a box below them—a container that looked vaguely familiar. Grospar picked it up. The clasp proving loose, the box opened, and man and cat looked inside.

Within lay six slender bottles, or maybe "vials" was the word. Each was frosted down its length, except for a space at one tip, but those areas were so small that they afforded no glimpse of the tubes' contents. The cargo master caught sight of markings on the nearest and held the box closer. Raven nearly lost his shoulder-seat as he leaned down to sniff.

The Free Trader glanced at the dealer, who was now collecting credit slips. Grospar did not know him, but that was not to say he was a jack dealing in stolen goods. The fact that he had openly displayed this container meant he believed he had nothing to fear. On the other hand, both box and contents were stamped "SURVEY PROPERTY," and such artifacts were usually strictly guarded.

"You have an eye for a mystery, Cargo Master?"

The booth-keep, Grospar guessed, was a fellow Solarian—from Mars, to judge by the brown skin that nearly matched his thinning hair.

"Mystery?"

"That there—" the dealer jabbed a showman's finger at the vial-holder "—come in 'bout ten days ago. Ast'roid miner found it hooked on the belt of a floater who'd got caught in the rocks he'd been blastin.'"

Grospar pointed in turn. "That's a Survey stamp," he said. "The law is—"

The hawker's laugh interrupted him. "Laws! They don't hold much, 'cept when a gov'ment man's there to back 'em up. Who's gonna make an extra flight to Jason or Silenea to turn in somethin' that little? Gimme ten credits, *you* can take it, and," his eyes narrowed shrewdly, "maybe get yourself a reward."

"Eight," the Trader countered, then automatically turned his head. "Worth that, Raven?"

The cat gave a small chirp of encouragement. There was something decidedly interesting about their find.

"Eight an' a half." The merchant fell into the natural rhythm of a sale.

The haggling went on for a few moments. When the cargo master left the booth, the box and some of the bone carvings were tucked into his shouldertote.

As the partners made their way back to the ship, Grospar stopped now and again to examine other offerings. Raven, however, paid no attention. He was keeping an eye on the bag that held his companion's selections and striving to pick up the thread of a very strange scent. Nor did he go off on his own when they were once again in the *Horus* but instead kept close to the cargo master's heels after he had leaped from his moving perch.

Grospar opened a chest built in under his bunk to stow away his most recent purchases, but before he closed the storage place, he opened the box again to view the six vials.

"*What—!*" The cargo master grabbed for a hand light and shone it into the interior, full on the transparent portions of the tubes. A— head? Some kind of carving?

There was no time now to make sure, for the liftoff alert had sounded, and that meant strapdown. He paused to boost Raven into the cat's hammock, then made his own preparations for ship-rise.

Raven wriggled until he could still see the box, which Grospar, for some reason had never placed in the chest. His lips shaped a soundless snarl. What was it? His feline senses were strained to the limit, but he was still frustrated. There had been no movement, no increase in that curious scent—nothing to sound the alarm, yet his inner warning system was clamoring ever more loudly.

The cargo master held the box with both hands, peering within. Carvings? No, he was seeing heads, with staring eyes—heads hardly bigger than his own thumbnails. Well, Survey often brought back samples of strange life—insects, plants—and this container bore their seal.

Found on a space-suited body... how long had its owner floated in the void, cast to a lingering and horrible death by some starship disaster? If the vials had once contained specimens living at that time, they were surely dead by now.

Once more Grospar inspected the tubes, tilting the chest to see their tiny clear windows. One of the half dozen had somehow worked loose. Before he could push it back into the padded crevice that had held it, the vial broke completely free and rose in the now-gravityless air of the cabin, moving upward with surprising speed.

The cargo master snapped the box shut and wedged it under his own body, lest another tube escape, then swept up a hand to snatch at the floater. It seemed to jerk, as though eluding his fingers.

But it did not escape Raven. Claws hooked, swung, and dragged the prize to the feline.

"Hold it, mate!" Grospar ordered. "Don't bite it through!"

As if Raven had any intention of doing *that*. Man's four-legged companions in space had been chosen because, among other traits, they possessed a well-developed sense of caution. The cat simply pressed the vial against the webbing in which he rested, summoning more strength to hold it there.

But the tube rolled, as though it had a will of its own and was fighting to escape. Raven stared into the unfrosted portion. Now he was sure he saw eyes—eyes that met his own. He blinked. They were—*no!* He would not—he would not!

Yet his warding paws moved against his wish, and the vial gained near-freedom even as the cabin was weighted once more with the partial gravity of ready-flight. As he fought to keep his trophy captive, his forelegs, insanely, did just the opposite of what he wanted: they opened. The tube spun lazily down to the floor—and met Grospar's metal-soled boot.

Raven snapped the safety catch of his hammock and leaped, only to pass through a puff of greenish vapor that burned his eyes and brought a squall of pain from him. He landed on the cabin floor and rebounded a little, dazed and limp. The cargo master caught him up, but seconds later the man began to cough with a force that made him drop the cat to gasp and clutch at his own throat.

The feline hit the floor again. Rubbing a paw at his smarting eyes, he let out another cry as Grospar continued to hack, collapsing back onto his bunk. The Survey box joined Raven on the floor, and a second of the vials was jarred loose.

Out of that tube's green gas skidded a reddish blur, an occurrence of which the sickened cat was only half aware. Then the blur made a scuttling approach to the container and its remaining vials. Raven strove to raise a paw but found himself unable to do so. However, while his eyes still hurt, his vision had cleared, and he could see what was happening around the mysterious cache.

The cargo master lay flat on his bunk, coughing in deep, racking bursts. But the tubes were all out of the case now, pulled free by the thing—no, *two* things—that had got out first. The breaking of each vial released more of the breath-stealing vapor to torment the rightful occupants of the cabin.

Those... creatures. The cat squinted. They were as large as his human partner's longest finger, and they had four appendages, but they moved so fast it was hard to see more than that they used an upright position as well as scrambled on all fours. He sprang toward them and, to his utter astonishment, missed.

The cabin door signal sounded a note. Grospar's head turned, and he tried to call out, but a strangled cough was the only sound he was able to make. However, it was a sufficient summons, and the door opened.

Raven squalled again—not in pain, this time, but at the thwarting of his performance of duty. Those elusive beings, avoiding Captain Ricer's booted feet, vanished past him into the corridor. Determinedly the cat started after them, but his steps wavered, and he did not get far before the captain scooped him up.

Thus began a reign of, if not terror, at least fierce frustration for the crew of the *Horus*. The creatures from the Survey box seemed not only uncatchable but unseeable as well; but the wrack and ruin they appeared to deliberately cause was more evident every day.

Some cabins had their furnishings nearly wrecked, while smaller treasures were either bashed beyond repair or disappeared altogether. Across the bunks where off duty crew members were attempting to rest, the things began to scuttle—and worse. The medic treated several nasty bites as best he could.

Raven grew thin, apt to hiss warningly when approached by even his favorite shipmates, and always he hunted. At last, however, he managed to comer one of the enemy in Supply Storage, while it was busy tearing at some packets of the captain's treasured Larmonte tea.

The cat had gotten his paws—or rather one paw—on the entity, only to be leaped upon by two of its kindred who had been devising devilment on a higher shelf. The impudent brutes had no fear of him but bit and snatched at his fur, tweaking tufts of it out of his skin. His battle cry soared into a yowl of pain, but he fought to hold his prize.

"What the—!" Rasidan, the steward and cook, loomed suddenly above the fray. Raven's prisoner bit, hard, into its captor's right front paw, and he snapped back, his teeth closing about one of the creature's forelegs. Then a smothering cloth descended upon feline and foe as they fought, and the warring beings were lifted into the air. Tenaciously the cat held his grip, even when the knot formed of himself and his keening captive was dropped onto a hard surface, and the fabric loosened to fall free.

They were in the captain's cabin, with crew members crowded around the pulldown leaf of the desk. Raven's prey went abruptly limp, but still he did not release his hold. It was Grospar who reached down for the small body. His furred partner growled, body tensed to spring away. He was going to finish this catch! That's what he was there for: to make sure that the ship—*his* ship—was free of such intruders.

"It's all right, Raven," the cargo master assured him quickly. "Let me have it."

The cat held on, studying the situation. He mistrusted Grospar's ability to keep a grip on the thing. It was far from dead, and he was sure that if he released it, it would vanish again. These invaders had already proved that they were too swift, too small to be managed by men.

"Raven!" Captain Ricer spoke now, and he held up a square of cloth. "I'm going to wrap this around it—then you let go."

That was a definite order—a captain's order—and even he had to obey. He ducked his chin, relaxing his jaws. As he did so, the being came to furious life, but the captain had it bagged. The cat edged back. His numerous wounds burned, and an evil taste filled his mouth; however, he had set his own mark on the menace. He moved forward again to lend the weight of his forepaws to the control of the heaving bundle, though his superior continued to pin it also.

"In that lower cupboard." Ricer was giving Grospar directions. "Yes—that's it!"

The cargo master had stooped and risen. What he placed upon the desk was equipment from his commander's own private hobby. The captain, when the *Horus* had time in port on a lesser-known planet, hunted flying insects, then studied them in holding boxes of his own design. Since some of his captives had not only been large in size but equipped with menacing jaws, claws, stingers, and whatever other defenses nature had chosen to give them, the cages were indeed right and tight.

The one Grospar held at the ready was a cube of heavy netting with a thick metal floor. Into this the captain now transferred the frantically-wriggling contents of the improvised bag.

The cargo master instantly slammed down the top of the box with force enough to make it catch and lock—and just in time, for the creature sprang, only to be knocked back by the lowered flap.

"Now, then—" Ricer beckoned forward those who wished a closer look at one of their miniature nightmares of days past. Those of the crew who had gathered in his cabin closed in, staring at the cage and its inmate. For the first time, since the things moved with such speed, they could all view a specimen as it tugged and hurled itself against the wire-net walls that now enclosed it.

The body was covered with what seemed to be matted brownish-red fur, but the front paws, shaped not unlike human hands, were equipped with pointed talons that were now hooked into the screen barrier. An open mouth displayed similar armament in the form of a set of needlelike teeth, which were dripping a green liquid. The nose was flat and the face hairless about the jaw, cheeks, and eyes.

Its first battle rage was stilled, but the small nightmare still clung to the wire. Glittering blood-red eyes were fixed upon Ricer as he knelt down to bring himself closer to the surface of the flap-desk. Without looking, he groped along its top, brought out a magnifier, and swung that circle of view glass between himself and the now-quiet prisoner.

Raven approached the other side of the holding box. He snorted at the musky odor that was so strong, then stopped, growling, as though he had come up against an unseen barrier. He sensed from the being an intense malignancy. He could pick up no fear whatever—only a raging fury.

"I—don't—believe—it—" Captain Ricer accented each word he spoke, apparently wanting to deny the report given by his eyes.

"Don't believe what?" questioned Medic Lothers as he pushed Raven to one side to better view the cage and its occupant.

"That," Ricer declared slowly, "is a *monkey!*"

"A what?" Lothers asked the question for everyone.

"If that beast were about a hundred times larger—" The captain let his sentence trail off unfinished as he swung away from the table. He opened a cupboard and reached within, emerging with a reader-tape from his personal library. This tape he slapped into the viewer that shared the desktop with the cage and its captive.

The cat paid no attention to his commander's behavior, not even to the picture that appeared on the screen as Ricer triggered keys. He was intent on what was happening before him.

The entity had released its clutch on the wires and dropped to the floor of the box, where it curled itself into a ball. All at once, Raven shook his head vigorously, feeling as though both his ears had been invaded by loudly-buzzing insects. After a moment, he realized that the creature was mindcalling—and in a manner he had never encountered before.

The feline could not interpret the sense of the message being sent, but he was certain that it was either a warning to the being's own kind to take cover or a plea to them for help. The thing turned its head, staring at him. Again Raven could sense no fear—only a consuming rage.

In any grouping of wildlife there was always a leader. Even in an assembling of ships' cats, such as occurred at times when a starport's fields were crowded, one or two would take precedence, and the others would accord them room, as was required. This angry alien was not such a dominant one, but it seemed to believe that its mental broadcasts would reach its fellows. And perhaps that vast hatred had, indeed, reached a level of force in its projection to where it would bring aid…

The men had moved away from the cage and were concentrating on the reader. Raven closed his ears to the argument that seemed to be rising among them—something about a comparison between the information on the tape and the size of the thing in the box. The cat was entirely intent on its broadcasting of near-insane anger.

Suddenly he made a move of his own. A sweep of paw struck the cage to the floor of the cabin, and an instant later he was beside it. A hand grabbed for the holding box; a second caught one of his own feet in a trap-tight clutch.

"What you trying to do, Cat?" It was Grospar who held and questioned him.

No time! Raven bit—hard. The cargo master yelled and loosed his grip. His furred partner offered no more aggression but rather jumped for the cage, sank teeth into its netting, and dragged it out into the passageway beyond.

The prisoner's kin—ones were coming—the cat could not see them, but he knew. He yowled, standing directly before the box, which he was using as bait to draw the rest of the creatures out of hiding. Then a pair of space boots grazed his tail as Grospar stopped just behind him.

"Stun him!" someone yelled.

"No!" shouted the cargo master. "He's got some sort of plan—I'll swear to it!"

The feline heard this exchange as though it were a rumble of distant thunder that had no meaning for him. He bobbed his head and gave the box another shove.

Within its enclosure there was no stir; the tiny intruder was still enwrapped upon itself, concentrating on its call. Not for the first time Raven wished he could communicate with his human crew-mates. True, he could convey broad outlines of feelings or ideas to Grospar, but not detailed ones such as he needed to share now. He could only—

The cat crouched down between the men and the cage. Should these invaders turn away from the summons and seek hiding places, it might be a long time before they would be found and routed out. Let them come into the open to free their fellow, however, and any member of the crew with a battle- stunner might take them.

"By the Last Ray of Corbus—look—they're coming!"

The cargo master had apparently sighted one of those scuttling shadows Raven had already sensed, though he was keeping most of his attention on the entity in its pen. The cat raised his still-bleeding forepaw and shook the box back and forth. The reaction was instantaneous—a fresh burst of defiance struck at him, revealing that the little brute was still both aware and angry.

The men had been exchanging a rapid-fire volley of suggestions, but a single word from the captain brought instant silence.

"Stunner—"

"*Here?*" challenged the medic immediately. Use of a stunner within the narrow confines of a corridor ran counter to all the never-questioned rules of ship safety.

The creatures were all in view now, though spread well apart. Once more Raven rattled the cage, then almost at once shook his head again. The original broadcast of wrath seemed a love pat compared to the silent waves of killing fury that now crashed into his mind, causing actual physical pain.

Through the red haze he forced himself to think: *Get behind the ones who would rescue their fellow—cut off any retreat.* But how could he achieve that position—and how would his own crewmates snare the things still loose? These were monkeys, with the intelligence of all their kind, but incredibly small in size and able to move at a speed too fast for eyes, human or feline, to follow—

Raven gave a last bat of his paw to the box, then turned around. As he had hoped, the cargo master was right behind him. With a swiftness rivaling that of the aliens, he leaped upward, hooking claws deep enough into Grospar's ship suit to pierce skin. The man gripped the cat and ripped him free.

For a second time, Raven bit the hand that held him, thus achieving part of his desperate plan. He was hurled away (a spluttered oath loud in his ears) to land some distance ahead, well past the pen.

Perhaps what the cargo master called "luck" was truly on his side, for the cat by his actions had now placed the invaders between himself and the crew. The creatures scrabbled frantically, but escape was impossible from the section of corridor into which the mind-call of the captive had brought them. One tried to dart in Raven's direction, and the feline responded with the hunter's reflexes of his kind: he did not try to pin this being down but swatted it, straight back at its companions.

The men of the *Horus* had spread themselves across the other end of the passage where they stood forming a barrier, space boot to space boot. Once more Captain Ricer spoke the word that told how he would deal with this situation, but this time, as he turned to exit the corridor, he was not inviting debate:

"Stunner!"

Raven uttered a yowl of agony. The free monkeys were not attacking, but the beat of rage inside his head from the confined one was almost enough to knock him down: Almost, yes—but not quite. A stunner, though—the cat knew what such a weapon might do if fired at close quarters.

Retreat? No—not for him. That was a very fleeting thought. This was his ship, his territory, *his*—!

The crew members on the other side of the cage drew back a fraction, and the creatures, who had seemed frozen in place by wariness, suddenly stirred. Raven felt a thrust of anger that was purely his own. Were Grospar and the rest going to give the enemy a chance to escape again?

But it was the captain for whom the men were making way. And he was carrying a tube that the cat had seen borne in action planetside only twice when lives had been threatened.

Instinctively he braced himself. There would be no sound, no visible shot fired—there would be—

Blackness swallowed him. The dark was painless, but it carried fear. He was in bonds, and he could not escape—not even open his mouth to cry out a protest! Panic had almost overwhelmed him when a familiar scent reached his nose, his brain. Grospar—? Yes, the cargo master had picked him up, was cradling him.

"Raven! Come on, li'l shadow—"

A quick sharp stab in his shoulder, and the helpless weakness began to fade.

"That ought to bring him around—"

Those words broke through the blind bondage that no longer held so tightly. Raven opened his eyes. Medic Lothers was watching him, and behind him stood the captain. Grospar gave his friend a last hug and laid him down on the softness of a bunk. His returning senses registered the odors of the captain's cabin.

"Got 'em—every one o' the buggers!"

Fortunately, because his head still felt too heavy to lift, Raven could see what was happening from where he lay. First the cage containing his "bait," then Ricer's insect-capturing net were being placed on the desk, and the bug-bag was bulging with inert bodies.

"Dead?" The cargo master, his hand still poised above the cat's head to touch him gently now and again, had asked that. The captain gingerly inserted fingers into the insect-net. Bringing forth one of the small bodies, he held it out to Lothers for a medical verdict.

"Well, it can evidently survive being stunned because it's still breathing," was the doctor's reply. "Can't tell whether it's damaged, though—too alien."

Ricer produced another collecting cage, then a third, and into these the creatures were placed. With the three miniature brigs lined up before him, the commander could finally perform a careful examination of the inmates.

"Survey can certainly have you," he at last declared to the entities who might or might not awaken from their enforced slumber. Then, his prison inspection concluded, the captain swung around to Raven. Standing at attention, he lifted his right hand and touched his temple in the formal salute offered only on state occasions to valiant beings in the Star Service.

"Ship's Guard," he said solemnly, "well done."

Grospar smiled, giving the cat a second, more intimate reward in the form of a rub behind the ears. "Lasseea was right, fur-friend," he said with a sigh of relief. "Your lucky star was our luck, too."

The weary feline lowered his head and closed his eyes. These attentions were very flattering, but right now he just wanted his shipmates to clear out and let him sleep. What nonsense humans talked, he thought. Suns in the heavens an influence on fate? Better the light-of-mind that was his kind's common sense. Were he to attempt such a farseeing as Lasseea's, though, he felt sure he could predict that Grospar would never go salvaging Survey-sealed material again. He, Raven, Ship's Guard of the Free Trader *Horus*, would personally make certain that there was no more such—what was the expression the men used for foolhardy activity?

Ah, yes (the cat wished he could smile)—*monkey business.*

Dawna Keen-Eyed is a weary, battle-hardened human mercenary swordswoman in a primitive, war-torn fantasy world. She is used to selling her sword to (hopefully) the "good" side in a land of constantly shifting warfare.

Cabbage Town may be an amusing name, but there is nothing funny about its inhabitants' mistreatment of their animals, especially their cats. Dawna objects, but it's ultimately the town's business. But when Dawna prepares to leave, she is taken aback when the cats want to hire her services.

Defender of the Small

by Jody Lynn Nye

Dawna Keen-Eyed upended her water skin and drank the few last drops. Walking the rough horse track between villages was thirsty work, but she was happy. It was better to be breathing country air full of the smells of new-cut hay, wood smoke and pig poop than blood, rot, burning oil and the smell of corpses beginning to decay. The way the land sloped the river shouldn't be far ahead, and by it the town where perhaps a decent meal and a clean bed waited. Her longsword, carefully cleaned from the last battle and wrapped in its oiled cloth, and her shield with its red stripe down the center bumped against the tall woman's back with every step she took. The red pennant that indicated her status as a mercenary fluttered from the hilt and tickled the back of her neck under her long, brown braid. King Drealin III himself had handed the pennant back to her with a brief statement of gratitude, at the same time that the paymaster gave her her fee. The money wasn't much, but it ought to last long enough for her to reach home. For the moment she longed to sit down. Her legs were tired, and she had finally worn through the thin place in the sole of her left boot.

Cabbage Town, the gold-lettered plaque read, as the track changed from mud to gravel at the edge of the village. Dawna glanced around with pleasure. Life was here, not death. It was market day. Hearty merchants wrangled with their customers, apple-cheeked women in kirtles and wimples, or tall men with colorful liripipe hoods. Farmers argued about the relative merits of this or that cow. Dogs slept in the sun.

A plump gray puss slept tucked up on a window sill beside a scarlet flower in a pot. An orange-striped mother cat, her teats heavy with milk, wound about the legs of the tables on which the merchants' goods were displayed.

A group of shouting and laughing children ranging in age from five to ten or eleven years old raced up the hill along a lane that led up from the river that Dawna could now see from the village's main street. They stopped to stare at the mercenary in armor with her pack and sword slung upon her back. She smiled at them.

"Good day to you," she said, shifting the heavy load to the other shoulder.

Immediately the children went wide-eyed with distrust and curiosity.

"Are you here to conquer us?" asked a little girl with long plaits tied with blue ribbon.

Dawna laughed. "No, I'm just back from the wars."

"You were fighting?" asked the biggest boy, hair the color of fresh wood and eyes of leaf green.

"Indeed I was. I killed eight men in the last battle at Songhelm. I and my fellow sell-swords were in the front line when we laid siege to the pirates' stronghold at Valorin on the coast. We broke the walls down in only three days, and saved the town."

"Ooohhh!" the children gasped, awed.

"Did you burn their boats? Did you meet the king? Did you find bags of gold?" Now that she had proved friendly, questions bubbled up out of the children like steam in a stewpot.

"Perhaps I'll tell you a tale or two later. I just want a rest now," Dawna said, with a smile. She turned back to the butcher, who was hacking a slab of meat into collops. "Where's a good place to get a meal and a bed for the night?"

The man stuck the tip of his carving knife into the chopping block and consulted the sky. "Oh, well, there's Brenner's tavern, or Mistress Peck's…"

The biggest of the boys, bored by such ordinary talk, picked up a stone and heaved it at the orange cat. It struck her in the side. She let out a cry and skittered underneath the weaver's table, next to the butcher.

"Stop that," Dawna ordered. The boys paid no attention. They picked up more stones and continued to pelt the cat, who mewed piteously, trying to find a place to hide. "For Gods' love, what's the matter with you? Whose children are those?" she asked the tradesfolk.

"Just children," the butcher replied, with a shrug. "Just a cat. What do you care?"

"It's wrong," Dawna exclaimed angrily. "Cats are the Gods' creatures, the same as we are."

The man blew a derisive raspberry. Dawna felt her temper flaring. Those brats were hurting an innocent animal, and he didn't intend to do a thing about it. After all the killing she had seen, senseless cruelty fired her blood.

"Mind that for me," she said, thrusting her pack into the butcher's arms. She drew her sword and stuck it, point quivering, into the nearest tree. No need for it in what she intended to do.

As she turned the children instantly divined her intention. They dropped the rest of their stones and fled down the street towards the river. A coracle lay on the churned-up mud bank. No doubt they intended to make their escape in it, leaving the woman unable to follow them in her heavy leather-and-bronze armor. They had the advantage of lightness, but her temper lent speed to her feet. With a surge of strength she hurtled down the hill, angling to come up in front of the largest boy, the initial stone-thrower.

"Now we'll see how much *you* enjoy a thrashing," she said, grabbing him by the arm. She sat down on the coracle's edge and swung him over her knee. "*That's* for assaulting a poor innocent beast. And *that's* for harming a mother. And *that's* for not listening to your elders." Her open hand smacked down hard on his upturned back-side again and again.

The other children fled as soon as their leader had been captured. By the time Dawna marched her captive up the hill, a crowd had gathered.

"What the hell do you think you're doing to our children?" demanded the weaver.

"They needed a lesson," Dawna stated, thrusting the boy toward the crowd. He immediately ran to a prosperous-looking man whose sandy-blond locks suggested to her that he was the boy's father. "Cruelty to animals is a sin." The gray cat had been awakened from his nap by the shouting. He wound around the legs of the crowd. The weaver distractedly aimed a kick at it when it brushed against him.

"Get away with you," he growled.

Dawna turned on him. "You're no better! Children learn from their elders. You should teach them kindness. These animals are your friends and protectors."

"Oh, please," the weaver groaned, rolling his eyes. "Don't spout your animist noises at me. The Father put all creatures under the command of humans. If He wishes us saved from plague He will be the one to save us, not some dumb animal." From the sound of the grumbling, the rest of the crowd agreed with him.

"Dumb! Can *you* catch a rat with your hands?"

"You're a fine one to talk about holding life sacred," a gaunt, gray-haired woman declared, shaking a finger at her. "That red flag of yours gives you away. You work for a price, killing for pay."

Dawna walked over to the tree beside the butcher's stall and pulled her sword free. The crowd watched with worried eyes as she sheathed it. "I accept a fee to defend what I think is right, goodwife. I only use my weapon in worthy service. I never harm anyone who cries me mercy and lays down his weapons. Thank you." She tugged her pack out of the butcher's limp arms.

"Fine words," the prosperous man said, "but you were quick enough to paddle a harmless boy."

"It's a lesson he had coming, if not from you, then from me," Dawna said frankly. "If the king's marshalls saw him he'd have gotten more than a swat, I can tell you that. His punishment was with my empty hand. I will never draw my sword against an unarmed man, woman or child." She sighed. "I am only passing through your town. I'm not looking for a fight. But don't doubt that I can defend myself well without it. I don't want a fight with you. All I want is to sup here and sleep, and I'll be on my way in the morning."

"Not in my establishment, you won't. You stay out of my inn," the wrinkled old woman ordered her.

"And mine," added a stout man.

"Leave our town," the boy's father declared, shaking his fist. "We don't want you here, sell-sword. No one here wants your services, or your presence."

Dawna growled to herself. If she hadn't been so tired she'd have given them *all* the flat of her hand. If anyone she'd ever met needed spankings, it was these people. "I'm on the common property, and I claim the king's peace." She raised an eyebrow, defying anyone to disagree with her.

No one did. The king's peace meant they couldn't drive her off the green or within a body-length of any public highway. Paying her no more mind the townsfolk closed up their market stalls and went in to dinner. Dawna watched longingly as a cluster of merry-makers followed Mistress Peck through the cheerfully-painted wooden door at the corner of the square. *Beer,* she thought, wistfully, *roast beef.* Tempting smells floated out to her on the evening breeze.

No chance getting a hot meal from Mistress Peck or the other innkeeper, nor of paying a villager for a share of their supper. Dawna sat down against a tree and began to rummage in her pack for dry, tasteless journey biscuit. It'd gripe her belly more than usual knowing that good food was so close by.

191

She jumped back in alarm as something cold and slimy fell on her hand. The tabby cat she had rescued sat at her feet with tail wound around its paws, looking up at her with big, green, saucerlike eyes. The thing that had now fallen off Dawna's hand was a freshly caught trout.

"Taking pity on the hungry traveler, eh?" she said, reaching down to scratch the cat behind the ears. "Thank you. It'll be most welcome."

With flint and tinder from her pack she struck a small fire, gutted and staked the fish over it to cook. It was delicious. The cat watched her eat, accepted a morsel and no more, rubbed against Dawna's knee, then disappeared into the darkness. Dawna banked the fire and settled herself uncomfortably against the tree. With the townsfolk unkindly inclined toward her she didn't dare strip off her armor. After a few drinks they might be bolder. She hated fighting with drunks; they always threw up on her, and bronze took so much polishing.

The blanket of twilight began to draw across the sky. Now that the sun was down the chill river mist was rising. She pulled her gray wool cloak out of her pack and wrapped it around herself, tugging the hood down over her forehead. Not warm enough, but it would have to do. She'd have to sleep with one eye open and her sword at her side. It'd be a cold night and a wakeful one.

* * *

Birdsong woke her at false dawn. Dawna's free hand clenched on something unfamiliar, which squirmed. She struggled to sit up. A heavy weight on her chest and legs shifted. Her hand fumbled for her sword. Instead of metal her fingers touched fur. Her eyes flew open. Green eyes in a wedge-shaped gray head regarded her from an inch away.

"Wha'?" Dawna sputtered, thrashing. "Gah?'

The gray cat was curled up just underneath her collar bone. More of the weight on her moved. She raised her head to look. Behind the gray cat a blanket of felines rolled or stalked off Dawna's body, leaving behind cold morning air. Dawna gaped in amazement. They had spent the night on her, providing her with a living blanket. But that was not all. From the protected hollow in the crook of her arm four kittens, two gray, one orange and one calico, looked up at her with trusting eyes. The mother cat unwound herself from a ball next to Dawna's head and came over to rub against Dawna's jaw, then began to lick the kittens vigorously.

"Well, so much for my reputation for vigilance," Dawna said, touching the little ones' delicate heads. The kits were so young their ears were still rounded. The mother cat's rough tongue pushed her fingers away from the calico's ear. "I'm glad my sisters-in-arms weren't here to see me sleep through that. Thank you for keeping me warm. I was comfortable. A kindness for a kindness."

The mother cat arched her back upward, stretched forward and back, then stalked away, leaving her kittens in the curve of Dawna's arm.

"Wait, I'm not a nursemaid!" Dawna called, then chided herself. How could she expect a cat to understand what she was saying?

It wouldn't be long before the townsfolk emerged to take up their chores for the day. If Dawna hung about too long they'd begin to gather in small groups, eventually working up enough mob courage to drive her out of the village. She intended to be on her way long before *that* psychological moment arose, but in the meanwhile, her damaged boot needed attention.

Gingerly, she peeled off the battered black shoe. It would have been nice to have the local shoemaker fix it for her, but under the circumstances he'd most likely be afraid to do business with her. Never mind: she had pieces of leather, waxed cord and a needle in her pack, same as she used for patching her armor.

The kittens crawled in her lap and batted at the end of the string. Dawna gently pushed them away as she took another stitch.

"You still here, sell-sword?" a voice demanded. Two very nice, honey-colored boots stopped just over a body's length from her knee. She'd have liked to have a pair like that. Dawna looked up, in no hurry. In them was the weaver, wearing a defiant expression, though his eyes were scared.

"I'll be gone soon enough," she said.

"Sooner's better than later," he replied. It *almost* sounded like a threat. Dawna went back to her work. The weaver hesitated for a moment, the beautiful boots rocking back and forth with indecision, then strode away. Dawna dismissed him. He wouldn't be the one to attack her, but he'd stand at the back and shout encouragement to the stupid ones at the front. Dawna knew his kind.

A soft but insistent mew interrupted her thoughts. The orange cat had returned, laying another fish at her feet. Her right paw was wet up to the shoulder, but the rest of her was dry. A good hunter.

"You've decided to feed me, eh?" Dawna said, picking up the fish. It was a mature brook trout, twice the length of her hand. Plenty of good meat on it. The cat chirruped, expectantly. "Is it out of gratitude?" Dawna asked. "Because you already thanked me last night."

The cat chirruped again, and settled down with her paws tucked under her breast. Dawna had had few dealings with cats except on her father's farm. They seemed curious, independent, brave and cowardly at the same time, taking their business and pleasure equally seriously, just like people. But she'd never taken the time to talk to one, assuming their comprehension was limited to their own language. This one listened carefully, her orange-striped head cocked to one side, almost as if she understood. Then, to Dawna's surprise, the cat walked from the fish to the pennant hanging from Dawna's shield and back again, rubbing up against the mercenary's knee with each pass. Dawna let the corners of her mouth perk up in amusement.

"You couldn't be...hiring me?"

The cat chirruped again.

"How can you understand what I said yesterday? How could you possibly know what I do?" The cat gave her a wise look. "What is it you want me to do, then? Protect you? Or you *and* your babies?"

It was a test. The cat passed it. She climbed into Dawna's lap, briefly licked the top of each kitten's head, then stared up at the warrior again as the kittens burrowed in toward the tabby's nipples. "By the Gods, I believe you *are* hiring me. Why not? Very well. It's a bargain." She put out a hand to seal the deal, as she did with her human clients, and laughed at herself as the cat sniffed her fingers. "Here, then," she said formally, unhooking the pennant. "My gage is the symbol of my service. Carry it until my duty to you is discharged."

She wound the streamer twice around the cat's neck, tying the loose ends in a bow. "A bit gaudy with your coloring, my lady, but not too bad."

The cat seemed pleased, and began to wash her wet paw. The kittens were well into their morning meal.

But how to discharge her commission? Dawna thought, pushing the needle through the hard leather. She could hardly follow the cat on her morning rounds, nor shadow her as she stalked vermin. The cat solved the dilemma by departing abruptly from the mercenary's lap, leaving the now sleeping kittens behind. The mercenary shrugged and went on with her repair.

As morning began, the smaller children emerged carrying slates and headed toward a house at the opposite corner of the square, where a goodwife was waiting with her hands on her hips: the village schoolteacher. The older children who were apprenticed were already on their way to and fro, discharging commissions for their masters. They all gave her a wary look as they passed her, sitting under the tree in the middle of the green, especially the blond boy whom she had spanked.

Once in a while the cat returned to feed her kittens. She had decided Dawna's lap was by far the best place for the job. The butcher passed by with a cart full of meat, saw the red streamer around the cat's neck, and snorted.

"How much is it paying you?" he asked.

"Two fish a day," Dawna replied. "I've had better wages, but I've had worse, too."

"You're mad," the butcher informed her. "That's the silversmith's cat. He'll do as he pleases with her, scarf or no scarf."

"If she has the wits to ask for my help, then she's master of her own fate," Dawna said.

Word spread quickly through the small town about her contract with the cat. From her vantage point on the green she could see all the comings and goings. Even the boy, who appeared to be apprenticed to the brewer, gave the orange cat a wide berth as he wheeled kegs of beer up and back from the brewery. The cat strutted, proudly displaying the red scarf around her neck as she went about her business.

One dark-haired lad did work up the courage to shy a stone at the orange cat. It just missed her, striking dust up from the pathway directly under her belly. The cat levitated in surprise, spun around to glare at her attacker, then she turned and stared directly at Dawna. No doubt remained in the warrior's mind that the cat understood what she had commissioned. Dawna, grinning, began to rise from her seat under the tree. The boy's face paled in fear, and he fled into an alleyway, his loose shoes pattering on the cobblestones. Dawna settled back again. She doubted he'd ever try again.

As long as she was there, that was. Dawna could not stay in Cabbage Town for long. By her reckoning she had perhaps a day, maybe two, before the townsfolk decided they were tired of the looming presence of an armed mercenary, one they thought was at least a little mad because she considered herself employed by a cat!

Shouting voices drew her attention to the river path. She saw nothing at first, but a small black-and-white cat came tearing up the hill, running full out. Its eyes were round with terror. It spotted Dawna and made directly for her. As it neared, Dawna saw blood, bright red on its fur. A cluster of children pelted up the hill ten steps behind it, throwing stones and clods of earth. By the time they reached the green the black-and-white was crouched underneath Dawna's shield, trembling. Its eyes lifted to hers, beseeching. The blood dripped from a cut in its side.

"I won't give you away, little one," she said, laying a gentle hand on its neck.

The children cast about, looking for their prey. "It got away!" one of them shouted. "Let's go find another!"

They shot Dawna defiant glances. So that was the way of it, she thought. As long as the orange cat was off limits, they were going to have their fun with other animals. She loathed this town and everyone in it.

She opened her pack. "Stay there, little one," she said, as the black-and-white began to edge away from the strange sounds. "I've got salve that will ease the pain and stop the bleeding." The little cat held still for its physicking, then lay purring weakly as Dawna tied a makeshift bandage around its middle. When the orange cat returned she touched noses with the newcomer, then gave it a good washing before lying down to feed her kits. Dawna had a new client.

* * *

"Nay, I'll not sell you red cloth, nor anything else," the weaver said severely, spreading his hands protectively over the stock on his counter. "I'd suggest you go visit the priests and see if they'll pray for your sanity. Now, leave."

Dawna gave up the argument and departed from the white-painted shop. She had not gone five paces out of the door when something bumped her leg. She looked down to see the gray cat, a long, red ribbon trailing from its mouth. It draped the end over her boot and blinked moonlike eyes at her. She groaned.

"Not you, too! Does no one treat their beasts with respect in this town?" Dawna glanced about to see if anyone was watching her. She took a small coin and wrapped it in a scrap of cloth. "Give this to your master for pay," she said. "I won't have either of us in trouble for theft. I accept your commission."

The gray cat dipped his head as if nodding, and trotted back into the store with the little bundle in its mouth. Dawna strode hastily up the hill, not wanting the weaver to come bursting out and accuse her publicly of sorcery.

Word had spread among the four-legged denizens of Cabbage Town, too. When she returned, her small camp was occupied by a dozen cats. Some of them bore the marks of recent ill-treatment; still others had old scars and limbs misshapen from being broken and left untreated. None of them had come empty-handed, or, rather, empty-mouthed. A little pile of offerings guarded by the orange-striped mother cat included sausage links, a raw chicken leg, a silk handkerchief, a child's purse containing one copper coin and a thumbprint-sized religious medallion depicting the Forest God. The length of red ribbon from the weaver's was barely long enough to make collars for all the worried-looking felines huddled near her. More clients. That night, they once again provided her with warmth, fresh fish, and not a few fleas. If she was going to be the protector of the local cats, she was going to have to pick them some fleabane.

* * *

"Rats!" the silversmith declared, confronting the warrior nose to nose as she stumped back up the hill after making a rough toilet at the river's edge. The orange cat followed her, her latest catch clasped proudly in her jaws. "There are rats in my shop, and *my cat*," he pointed accusingly, "has spent all the last day up here with you. Release the witchery you've placed on her so she can do what I keep her to do!"

"There's no witchery," Dawna replied, glancing at the cat, who'd taken her favorite spot among the knobby roots of the tree. Her kittens, looked after by her other charges, played with their mother's tail, a leaf and a strand of hair from Dawna's comb. "She'll go, but your son must promise not to abuse her."

"Er…" the silversmith began. If he thought it was sorcery how could he argue? "Er. Done, then."

He rushed away. Dawna glanced at the orange cat. "In your own good time, then. We'll see if his word's his bond."

She was beginning to enjoy the company of cats. In many ways her little enclave on the hilltop reminded her of the war camp she had just left. Each warrior had her job to do, but was glad of the society of fellow warriors at the end of the day. She wished they could talk as well as understand. Dawna missed human conversation. Her keen hearing allowed her to eavesdrop on the innkeeper's guests at the edge of the green.

"…Say the war's over, so I guess that female up there was telling the truth…"

"…Raspberry season down south. It'll start here soon…"

"…Sixty dead in one town. Can't tell *me* that's not sorcery from the enemy!"

"…Never happen here. Come on, let's have another drink."

* * *

By the next morning Dawna could feel that the town's tolerance limit had been reached. Though they couldn't tell she knew what they were doing, the adults went about furtively, peeking at her from behind trees, ducking into one another's shops and homes, coordinating what they planned to do, to drive away the invader. She had plenty of time to divine their intention. By the time they'd formed up into a mob, three hours after they had begun, she had had time to bathe, enjoy a hearty breakfast of grilled fish and purloined sausage, pet and doctor all the cats, and don her full armor, including her buckler and newly-polished sword. The gleaming hilts of dirks poked out of both boot tops, and a war hammer, her least favorite weapon but a good one of last recourse, hung ready at her belt. She had fifteen cats with her now. Most of the adult felines of the town had come to her during the last day, bringing an offering, hoping for protection. They clustered behind her heels.

Led by the silversmith nearly the entire human population of Cabbage Town stalked into the common and surged partway up the hill where she held her vigil. They were carrying tools of their trades, such as shears and hammers, or garden implements like hoes and spades. Only two bore themselves like former soldiers: the school teacher and the dyer, who both carried short-swords of uncertain age. The rest held their makeshift weapons with no conviction. Dawna felt certain she could defend herself if it came to a fight, but she intended that no fight should begin. A few of them stopped dead when they saw how she was attired. She smiled. Half the battle was already won.

Pushed by the others, the silversmith finally stepped forward out of the mob. He cleared his throat.

"Sell-sword, we've concluded...all of us," he turned to gesture at the crowd, "that, er, it is disruptive to the, er, well-being of our town, of which you are not a citizen, that...that..."

"That I should leave?" Dawna finished for him.

"Um...er...yes," the silversmith squeaked out, surprised at her capitulation. He seemed to take heart. "I mean, that is, forthwith. You must be on your way at once. Carrying only what you came with. Er. Yes. You must leave our cats behind."

"Very well," Dawna said, crossing her arms. "I won't touch a single one." Muttering erupted amongst the townsfolk. She had agreed so easily. What were they missing? They would be missing quite a lot, soon, if she was not wrong. She raised her voice. "I've got a few words to say that I want everyone to hear. I wish to thank the citizens of Cabbage Town for the use of your green for the last two nights. It would have been a cold and uncomfortable place to stay, if not for the hospitality of your cats. They've shown me the common courtesy that I thought humans owed to one another, certainly that which one might expect to be extended to fellow subjects of this kingdom.

"To my hosts and clients, then," and she turned to look into the round eyes of the cats huddled at the foot of the tree, "I depart now for my home town of Marigold Down. If you are afraid to remain here, you may come with me. I'll find you somewhere better to live where you need never again fear a boot or a stone. I know my father would be grateful for good hunting cats. His barley harvest is much troubled by rats."

"Now, sell-sword!" the silversmith protested. "Didn't you just agree not to take our cats with you?"

"Now, silversmith," she countered, turning to face him. "They're dumb creatures, aren't they? You've all said as much for the last two days. You don't honestly believe that they can *understand* me, do you?"

"Uh. Er. No. I suppose not." The muttering in the crowd got louder. Dawna pitched her voice so it could be heard clear down to the bottom of the hill.

"I swear to you by my soul that I will not take a single animal out of this town. If any follow me, it will be by their own volition. Will that satisfy you?"

"Not me," the butcher growled, stepping forward with a cleaver in his hand. "I'll see you to the edge of town, mercenary, just to make sure you don't steal anything of ours."

"And I!" exclaimed the weaver.

"And I will, too," said the barber-surgeon, a dark-complected man with beefy arms. In all, six of the boldest elected to act as her escort. Dawna glanced back as she marched down the hill with her honor guard trailing behind. All of the cats who had been there had melted away into the undergrowth.

"Go on about your business," the butcher ordered the rest of the crowd. "We'll see she doesn't turn back."

Dawna led the six townsfolk toward the northern edge of town. Six days' march would bring her within sight of Marigold Down, and another half day to her father's home to the northwest.

"Goodbye," she said, nodding to her escort.

"Good riddance," the butcher said. As one, the men turned and stumped back toward town.

"Same to you," Dawna said under her breath. The sooner she shook the dust of Cabbage Town off her feet, the happier she would be. And now to see if her speech had had any results.

It had. As soon as she left the clean, gravel track for the muddy forest path, cats began to appear like magic out of the surrounding undergrowth. The orange cat popped out from beneath a flowering gorse bush with her kittens marching in a file behind her, and claimed the warrior with a cheek-swipe along her boot top. Dawna stopped only long enough to scoop up the little ones and put them in a makeshift sling made of a fold of her cloak. The gray cat and the injured black-and-white came running from another hiding place. In all, eighteen cats and a couple dozen half-grown kits would be making the long journey northward with her. As soon as she felt safe stopping she would tie red ribbons around the necks of each to show the people they met that these cats were under her protection. She hoped she wouldn't run into anyone as thick as the denizens of Cabbage Town.

"Come along," she said to the cats, setting a light pace once she was out of sight of the town. "We've got a long way to go, and I've always found a story helps to pass the time. Now, let me tell you about the siege of Valorin…"

The kittens against her chest purred their approval.

Here is another story about a lucky ship's cat—with a difference. "The Luck of the Dauntless" is set in a fantastic world where the ships are living sea dragons. The silver-furred, blue spotted Rex isn't any ordinary cat, either. Rex the Mau cat and Dauntless the dragon/ship make a unique and effective team.

James M. Ward's "The Luck of the Dauntless" is a standalone story, with different characters, set in the same world as his two novels Midshipwizard Halcyon Blythe *(Tor Books, August 2005) and* Dragonfrigate Wizard Halcyon Blythe *(Tor Books, November 2006).*

The Luck of the *Dauntless*

by James M. Ward

I wasn't happy, and I made sure all the pets scurrying around on the dock knew I was displeased. There's no sense being royalty if you don't demand and receive royal treatment.

"Move it ya swab! The faster you climb these ratlines, the faster we get this here duty done," Leading Seaman Handel Thune barked to his mate.

Rough sailors, as noted by their drab brown work trews, they'd taken the cat cage from the jolly boat to the sea dragon's side and then carried it onto two rope ladders on the side of the dragonfrigate.

"Orders, by the sea gods that made me, these are the silliest orders we've ever carried out. Who ever heard of putting a caged cat through a captain's ship window?" Junior Seaman Turlor Tuttle whined. "What's wrong with using the door?"

Thune stopped on the rigging, an expression of amazement plain on his face. One of Thune's hands held the rope ladder and the other held one-half of the large cat cage. "Don't ya know nuthun about cats?"

"What I know about cats, I can see for myself. This cat has blue spots on its silver fur. I ain't never heard of a blue spotted cat before." Tuttle gave an uneasy look to the cat in the cage.

The feline hissed at both of them, but the cage looked solid, so the men ignored it.

Suddenly the great sea dragon shivered and belched a satisfied roar, more of a loud purr than a scream, as the hay barge rowed up and presented bales of hay for the dragon to feed on. The entire forty-four blast-tube war frigate shivered on the back of the dragon as it ate its fill of lush, fresh-cut hay. Its tail slapped the water loudly and happily, raising a large plume of water that got the two sailors hanging from the back of the ship thoroughly wet.

The men ignored their living ship as well as the cat and kept talking, suspended on the side of the breathing war vessel by two ladders. They were used to the ways of the sea dragon as it fed. The poor cat was thrown to the back of its cage. Stunned, it shook its body to clear the stars spinning all around its head.

"Cats are the luckiest critter you can have on a full-rigged ship 'o the line," Thune explained. "Sure the blue spots are a bit odd, but that just makes it more magical, doesn't it? We're putting it through the Captain's window because everyone knows that keeps the cat from straying off the ship."

"That's superstition," the other muttered.

Thune shook his head. "And ya think on this, me boyo, if a cat walks in front of a sailor, it brings good luck. If you rub the tail of a cat over a sore eye, that eye ain't sore no more. A wailing cat warns you that a false friend means you harm. You tellin' me you ain't never heard these things about cats?"

"I've heard all those old wives' tales. But who can believe them?" Tuttle was clearly not convinced.

Handel chimed in: "That ain't even the half of it. Cats can store the blazing light of the setting sun in their eyes all through the night. Cats can forecast the weather with a washing of their ears or by laying on their paws and falling asleep. Never kick a cat, because the leg that kicks it is going to suffer."

"I'm from Gold City, and if I ain't seen it fer meself, I'm not a believing any of it!" Tuttle rested against the scaly, living flesh of the frigate's side.

"Believe what you want!" yowled Captain Alex Tobin from the railing of the quarterdeck high above their heads. He leaned down to watch the loading of his Mau cat. "Just get my cat in that window yesterday, if not sooner! Rest on your own gods-be-damned time! If that cage hits the water or gets any wetter, I'm feeding you to the dragon, mark my words!"

The men jumped to action at the barking order of their new Captain, having no doubt they would be dragon food if they made a mistake.

"See what you did," Tuttle whimpered.

"I've heard this cat has been in the Captain's family fer three generations. I've never seen a spotted cat, have you?" Thune asked.

I looked at them from behind my bars, amazed that they weren't moving faster. Usually when my Captain-pet hissed loud orders at the other pets, they stopped talking and moved as quickly as their sluggish pet natures allowed.

Finally, they had my locked home through the window and the ancient rite of special care was finished to my satisfaction. I was honor-bound to stay in the territory of my Captain-pet as long as he observed the special care needed in settling me into my new home. It's good to be a cat.

My Captain-pet was there to greet me as other lesser pets positioned my metal home in the corner of the den.

"Rex, there's a good cat. Come to me," the Captain-pet begged as he opened the cage door.

As pets go, Captain Alex Tobin is pleasant. I'd been with this family for one hundred years. I'd seen other Tobins command other pets onboard ships during the years. I'd helped all the members of my adopted human family gain control of ships and become what my pet calls a Captain.

"Giant snake!" *I howled a warning and leapt into the arms of the Captain-pet. I summoned magical, destructive energies into my body ready to blast whatever dragon or other snaky monster lay somewhere in the cabin. I could smell the monster, but I couldn't see the creature just yet.*

"What's wrong with it?" First Officer Nevets Tangle scowled. It was obvious he didn't like animals in general, and this odd spotted cat left him unsettled.

"Oh, I suspect Rex has only now sensed the sea dragon," Captain Tobin replied. "My cat has never been inside the bowels of a monster. As the bulkheads all around us are the living flesh of the dragon, I'm sure Rex thinks there is an enemy all around him. You don't like cats, do you, First Officer Tangle?"

The first officer stood silent for a moment, looking over his new Captain and trying to judge the man after speaking only a few sentences with him. Tangle didn't like what he saw. The Captain was a large man, well over six feet tall, but the cat easily filled even his muscular arms. Tangle didn't like the way the cat hissed as it looked around the cabin. Nevets had never seen a spotted cat—nor any cat so huge.

"Sir, I'm just not used to pets onboard ship. I'm sure if you like to have them, then they're fine. If you need nothing else sir, the men and I will tend to our duties while you square yourself away." Tangle made this sound more like a question than a statement.

Tobin noted the look of distaste on the first officer's face. He became more brisk with the man. "Carry on, get the ship ready to sail. I'll be up shortly."

"Aye, aye, sir." Tangle and the others left the cabin.

Captain Alex Tobin looked at the retreating form of his new first officer with a sense of unease. There was something about the man that would bear watching.

"Rex, we've been in many a scrape, and a living ship 'o the line isn't going to give you any problems. Let's get on your collar and leash and take you on a tour of the ship." Tobin had a soothing voice that seemed to calm the frightened cat.

The collar was spiked and protected my neck from rat and dog bites. I quite liked its feel. I still couldn't find the giant snake, but I feared it would take a bite out of my Captain-pet, as it held my leash, before it would attack me. I was ready with powerful magics for that attack. I knew there were other Tobins working on their captaincies that I could flee to if this one chanced to die. Pets were such fragile creatures, even when you took loving care of them.

The walk about the ship was a tradition I demanded of every Captain-pet. As I regally passed from cabin to cabin and deck to deck, leading my Captain-pet, the act of walking itself let all the other pets know who the boss was.

Still smelling giant snake, I moved to the blast-tube deck. I would have to find it and kill it. From the blast-tube deck, I insisted on going below to the lowest deck, the orlop deck. I was sure I would find my enemy there.

From the companionway, as I adroitly leapt from the ladder to the deck, my delicate paws touched the flesh of the creature. Up until then I'd been walking on solid Arcanian planking. I screeched another howl of warning and bit and clawed at the creature. My needle sharp fangs didn't make a dent on the huge scales of the monster dragon.

"Rex, stop it this instant!" my Captain-pet suggested, tugging on my leash. "That's our dragon and I won't have you eating it. Quit your fussing and move along."

More slowly now, I advanced through the lower deck, digging my claws in with every step, but knowing they didn't penetrate very far. Then we came to a chamber I'd never seen before. Whatever was behind the large hatch smelled delightful.

"Marine, you are never to allow my cat in this chamber. Are we clear?" Captain Tobin ordered.

I had no idea why he would give such a silly suggestion until the hatch opened and I saw an amazing lunchtime sight. A huge heart beat slowly in the middle of the chamber. Delicious dragon blood could be smelt pumping through outer veins and arteries. It would take me weeks to eat all of that.

"YOU MAY NOT EAT MY HEART OR MY LIVER," thought an intruder into the cat's mind.

I backed up and hissed, looking all about the chamber, finding nothing to kill, but knowing there was something here. The Captain-pet tried to drag me through the other side of the cabin and through the other hatch. I wasn't having any of that at the moment.

"WHILE I'M NOT OF ROYALTY AS YOU ARE, I COME FROM A NOBLE LINE OF SEA DRAGONS. I INTRODUCE MYSELF AS DAUNTLESS. WOULD YOU CARE TO TELL ME YOUR NAME?" the now named intruder asked.

"My name is King Rexmet Fuatic Rifai, but I allow my pets to call me Rex," I replied. "I've never heard of a creature calling itself the Dauntless. Isn't that the name of this warship?"

"COME TO THE FORECASTLE AND LET ME PROPERLY INTRODUCE MYSELF. I AM THIS SHIP AND THE SEA DRAGON YOU HAVE BEEN SO READY TO KILL WITH YOUR MAGIC," replied the Dauntless.

The cat moved quickly from the orlop deck up to the front of the ship and onto the forecastle. Rex didn't even stop in the liver chamber, as tantalizing as that was, since he wasn't going to be allowed to eat any of that giant delight, either.

The huge head of the sea dragon lay resting on the deck with its serpentine neck twisting off over the prow of the ship. Large, unblinking sea-green eyes focused on the cat. Each orb was larger than the cat itself. Strange long whiskery tentacles lay matted to the dragon's face. Its mouth was closed, but the giant fangs couldn't be hidden. A large fin of bright green flowed back from its head and along its long neck.

"Dauntless, I'm glad you're here. Let me introduce my cat, Rex. Rex, this is the sea dragon Dauntless. I've no doubt you both will become fast friends."

"Nice fangs; you said you came from a noble line?" I used my mind to communicate, rather than my usual chirps and meows. If the dragon truly came from a noble line, I would have to treat it with more respect than I tend to show my other pets.

"WE SEA DRAGONS TAKE ON THE NAME OF THE SHIP. I'M THE DAUNTLESS NOW. MY LINE STRETCHES

BACK TEN THOUSAND YEARS, YOUR MAJESTY," replied
the sea dragon.

*"You may have all the others on this ship as pets. I will share them
with you. However, you may not have the Captain- pet as yours. His
family has been mine for more than one hundred years. Are we clear
on this?" I was ready to defend my special pet with all the magic at my
command.*

*"I UNDERSTAND AND APPRECIATE YOUR
GENEROSITY. IF I CAN BE OF HELP TO YOU, YOU HAVE
BUT TO ASK,"* the dragon thought. With that, it raised its head
and left the forecastle.

"What in the world happened there?" asked Tuttle.

"Blimey if the cat wasn't getting the best of the old sea dragon
he was," laughed the amazed Thune. "We got a lucky cat in that one,
mark my words. This ship is going to have an amazing cruise, see if
it don't."

The men got back to work.

"Rex, I'm very proud of the way that meeting went. The dragon
clearly likes you. Let's get you something to eat, shall we?" The tension was gone from Tobin's face. He'd been very worried how his cat
and the sea dragon would get along.

"Food at last," I purred.

*A week later, I roamed the lower decks without my Captain-pet. "I
shouldn't have eaten that last rat's liver. Now I don't have anything else
to munch on."*

*"I'VE GOT SOME UNUSUALLY LARGE SEA LICE
UNDER MY SCALES ON THE FORECASTLE IF YOU'VE A
MIND,"* thought the *Dauntless*.

*"Please, I have my limits and grooming great, even noble louts isn't
one of them. Besides, you couldn't groom me in return, and what's the
fairness of that?"*

Rex ambled into the ship's galley hoping to get some tidbit worth
eating.

"Get out of here, you great blue creature!" barked the cook as Rex entered the galley. He tried to kick the cat away, but the Mau refused to be rushed, and deftly avoided the flailing boot.

"I'll not have cat hairs in my food!" shouted the cook.

"Dauntless, *would you mind suddenly twitching to port?*"

"OF COURSE, MY KING," replied the sea dragon.

In a very humanlike voice, Rex magically meowed, "Servium oct sept!"

Suddenly the cooking hat jammed tight over the face of the cook, just as the man was trying to again kick Rex. The ship lurched, causing the cook's leg to smash hard into the bench with a very satisfying CRACK!

The cook fell moaning to the deck with a severely broken leg.

"My work is done here, I think I'll see what my Captain-pet is doing on the quarterdeck."

As soon as I came onto the bright upper blast-tube deck, I could sense the coming storm. It didn't matter that the skies were currently cloudless. There was a huge gale coming, and it would reach the war vessel just after sunset. The Captain-pet would need a warning of the coming storm.

Rex deftly climbed the ladder onto the quarterdeck and leapt up on the chart table in front of the ship's helm. The bright afternoon sun was warming the deck, and the wood of the chart table felt deliciously warm.

Rex could have put the thought of the approaching storm into the mind of his pet, but what was the art of that. Pets needed training and Rex was more than up to the task of making sure his Captain paid the proper attention to his master. Other pets were working all around the table.

A ridge of fur rose on Rex's back.

There was a feeling of evil somewhere in the area, but I couldn't pin it down. Sensitive to malicious thinking, there were just too many foolish pets moving around the quarterdeck for me to tell who was thinking what. Someone meant ill to the crew and more importantly to my Captain-pet. That would need some attention. As I closed my eyes and relaxed for the first time that day, I would hear my Captain-pet talking.

"Well done, midshipmen. Taking sights on the sun and working on your navigation skills at all times of the day is extremely important." Tobin was addressing six young naval officers. "Midshipman Withers, what the devil is wrong with your eye?"

The thirteen-year-old came to attention. His right eye was all red and crusty with yellow matter filling his right eyelash. "I don't know, sir. I woke up with this and it just won't go away. It doesn't hurt enough to see the surgeon." The boy was trying to put on a brave face.

"Nonsense, midshipman, there's no sense suffering when your relief is right at hand . . . or I should say tail. Come here," ordered Tobin.

Rex knew what was coming and stood up and came to the edge of the table.

First Officer Tangle looked on in distaste. His thoughts were plain on his face. The cat was allowed on the ship, but allowing it on the chart table was a bit much. The man didn't say anything, as there was always a look of pride on the Captain's face when the cat was involved. Pride in what, Tangle's face expression showed he had no idea. When I become Captain of the *Dauntless*, he mouthed, that cat is going over the side.

Even at thirteen, Withers stood a lanky six feet. Captain Tobin grabbed him behind his head and forced his face down by the cat. "Just close your eyes and my Rex will do the rest."

Tuttle and Thune were in the rigging of the mizzen sail above the heads of the officers. Thune could easily hear everything said on the quarterdeck. Normally he didn't pay any attention, as it was officer stuff, but Thune perked up at the mention of Rex. It seemed that every day Thune pointed out some thing the cat was doing, and Tuttle had to watch and remark that it was nothing unusual.

"That cat's got magic in it," Thune said.

Tuttle just shook his head.

Rex was only too happy to use some of his minor magical powers to heal the midshipman-pet. Eye problems could turn into major ills for the entire crew in short order.

The cat purred healing magics through his tail and forced the malign spirits in the eye of the young pet out and away from the ship. As the cat rubbed his tail on the eye of the young man, all the yellow matter fell away. Withers gave up a great sigh of relief.

"Amazing, Captain, my eye feels much better!"

"Of course, Midshipman Withers. Rex likes helping the men." Captain Tobin rubbed Rex's ears.

The cat responded by going to the edge of the chart box and lying down, as if to sleep.

"*I WONDER IF MY TAIL COULD HEAL LIKE THAT?*" thought the *Dauntless*.

"*Your tail would smash that young pet into a red smear on the deck. Your tail must weigh ninety stone. Such healing requires a delicate touch, don't you know.*"

"*I DON'T KNOW. DO YOU THINK I COULD LEARN THE MAGIC YOU USE?*" "*Of course you could. All you have to do is lay on the chart table with me and I'll teach you. Oh, that's right . . . you're too big to do that. Well, all you have to do is be a thousand-year-old Mau.*"

"*I GET IT, MY KING. I'M NOT BLESSED WITH BEING A CAT,*" sighed the sea dragon.

"*I must tell my Captain-pet of the coming storm. Enjoy the after-noon; it's going to be a nasty night,*" thought Rex.

"*I DON'T SEE YOU TELLING HIM ANYTHING. ALL I SEE YOU DOING IS FALLING ASLEEP IN THE SHELL,*" observed the sea dragon.

"*What's this shell business? I don't see a shell anywhere.*"

"*THIS THING ON MY BACK WHERE YOU LIVE IS MY SHELL. LOTS OF ANIMALS IN THE SEA HAVE THEM.*" The dragon paused. "*WHAT STORM?*"

"*Ship or shell, it's really all the same I guess. About the storm . . . you must watch and learn, young dragon, watch and learn,*" replied the cat sleepily.

Captain Tobin loved his cat and knew the creature well. Seeing the cat sleeping with all of its paws tucked under its body told the observant man that a storm was brewing. When all four of the cat's paws were under its body, it was going to be a savage one. Tobin first saw the Mau do this when he worked as a cabin boy on his uncle's ship. It didn't take many storms for him to realize what the cat was warning.

He went to the railing and shouted down to the ship's chanter. "Chanter Salt, sing out Ring the Bell."

The singer looked up into the clear sky.

"Wonder why you have to sing about storms and rain," mused a nearby sailor.

Chanter Salt didn't reply, he just did what he was told. Salt had been a chantey singer for all of his forty-four years at sea. Such men were prized on a ship's crew, as they got the men working together on the many difficult projects from pulling ropes to loading cargo. The sea chanteys coordinated the work of the ship. In the rhythm of the song, the men worked all at the same pace. Singing could lift the spirits of the men, as well. There were specific songs for raising the sails and lowering the sails, for rising and lowering the anchor. There were songs for when the men were on the last leg of a long cruise. In this case, there was a chantey for getting the ship ready for a violent storm.

Aft on the poopdeck
Walking about
There is the second mate
So sturdy and so stout

What he is thinking of
He only knows himself
Oh, we wish that he would hurry up
And Strike, strike the bell.

Strike the bell, second mate
Let us go below
Look away to windward
You can see it's going to blow
Look at the glass
You can see that it is fell
We wish that you would hurry up
And Strike, strike the bell

As the chantey began, the crew showed its surprise at the subject, but joined in the singing nonetheless. The chantey meant one thing, there was a bad storm coming. Every man knew the drill for a storm, and they started working from the tops and the rigging to the orlop deck at the bottom of the ship.

Sails furled, except for the jibs at the front of the ship, the mainstaysail in the middle of the ship, and the spanker at the stern. These sails were low to the deck and would help the ship make way in the most violent of gales.

"Sir, may I ask why we're preparing for a storm with the sun at our backs?" First Officer Tangle's voice was skeptical.

"Of course you can ask. Rex informs me that we're in for a nasty blow. I want to be prepared for it."

"Your cat, Captain?" Tangle couldn't keep the distaste out of his words. "You've got four hundred men working at top speed to prepare for a storm on the intelligence of your cat?"

Captain Tobin ignored his first officer, closed his eyes, and enjoyed the singing of his men.

Down on the main deck

Working at the pumps
There is the larboard watch
Ready for their bunks
Over to windward
They see a great swell
They're wishing that the second mate
Would Strike, strike the bell.

Strike the bell, second mate
Let us go below
Look away to windward
You can see it's going to blow
Look at the glass
You can see that it is fell
We wish that you would hurry up
And Strike, strike the bell

Tangle had more questions; Captain Tobin could see it on his face and in his stance. It would be impossible to explain to a noncatlover the faith Tobin placed in his cat.

"First Officer, check the ship before the coming storm and report back to me."

"Aye, aye, Captain," Tangle had to reply. "Boatswain Gray, go aloft and inspect the luffing and report to me."

Tangle went down to the blast-tube deck to observe the men lashing down the tubes. Each long tube was made of tons of metal on short wheels. They couldn't be allowed to sway with a storm and were now being lashed tight to the dragon railings. In the middle of a raging wind, if such a weapon broke lose it could destroy masts and kill any man it smashed against.

Tangle observed the hatches, as crewmen covered them in thick leather covers. He went below to personally see to the quenching of the galley fires. The final meal of the day was at four bells, and that was an hour ago, so the men had a hot meal and grog in their bellies—it should hold them if a storm did come. The barrels of the orlop deck were lashed, and the animals were slung so that they wouldn't crash to the deck in the rolling of the sea. There were only two steers left, as the pigs and chickens had been eaten already.

With everything ready for a storm, Tangle went back to report to Captain Tobin.

The men on deck and in the rigging were now wearing rain slickers. Safety lines were strung on the port and starboard sides of the ship as well as down the middle and around all of the masts.

As topsmen, Tuttle and Thune made sure their sails were tied tight, and then they checked the ties of the other sails up and down the mizzen mast.

"Why are we wearing these slickers? There isn't a cloud in the sky," Tuttle complained.

"It's the cat again, may the gods bless it. The Captain's cat knows there's a bad one brewing. Look at it," Thune pointed down on the quarterdeck and toward the Mau.

"It's a bloody sleeping cat, Thune. That's what cats do. They sleep a lot," Tuttle sounded as if he'd suddenly becoming a cat expert.

Thune shook his head. "They sleep on their sides in the sun. Look at it now. The cat is sleeping on all of its paws. I told you that's a sign of a storm. You mark my words, we're in for a blow."

It was an hour until sunset, and suddenly the breeze picked up.

Seven hours into the night, *Dauntless* was in fear for its life. The sea dragon swam through the black pitch of night as terrible waves smashed against him with bruising force.

"*HELP, MY KING, HELP!*" thought *Dauntless* to the cat.

The Mau was below decks weathering the storm in the Captain's locked cabin. Somehow he knew it was time to join the Captain-pet on the quarterdeck.

"*Help you with what? We're in a bad storm. I've weathered many a storm like this. You'll just have to keep heading into the waves,*" assured Rex.

"*MY KIND GOES UNDER THE SEA DURING STORMS LIKE THIS. I CAN'T BECAUSE MY HEART AND LIVER ARE EXPOSED. I WASN'T MADE TO SWIM ON TOP OF THE WATER DURING A STORM,*" whined the dragon.

"*Quit your belly aching, you great lummox. We'll be fine, but there's something odd going on near my Captain-pet. Can you tell what it is?*"

"*THE CREW IS THINKING DARK THOUGHTS. SOME BLAME THE CAPTAIN FOR THE STORM AND WANT TO BEACH ME. THE CAPTAIN WON'T LET THEM FOR FEAR THAT IT WILL RIP OUT MY BELLY.*"

"*Testy things pets are. Sometimes no matter how well you treat them they try to scratch your eyes out. There will be no clawing or biting on my ship tonight,*" snapped the Mau.

On the quarterdeck, Tangle cupped his hands and hollered into the ear of Captain Tobin. It was the only way he could be heard through the noise of the thunder and lightning. Waves continually crashed across the decking, constantly pulling the men tight on their safety lines. "Captain, we have to beach the *Dauntless*. It's the only way for us to survive this storm!"

In the dim light of two lanterns, Tobin could be seen shaking his head 'no' at the plea of his first officer. Tobin helped the boatswain and the second officer at the helm of the ship. The two great wheels of the helm controlled ropes and pulleys in the bowels of the vessel and forced the fins of the sea dragon to turn the ship in the direction the humans wanted to go. Normally, the dragon would have never fought the sea. The great beast would have flowed with the sea until the storm blew its course.

While it was difficult to see, the wind and waves made it easy to judge the direction for the prow of the ship. Captain Tobin kept in mind the nautical map of the area and didn't let the ship get too close off the coast of Elese. A lantern by the binnacle compass and constant glances into the glass kept the ship from heading east, no matter where the storm blew.

The flying jib ripped away in the wind, and Tobin didn't have the heart to order a replacement. The other staysails and the mizzen sail were still drum tight in the gale. It was then that Tobin saw his cat and grew worried for the first time. Rex never showed himself in a storm unless there was trouble the cat needed to handle. The Captain sent up a prayer to the gods.

Rex was down on the blast-tube deck heading for the quarter-deck. The cat glowed with magical energies and clearly showed up in the darkness of the storm.

Rainstorms weren't to the Mau's liking.

"I'm getting wet here."

Only Tobin knew what the cat was feeling. The poor thing hated to get wet.

Another wave brought a great force of water over the deck. As one, the men held their breath and held on for dear life to their safety lines. The cat couldn't be bothered with the thunderous force of the watery blow. It deliberately walked in front of its Captain-pet, imparting a great deal of luck to Tobin that would last for hours.

A blue nimbus of magic surrounded Rex's body, chasing the water from his fur and keeping the wind from buffeting him. His paws left dried marks on the wet deck as he padded his way up through the feet and lines of the quarterdeck to a higher position on the stern.

"Evil!" screeched the cat in a human voice that easily carried to all the ears of the crew and officers of the deck. "I smell evil!"

Thune looked at Tuttle as they stood on the foot-lines of the mizzen staysail in case that sail needed repairing or furling. There was an I-told-you-so look from Thune. Tuttle wasn't in the mood for the silent lecture.

"What is that cat doing here?" snarled Tangle to the uncaring wind and sea.

"What are you trying to tell me?" Captain Tobin to the cat.

"SOMEONE THERE MEANS TO HARM YOUR PET," warned the *Dauntless*.

"*I know that. Why do you think I'm here?*"

For hours now, Tangle had tried to work up the courage to take advantage of the storm. The presence of the cat unnerved him, and so he rushed into his plan.

As the next crushing wave struck the ship and crew, and tons of water engulfed the men, Tangle drew a hidden ship's knife and cut the Captain's lifeline.

"MEROWER!" Rex screamed, as a blaze of light as bright as the sun erupted from his eyes and bathed the entire quarterdeck in a glow as bright as the day. Rex had deliberately positioned himself at the far stern of the ship on the spanker boom.

In the magical light of the cat's eyes, everything stopped moving. The wave stopped in mid strike. Captain Tobin clutched at his cut rope at the railing on the port side, a second away from being forced into the sea.

The storm still raged around the ship, but everything was still and unmoving on the quarterdeck of the *Dauntless*.

"*A NEAT TRICK THAT. ARE YOU SURE I CAN'T LEARN HOW TO DO THAT?*"

"*This is a little something I learned from my mom, the goddess. I'm fairly sure you have to be part of the family to pick it up.*"

With a blink of enchanted cat's eyes, Rex magiced Captain Tobin into exchanging places with Tangle.

"*Normally, I would never move to harm one of your pets, dragon, but this one dared to try to kill my Captain-pet. I apologize for the action.*"

"THINK NOTHING OF IT. I WOULD HAVE EATEN HIM LONG AGO, BUT THE MAGIC OF MY PETS STOPS ME FROM DOING WHAT I WOULD LIKE."

Tendrils of blue enchantment streamed from the body of the cat and up into the storm, begging the spirits of the air to stop their play around the ship. The spirit royalty of the air was only too willing to comply. It was seldom they could grant a favor to the royalty of the felines.

In the next instant, the final wave of the powerful storm washed Tangle into the dark sea. A passing shark was happy to take the offering in one pleasant gulp.

A moment later, Rex closed his eyes and ended the magic holding the quarterdeck.

None the wiser for the experience, the men breathed easier as the storm blew itself out.

Rex came up to his Captain-pet and waited for a moment for the expected scratch under the chin.

Tobin refused to wonder how his cat got out of the locked cabin and up on deck.

It wasn't until morning that they discovered Tangle missing. The man was mourned, but these things happened in a storm.

The cats of a nameless human city call it Catopolis. Just like the humans, the cats have their politics, their social cliques – and their organized crime.

The cat boss of Catopolis is Don Luigi, a Russian Blue. He speaks "with a thick accent, sort of gravelly like Marlon Brando in the *Godfather* movies." He has pretensions of culture, and when a traveling museum exhibit brings a priceless item to Catopolis, he wants it! Vinnie the Mouser, one of his henchcats, is assigned to get it for him.

After Tony's Fall

by Jean Rabe

Luigi had a dense, blue coat with silvery-tips that gave it a lustrous sheen. Like all of his kind—Luigi was a Russian Blue—he had large, round eyes the shade of a just-misted philodendron. His head was broad, his rakish ears sharply tapered, and he was fine-boned, yet powerfully built.

Luigi had the most regal appearance of any cat in my acquaintance.

Though I knew he could trace his ancestors back to the Royal Cat of the Russian Czars, he claimed to be Italian—and I'd never heard anyone argue the point.

Luigi spoke with a thick accent, sort of gravelly like Marlon Brando in the Godfather movies. He lived in a spacious apartment above an Italian restaurant in an Italian neighborhood in what the humans had dubbed "Little Italy."

"Don Luigi" the cats in the 'hood called him.

I just called him boss.

He'd named me Vincenzo the day I came to work for him—that was a wintry morning nearly three years past when he'd caught me nibbling on some Fettuccini Alfredo that had been tossed into the garbage behind the restaurant. He offered me a job, and I was quick to accept.

"You're very kind," I told him. Now I can say it in his preferred tongue: *Sei molto gentile!*

The boss never asked my real name. Probably like T.S. Elliot, he figured it was only right that we cats have three—my original moniker, Vincenzo, and Vinnie the Mouser.

The latter is what I usually go by. Has a nice ring to it, don't you think?

I'm not really Italian either, being a Bombay, or Black Burmese, but I love the food. Lasagna, Ravioli, Gnocchi Riplieni, Cappellacci Al Vitello E Spinaci, and Tortellini Campagnola are often on the menu.

Last night it was Vitello Barolo—oh-so-tender veal with portabella and shitake mushrooms in wine, with just a touch of cream. The night before that was my favorite—Calamari Riplieni, sweet squid stuffed with cheese and bread crumbs in a delicate tomato sauce.

Per questa sera... I've no idea what will be on the menu tonight. *Per domani sera...* or tomorrow night for that matter. But I'm certain I will find everything tasty. *Mi piace l'italiano*, after all.

It is a good life, being Don Luigi's number-one cat—his enforcer, confidant, and appropriator. In exchange for my loyalty and service, the boss makes sure that when I say *Sono affamato*, I'm hungry, I am given something good to eat. Too, he has provided me a fine, dry place to sleep... on a thick velvet cushion in the attic above his apartment. From this lofty perch I can hear the boss's natterings with Guido, Nino, and Uberto, the Siamese triplets that collect the Don's take from the businesses in Little Italy. I can hear the passionate yowls from his late-night trysts with Mariabella, the Himalayan madam from around the corner, and with Tessa Rosalie, the sleek orange tabby who recently moved into the flower shop across the street.

Best of all, I can hear the boss play.

I'd not heard a cat tickle the ivory before coming into the Don's employ. The boss's tail is muscular enough to join his paws and make chords on the keyboard of a 1920 walnut Italian Florentine baby grand. The boss only plays the music of Italian composers; he says playing anything else is a waste of time. He just finished the main theme from Giacomo Puccini's *Manon Lescaut*. Before that he performed a piece from the unfinished *Turandot* and a few dozen bars from *La Boheme*.

It's like Heaven opening up when the boss plays, the rich notes swirling around the apartment and rising into my attic, consuming me and bringing tears to my eyes. No other sounds are so enchanting.

I live to hear the boss play.

He explained to me once that Italy gave the world the best composers and the best instruments, that piano is a short form of the Italian word *pianoforte*, which in turn comes from the original Italian term for the instrument—*clavicembalo col piano e forte*.

I could care less what you call the thing... I just love the way it sounds when the boss sets his paws and tail tip to it.

In the back of my mind I can still hear the notes. I've set my pads in time to the imagined music as I head down the street, looking over my shoulder once to see him looking out the window... not looking at me, but surveying his domain.

"*Buon compleanno!*" I hear him call to the long-legged Bengal on the sidewalk. Happy birthday.

"*Congratulazioni!*" he shouts to the Persian outside the used book store. I'd heard she'd recently had kittens.

Imparo I'taliano... I've been learning Italian ever since ingratiating myself with the boss, and I'm pleased that I've gotten quite fluent. *Mi piacerebbe visitare I'talia un giorno di questi!* Yeah, I would like to stroll down the sidewalks of Italy with the Don someday and sit high in a balcony during a performance of Gaetano Donizetti's *La Fille du Regiment*. He promised to take me and Guido next year if things work out all right.

I hear a shrill whistle and my head snaps around. It's Bianca, the beautiful bicolor Ragdoll who I visit when I go to Madam Mariabella's. I know that Bianca shares her affections with whoever meets the madam's price at the cathouse, but she claims to have a special spot in her heart just for me. I'd love to take her to Italy with me and the boss, but I know it's going to be a business trip, and so dalliances won't be allowed.

I flick my tail at her in a friendly greeting, and then pick up the pace. I'm not as fast as I used to be, but I can push my muscles when the need arises. You see, I've got quite a ways to go on this particular mission, which is why I set out before sunset. It means I'll be eating late when I get back; I've done that numerous times before, and so far it hasn't upset my delicate digestive tract.

I smell things along the way, the trace of Bianca and the other females at the cathouse, some clearly in heat; the daily specials from the flower shop… so many scents I can't differentiate one kind of bloom from another; the sharp and bitter pong of soap from the laundry; and rotting fish from the alley off S'hang's Sushi Bar, which has no place being in Little Italy. The farther I get from the Italian restaurant, the worse things smell.

So I concentrate on the sights instead, the garish, clashing colors of window boxes and signs, the graffiti scrawled here and there, the freshest in day-glow green.

And I focus on the sounds… car horns blaring from blocks away, babies wailing, a boy hawking newspapers on a corner, the slam of a door. There's music spilling out of an upper floor window, some rapper spitting out hippity-hop words like they are pieces of bad meat—Lay-Z or Forty-Cents, I can't tell them apart. They're certainly not in the class of the boss's *pianoforte* playing, and so I ignore the thumping racket.

I stick to the shadows whenever possible—being black has its advantages when you're into a bit of skullduggery. And I continue on my way, remembering the boss's gravelly words:

"*Vada dritto! e poi giri a destra!*"

Go straight—all the way down to the fire station—then turn right. It would be a whole lot of straight again after that—blocks and blocks and blocks of it.

The boss hadn't needed to give me directions, as I'd been to the museum once before when I had a fling some years back with an

Angora who lived in the area. Wonder what's become of her? I shake my head to chase away the sweet memory.

I was proud that the boss had entrusted this very special assignment to me. It deserved all my attention.

"You get this for me, Vinnie, this one precious thing, and I'll reward you well," he told me this afternoon. "I have the other three. I just need the fourth to complete the set."

I well knew that he had the other three; he'd shown them to me, taking them out of the chest and lovingly running his whiskers across them before replacing them.

"I just need the fourth. The missing piece. You understand? It will complete the year." His large, round eyes didn't blink. This missing piece was terribly important to him.

I told him I understood.

"*Buona fortuna*, Vincenzo," he said.

I didn't need luck, I'd mentally returned. I'd just need a big plate of pasta upon my return. Maybe I could order up something special—Polpo Alla Griglia, octopus charcoal broiled and dabbed with balsamic vinegar and olive oil. Yeah, that would hit the spot after a long mission like this.

The sun was all the way down by the time I'd left Little Italy behind and reached the museum. It was closing for the day, and I watched from behind a fir tree as the school groups and retired folks spilled out and down the steps. If I timed it right, I could snake my way between the young ones' feet and slip inside the lobby. A good plan, I decided, but then I quickly dismissed it when I noticed there were two guards at the entrance, and one of them had a gun at his waist. Better not to take the chance that one might scoop me up or shoot me.

I hack up a hairball that had been bothering me and shimmy around the side of the monstrous building. Well, truth be told, it wasn't that big of a place, but it was the most imposing structure in this part of town, all cement and iron, ugly and drab. A monstrosity of a building would be a better term.

The sounds of the city intruded—more car horns, people shouting. I shuddered: there was a dog barking nearby. I hated dogs almost as much as I hated rap music. I heard a door slam, and then another, a van from the sound of it, and I poked my head around the back corner to see a cleaning crew getting out of a rust-dotted Chevy Econoline. There were four men, all dressed in gray coveralls, and after picking up buckets and boxes, and after the smallest perched a boombox on his shoulder, they headed across the employee parking lot and to the museum's backdoor.

Buona fortuna was mine indeed.

I hurried, as much as I could because the trip here had winded me, and was just able to dart inside before the door closed. Lights still glared from the ceiling and bounced off a tile floor that as far as I was concerned didn't need to be polished. No shadows to hide my furry black self, I ducked into the first open doorway and discovered a janitor's closet. This hiding place would do until they turned off some of the lights and the museum staff filed out. I just had to make sure no one shut the door on me.

As I rested and waited, I dreamed about Bianca and her pretty spots, and about what I might have for dinner. An appetizer of Vongole Gratinate, juicy clams, would stop my growling belly right about now. I also thought about Italy, the real Italy that the boss would take me to, not the Little Italy we lived in. I heard music, muted, more of that rap crap, and the gentle shushing hum of what I guessed was a floor polisher or vacuum. The steady click of heels in the hallway beyond this closet, and the regular opening and closing of the back door told me the curators and secretaries and such were leaving.

Finally, all I could hear was the rap, and it was so soft now I had to strain to pick it out. The cleaning crew had moved farther away, and so I was relatively alone in the museum.

In a short while I would have the final piece to the boss's magnificent puzzle. He would be a very happy cat, and I would have my pick of anything off the menu.

I left the closet and hugged the wall, following it until a great room opened up before me, bathed in the soft glow of security lights. Suits of armor were spaced here and there between glass cases holding weapons and pieces of jewelry. A glittering crown sat on a pillow that I thought might be comfortable. A scepter lay next to it. The object of my quest was nowhere to be seen…but my keen eyes lit on something that would help me find it. I padded toward a placard touting the rotating displays.

Not all cats can read, but I found it a necessary skill to acquire in the boss's employ, and so I had let Guido teach me two summers past. The placard read:

Special Exhibit
The Life, Times, and Works of
Il Prete Rosso, the Red Priest
Second Floor, Main Hall

I passed by the elevator and took the winding staircase, careful not to slip on its newly-polished marble steps. Rap music drifted down from above—the cleaning crew had obviously preceded me.

One man was wielding a big floor buffer, moving it from side-to-side in time with the godawful beat. Two were dusting the wainscoting that ran around the room and down the hallways that led away to the north and the south. The third man was in the bathroom; I heard the toilet flush.

Occupied, they didn't notice me. I drifted from one display case to the next, slinking as much as possible. I looked through the glass of a low shelf, squinting in the dim light to see decorative red and white and green satin ribbons, and to make out the words on a card in front of a battered violin:

IL PRETE ROSSO, THE RED PRIEST, HE WAS CALLED, A VENETIAN PRIEST AND BAROQUE MUSIC COMPOSER WHO WAS ALSO A VIRTUOSO VIOLINIST. THIS VIOLIN WAS THE LAST HE PLAYED BEFORE HIS DEATH.

A card in the next case read:

BORN MARCH 4, 1678 IN VENICE, THE DAY AN EARTHQUAKE SHOOK THE CITY. HE DIED JULY 27 OR 28, 1741. HIS FATHER, GIOVANI BATTISTA, WAS A PROFESSIONAL VIOLINIST AND FOUNDER OF A TRADE UNION FOR MUSICIANS WHO TAUGHT HIM TO PLAY. HE BEGAN STUDYING FOR THE PRIESTHOOD AT AGE FIFTEEN, AND HE WAS ORDAINED TEN YEARS LATER. IT IS BELIEVED THAT HE WAS CALLED IL PRETE ROSSO BECAUSE OF HIS RED HAIR.

The next case, where a small painting was displayed:

IN 1704 HE WAS GIVEN A SPECIAL DISPENSATION FROM CELEBRATING MASS BECAUSE HE WAS ILL. RECORDS SHOW HE SUFFERED FROM SOMETHING SIMILAR TO ASTHMA. TWO YEARS LATER, HE LEFT THE PRIESTHOOD AND CONCENTRATED ON MUSIC.

Music! That's what I was looking for. And not that damnable rap crap. One of the men had turned it up louder. I couldn't understand the words, and it was hurting my delicate ears.

I continued searching the room.

Another card, this in the largest case, and one in which I had to stand up on my back paws to read:

LE QUATTRO STAGIONI, THE FOUR SEASONS, IS HIS BEST KNOWN WORK. THE SET OF FOUR VIOLIN CONCERTOS BY IL PRETE ROSSO, ANTONIO VIVALDI, WERE ORIGINALLY PUBLISHED IN 1725, EACH IN THREE MOVEMENTS. ON DISPLAY HERE IS ONE OF THE ORIGINAL WORKS, BELIEVED TO BE PENNED BY VIVALDI HIMSELF, TRANSCRIBED FOR PIANO.

Concerto No. 3 in F major, *L'autunno*, Autumn.

That's it! I practically shouted out loud.

Tony's Fall.

The boss had sent me here to this ugly museum after *Tony's Fall*, and there it was in all of its tattered parchment movements—allegro, adagio molto, and allegro again, on the top shelf of the display... where I couldn't reach it.

The card went on to explain that the matching piano music for the other seasons—spring, summer, and winter—had been lost through the ages. They weren't lost. They were safely kept in a chest in Don Luigi's apartment above the Italian restaurant that must be serving something absolutely delicious at this very moment.

My stomach rumbled and the floor buffer sounded louder. The machine was sweeping closer.

"A kitty cat!" called the man gripping the handles of the infernal machine.

"A black cat. A big one." This came from the one just emerging from the bathroom. "Don't let it cross your path. That'd be six years of bad luck."

"Seven," corrected one of the men dusting the wainscoting. "Seven years of bad luck, just like if you broke a mirror."

I summoned my strength and bolted toward the floor polisher, the pads of my feet slipping and sliding and threatening to send me sprawling. One leap and I was riding on the base of the thing, shushing back and forth as the man wielding it cursed in a language I could not fathom.

I reared up and hissed at him, digging my rear claws into a strip of rubber. I hissed and snarled, laid my ears back and appeared menacing. I well knew how to act menacing—after all, I am the boss's chief enforcer.

"It's rabid!" one of them shouted. I couldn't tell which one hollered, I was holding on for my proverbial dear life, as the buffer-wielder rammed the machine first one way and then another trying to dislodge me.

I hissed again, but it was a panicked hiss, not a mean one. Doubtless he could not tell the difference, though, as he jerked the machine forward and back, faster now, and then out of control, nearly causing me to lose what I'd eaten for lunch. One more jerk and the buffer-wielder slipped on a newly waxed patch of tile. The machine shot forward, humming and jostling and then colliding into the largest of the display cases in the hall. An alarm went off as the glass broke, a harsh claxon that drowned out the damnable crap-rap music and was punctuated by the sounds of thick glass shards hitting the buffer and the floor.

I winced when a shard lanced my back, and I yowled shrilly in pain, adding to the cacophony.

The cleaning men were shouting, all in the language I couldn't understand, and the buffer continued to whir, though now it was going nowhere. And faintly, from below, came the staccato barks of what I guessed were museum guards.

Despite the pain in my ears and my back I was well aware of my *buona fortuna*. I pushed off the whirring contraption and landed inside the now-open display case, climbed up to the second shelf, and then the third, where my prize awaited. Gently using my teeth and front claws, I rolled up *Tony's Fall* and tied it with a piece of ribbon that had been a decorative touch in the case.

All the while the noises continued, the alarm accompanied by a second one that had started somewhere on the floor below. Feet pounded up the stairs, and my mind whirled with thoughts of escape. I hadn't given any thought to that notion as I'd waited in the janitor's closet. I'd been thinking too much about dinner.

Tony's Fall secured, and my teeth securely fastened to the ribbon around the parchment, I jumped from the shelf and onto the back of one of the wainscot dusters. I dug my claws in, finding flesh beneath the shirt, and discovering that the man could shout louder than the rapper who'd begun to sing about jacking fancy cars.

He called to his fellows in the foreign tongue, and gestured wildly. In that moment, two guards reached the top of the stairs. Also in that moment, I leapt away and headed toward the bathroom. The door to it had been propped open, and I took full advantage.

I figured there would be a window in here, one which I could use my bulk to barrel through and find freedom. But there was no window, only mirrors and toilets and sinks and a floor that thankfully had not yet been polished. There was also a vent, and this I vaulted up to by propelling myself off the register and onto a sink, then up to a pipe. It had been some time since I'd been involved in this much activity, and my sides heaved. But my prize was worth the effort.

Tony's Fall, the last piece to the boss's magnificent puzzle, would soon be his, and a wondrous culinary reward and talk of a trip to Italy would be mine.

My front paws wrestled with the latch on the vent. They were a black blur that clawed and tugged and finally met with success.

The rap music stopped just as I shot inside.

The hollering continued.

The alarms still blared.

I heard the sharp click of heels come into the bathroom, knowing this would be one of the security guards; the cleaning men wore tennis shoes.

Branzino Alla Griglia, Chilean sea bass grilled perfectly with oil and garlic and served warm with beans, might be mine when I deposit this musical manuscript at the boss's feet.

All I need do is shimmy through this duct.

Shimmy.

Shimmy.

Merda.

I was stuck.

I sucked in my breath and pushed, let out my breath and wriggled. *Tony's Fall* still held by the ribbon between my teeth, dangling sideways in front of me.

Stuck.

Stuck.

"I see him! It's a cat!"

"Cat burglar more like." I knew this came from the other guard, though I could see neither of them.

"He's wedged in there pretty good and tight. He's a pudgy one, this cat. Don't know if I can get him out."

Merda. Merda. Merda.

He dug his hands into my side and squeezed, tugging and tugging and finally pulling me out, and then holding me in front of him, where my claws couldn't reach, too tight for me to wriggle free. The other guard plucked *Tony's Fall* from my jaws and retreated with it.

Merda. Merda. Merda.

One too many plates of Petto Di Polla Alla Senape. In my younger years—before I'd found that Italian restaurant—I was lean and would have been able to fit through that duct with no effort.

Merda. Merda. Merda.

"Wonder why a cat would want some old sheet music," my captor mused as he carried me from the bathroom and through the hall, where his fellow was replacing *Tony's* precious *Fall* and attempting to smooth it out and brush away the broken glass. I didn't see the cleaning crew, and thankfully someone had shut off that hurtful alarm.

I fought with the guard all the way to the bottom of the stairs, but it had taken most of my energy just to reach the museum and snare my prize. He tossed me in the janitor's closet and shut the door, told me through the crack that he'd call the Humane Society for me first thing in the morning.

No vent in here. No chance of escape. Even if there was a vent, I doubt I could have fit through it. Too many raviolis. Too many plates of spaghetti and rigatoni. It was blackest-black, the air dead still, and not even my keen eyes could pick through it. I could smell all the astringent cleaning supplies, and my paws brushed against the ropy tendrils of a mop. My nose touched a tool furry with rust.

I wasn't paying attention to the passing of time. My mind whirred with a mix of hopeful and horrid possibilities.

Maybe I could slip by the guards in the morning, when they opened the door to present me to the Humane Society. Maybe I could dart out between their legs and out the back and return to the safety of Little Italy.

Then I could hear the boss play *Tony's Spring* and *Summer* and *Winter* again, and promise to go after *Tony's Fall* once more. Just a few less tortellini helpings, and I'd be able to fit through that duct.

The godawful crap-rap music started up again, Forty-Cent wailing about a woman who dumped him. I closed my eyes and shook my head and tried my best to imagine the boss's talons and tail tip tickling the ivory.

The music came louder, and I paced, bumping into this and that. Suddenly the door opened, and one of the wainscot dusters flipped on the light switch and stared at me, the dim light of the hall haloing a head of bushy hair. I took only a heartbeat to register his kind face and thin lips, and then I was through his legs.

"I need to find some turpen…cat." He said something else, but I couldn't hear it over the cacophony of rap, which was loudest in the main hall where the other three were now working.

The cleaning men didn't notice me this time, so intent on bobbing their heads in time with the crap-rap and polishing the cases and the floor.

I shot up the stairs.

A great part of me thought I should instead look for an exit… right this very moment. Forget *Tony's Fall*, as I'd already taken a fall for trying to nab it. Get out and tell Luigi it couldn't be had, not this time and not at this museum. There was too much security. I wouldn't tell him about the too-narrow ducts which were no doubt in violation of some building code. I should turn around and hover at the back door, wait for the cleaning men to finish and open it and head toward their van.

I'd head back to Little Italy.

But I was, above all else, loyal to the boss. No one tells the Don they'll do something and then not do it. And I'd told him I'd go after *Tony's Fall*.

And so that's just what I was doing.

I don't know where my energy came from, maybe birthed from mind-numbing panic. I didn't want to be caught again; in my heart I knew a trip to the Humane Society wouldn't be humane, not for an aging overweight cat like me. It'd be the needle.

Thoughts of the needle spurred my paws faster.

A moment more and I was at the top of the stairs and slipping to the side of the closest Red Priest display case. The security man who'd nabbed me earlier was there, with a short fellow in a similar uniform. They were picking up the shards of glass. The short one stopped and talked into a little radio he pulled from his pocket. I didn't pay attention to the conversation; my heart was hammering so loudly I could barely hear Forty-Cent shouting the lyrics from the boombox below.

The glass shards they collected glimmered in the pale lighting of the hall.

So much glass.

A pity I was responsible for the mess. I glanced around. Only the two guards; it wasn't a terribly large museum, and so probably this pair constituted the entire night force. There would be many more people working here come morning. Through a trio of narrow windows on the east wall I saw that it was late, the sky black and moonless and filled with a scattering of stars.

I waited.

And after several minutes I slunk around behind the display case. The guards were moving, one of them picking up a bucket filled with the broken glass. They'd made no attempt to secure *Tony's Fall*, but I was certain that would be taken care of before the doors opened in the morning.

"Damn music." This came from the one who'd caught me. "Wish they would play something else. Boz Scaggs, Elton John."

"Country," the short one said. "I like Gretchen Wilson and that blond from Sugarland, and a little Faith Hill thrown in for good measure. Now that's music."

Did none of them have any taste? What the boss played was music. Real music. He produced notes so sweet and Italian that they didn't need someone singing along to dilute them.

"Got someone from Consolidated Glass coming in a few hours." Again, my once-captor spoke. "We've gotta get this case fixed and hooked to the alarm system before breakfast. Gotta get the cleaners up here one more time for another pass with the sweeper."

"Martina McBride has got pipes, I tell you. Heard her once at the county fair grounds. Dolly, she's okay, too."

"Nah, Bruce Springsteen."

The security guards continued their discussion of music as they finished their tidy of the room. Each took a different hall away from the gallery, and I took the shortest path back to the broken display case. No alarm to worry about, I leapt onto the top counter, my leg muscles still fueled by fear of the Humane Society's needle. I had to roll the sheet music up again, and this time I secured it with two ribbons. Then I was down the stairs again, and quick to hide behind a suit of plate mail.

I tried to catch my breath—a difficult thing to do considering my chest felt tight and on fire, my mind remembering the security guard's hands squeezing my well-padded ribs. Someone was running a vacuum cleaner. I couldn't see it, but I saw a long, red cord that snaked from the wall and meandered like an old snake down a corridor. There was wainscoting along that hall, and a man was polishing it. That left two unaccounted for. But they had to be nearby, that jarring hip-hop refrain was echoing off a wall, a woman's voice this time. Her rhythmic wail felt like pins against my paws.

Once more I thought of that lethal needle.

I flexed my claws nervously, unsure of what course I should take. Then indecision was ripped from me; the security guards were coming down the stairs.

I summoned all the strength remaining in my fatigued muscles and sprinted across the floor, slipping and sliding over the fresh wax and nearly caroming into a suit of samurai dragon armor. One of the guards must have spotted me, my original captor I'll wager. I barely heard his shout above the woman rapper.

My chest and legs burned, my heart hammered even faster, and my paws somehow found just enough purchase so I could speed down the hall and past the hated janitor's closet…and then through the back door that one of the cleaning men was opening. I thought he smiled at me as I galumphed past.

I didn't wait to see if anyone else spotted me, though I knew I should have. I took a risk heading straight back to Little Italy with my hard-won prize. What if one of the security guards had followed me? What if I had led someone straight to the Italian restaurant and to the wooden stairs at the back that led up to Luigi's spacious apartment? What if they'd discovered the rest of Tony's seasons hidden there and confiscated all of them?

But that didn't happen. I was "free and clear," as they say.

Sitting outside the door, I closed my eyes and thanked God that this fat cat burglar had escaped unscathed. I must have dozed or dropped off from sheer exhaustion, as when I opened my eyes the sky was lightening and full of birds. I heard a car horn, and then another.

I scratched at the door, still holding the ribbons in my teeth. After a moment, the boss let me in. I deposited the sheet music at his feet in much the same manner as one might drop a mouse at the toes of a human.

He grinned.

"Come, Vinnie," he said. "Let me order you something fine to eat. I will play this for you while you decide what you want."

He reverently carried the music to the piano and unrolled it, settled himself on the bench, and looked at me.

"An Italian tomato salad," I said, having already made up my mind. "With a few diced peppers, lots of celery, and a little basil. A small salad, boss, and have them hold the anchovies."

Don Luigi was into his fourth run-through of *Tony's Fall* before my scant meal arrived. The notes were worth everything I'd been through.

I climbed the stairs to the attic and gacked up a hairball, curled on my cushion, and listened.

The boss was just starting in on *Tony's Spring*.

I told you earlier that it's like Heaven opening up when the boss plays, the melody swirling around his apartment and rising into my attic, consuming me and bringing tears to my eyes. No other sounds are so enchanting.

I live to hear the boss play.

This is the only story here that might be called human-interest, although it's about a cat. No magic. No outer space setting.

Magtwilla is just a mother cat who loves her three babies. She is distraught when her human owner gives them away. Magtwilla finds something else to lavish her maternal instincts upon.

Magtwilla and the Mouse

by Mary E. Lowd

Heavy with kittens, Magtwilla made a choice. She'd been a housecat before, and she'd spent time being feral. Although she disliked the restrictive interference of the clothed primates, she had to admit that their houses with reliable food and warmth would be the better environment for a litter of kittens. So, Magtwilla selected a nice house and set about the work of charming the clothed primate who lived there. In mere days, the primate took her in, strapped an offensively pink collar around her throat, and took to calling her Jenny. Todd was laughably easy to manipulate with a simple purr. Magtwilla felt she'd done well by her unborn kittens.

The litter of three was born in a cozy sock drawer. Warm, soft, and infinitely precious, the three tiny kittens gave meaning to a life that had previously been nothing more than a fight to survive.

The clothed primate called her darlings Socks, Boots, and Mittens. Magtwilla appreciated his enthusiasm for his role of provider for her and the kittens, but his idea of a good name was terrible. Magtwilla gave each of her kittens a proper feline name in the traditional ceremony held when a kitten first opens her eyes.

Twillatha was a gray tabby, just like the handsome tom who fathered her. Magtori was a calico girl like her mother. And Jenwilla was a solid gray who bonded almost instantly with the clothed primate. Magtwilla had to tolerate Todd holding her much more than she would have liked.

Nonetheless, those early weeks of her litter's kittenhood were the happiest of Magtwilla's life. Twillatha, Magtori, and Jenwilla filled their mother's heart with love and pride. Every day, she overflowed with purrs, watching her kittens stumble about, pouncing, playing, and learning the nature of their world. As the kittens grew steadier on their paws, Magtwilla began teaching them what they'd need to know to survive when they escaped from Todd's house.

Twillatha took to her mother's teachings the best. She wiggled her tabby haunches like a pro and could track a single dust mote, falling through a shaft of sunlight, only to pounce on it perfectly as it hit the floor. Magtwilla would never have to worry about Twillatha being able to feed herself. She would be a natural huntress.

Magtwilla didn't worry about Magtori either. While the baby Calico showed less interest in hunting, preferring to stay cuddled close to her mother, a true mama's little kitten, she was wise and cautious beyond her age. She listened closely with wide golden eyes— both to the lessons her mother told her and to the signs and tiny noises in the environment around her. Her ears constantly tracked the sounds of passing cars on the street outside Todd's house, and the sound of Todd's footsteps always sent Magtori darting to her mother's side.

Jenwilla, however, worried her mother greatly. It was as if she'd been born more domesticated than the others. She was too comfortable sleeping on cushions and eating dried pellets from ceramic bowls. She was too comfortable with Todd's ungainly primate hands on her. And when Todd brought a group of clothed primates to visit them all, Jenwilla showed a bizarre and unnatural interest in them.

Magtwilla didn't know why, but it gave her stomach butterflies to watch her cloud-gray baby skitter and play for the visiting primates, batting at string and purring loudly when they petted her. She wanted to call her daughter away from them, but her own fear of the visitors kept her back. So, when they left Todd's house, holding her daughter in their grabby primate hands, she was cowering in the corner, between the sofa and the wall. Magtori cuddled next to her. Twillatha was busy stalking a mouse that lived behind the refrigerator in the kitchen.

When the front door opened again, Todd returned without the other primates. And without Jenwilla.

Magtwilla cried out piteously, and she rushed to the front window, only to watch one of the primate's mechanical monsters pull out of the driveway and drive away. She sat in the window all night, spurning Todd's offers of tuna water. By the early hours of the morning, she felt haggard and hopeless. Unable to do anything to bring her Jenwilla back. She'd made a deal with the devil, and one of her three precious kittens was gone.

Magtwilla spent the whole next day bathing her remaining kittens, against their strenuous dissents. As the soothing rhythm of washing their warm, struggling bodies, dragging her rough tongue over the soft napes of their necks, brought Magtwilla back to herself, she began to form a plan.

It was time to escape. Whether her two kittens were ready for life outside or not, it was better than the risk she ran if they stayed. So, Magtwilla set about finding a way out of the house she'd adopted for her kittens' nativity.

Unfortunately, leaving Todd's domicile turned out to be much harder than working her way into it. The windows and doors were all kept tight shut, except when Todd walked through the front one. She'd tried darting through the front door, but he always blocked her deftly with his feet. She'd never known of another primate who was so fastidious about keeping a cat inside its house! There were vents in the floor, but they were much too heavy for her to remove and their grates too fine to reach more than a single paw through. She tried all the cupboard doors, but they only led to cupboards. And when she tried clawing up the carpet around the edges of the room, the floor underneath was hard and solid. No escape there.

Exhausted, Magtwilla vowed to explore behind the refrigerator after a decent night's rest. If the invading mouse had found a way in, there must also be a way out. Hopefully, it would prove to be cat-sized. Not merely mouse-sized.

The next day, though, was not soon enough. For Todd brought more clothed primates to visit them, including more of the boisterous short ones who moved in startling, jerky ways. Magtwilla spat at them, and Magtori followed suit. But one of the shortest primates dragged a piece of ribbon over the floor in a halting, stop-start fashion that completely charmed Twillatha. The tabby baby's hunting instincts took over, and she pranced entrancingly for the primates.

Magtwilla watched her second daughter's goodbye dance in horror, presciently guessing what was coming this time. She steeled herself to attack the visiting primates, but Todd chased her and Magtori off before her claws found a solid, fleshly purchase. She heard them leave with Twillatha while she was still recovering in the next room.

She didn't wait in the window this time. Her first daughter had been gone for days. She knew that her second one wouldn't return either.

After many dark hours, while Magtori's soft purring and beseeching gold eyes couldn't console her, Magtwilla resolved that she would escape Todd's prison of a home and find her daughters. Wherever the evil primates who took them had gone, Twillatha and Jenwilla must be findable. She was a good hunter. She would track the mechanical monsters that had borne her kittens away, and they would all be reunited. They would live a wholesome, righteous life in the wild, far from the primates who tempted with easy food and damnable cages.

Magtwilla told Magtori her plan. Perhaps the kitten was too young to understand. Perhaps she was too used to the cushy life the devilish primates offered. Perhaps she was simply frightened by her mother's frantic demeanor and bored by a long morning of searching for a seemingly non-existent mouse hole behind the refrigerator. Truth be told, Magtori wasn't even sure that the mythical creatures that her mother called 'mice,' and her missing sister pretended to stalk, even existed.

She did know that the old lady who Todd brought to visit her smelled pleasantly of milk and fresh bread. This older primate moved slowly and steadily, unlike the younger ones, and Magtori was drawn to her long white hair. The silvery strands escaped from a waist-length braid in a way that intrigued Magtori. She felt drawn to approach the older lady and touch that braid, gently, with a claw-sheathed paw. It was love at first sight, between Magtori the shy baby Calico and this woman who'd come to visit her. As pure a love as ever forms between cat and human.

Magtwilla watched it happen, helpless to affect it. She sat on the floor, in the middle of the room, too numb to hide. She'd brought her kittens to this house to protect them. She'd chosen to raise them in a place where they'd be safe and warm, and she had kept their bodies safe. Yet, the insidious nature of the primates had wormed its way into her kittens' hearts and minds. She had lost them as surely now as if all three had died in the cold.

Todd returned from walking the demon-shaped-like-a-harmless-old-woman out with Magtori, and he scritched Magtwilla behind the ear.

"It's just us now," he said. "You're a good kitty, Jenny, and you don't want those tiresome kittens wearing you out."

Magtwilla miaowed, a hollow sound, filled with sadness. The human who had entrapped her didn't understand its meaning, but the mouse who lived behind the refrigerator was watching. And he did.

As the hours progressed to days, the mouse watched Magtwilla begin to waste away. She sat in the window dreaming of her kittens. She wouldn't touch the food Todd brought her. The mouse feared Magtwilla, but his stomach was empty and a poorly-healed broken paw kept him from returning outdoors. The more food he'd stolen, the more careful Todd had become with his pantry. Now all the food was locked up tight, except for the bowl of milk and fish that perennially sat before the fading cat who disdained it.

Tiny brown eyes cautiously watched wide golden ones as the mouse began to dare approaching his natural predator. With each step, his heart beat faster, and his paws quivered worse. When the gold eyes finally turned and saw him, the mouse froze. But Magtwilla did not attack. She didn't raise a paw to strike him, and his hunger slowly conquered his fear. The small brown body crept up to Magtwilla's bowl. He placed his paws on the edge, and he stared into eyes that had spent days searching for something they would never find.

The brown mouse was nothing like her kittens, and, yet, he was small and soft and warm. "Are you a kitten?" she miaowed.

The mouse shook all over, but it dared the horrible impudence of squeaking in its rodent's voice, "Yes."

Magtwilla tilted her head, skewing her left ear to the side. She knew the mouse wasn't her kitten. Or a kitten at all. At least, certainly not a healthy, beautiful one. She remembered Twillatha hunting this very rodent, and, somehow, that connection to her kittens was enough.

Magtwilla stretched out, relaxing for the first time since Magtori left. If this deformed rodent of a kitten meant to be hers, then it would need bathing.

The mouse thought he would die of fear as Magtwilla's sharp tooth-filled mouth approached him, but it was a warm, rough tongue that he felt. Not the points of her teeth. She bathed him thoroughly, and watched him eat. When he'd had his fill, before the mouse could skitter away, Magtwilla bit him gently at the nape of his neck. She carried him with her mouth to her favorite sock drawer where she performed the secret ceremony for naming a new kitten.

This was a kitten she could keep hidden from Todd. This was a kitten she could keep. And as they slept together, predator and prey side-by-side, the mouse willed his heart to stop racing. This dangerous foster mother could eat him whole in one bite, if her heart ever healed and she regained her mind. However, she could keep his belly full of good food until then, and he didn't mind her calling him Twilltori. Even if it wasn't his true name.

Dusty Rainbolt is a self-professed lover of, besides cats, 1950s sci-fi horror movies about giant menaces. Them! Tarantula. The Beginning of the End. Attack of the Crab Monsters. But what if the monster isn't a ferocious humongous ant or spider or grasshopper, but a loveable kitty-kat?

Fluffy just wants to play. Unfortunately, Fluffy is the size of a Tyrannosaurus Rex. His idea of being cute leaves a lot of broken bones and tumbleweed-sized furballs behind him.

A Spoiled Rotten Cat Lives Here

by Dusty Rainbolt

Etta May Bagley peered through the screen door. She wore an embroidered apron and lodged a Bagley Insurance ballpoint pen over her right ear. "Can I help you?" She blinked innocently.

Her next door neighbor, Arlan Dingle, stood on the porch, his fist pounding on the door frame and his spine stiff as a broom stick. He had a permanent scowl etched into his sixty-something year old face. Today his frown lines looked more severe than usual.

Beside Arlan stood Vale Verde County's youngest Animal Control Officer. Late afternoon sunlight reflected off the kid's name badge that read "BECKMAN." Beads of perspiration dripped down his perfect twenty-year-old face, and fresh underarm sweat stains soiled his otherwise clean khaki uniform.

"Mrs. Bagley, I hate to bother you—" Young Lewis Beckman's voice was tinged with hesitation.

"I don't," Alan interrupted. "Now get to it. That cat's a menace."

The young officer glared sideways at Arlan, then continued. "Mrs. Bagley, we've had a complaint against the pet you call—" He scanned his complaint form, but he didn't need to. He knew the name. "—Fluffy."

Etta May took a deep breath. "Oh, dear. What's he done this time?"

"My baby. He's killed my *baby!*" Arlan held up the top half of a black leather-covered steering wheel.

Old wood planks squeaked as Etta May joined the men on the porch. She glanced to the east. Furry orange tumbleweeds the size of a large German Shepherd hung from shrubs and tree branches, as well as the barbed wire fence that separated their property line. It was March after all, and this time of year Fluffy shed his coat faster than a cheerleader on prom night. An especially large wad of cat hair clung to the serrated teeth of the piranha weather vane mounted atop Arlan's barn roof.

Parked next to the house was Arlan's 1968 candy apple red convertible. Sure enough, a fresh three-foot long tube of slimy orange cat fur protruded through the broken windshield. The mass looked remarkably similar to the stillborn alien Etta May had once seen in a jar of formaldehyde at a Sinclair station outside of Roswell, New Mexico.

"That mutant nearly killed my wife." He pointed to a trembling woman standing near the car. She held an ice pack to her cheek.

"Poor thing," Etta May said sincerely. Then she called over the fence to her neighbor, "Sorry about the black eye, Mrs. Dingle."

"That animal should be shot," Arlan insisted.

Etta May wiped her damp hands on her apron bib. "As I recall, Arlan, you've tried that a couple of times. It didn't do anything but make him mad."

Speak of the devil. A T-Rex-sized creature trotted into the Bagley's front yard, and dropped his bottom to the ground. Oblivious to the heated conversation on the porch, Fluffy ran his moistened paw daintily across his face. Obviously he was reloading for round two of the Olympic event, Projectile Vomiting at Five Meters.

Fluffy was just your average domestic shorthair, mostly, but he stood twelve feet tall from the tip of his orange tabby ears to the pads of his basketball-sized paws.

Arlan's face flushed until he turned the most interesting shade of cerise. "Arrest her!"

The young Animal Control Officer pursed his lips. "Mr. Dingle, I don't have the authority to arrest Mrs. Bagley."

Arlan's hand formed a fist and he shook it in the air. "Then, impound that cat."

Lewis' eyes grew wide. "Just how do you propose I do that?"

Etta May looked at Lewis and then at the animal control truck. It was standard issue, just like the trucks driven by dedicated ACO's across Texas. It would hold Irish Wolfhounds, and maybe even a small pony, but the vehicle's designers never intended it to contain Fluffy.

"Arlan, stop bullying the boy. You know my insurance always pays for the damage. Now quit whining, and get an estimate. You'll get a check in a week or so."

Etta May looked past the men at Fluffy. He had abandoned the spit bath and had rolled over on his back to take a sand bath. Etta May moved down the cinder block steps and across her front yard where Fluffy had stirred up a cloud of dust. The two men followed her.

The Morris-the-Cat lookalike kicked around and rolled upright, assuming a Sphinx position, only to one-sixth scale. Lewis cautiously approached Fluffy and allowed the kitty to sniff the end of the cattle prod. Fluffy leaned into the pole, rubbing his chin against the metal prongs.

"Well?" Arlan insisted. "Do something!"

"Look, Mr. Dingle, I have plenty of other problems." Lewis carefully positioned the prod to the cheek area, then moved the contacts up and down. Fluffy dropped his head against the stick and allowed the officer to give him a good scratch. "The coyotes are so thick in this county the feds have decided to count them in the next census. They're eating everything that's not armed." The young officer turned to Fluffy's owner. "Mrs. Bagley, I know the Vale Verde

County doesn't have any leash laws for cats, but could you please try to keep Fluffy in your yard?"

Etta May sighed. "I'll try, Lewis. I don't know why he likes Arlan's property. He doesn't bother any of the other neighbors."

"They're having a county commissioners' meeting tomorrow night about dealing with nuisance animals," Lewis said. "Mrs. Bagley, could you please come to it? Maybe we can come up with a solution."

* * *

Etta May eased down Main Street of Del Rio, Texas, in her twenty year-old Ford pickup truck. Behind it rolled an open trailer usually used to haul hay. Tonight the trailer overflowed with an orange cat curled up on a bed of hay, snoozing. Moving along the main drag, Fluffy's presence inspired two opposite reactions from mothers with small kids. One woman used her own body to shield her children as she urged them into the first available unlocked door. In this case, the establishment was What's New Pussycat?, which provided one hundred percent fabric-free entertainment.

A more adventurous mom dashed to the curb and pointed. "Look, Johnny. See the big kitty?" Her excited toddler waved at Fluffy and squealed, "Kitty!" The youngster's exuberant shriek woke Fluffy, who flicked his ear, dislodging a horsefly.

Finally, the old Ford pulled into the courthouse parking lot. As the trailer screeched to a stop, Fluffy held up his head and yawned. He jumped off the trailer, then he trotted over to his favorite scratching post: the county's four-hundred year old live oak tree, Big Oak. He dug in his T-Rex-sized claws into the tree trunk, arched his back, and stretched every vertebra before debarking the county's historical landmark.

"Fluffy! Come here." Etta May gave the tow chain attached to his collar a solid yank.

The county officials and an assembly of curious residents filed out of the old stone courthouse when they heard that Fluffy had arrived.

County commissioner Utah Walker, who really hailed from Rhode Island, stopped his monologue with Texas Fish and Game director Evan Gonzales, to watch Fluffy desecrate the living treasure. When Etta May and Fluffy approached them, a devious grin spread across Utah's face. Fluffy leaned down, sniffing Utah, then giving the older man a vigorous shove with his enormous pink nose.

"I can't keep anything from him, can I?" He pulled out a Kentucky Fried Chicken box and held up a drumstick by the very tips of his fingers. Fluffy snapped the treat out of his fan's hands and gulped it down without even chewing it.

Evan dashed behind Utah, using the commissioner's five-foot-eight frame as a human shield.

Utah laughed. "Aw, come on, Gonzales. Show some balls. He's just a plain old domestic cat." He turned to the woman holding the end of Fluffy's chain. "Hey, Etta May, is he still growing?"

"Might be," she answered. "I did have to let his collar out the other day. I thought he was just getting fat."

After introductions had been made, Evan said, "Are you telling me this monster is a domestic cat? He couldn't be."

Etta May smiled. "Don't worry, Mr. Gonzales. Those vets at Texas A&M did DNA testing on him and said genetically he's the same as that little kitten who sleeps on your sofa."

"Impossible!" Evan peered cautiously from around Utah's shoulder.

Etta May nodded. "They said that all that radiation he was exposed to as a kitten affected his pituitary gland. So now, he continues to grow. They said unlike most giants, he could live to be a hundred."

"Radiation?" Gonzales backed away. "In Texas? Where?"

"Oh, heavens, no." Etta May opened her purse and dug through her accumulation of bills and receipts until she located her wallet. It contained a plastic sleeve holding a black and white picture of a much younger Mr. and Mrs. Bagley petting a beagle-sized cat in front of a sign that said, "NEVADA TEST SITE: No Trespassing." "We found him on vacation to the Nevada Proving Grounds right after an atom bomb test. You'd think watching an atomic explosion would be an awe-inspiring sight with that ball of fire rising up in the sky in the shape of a giant salad fungus. Instead we got to witness the country's very first underground atomic bomb test. I've seen more impressive detonations at the Val Verde County Farting Competition. So much for our once-in-a-lifetime vacation. But I digress.

"Finding that poor kitten was the only good thing that happened on that vacation. Roy named it Fluffy. My perceptive husband was not only under the mistaken impression that Fluffy was a girl, but that he would develop a long, voluptuous coat. Neither point turned out to be true."

The front door to the courthouse opened and a large Latino man exited the building. "There's that cat!" shouted Butch Seguin as he descended the courthouse steps. He approached the cat wielding a garden rake. "I hear your cat's been causing problems again, Etta May."

"It's shedding season." She shrugged.

"Come here, Fluffy." He shook the rake in the cat's face.

Seeing Butch, Fluffy flopped over on his side. Butch ran the rake down the cat's torso, catching a huge wad of loose orange fur. He held up the rake. A gust of wind caught a fluff of fur and sent it floating down the street.

Etta May watched the grooming session. "While you're at it, maybe you could trim his nails." She glanced at Big Oak, then picked up the cat's paws. Using her thumbs, she pressed the softball-size toe pad with all her strength exposing claws longer than a railroad spike. "I guess he could use one right now."

Gonzales eyed the cat's feet. "How do you cut his claws?"

"With bolt cutters, of course."

After a few more minutes of raking, Butch broke out into a sweat and his arms grew tired. "That's it for today, little buddy. Come next door tomorrow, and we'll play Chase the String."

Etta May turned to the other men. "Butch attaches a tow chain to his riding lawn mower and drags it along behind. Fluffy takes out after him. Sometimes they spend the whole afternoon playing with 'string'." She turned to Butch. "That game of yours has spawned some really bad behaviors. Every week or so Fluffy drags home some kind of farm machinery. Occasionally the farmer is still onboard. We free him, give him a good stiff drink of bourbon and take him home. They're always a little shaken the first time, but they get used to it. He never does any *permanent* damage. Fluffy's pretty gentle as long as you don't run away from him."

Eddie Dodd, an elderly gentleman leaning on a cane made of longhorns, interrupted the conversation, demanding, "Mr. Gonzales, what is the state going to do to help us with our coyote problem? Ranchers are losing half of their calves to those varmints. What about you, Etta May? How many calves have you lost this year?"

"None," Etta May said proudly.

"Me neither," Butch added.

"Really?" Old Dodd coughed an old man cough.

"Haven't even lost so much as a chicken," Etta May said.

"Really? What's your secret?" Gonzales asked her.

She took a thigh out of Utah's chicken box and offered it to Fluffy. "You're looking at him."

"Really?"

About that time, Fluffy began coughing with so much force he knocked over the county attorney. When he dropped his head and began to back up, townspeople scattered for their lives. Then with catapult tension, Fluffy hocked up another alien abortion, springing it a good ten feet before it landed in the Ladies Auxiliary's garden, freshly planted with Texas primroses.

"*There's* your problem." Utah tapped the slime wad with his long-horn walking cane. Buried within Fluffy's furball was an intact, semi-digested coyote.

Evan stared at the mass and then looked Fluffy up and down. Finally the Texas Fish and Game director took Etta May by the elbow and led her away from the other residents. "The State of Texas is interested in buying Fluffy from you."

Etta May smiled. "Sorry Mr. Gonzales. Fluffy's part of our family. He's not for sale."

* * *

Etta May answered the knock at the door. *Now what!* This time, fortunately, it wasn't Arlan. Looking down through the screen door she saw a tiny fist poised to knock again. It was Mattie, Butch Seguin's granddaughter.

"Come in, Mattie." Etta May opened the door. "Don't forget to wipe your feet on the welcome mat."

"Mrs. Bagley," the kid said excitedly as she handed Etta May her mail. "Fluffy ate another drug lord."

Etta May folded her hands together reverently. "Thank you, Jesus. Those dealers have sure kept our cat food bills down."

Once the four-legged coyote population began to dwindle, Etta May had to supplement Fluffy's hunting soirees with a side of beef every week. Since he acquired a taste for two-legged coyotes, the feed bills were manageable again.

After Mattie left, Etta May sat down and opened her mail. "What the heck?" She stared at the letter with a return address that simply said "Immigration and Customs Enforcement, Washington, D.C." "No street address, just Washington, D.C. Who do they think they are? Santa Claus?"

Somehow the U.S. border patrol got word about Fluffy's penchant for Mexican food. Now ICE wanted to buy Fluffy for a million dollars. After she said "no" they sent her this letter threatening to seize the kitty under eminent domain.

She scanned it over it one more time just to make sure she'd gotten it right.

"*One of your neighbors informed us that an orange tabby cat named Fluffy has been consuming undocumented immigrants crossing the Rio Grande into Val Verde County. This is a federal issue and said feline must cease and desist from ingesting any more Mexican nationals. ICE requires you to turn Fluffy over to U.S. Customs officials or face a ten-thousand-dollar-a-day fine.*"

"Three guesses who the neighbor was." Etta May mumbled to herself as she returned to the supper simmering on the stove.

As Etta May stirred the okra, she heard a terrible commotion outside. She rushed out just in time to see the metal outbuilding behind Arlan's home collapse into a heap of splinters and corrugated tin.

Arlan crawled out from under the debris pile. Fortunately it looked like he only suffered a few bruises.

"What a shame about the building." Etta May picked up a broken red-painted pine two-by-four and tossed it back with the other debris. She pulled an insurance claims form from the pocket of her apron and licked the tip of the ballpoint pen she always kept over her ear.

Arlan picked up a crumpled piece of corrugated tin and shook it at Etta May. "He's destroyed my darkroom. How am I going to develop my film?" Arlan whined.

"Arlan, who uses a darkroom these days? Haven't you ever heard of Photoshop?"

"I don't have a computer." Arlan picked up a loose roll of negatives peeking out from under a pulverized enlarger. He held the already processed film up against the sunlight and quickly pocketed it. "I don't know a computer from a cash register. Besides, I like to take artistic photographs. You have to dodge and burn them to make them look good. Like Ansel Adams did."

"Well, Ansel, I guess for the next couple of weeks you'll just have to take your film to the drug store like everyone else stuck in the 1960s. You'll be up and running again soon enough."

"I was, uh, pulling proofs when that beast jumped up on the roof and started purring. It was like listening to a jackhammer. Dust crumbled down from the ceiling; cracks appeared in the corner and the light fixture started shaking. The next thing I know the walls caved in around me. Lucky thing I wasn't agitating the film." Arlan pointed at the far corner that was squashed flatter than a supermodel.

"Come on, Arlan." She kicked a fragment of a brown glass jug. "The building was full of dangerous chemicals. It could have blown it up."

"It didn't. It was that damn cat what did it. I coulda been killed."

"Too bad." Etta May smiled for a moment, then forced a grim expression.

"What?"

"Too bad about your darkroom."

* * *

A few days later ICE tried to make good on their seizure threat. Etta May stood defiantly in the center of the circular driveway with her arms crossed over her ample bosom. "The only way you'll get Fluffy is over your dead bodies," she warned the agents.

"Mrs. Bagley, is that a threat?"

"Of course not. Just a fact."

When they tried squeeze Fluffy into a shipping container made for elephants, they found out Etta May wasn't kidding. Without her lifting a finger or uttering a word, Fluffy buried one ICE agent alive in the sand box. The big game hunter hired to implement the plan was thrown twenty feet in the air, like a toy mouse.

After the bureaucrats removed a coworker from the top of a fifty-year old mesquite tree, ICE agents ran up the white flag and surrendered before Fluffy eviscerated a whole new generation of civil servants.

* * *

A few days later, Etta May finally convinced the Environmental Protection Agency to declare Fluffy a protected species because he was the only one of his kind. With EPA protection, Fluffy could live unmolested in his own habitat.

Finally Uncle Sam came to an agreement with the Bagleys. Once a year they'd be permitted to take blood samples from Fluffy so they could try to clone him.

"Can you imagine what would happen to the world with unsocialized Fluffies wandering the landscape?" Etta May asked her husband Roy. "It would be like watching one of those old Japanese horror movies from the sixties. Cat-zilla verses Washington." The farm lady rubbed her hands together. "My money's on the cat."

* * *

A week after what came to be known as the Great Darkroom Incident, rumors stirred up around Del Rio. For once they had nothing to do with the Bagleys or overactive feline pituitaries. Nobody had ever thought too much about Arlan's darkroom until Mildred Newberry, the busybody clerk at the drugstore, went through Arlan's pictures after she printed the photographs. Right in middle of the roll Mildred found some photos of ten-year-old Mattie Seguin with her tank top off. One shot looked like Mattie was trying to run away.

Before Sheriff Cade could arrest Arlan, he located the pervert's red convertible abandoned on Etta May's property. Next to the car, the sheriff found Arlan's broken sunglasses, a cattle prod, a Hawkins fifty-caliber rifle and a puddle of blood, but no Arlan. A few hours after the sheriff's cryptic discovery, Etta May became the recipient of a very special gift: Arlan's head and what looked to be entrails laid out neatly on the welcome mat that said, "One spoiled rotten cat lives here."

"What's going to happen to Fluffy?" Etta May asked the animal control officer Lewis Beckman as the ambulance carted off the remains of her neighbor. "His eating Arlan and all."

Lewis shrugged. "I don't know. It's up to the sheriff. If he's current on his vaccinations, we'll only have to put him in rabies quarantine for ten days."

All of Etta May's fretting about Fluffy's fate was for naught. Little Mattie's father Butch Seguin happened to be the county medical examiner. He autopsied what was left of Arlan and determined the death was accidental, the result of a mountain lion attack.

But even after the ME's report absolved Fluffy of the death, Etta May worried about Mrs. Dingle creating a stir.

The afternoon of Arlan's funeral, Etta May brought an okra and squash casserole to the Widow Dingle. As she waited for Mrs. Dingle to answer the back door, Etta May noticed a well-tended herb garden planted with nothing but catnip.

Mrs. Dingle offered a gift of her own. "Give this to Fluffy." She handed Etta May a handmade fabric beach ball filled with fragrant catnip. "Tell him he's welcome here anytime, now."

Suddenly, Fluffy became a celebrity. Etta May and Fluffy appeared in *Time*, *People*, and the *National Enquirer*. Finally came the crème-de-la-crème of interviews, *Cat Fancy Magazine*. The interviewer spent several hours drinking lemonade on the front porch, speaking with Etta May and photographing Fluffy with a wide angle lens.

Finally, Etta May checked her watch and stood up. "Well, I'd love to talk to you all day, but this is a working farm, and I still have a long list of chores to do before the sun goes down. You know how to get to the main road, don't you?"

The reporter nodded and Etta May walked her to the car.

"Great. First thing I have to do is scoop the cat litter." She fumbled around the pockets of her apron. "Let me see, did you see where I left the keys to my bulldozer?"

Up to now, "cats" have meant domestic housecats. But there are also the so-called "big cats". Lions. Cheetahs. Leopards. Cougars. Tigers.

Renee Carter Hall's "The Emerald Mage" is narrated by Jiro the snowcat, the companion (familiar) of Korrinth, the Emerald Mage of a fantasy world. Jiro has been Korrinth's loyal companion for many decades – so long that he has imperceptibly become Korrinth's nursemaid as the once-powerful Emerald Mage has slowly sunk into senility. Jiro has been secretly performing Korrinth's wizardry for him to keep up his reputation. But when the old wizard insists on going to the annual council of all the Mages, the snowcat is hard-pressed to keep up the deception among the wizard's peers, at close range.

The Emerald Mage

by Renee Carter Hall

We snowcats may be born for swirling blizzards and icy cliffs, but for myself, I'll take a cozy cottage hearth any day. A bellyful of roast rabbit, a fire of crimson embers, the old rug covered with layer on layer of my gray-and-white fur—*that's* comfort.

I was stretched out on that rug, dreaming of yellow butterflies, when the explosion woke me. There was no question where it had come from, and in a matter of seconds I'd already raced across the one-room cottage, shouldered open the door, and headed for Korrinth's workroom. It was actually larger than the cottage, with the same rough shutters and thatched roof. All looked well outside, and there was no smoke pouring out from anywhere, so I hoped those were good signs.

Inside, Korrinth's chair was knocked over and his worktable covered with shards of pottery, but the oil lamp was still upright, and thankfully so was the mage himself. His complexion looked a little gray, but then I realized it was just the powdery ash of whatever he'd been mixing. His curly white beard was singed and his eyebrows were gone, but otherwise he looked all right.

"Korrinth—are you hurt?"

His cloudy green eyes focused on me. "Hurt? Why would I... No, my boy, I'm perfectly fine. Just..." He looked at the shambles on the

worktable as if someone else had put the mess there. "Something…
didn't work right."

I took the back of his chair in my teeth and managed to get it
upright. "Here. Sit down and rest a minute."

It was hard to tell if anything else in the room had been damaged. I remembered the days when everything was neatly labeled and
stored away on the shelves and in the cupboards. Now half the clay
jars had faded labels, bundles of herbs were lying around in piles,
and stacks of books teetered next to stale bread crusts and teacups
with dried leaves stuck inside.

I couldn't help wondering if the wizard's mind now looked much
the same way.

I turned back to Korrinth. "I was thinking… It looks like it might
rain tomorrow. Maybe we should send a message to the council and
stay home this year. It's such a long journey for bad weather."

"Stay home? Nonsense! We have to be there."

"Oh, now, you said yourself last year it was just an excuse for
all the high mages to get together and show off and bicker about
nothing."

"Did I? Well. It's still important. I'm the emerald mage, after all.
Can't have any empty chairs." His eyes lit suddenly. "Oh—I almost
forgot. I have to make the tonic for Myomé's companion." He stood.
"Now… Where did I put the flameroot…"

So that's what he'd been doing. As he rummaged through the
cupboards, I sniffed the remains of the bowl. Sparkweed instead of
flameroot. No wonder it had gone up. We were lucky it hadn't taken
the roof off. Or his head.

It was my fault, really, dozing at the fire instead of keeping an
eye on him, knowing his mind wandered too much anymore for him
to be safe working alone. I looked through his recipe book, as he
called it, until I found the right one, and we gathered the ingredients
together.

Korrinth picked up a jar, squinted at the label, put it back, and
picked up another. The clay lids rattled as his hands shook. "Oh—"

I glanced up just in time to see the jar fall. Before it hit the packed floor, I seized the jar with my mind, slowed its descent, and righted it so that it came to rest without breaking.

Korrinth gazed at it a moment, obviously puzzled, then picked it up and went on. I turned back to the recipe book, trying not to pant with the sudden exertion, the pads of my paws slick with sweat. He wouldn't put it together. Maybe he'd think he did it himself by instinct. I hated keeping secrets from him, but like so many things these days, it was for his own good.

I'd been the emerald mage's companion since he'd found me as a starving cub, lost or abandoned in the northlands. I had more memories of snuggling against his green wool cloak than I did of my mother's fur. He'd been a waywalker in those days, no settled hearth of his own, and he'd thought a fierce male snowcat would make for good protection. He named me Jiro, after a silver flower that grew in those mountains, the only one that bloomed in winter. By the time I was grown, my head came to just above his waist, he'd spelled me to speak and taught me to read, and though I saved his life a time or two in the mountains, fighting off frost-wolves and keeping him warm at night when we couldn't risk a fire, I did it not from duty or command, but out of friendship. Out of love.

Once the tonic was finished and poured into its blue glass bottle, we went back into the cottage. Korrinth sat in his chair by the fire, intending to read, but he was asleep in moments. Grateful I could use magic now instead of my teeth, I took the book from him and placed it on the side-table, drew a blanket gently over him, and went outside to finish the day's chores. A pair of leather gardening gloves, roused with a few whispered words, became my hands, and I drew water from the well, brought in a few more sticks for the fire, and milked Penelope, our goat. It had taken a little while for her to get used to me, and a good while longer to get used to being milked by a pair of enchanted gloves instead of warm human hands, but now she stood placidly by until I was done.

All through the chores, I worried. Some days he was fine, others not. It was two days' journey to the hall where the mages' council was held—would those be good days or bad? And the council itself… When we were alone, I could help him without him noticing, but the other mages wouldn't be so easily fooled.

I put the gloves away. By now, they felt like they were made of stone, and my head ached. I wasn't born for magic, and I'd never meant to learn it, but something had had to be done. Even though it was forbidden for a mage's companion to learn, I'd had no choice— or so I told myself. I tried to ignore the fact that, tired as I was now from the chores, I was proud of how much I could do, and satisfied by how well I did it. I *liked* doing magic, but that, above all, was what I could admit to no one. Not even myself.

* * *

Dawn came rosy and fair, and we set out, Korrinth with his walking stick in one hand and the other resting between my shoulders. It looked to be a good day in more than just the weather. I'd double-checked his pack and found our supplies in good order, he hadn't forgotten the tonic, and now he was even humming an old road-song from his waywalker days. I joined in with the chorus as we walked, and he laughed and rumpled the thick fur at my nape. "Like old times, isn't it?" he said, smiling, and happily I agreed that it was.

The second day grew cloudy. A sudden shower in the early after-noon forced us to shelter in a grove of pines. Korrinth and I gathered dry branches, but when he tried to get a fire going, he couldn't recall the name of fire and instead kept repeating variations on a word used to snuff candles, getting more and more frustrated. Finally I muttered the right word under my breath, and the flames sprang up and blazed.

"There." Korrinth crossed his arms and settled back against a log. "Must have been a bit damp."

He dozed a bit, and I relaxed, enjoying the snap of the fire and the patter of rain. Just as I was drifting off, though, Korrinth stood, looking around.

I stretched. "What is it?"

"We have to get home. It's getting late." He picked up his walking stick and looked around for his pack.

"No, it's all right. We're going to the council, remember? We'll be there tomorrow morning."

"The council." His eyes went unfocused a moment. "But Penelope—"

"Sadie has her. Sadie Cross-Creek? She's keeping her for us. She's going to make you some of that cheese you like from the milk. The kind with the herbs in it?"

"Oh." Korrinth sat back down on the log, slowly. "Yes. I suppose." He still clutched his walking stick, looking down at his hands like he wasn't sure they were his. I wondered if he expected them to look younger, stronger, the way he remembered them—the way I remembered him.

The shower passed, and we came out of the pine grove into a rainwashed meadow. Back on the road, I felt better, though I was already vowing that, one way or another, this was going to be our last council. We had walked perhaps half a mile when Korrinth slowed and stopped, leaning on his stick.

"Should we rest a bit?" I asked brightly.

Korrinth shook his head. He gazed at the horizon a moment, frowned, turned to the right, and stopped again.

"What's wrong?"

He looked back at me, and I ached at the sadness in his eyes. "I'm sorry, Jiro. I'm… not quite certain where we are. We should be near the second marker by now, but I don't…" He looked back at the horizon. He sounded tired. "I'm afraid I don't remember."

"Hush." I nudged his hand. "All these stupid fields look alike anyway, you know that. We can't be too far off."

"We'll be late." He looked down at the road. "We'll be late, and it'll be my fault."

I pressed against him, purring. "Then they'll just have to wait for the emerald mage. It'll be good for them."

As I spoke, I tried to push aside fear and worry and sorrow to clear my mind enough to search for the second marker. The first one the day before had been a chunk of amethyst crystal wedged high up in a tree to mark the path, so suffused with magic it practically hummed. Here I felt nothing, but it was hard to clear my mind when all I could feel was Korrinth's frail hand on my back, gripping my thick fur as if it kept him from being blown away like dandelion fluff. I buried my nose in his cloak, smelling pinesmoke and a leaf of sage caught in the wool from home.

Scent. That was it. Strong, concentrated magic like the markers had its own scent, something like a cross between rosemary and the air after a storm. I whispered a spell I'd learned the week before, to increase my sense of smell tenfold, and hoped it would work.

It was as if all the colors around me brightened as every scent grew sharper. I sneezed twice, then sniffed the next breeze. Yes— there. It was faint, but I could follow.

"Come on." I tugged gently at Korrinth's cloak. "Let's try this way." Thankfully, he followed without question, and I mock-wandered a bit, moving toward the marker's scent. I didn't know how long the spell would last, or if it would work a second time. Some seemed to be single-use only, though for some maddening reason they never told you that in the books. Maybe they didn't work the same way in nonhumans.

Finally, just as the spell seemed to be fading, Korrinth jerked a bit, as if woken up. "There it is! Clear as a bell—and there's the path." He smiled down at me. "Maybe I'm not so worn out after all."

In the old days, I might have nipped his hand playfully, but his skin was too thin for that now, so I brushed it with my whiskers instead. "You're just fine."

* * *

The council hall was actually a castle—or at least what remained of one, high on a green hill. It had been a place of ancient magic and storied battle ages ago, and now only its great hall still stood, surrounded by weathered gray stones with weeds and ivy growing between. Inside, though, the hall itself appeared untouched by time. Tapestries covered the walls, the rushes on the floor were strewn with fresh mint, and a great table of dark, gleaming wood nearly filled the room. Around that table, Korrinth and the other four mages of the council took their places.

Myomé, the crimson mage and the highest among them, took her place first. She was nearing her three hundredth year, but her dark brown skin remained unlined, though she had grandsons now who were waywalkers themselves. Her companion, a little red dragon named Reza, had already staked out a spot at the massive hearth, and when she saw me, she puffed out twin curls of smoke in greeting.

Beside her sat Sterlan, the indigo mage, with ice-blue eyes under sharp brows and glossy black hair. His companion, a silver falcon, perched on his forearm, as if they were out hunting. I'd never felt comfortable under that bird's gaze, and now that I carried my secret, I shivered a little when the falcon's dark eyes locked on mine.

Brant, the blond-haired yellow mage, was the youngest of the group in both age and appearance. His chair was empty at the moment because he was, as always, chasing after his companion, which was apparently some sort of cross between a lemur and a demon. It had already eaten half the mint out of the rushes, upset all the chalices on the table, and was now clawing its way up the largest tapestry, defecating copiously as it went. Brant's magic lay in song, and I hoped before things got started he'd take up his lute and spell the thing to sleep for the duration of the council. Or preferably forever.

The last of the company was Neely, the Beige. He was pleasant enough but had a way of fading into the background, and had he been absent, I doubt anyone would have noticed. His companion was a small rodent of some sort from its scent, though all we ever saw of it was him apparently feeding sunflower seeds to his sleeve.

Korrinth took his seat, and I settled down next to Reza by the hearth. I was glad she was there; it was good to have someone to talk to. (Technically, Brant's thing could talk, but its vocabulary was limited mostly to the words "give," "mine," and "hungry.")

"You look awful," she said, but she said it kindly.

I stretched out all the way, spreading my toes, and sighed, feeling the warmth of the fire seep through my fur. "It was a long journey. He gets tired a lot sooner now."

"And you're exhausted yourself."

"Just need a nap. I'll be fine." I could tell she wanted to say something else, but whatever it was, she let it go and curled up next to me. We rarely saw each other outside of the councils, but whenever we met, it was as if we picked up right where we'd left off.

I drifted in and out of sleep until Myomé rapped her staff against the stones to call the council to order. Brant had managed to subdue his companion enough to have it sitting on his shoulder gnawing an apple. I hoped he had a whole bushel with him.

"Ever wonder what that thing would taste like?" Reza murmured. "Stuff it with apples, roast it nice and slow…"

I chuckled despite my worry. Maybe things would be all right. The castle's magic was deep and strong; maybe it would strengthen Korrinth somehow. Maybe it really would be like old times.

Myomé's voice rang through the hall. "I call upon each mage to bind their word to the will of this council. Sterlan, the Indigo."

"I am thus bound."

"Brant, the Yellow."

"I am—ow! you stupid little—"

Myomé's expression looked carved into her face, though there was a hint of mirth in her eyes. "Brant, the Yellow?"

The young mage turned red enough to have been called Brant the Scarlet. "I am thus bound."

"Neely, the Beige."

Neely coughed politely. "Madame Crimson, if you please—"

"What color is it really this time, Neely?"

"I rather think it tends more toward ecru, you see, because—"

"Very well. Neely, the Ecru."

"I am thus bound."

"Korrinth, the Emerald."

"I am thus bound."

I hadn't realized I'd been holding my breath until I released it.

"As am I, Myomé, the Crimson. So we proceed."

The first order of business was from Neely, a question about whether some sort of magic hedge had grown too tall and exactly who was responsible for pruning it. I rested my cheek against the warm stones by the hearth and sank gratefully into sleep.

* * *

"Jiro." Reza's voice, low and insistent. "Wake up."

"Mm?" I yawned. "Was I snoring?"

"No. Listen."

I turned my attention back to the table. Things had apparently gotten a bit livelier than magic horticulture while I'd been asleep. Sterlan was leaning forward, obviously irritated; Brant was frowning (at least his lemur-thing was asleep now); and Neely looked worried (though, to be fair, Neely always looked worried). Myomé was calm, but that too was no surprise; she was like the eye of a storm given human shape. But Korrinth was pale, and I didn't like that anxious look in his eyes. I growled softly and padded over to the table to sit by his chair.

"Those wards have been getting weaker by the day," Sterlan said. "Your border might as well be unwarded—any shade with more strength than a butterfly could get through by now."

The wards. My stomach lurched. I couldn't help Korrinth maintain them; only the true emerald mage could weave and hold that magic. I'd reminded him about them a few times, but apparently he either hadn't kept them up or hadn't the strength to do it as well as before.

Korrinth's gaze hardened. "I know how to protect my own border."

"Then do it. If you can."

A snarl welled in my throat. Korrinth put a hand on my head, lightly, but I felt no reassurance from it. "You have some concern regarding my abilities?"

"I have some *concern*," Sterlan said, "about this whole council. Have we all forgotten that we're guardians? That our wards keep this land safe? If any of us neglects that work"—he eyed Korrinth—"or no longer has the capacity to do it properly, we leave all our lands open to shadow. Have we forgotten the war my father fought in— was lost in—battling those forces?"

"We have not." Myomé spoke quietly, but her voice still seemed to come from the very stones of the hall. "And some of us lost as much. Or more."

I wondered if Sterlan remembered that Myomé's husband had also been lost in the Shadow War. It seemed he didn't, because he barreled on.

"These are not merely titles; these are not amusing tricks we do. Lives depend on us, and we cannot risk failing them."

"If you have a point," Myomé said, "this would be an excellent time to present it."

There was no hesitation. "I charge Korrinth the emerald mage to prove potency by ordeal."

The hall went still as ice. Only apprentices had to prove their powers; as far as I knew, it had never been asked of any mage, let alone a high mage of the council. But now it had, and if Myomé allowed it—and if he wasn't strong enough—

I couldn't bear to finish the thought, couldn't bear to think of him so defeated. I wished I could will him some of my strength, some of my new magic's power, but that was in the realm of magical healing, and far beyond the meager skills I had.

"This is a serious charge," Myomé said. "Are you certain you wish to pursue it?"

"Absolutely."

I imagined what his bone might feel like against my teeth.

"Maybe we should take a break," Brant said. "Have some time to rest."

"Oh, of course," Sterlan said sweetly, "because when the shadow forces creep across the border, they'll allow him some time to rest up before they attack, won't they?" He seemed to be speaking more to his falcon than to anyone else in particular. "Of course it doesn't matter that one of our high mages is fading—why, we've got minstrel boy the monkey trainer and Fruitcake the Taupe to keep us safe—"

"Ecru," Neely muttered to his sleeve.

"You've made your point," Myomé said. "Speak further, and you'll certainly dull it." She paused, and I saw pain flicker across her face before she composed herself again. "Reza, bring the testing-stone."

The little dragon gave me a sympathetic glance, then slipped out of the hall and returned a few moments later with the stone. It looked like nothing more than a cabochon of clear glass the size of my paw, set in a silver frame, but from my secret reading I knew it was a type of stone rarer and clearer than diamond, one of only seven in the world, worthless to average humans but precious to mages for its ability to perfectly reflect power without amplifying it.

Reza placed the stone on the table before Korrinth.

"A waste of valuable time," Korrinth said, "but if I must..."

"Please," Myomé said.

All grew quiet again. Korrinth focused on the stone. Threads of pale green light danced through it, quivering, entwining. Gradually the color deepened, and the light grew brighter.

I stared at the stone as if doing so would somehow help him, as if by sheer will I could force it brighter. By now it glowed faint green throughout with deeper sparks flashing within. It would have been an impressive show for an apprentice. For a mage…

The glow intensified, as if a green flame had been lit inside the stone. Then it grew brighter still. Hope set my heart pounding. A little more, just a little more, and that would shut Sterlan's mouth and everything would be all right.

I glanced at Korrinth. His face was a blank slate, but I saw strain in the muscles around his eyes. His hands were in his lap, and from where I sat next to him, I could see them trembling. The emerald light in the testing-stone was steady, but it wasn't enough. I saw a sudden desperation in Korrinth's eyes, saw him struggling to hold even the light that was there. I couldn't bear it, couldn't bear that pain, couldn't bear to watch him on the verge of humiliation, of defeat, when he was as good as any of them had ever been—

Something jolted through me, searing my chest like a spear of fire. The testing-stone blazed, too bright to look at directly, and sent an emerald beam straight up to the ceiling, clear and sharp and true.

Korrinth sat back heavily, sweat shining in the lines on his pale forehead. The stone went dark.

"I hope," Korrinth said, his breaths short and wheezing, "that was enough for your satisfaction."

I stared at the rushes on the floor, heart racing. That hadn't been Korrinth at the end. Somehow that had been me. Had anyone guessed? I scanned their faces and saw no suspicion—except for Sterlan, who was in a cold fury now, fists clenched as if he were determined to fight someone but wasn't sure who. Then he snatched up his silver chalice, still half full of red wine, and threw it directly at Korrinth's head.

Korrinth put his hands up to block it but didn't have the strength to divert the object instantly and harmlessly, as any other mage would have. The chalice struck him on the temple, and I heard him cry out in pain.

I felt the roar in my chest before I heard it from my lungs, and in my rage I seized the chalice and flung it back hard at the indigo mage. He deflected it without even wincing—as simple a reflex for a mage as someone putting up their hands—and it clattered to the stone floor.

I turned back to Korrinth, purring hard, sniffing for blood, pressed against his chest, trying to climb into his lap as if I were a cub again. I wasn't sure whether I was comforting him or looking for reassurance myself. A hard welt was rising above Korrinth's eye, but that wasn't the worst. He'd passed the ordeal of the testing-stone but failed this simpler test. He knew it. They all knew it. The emerald mage sat crumpled in his chair, hand to his head, tears on his sunken cheeks. For the first time since I had known him, he looked like nothing more than an old man.

It wasn't until Myomé inspected and healed Korrinth's wound that I started to worry whether anyone knew I'd been the one to throw the chalice back at Sterlan. Certainly they wouldn't connect it to me. It could have been any of them, and it wasn't like Sterlan had been hurt. I glanced nervously at Sterlan's falcon, but it was paying no attention to me. I took a slow, deep breath and tried to relax.

And then I looked to Reza, sitting back by the hearth, and her eyes met mine, and I knew she'd seen everything.

* * *

Myomé halted the council until the next morning and went to speak with Sterlan in private, and the other mages went to the various shelters and tents they'd set up among the ruins. Myomé gave Korrinth a draught from a gold flask she carried, and only when I was sure he was sleeping soundly did I finally leave his side and look for Reza.

She was sitting at the edge of the ruins, perched on a crumbling wall of wide stones. In her claws she held the blue glass bottle of tonic we'd brought her, and when I climbed up next to her I saw it was still full. Before us, sunset glowed pink and gold in the clouds, reminding me too much of the testing-stone.

"Is Korrinth all right?" she asked.

I nodded. "He's sleeping."

"I'm sorry about…" She didn't seem to know how to finish, but I knew what she meant. Sorry your mage isn't going to be a mage anymore, whatever that would mean. I didn't know who the new emerald mage would be or how any of it worked, but I didn't care. All I wanted was to go back home with Korrinth, and take care of him, and never mind what he was or wasn't, except the closest friend I'd ever had.

"Reza…" I wasn't sure where to start. What if she really hadn't seen anything? "Back there…"

She smiled, but her eyes were sad. "How long?"

"Months. Just to help things along, that's all. I didn't mean to…" But of course I had. You didn't stay up nights reading spellbooks in secret just to help things along.

"But why can't we?" I asked. "If it can be taught, why can't we learn?"

She looked down at the bottle, tipping it gently back and forth, watching the liquid swirl inside. "Magic's for humans."

"But *why?* There has to be some good reason."

She shrugged, still gazing at the bottle.

"Reza…" A vague suspicion teased at the edges of my mind. "What does that tonic do?"

It was a long time before she answered, and when she did, her voice was quiet and flat. "Dragons are magic. We're born with it. This… keeps things under control."

"Keeps you from being able to use magic."

She wouldn't look at me. "Yes."

"That you were born with."

"Yes. But—"

"And if you didn't take it?"

She was silent. Then she turned to face me, and her pale gold eyes held mine. A door opened in her mind, and for an instant I was able to look through it.

I gasped. I felt like I was falling, though I knew it had nothing to do with my physical body. The magic in her was a landscape, a vista of towering red cliffs, a power from within the very earth that simmered in her veins. Just trying to grasp the scope of it was overwhelming.

She closed the door. A shudder ran through me from nose to tail. If she didn't drink that tonic, she could be the crimson mage herself. Or something even greater.

"Reza…" I had no idea how to convince her. I couldn't believe she'd kept so much power pent within her for so long, hidden from everyone, maybe even from herself.

Again she gave me a sorrowful smile. "I'm not as brave as you are, Jiro."

There was nothing else to say, and it was getting dark. As I left her, I heard the soft pop of the cork being pulled.

* * *

I lay awake most of that night, exhausted but unable to sleep. When I did doze off, I dreamt of wandering the landscape I'd seen in Reza's mind, red cliffs and deep caves and tendrils of lava, with shades chasing me at every turn, creatures I could feel but never see. Dawn was a mercy, though I had no idea how I was going to get through the day. I helped Korrinth wash and dress; he was wandering badly, probably from the strain of the day before. I hated Sterlan all over again, even if what was happening to Korrinth wasn't really the indigo mage's fault.

I was taking a currant bun from our pack for Korrinth's breakfast when he spoke.

"Jiro…"

I dropped the bun and went to him. He held my face in his hands a moment, then stroked my head.

"I wanted to thank you, for what you've done. What you tried to do."

It took a moment for me to realize what he meant. I'd never wanted him to know I was helping. I didn't want him hurt that way.

"It's all right. I'm not angry. You would have made a good apprentice." He smiled. "And you have marvelous aim."

I tried to laugh, but the sound choked in my throat. I rested my chin on his shoulder, and he stroked my fur like he had when I was little, humming the old road-song again, the words all coming back to him safe and true, and we sang it softly, for the new road, together.

* * *

When I saw Myomé's face at the council later that morning, I knew Reza had told her everything. I felt like I should be angry, or at least afraid, but all I could manage was a kind of numb resignation. I didn't know what the penalty was for companions practicing magic, but my only concern was who would look after Korrinth if I were jailed or executed. What happened to me didn't matter.

Myomé rapped her staff against the stones. "Jiro, come forward."

I went to her side. She took something from a bag on the table and laid it on the floor before me.

The testing-stone.

I looked up at her, trying to read her expression, but she was as impassive as the stone itself. I looked at Reza, but she seemed to have become a dragon statue.

I thought of the landscapes in Reza's mind, and then I saw something different. Snowy mountains. Icy crags. All the vistas in myself I longed to explore.

Whatever the cost, I wasn't going to lock them away.

I looked back at Korrinth. He smiled, and then he nodded.

I closed my eyes and cleared my mind. I could smell the snow in the air, could feel the sharp wind ruffling my fur.

I opened my eyes and focused on the stone. It glowed, then flared, then burst into a green so bright it blinded me. When my vision cleared, the beam was still there, a beacon in the stone hall, lighting the way to the path inside myself.

Myomé smiled slow and wide. "Well proven. Take your place, Jiro."

I stared at her. "Take...?" I looked back at Korrinth. He was standing behind his chair now, and though there were tears in his eyes, he was smiling, too.

I padded over to the chair and jumped up, my claws scraping the wood as I found my balance. Brant grinned at me. Neely smiled uncertainly but waved. Sterlan wouldn't look at me, but I was perfectly fine with that.

Myomé's staff struck the stones. "I call upon each mage to bind their word to the will of this council. Sterlan, the Indigo."

"I am thus bound."

"Brant, the Yellow."

"I am thus bound." The lemur-thing chittered at me. I hissed at it, and it shut up.

"Neely, the—yes, I know—Ecru."

"I am thus bound."

"Jiro, the Emerald."

I tried to speak, but nothing came out. Myomé's gaze softened, and she spoke again, slowly, kindly.

"Jiro, the Emerald."

I sat up straighter. "I am thus bound."

"As am I," Myomé said, and the council proceeded.

* * *

That evening, with my head still buzzing from a combination of magic, giddy disbelief, and sheer shock, I met Reza at the wall again. The bottle of tonic sat beside her, and when I came closer, she uncorked it and poured the contents into the weeds.

"I thought you—"

"I did take a sip," she confessed. "Just to keep it all from being so… big."

I could understand that. The world hadn't felt this huge and scary and wondrous since I was a cub.

Reza set the empty bottle aside. "Myomé says it might be hard for me to control at first, but she's going to help me."

"You must have told her a lot."

She nodded. "We talked a long time last night. Almost all night. And argued. And cried. And laughed." She sighed, sending wisps of smoke into the twilight. "And so I'm an apprentice now." She laughed. "Can you believe it?"

We sat and watched the stars come out, all the new worlds glimmering over our heads. "Actually," I said, "I can."

* * *

And now it's been almost a year since my first day as the emerald mage. I'll go to the council hall alone this year, and Sadie Cross-Creek will come to look after Korrinth as well as Penelope. Sometimes Korrinth thinks he's still the emerald mage, and I've finally had to lock the workroom door with a spell to keep him from wandering in.

There are still good days and bad days on this road, and I know soon enough the bad ones will outnumber the good. But like all the other journeys we've taken, we'll reach the end together, and as I lie before the fire in our hearth, Korrinth stroking my fur, the landscape in my mind is calm and quiet, and snow falls gently, and all is well.

This was originally rejected for a furry fan convention's souvenir book. It was written as an introduction to the fandom for the neofan attending his or her first furry convention. You probably already know most of this, but you may not have realized how much furry fandom has been based upon cats.

Furry Fandom and Cats

by Fred Patten

You might say that a cat was responsible for furry fandom.

It all started with a painting in the Art Show at the 1980 World Science Fiction Convention, in Boston. The painting, of a funny-animal cat military pilot standing next to a photo-realistic futuristic warplane, was by Steven A. Gallacci, a USAF technical illustrator. He explained that he was working on a s-f series about a far-future interstellar civilization of bioengineered animal people that had forgotten their origins. Several fans got to talking, and discovered that their favorite stories were s-f about bioengineered or "uplifted" animals, and fantasies about anthropomorphic animals like Puss in Boots in the modern world. One thing led to another; the first all-furry convention was in Southern California in 1989; and today there are over 110 furry conventions around the world. The largest is the Anthrocon in Pittsburgh over the July 4th weekend, with 6,389 attendees in 2015, including 1,460 in full-body mascot-like "fursuits". Estimates of the total number of furry fans range from 60,000 to 100,000. In 2013, the Canadian government's Social Sciences and Humanities Research Council gave a C$75,000 grant to the International Anthropomorphic Research Project, headed by Dr. Kathy Gerbasi, a professor at the Niagara County [New York] Community College's psychiatry department, to study the fandom.

What is furry fandom? Wikipedia's definition is "a subculture interested in fictional anthropomorphic animal characters with human personalities and characteristics. Examples of anthropomorphic attributes include exhibiting human intelligence and facial expressions, the ability to speak, walk on two legs, and wear clothes. Furry fandom is also used to refer to the community of people who gather on the Internet and at furry conventions." Examples of furry characters range from talking but otherwise realistic animals like the rabbits in *Watership Down* by Richard Adams, and Einstein, the intelligent golden retriever in Dean R. Koontz's best-selling thriller *Watchers*, to comic-book and animated-cartoon characters like Bugs Bunny and Pogo Possum.

Furry fandom activities range from informal gatherings at fans' homes and public parks for picnics and BBQ cookouts, to outdoor camps of several days such as Canada's annual Camp Feral! and Brazil's Abando, or Zillercon, held each January at a lodge in the Austrian or Swiss Alps for skiing and other Winter activities (some in fursuits), to the conventions of hundreds or thousands held in large hotels. The annual Eurofurence has grown from nineteen fans in a German fan's parents' farmhouse to over 2,000 fans in the largest hotel in Berlin. Furry conventions almost all have an Art Show for paintings and sculpture of anthropomorphic characters, a Dealer's Den for anthropomorphic merchandise (including faux-fur animal ears and tails for those who do not have their own fursuits – real fur is condemned as barbaric), a Fursuit Parade for those with at least animal heads, paws, and tails, and a charity auction usually for a nearby animal care center or activity like guide dogs for the blind. Anthrocon 2015 donated $35,910 to the Western Pennsylvania Humane Society.

Furry fandom is unusual in being a fandom of original creations rather than of any famous (and copyrighted) animal characters. The fans who develop their own characters, rather than admiring high-profile funny animals or animated features with animal casts like DreamWorks' or Pixar's*, often build their own fursuits (a recent high-profile but tragic example was the neon-furred Lemonade Coyote, in real life Timothy C. McCormick, an Indianapolis Emergency Medical Services technician, killed in a traffic accident in 2013 – in this case, although he was a prominent performer in fursuit events, he had not built his own full-body fursuit; he had commissioned it from another furry fan), or write & draw their own Internet comic strips. Two leading examples are the U.S.'s *Housepets!* by Rick Griffin, and Australia's *Doc Rat* by "Jenner" (in real life a Melbourne General Practitioner).

* Despite this, many furry fans regularly watch *My Little Pony: Friendship Is Magic* or *Regular Show* and collect their comic books.

For the past fifteen years, furry fandom has had an often adversarial relationship with the press and TV media. This started in the late 1990s when the first "mainstream" articles appeared about people who dress in animal suits. It crystallized when Vanity Fair published "Pleasures of the Fur" in its March 2001 issue, making it look like all furry fans were sexual perverts who gathered at conventions to hold orgies while dressed in fursuits. Other publications and TV programs jumped on the bandwagon, such as the CSI: Crime Scene Investigation TV drama with its "Fur and Loathing" episode first broadcast on October 30, 2003, which brought its fictional detectives to a supposedly-typical furry fan convention to discover little more than fursuited sex orgies. The result was that many genuine furry conventions banned the press for years to discourage false "exposés".

This attitude has not disappeared. The *Fursday* Internet blog recently published "Eurofurence 2014: A Tale of Two Newspapers", about the British press' differing coverage of the 2014 furry convention in Berlin on August 20-24. *The Independent's* lead paragraph was a neutral, "This weekend 2000 self-proclaimed 'furries'—fans of anthropomorphic animals in cartoons, anime movies, literature and computer games—checked into a conference hotel in Berlin for Eurofurence, Europe's largest furry fandom convention." But *The Daily Mail's* lead paragraph was, "Grown adults dressed as sexualised cuddly toys met at a gathering for 'furries' in Germany at Eurofurence, Europe's largest furry fandom convention."

Even the favorable articles give the impression that almost all furry fans are full fursuit wearers, and that every furry fan's goal is to have his or her own fursuit. This ignores the many furry artists and writers, and those who just enjoy the social atmosphere without any desire to dress up. Several furry artists specialize in anthropomorphized feral and civilized felines, and earn a good part of their income from commissioned work. Furry fandom has two annual awards; the Ursa Major Awards (since 2001), a popular vote award administered by the independent Anthropomorphic Literature and Arts Association (ALAA), and the entirely literary Cóyotl Awards (since 2012), voted upon by members of the Furry Writers' Guild. The Ursa Major Award includes a Best Published Illustration category; the 2014 winner, Sabretooted Ermine, won with a cover painting showing mostly anthropomorphic felines at a snowy Christmas festival. Furry fandom supports three small presses: Sofawolf Press (since 1999), FurPlanet Productions (a book publisher since 2008), and Rabbit Valley (a book publisher since 2012).

Furry fans seem most drawn to feral animals like foxes, wolves, and bears. But there are plenty of cats among them, from Steven Gallacci's 1980 pioneering *Erma Felna of the EDF* (Extraplanetary Defense Force) to Mary E. Lowd's current Kipper Brighton and Lashonda Brooke, in such novels and short fiction as "When a Cat Loves a Dog". The favorite pets of a furry fan are often one or more cats. This is not surprising considering the popularity of anthropomorphized cats in mainstream culture: the newspaper strip, TV cartoon, comic-book, and Internet feline stars like *Garfield*, *Heathcliff*, and *Nyan Cat* (going back to the 1920s *Felix the Cat* and *Krazy Kat*); the old Hanna-Barbera *Top Cat* given new life as a 2015 computer-animated feature; the live-action theatrical and Internet favorites like *Grumpy Cat*, the cat villains of the two *Cats & Dogs* movies; the *Lolcats* and "I Can Has Cheezburger?"; and so much more.

Do you want more fantasy cat stories? Here are some.

A Bibliography for Bast

by Fred Patten

Here are all of the cat-fantasy short-fiction anthologies and collections from which many of these stories have been taken. A few are reprint volumes featuring classic cat fantasies by Stephen Vincent Benét, Algernon Blackwood, John Collier, Walter de la Mare, Stephen King, Saki, and others; or the cat-themed s-f of genre authors like Isaac Asimov, Ursula K. LeGuin, Fritz Leiber, Edgar Pangborn, and Cordwainer Smith. Too many have featured all-original stories that were published once and then have been forgotten. If you want more short cat fantasies than are in *Cats and More Cats*, here are where to look.

This does not include the anthologies and collections in which the majority of the stories may feature normal, unanthropomorphized cats, such as the *Cat Crimes* series edited by Ed Gorman & Martin H. Greenberg.

Bedtime Stories for Cats. Leigh Anne Jasheway. Andrews McMeel Publishing, April 1997.

Cat Futures and Other Feline Fiction. Nancy Fulda. AnthologyBuilder, September 2012.

The Cat Megapack; 25 Frisky Feline Tales, Old and New. Robert Reginald & Mary Wickizer Burgess, eds. Wildside Press, July 2013.

Cat Tales: Fantastic Feline Fiction. George H. Scithers, ed. Wildside Press, September 2008.

Cat Tales 2: Fantastic Feline Fiction. George H. Scithers, ed. Wildside Press, April 2010.

Catfantastic: Nine Lives and Fifteen Tales. Andre Norton & Martin H. Greenberg, eds. DAW Books, July 1989.

Catfantastic II. Andre Norton & Martin H. Greenberg, eds. DAW Books, January 1991.

Catfantastic III. Andre Norton & Martin H. Greenberg, eds. DAW Books, February 1994.

Catfantastic IV. Andre Norton & Martin H. Greenberg, eds. DAW Books, August 1996.

Catfantastic V. Andre Norton & Martin H. Greenberg, eds. DAW Books, August 1999.

Catopolis. Martin H. Greenberg & Janet Deaver-Pack, eds. DAW Books, December 2008.

Cats in Space and Other Places. Bill Fawcett, ed. Baen Books, April 1992.

Cats Triumphant! Jody Lynn Nye. Darkstar Books, December 2012.

A Constellation of Cats. Denise Little, ed. DAW Books, November 2001.

The Enchanted Cat. John Richard Stephens, ed. Prima Publishing & Communications, October 1990.

Fantastic Cat. Andre Norton & Martin H. Greenberg, eds. I Books, July 2004. (A retitled reprint of *Catfantastic II.*)

Feline Fetishes: Erotic Tales of Science Fiction. Corwin, ed. Circlet Press, May 1993.

Five Feline Fancies, by Kristine Kathryn Rusch. WMG Publishing, August 2012.

Furry Fantastic. Jean Rabe & Brian M. Thomsen, eds. DAW Books, October 2006.

Ghost Cats of the South. Randy Russell. John F. Blair, Publisher, October 2008.

Magic Tails. Martin H. Greenberg & Janet Pack, eds. DAW Books, September 2005.

Magicats! Jack Dann & Gardner Dozois, eds. Ace Books, July 1986.

Magicats II. Jack Dann & Gardner Dozois, eds. Ace Books, December 1991.

The Mystical Cat: An Anthology of All Things Feline. Dusty Rainbolt, ed. Sky Warrior Book Publishing, January 2013.

The Necromouser and Other Magical Cats. Mary E. Lowd. FurPlanet Productions, September 2015.

9 Tales o' Cats. Elizabeth Ann Scarborough. Amazon Digital Services, October 2011.

The Second Cat Megapack; 26 Frisky Feline Tales, Old and New. Robert Reginald & Mary Wickizer Burgess, eds. Wildside Press, July 2013.

Supernatural Cats: An Anthology. Claire Necker, ed. Doubleday, November 1972.

Tails of Wonder and Imagination: Cat Stories. Ellen Datlow, ed. Night Shade Books, February 2010.

The Third Cat Story Megapack; 25 Frisky Feline Tales, Old and New. Robert Reginald & Mary Wickizer Burgess, eds. Wildside Press, November 2013.

Twisted Cat Tales. Esther Schrader, ed. Coscom Entertainment, February 2006.

Twists of the Tale: An Anthology of Cat Horror. Ellen Datlow, ed. Dell, October 1996.
Weird Tales of Weird Tails: A Fine Selection of Supernatural Short Stories About Were-Cats and Other Ghoulish Felines. Read Books Design, July 2013.

Is the cat-fantasy short fiction an English-language literary quirk? All of these anthologies consist of American and British stories; there are none translated from other languages. The only French anthologies of which I know are filled with translated English-language stories. The exception is with German *katzenkrimi* short stories, and they have all been written since 2010, too late for most of these English-language anthologies.

Les Chats Fantastiques. Xavier Legrande-Ferronnière, ed. Jöelle Losfeld, September 1998. [French]

Les Chats Fantastiques: volume 2. Xavier Legrande-Ferronnière, ed. Jöelle Losfeld, May 2000. [French]

Auf leisen Pfoten kommt der Tod: 12 Katzenkrimis [*Death Comes on Silent Paws: 12 Cat Crimes*]. Tessa Korber, ed. Ars Vivendi Verlag, October 2013. [German]

Krimikätchen: Spannende Katzengeschichten [*Kitten Crimes: Exciting Cat Stories*]. Jone Heer, ed. Piper Verlag, February 2014. [German]

For those who want a fantasy or science-fiction complete novel (as opposed to a short story) featuring one or more talking cats (or other felines such as lions), I recommend the following. These are first editions; a reprint may be more easily available today. This list does not pretend to be complete; you may have other favorites.

Omitted are the popular mystery series told from a cat's viewpoint in which the cat investigates human crimes, or tags along while the human amateur detective, almost always a young woman, does so. Often the cat protagonist talks intelligently to the reader, or with other animals, but seldom to the humans. Examples include the *Mrs. Murphy* series by Rita Mae Brown, the *Midnight Louie* series by Carole Nelson Douglas, the *Magical Cats Mysteries* by Sofie Kelly, and the *Joe Grey* series by Shirley Rousseau Murphy. The first two currently include around two dozen novels each; the latter almost twenty. It's easy to get information about those. Other "cat cozies" only feature the human amateur detectives, with the cats as secondary characters.

The Abandoned. Paul Gallico. Knopf, September 1950.

The Adventures of Samurai Cat. Mark E. Rogers. Donald M. Grant, Publisher, May 1984.

The Autobiography of Foudini M. Cat. Susan Fromberg Schaeffer. Knopf, September 1997.

Between Darkness and Light. Lisanne Norman. DAW Books, January 2003. (Sholan Alliance #7)

The Big Catnap: A Sam the Cat Mystery. Linda Stewart. Cheshire House Books, August 2000. (Sam the Cat Detective #2)

The Big Meow. Diane Duane. Free e-book, February 2011. (Feline Wizards #3)

The Book of Night With Moon. Diane Duane. Hodder & Stoughton, July 1997. (Feline Wizards #1)

Breed to Come. Andre Norton. Viking Press, June 1972.

The Cat. Pat Gray. Dedalus Ltd., March 1997.

Cat House. Michael Peak. Signet Books, September 1989.

Cat Out of Hell. Lynne Truss. Hammer Books, March 2014.

Catacombs: A Tale of the Barque Cats. Anne McCaffrey & Elizabeth Ann Scarborough. Del Rey Books, December 2010.

Catalyst: A Tale of the Barque Cats. Anne McCaffrey & Elizabeth Ann Scarborough. Del Rey Books, January 2010.

Catamount. Michael Peak. Roc Books, March 1992.

Cathouse. Dean Ing. Baen Books, May 1990.

Cats in Cyberspace. Beth Hilgartner. Meisha Merlin Publishing, September 2001.

Chanur's Homecoming. C. J. Cherryh. Phantasia Press, July 1986. (Chanur #4)

Chanur's Legacy. C. J. Cherryh. DAW Books, August 1992. (Chanur #5)

Chanur's Venture. C. J. Cherry. DAW Books, September 1984. (Chanur #2)

The Children's Hour. Jerry Pournelle & S. M. Stirling. Baen Books, November 1991.

Clan Ground. Clare Bell. Atheneum, October 1984. (The Named #2)

Dark Nadir. Lisanne Norman. DAW Books, March 1999. (Sholan Alliance #5)

An Edge of the Forest. Agnes Smith. Viking Press, April 1959.

Father Christmas: Spam the Cat's First Christmas. Elizabeth Ann Scarborough. Gypsy Shadow Publishing Company, February 2012. (Spam the Cat Purranormal Mysteries #2)

Fearful Symmertries; The Return of Nohar Rajasthan. S. Andrew Swann. DAW Books, April 1999.

Felidae. Akif Pirinçci. Villard Books, February 1993. (Felidae 1; originally published in German, July 1989)

Felidae on the Road. Akif Pirinçci. Fourth Estate, July 1994. (Felidae 2; originally published in German as *Francis: Felidae II,* January 1993)

Feline Online: What Happens When a Smart Cat Surfs the Internet? Elyse Cregar. Tamerac Publishing Co., June 2001.

Fire Margins. Lisanne Norman. DAW Books, November 1996. (Sholan Alliance #3)

Forests of the Night. S. Andrew Swann. DAW Books, July 1993.

Fortune's Wheel. Lisanne Norman. DAW Books, August 1995. (Sholan Alliance #2)

The Girl Who Bit Back; The Adventures of Benedict and Blackwell [#2]. E. Earle. CreateSpace, August 2013.

The Girl With Nine Lives; The Adventures of Benedict and Blackwell [#1]. E. Earle. CreateSpace, June 2013.

The Girl With Ten Claws; The Adventures of Benedict and Blackwell [#3]. E. Earle. Court & Earle, April 2014.

Godsfire. Cynthia Felice. Pocket Books, June 1978.

The Golden Cat. Gabriel King. Century, November 1998.

The Great Catsby. Linda Stewart. Cheshire House Books, September 2013. (Sam the Cat Detective #4)

The Great Purr. Catherine Holm. North Star Press of St. Cloud, June 2014.

Guardian Cats and the Lost Books of Alexandria. Rahma Krambo. Reflected Light Books, June 2011.

Haydn of Mars. Al Sarrantonio. Ace Books, December 2004.

Huntress. Renee Carter Hall. FurPlanet Productions, September 2015.

In the Long Dark. Brian Carter. Century Hutchinson, November 1989.

The Jaguar Princess. Clare Bell. Tor Books, October 1993.

James, Fabulous Feline: Further Adventures of a Connoisseur Cat. Harriet Hahn. St. Martin's Press, June 1993.

James the Connoisseur Cat. Harriet Hahn. St. Martin's Press, October 1991.

Jennie. Paul Gallico. see *The Abandoned.*

Keeper of the City. Peter Morwood & Diane Duane. Bantam Spectra, August 1989. (a.k.a. *Guardians of the Three*: volume II)

The Kif Strike Back. C. J. Cherryh. Phantasia Press, April 1985. (Chanur #3)

The Kitty Killer Cult. Nick Smith. Luath Press Ltd., October 2004.

The Life and Opinions of the Tomcat Murr [*Lebens-Ansichten des Katers Murr*]. E. T. A. Hoffmann (translated by Anthea Bell). Penguin Classics, November 1999.

The Lighthouse, the Cat, and the Sea. Leigh W. Rutledge. Dutton, October 1999.

Majyk by Accident. Esther Friesner. Ace Books, August 1993.

Majyk By Design. Esther Friesner. Ace Books, November 1994.

Majyk by Hook or Crook. Esther Friesner. Ace Books, May 1994.

The Maltese Kitten. Linda Stewart. Cheshire House Books, December 2002. (Sam the Cat Detective #3)

A Manx McCatty Adventure: The Big Scratch. Christopher Reed. Ballantine Books, November 1988. [This has a sequel published only in Germany: *Der Fluch der Weißen Katze: Ein Katzenkrimi mit Manx McCatty* (Bastei Lübbe Verlag, October 1996).]

Milk Treading. Nick Smith. Luath Press Ltd., May 2002.

Mort(e). Robert Repino. Soho Press, January 2015.

The Nine Lives of Catseye Gomez. Simon Hawke. Warner Books/ Questar, October 1992.

Nine Lives to Murder. Marian Babson. HarperCollins, October 1992.

Off Leash. Daniel Potter. Fallen Kitten Productions, July 2015.
On Her Majesty's Wizardly Service. Diane Duane. Hodder & Stoughton, July 1998. (Feline Wizards #2)

Pet Noir, by Pati Nagle. Book View Café, August 2013.

PKP for President. Beth Hilgartner. Brigantine Media/Voyage, December 2011.

The Pride of Chanur. C. J. Cherryh. DAW Books, January 1982. (Chanur #1)

Queen of Mars. Al Sarrantonio. Ace Books, June 2006.

Ratha and Thistle-chaser. Clare Bell. McElderry Books, April 1990. (The Named #3)

Ratha's Challenge. Clare Bell. McElderry Books, January 1995. (The Named #4)

Ratha's Courage. Clare Bell. Imaginator Press, October 2008. (The Named #5)

Ratha's Creature. Clare Bell. Atheneum, March 1983. (The Named #1)

Razor's Edge. Lisanne Norman. DAW Books, December 1997. (Sholan Alliance #4)

Rememory. John Gregory Betancourt. Popular Library/Questar, October 1990.

Reserved for the Cat. Mercedes Lackey. DAW Books, November 2007.

Salve Roma! Akif Pirinçci. Amazon Digital Services, May 2012. (Felidae 5; originally published in German, March 2004 – Felidae 3, 4, 6, 7 and 8 are not yet translated into English)

Sam the Cat: Detective. Linda Stewart. Scholastic, Inc., February 1993. (Sam the Cat Detective #1)

Sebastian of Mars. Al Sarrantonio. Ace Books, October 2005.

Shades of Gray. Lisanne Norman. DAW Books, August 2010. (Sholan Alliance #8)

Shakespeare's Cat: A Play in Three Acts. Malcolm Willits. Hypostyle Hall, September 2004.

Solo's Journey. Joy Smith Aiken. Putnam, November 1987.

Spam Vs. the Vampire. Elizabeth Ann Scarborough. Gypsy Shadow Publishing Company, April 2011. (Spam the Cat Purranormal Mysteries #1)

Stray. A. N. Wilson. Walker Books Ltd., April 1987.

Stronghold Rising. Lisanne Norman. DAW Books, June 2000. (Sholan Alliance #6)

Sue Slate, Private Eye. Lee Lynch. Naiad Press, November 1989.

Tailchaser's Song. Tad Williams. DAW Books, November 1985.

To Visit the Queen. Diane Duane. see *On Her Majesty's Wizardly Service.*

Tomorrow's Sphinx. Clare Bell. McElderry Books, November 1986.

The Tour Bus of Doom: Spam and the Zombie Apocalyps-O. Elizabeth Ann Scarborough. Amazon Digital Services, September 2012. (Spam the Cat Purranormal Mysteries #3)

Turning Point. Lisanne Norman. DAW Books, December 1993. (Sholan Alliance #1)

Umbulala: Through the Eyes of a Leopard. Lena Godsall Bottriell. Questech Productions, November 1993.

Waiting for Gertrude: A Graveyard Gothic. Bill Richardson. Douglas & McIntyre, October 2001.

The Wild Road. Gabriel King. Arrow Books, November 1997.

Many of the above books have fine cat-themed cover paintings. Unfortunately, there are almost no fantasy cat art books for adults, with the exception of Susan Herbert's works. She specializes in "artistic reinterpretations" of famous paintings (and sometimes also movie posters) with their human subjects turned into anthropomorphic cats, and similar original works such as her *Opera Cats* with scenes from famous operas featuring anthropomorphized cats. Although it is not specifically about fantasy cats, *A Clowder of Cats* by Bryan Holme is an excellent collection of cat illustrations over the ages on sculptures, porcelain, paintings, dolls, postcards, posters, and more.

The Catropolitan Opera: The Centenary Celebration of the Grand Catropolitan Opera Company. Susan Herbert (text by Bill Meadowcane). Bulfinch Press, September 1997. [See also *Opera Cats*.]

The Cats Gallery of Art. Susan Herbert. Thames & Hudson, April 1990.

The Cats Gallery of Western Art. Susan Herbert. Thames & Hudson, March 2002.

Cats Galore: A Compendium of Cultured Cats. Susan Herbert. Thames & Hudson, September 2015.

The Cats History of Western Art. Susan Herbert. Thames & Hudson, March 1994.

A Clowder of Cats. Bryan Holme. Herbert Press, October 1985.

Diary of a Victorian Cat. Susan Herbert (text by Stanley Baron). Thames & Hudson, September 1991.

Impressionist Cats. Susan Herbert. Thames & Hudson, September 1992.

Medieval Cats. Susan Herbert. Thames & Hudson, March 1995.

Movie Cats. Susan Herbert. Thames & Hudson, August 2006.

Opera Cats. Susan Herbert. Thames & Hudson, September 1997. [This presents Herbert's paintings from *The Catropolitan Opera* without Meadowcane's text.]

Pre-Raphaelite Cats. Susan Herbert. Thames & Hudson, May 2014.

Shakespeare Cats. Susan Herbert. Thames & Hudson, April 1996.

Since *Cats and More Cats* is intended for adults, this list does not include many excellent children's and Young Adult fantasies such as the dozens of *Warriors* novels by "Erin Hunter" (Kate Cary, Cherith Baldry, and Tui Sutherland, coordinated by HarperCollins editor Victoria Holmes); the four *Catwings* novels by Ursula K. LeGuin; the four *Space Cat* novels by Ruthven Todd; the three *City Cats* novels and the three *The Lions of Lingmere* novels by Colin Dann; the three *Windrusher* novels by Victor DiGenti; the three *Toby, Apprentice*

Cat novels by Virginia Ripple; the three *Carbonel* novels by Barbara Sleigh; the two *Tygrine Cat* novels by Inbali Iserles; the two *Varjak Paw* novels by S. F. Said; or many stand-alone novels like *Time Cat* by Lloyd Alexander, *The King of the Cats* by P. T. Cooper, *The Cats of Tanglewood Forest* by Charles de Lint & Charles Vess, *Grimbold's Other World* and *The Stone Cage* by Nicholas Stuart Gray, *Captain Kidd's Cat* by Robert Lawson, *The Cat Master* by Bonnie Pemberton, *The Amazing Maurice and His Educated Rodents* by Terry Pratchett, *The Cats of Seroster* by Robert Westall; and, of course (even if it's not a novel) *Old Possum's Book of Practical Cats* by T. S. Eliot. Ask your public library's children's librarian for recommendations.

I would be remiss if I did not at least acknowledge the "paranormal romance" genre for women. These traditionally feature steamy romances between a human woman and a hunky, super-hot cat-man (in this case; there are also wolf-man, stallion-man, bear-man, zebra-man, and other species; plus centaurs, dinosaurs, dragons, Minotaurs, vampires, yetis – you name it), or a werecat or other feline shape-shifter. Sometimes they are about a woman who finds herself as the lone human in a clan of oversexed cat-men and –women. Examples: *Lion Eyes* by Jennifer Ashley, *Lion's Love* by Kate Kent, *Chasing Tail* (plus "Quick and Furry" sequels *Tailing Her, On Her Tail, Heads or Tails*, etc.) by Celia Kyle, *When an Alpha Purrs* by Eve Langlais, *Lion in Wait* by Lynn Red, or *The Lion God* by Ellie Saxx (lion-men), *The Panther's Desire* (a.k.a. "Were-Cats of Apple Creek" #1) by Emerald Ice or *Make Him Purr* by Anya Nowlan (panther-men), *Once a Cheetah* by Lola Kidd, *Tigress for Two* by Marissa Dobson or *Tiger Mine* by Angela Castle, *The Bobcat's Tale* by Georgette St. Clair, and many, many more. Practically all are self-published e-books; many are written under pseudonyms.

No attempt has been made to include fantasy cat novels in languages other than English. For the record, though, there is a tremendous number of untranslated original German detective novels featuring cat sleuths, usually called *katzenkrimi Bücher*. Examples include the *Kater Serrano* novels by Christine Anlauff, the *Felidae* novels by Akif Pirinçci, and the *roten Katze* novels by Catherine Ashley Morgen; and single novels such as *Kater Brown und die Klostermorde* by Ralph Sander. There are also German *Katzenromanen*; women's romances with sentient and often magical cats. Andrea Schacht specializes in those, such as her *Hexenkatze, Die Katz mit den goldenen Augen, MacTiger; Ein Highlander auf Samtpfoten* (set in Scotland in 1744), *Die Spionin im Kurbad, Zauberkatze,* and over a dozen others. Amazon.de has them all.

About the Authors

Clare Bell

Clare Bell (1952-current) is known for her *Ratha* series (also called the *Books of the Named*) about a society of prehistoric intelligent self-aware big cats and their female leader, Ratha. To create the Named, Bell carefully researched fossil species as well as modern lions, cheetahs, and pumas. The first, *Ratha's Creature*, appeared in 1983; the latest, *Ratha's Courage*, in 2008. Bell also wrote short stories for Andre Norton's anthology series *Catfantastic*, including "Bomber and the *Bismarck*". Set during WW II, this tale unveils the real heroes of the Allied action against the powerful German warship; an antiquated torpedo biplane known as a "Stringbag", a daring British pilot, and Bomber, a cat with an unusual magical gift.

Bell's current projects include a graphic novel adaptation of *Ratha's Creature* and a new book in the *Named* series. For more detailed information, series history, and bibliography, please see Wikipedia http://en.wikipedia.org/wiki/Clare_Bell

Bryan Derksen

Bryan Derksen (1976-current) hails from the far-off snowy north of Edmonton, Canada. (He started out in Winnipeg, but that was too snowy even for him.) His first love was the study of genetics, and during his university days he spent his spare time writing stories for his own amusement. But it turns out careers in writing or the study of genetics are hard to come by, so when it came time to venture out into the real world, he went with his love of programming instead. Fortunately, he landed a job with the game company

BioWare, where he was able to use those skills to help stories come to life—and also avoid getting too much of the real world on him in the process. He still fondly remembers the olden days of writing. Perhaps some day he will pick up the pen again to write a few more of his own.

P. M. Griffin

Pauline (P. M.) Griffin (1947-current) has been writing since her early childhood. She enjoys telling a good tale, and since she always works with characters and situations deeply interesting to her, she finds the research as rewarding as the scribbling/keying. Griffin's Irish love of story telling coupled with her passion for history, the natural world, and the above-mentioned research have to date resulted in twenty-one novels and twelve short stories, a number of award winners among them, all in the challenging realms of science fiction and fantasy. She has also written several nonfiction articles, primarily for the Brooklyn Aquarium Society's publication *Aquatica*, several of which have won the Editors Choice for Excellence Award.

She lives in Brooklyn, New York, with her cats Nickolette and Jinx and three tropical fish aquariums. Her website is www.pmgriffin.com

Renee Carter Hall

Renee Carter Hall (1977-current) works as a medical transcriptionist by day and as a writer, poet, and artist all the time. Her short fiction has appeared in a variety of publications, including the magazines *Strange Horizons, Daily Science Fiction,* and *STRAEON Quarterly,* and the anthologies *Bewere the Night,* ed. by Ekaterina Sedia (Prime Books, April 2011), *Hero's Best Friend; An Anthology of Animal Companions,* ed. by Scott M. Sandridge (Seventh Star Press, February 2014), *PULP! Two-Pawed Tales of Adventure,* ed. by Ianus J. Wolf (Rabbit Valley, September 2014), and *An Anthropomorphic Century,* ed. by Fred Patten (FurPlanet Productions, July 2015). She also has two novels available from furry publishers, the medieval fantasy *By Sword and Star* (Anthropomorphic Dreams Publishing, February 2012) and the tribal coming-of-age fantasy *Huntress* (FurPlanet Productions, September 2015). Her stories often include feline characters, and she's owned by a dilute calico who serves as her first beta reader. (If the cat falls asleep on the printout, it's good.)

She lives in West Virginia with her husband, their cat, and a ridiculous number of creative works-in-progress. Readers can find her online at www.reneecarterhall.com, on FurAffinity as Poetigress, and on Twitter as @RCarterHall.

John E. Johnston III

John Johnston III was born in East Los Angeles in 1953. He actually was a member of a famous L.A. County street gang for years. Eventually escaping to Texas in the seventies, he hung out at Tex-Mex restaurants, had too much fun at the Armadillo World Headquarters, supported Oat Willie, learned The Zen Of The Cowboy, mastered barbecuing, and finally finished graduate school at the University of Texas.

After that he gave up on fun for marriage, a career, teaching at Louisiana State University, and the occasional spasm of fiction and non-fiction. He lives on a Louisiana bayou near the LSU Lakes and has four dogs: Lady, a Dalmatian/spotted killing machine (Lady 12, poisonous snakes 0, 4th quarter); Oscar, the grouchy dachshund-in-charge; Kate, the Amazing Watchdachshund; and Zoey, a wonderful tiny miniature Chihuahua who is - of course - everyone's favorite.

Mary E. Lowd

Mary E. Lowd writes stories and collects creatures. She's had more than sixty short stories and three novels published, including her collection of cat stories, *The Necromouser and Other Magical Cats* (FurPlanet Productions, September 2015). Her fiction has received an Ursa Major Award and two Cóyotl Awards. Meanwhile, she's collected one husband, two children, and a bevy of cats and dogs. The stories, creatures, and Mary all live together in a crashed spaceship disguised as a house in Oregon. Find out more at www.marylowd. com.

Andre Norton

Andre Norton (1912-2005) was born Alice Mary Norton. In 1934 she legally changed her name to Andre Norton; her first published book that year was under that name. She wrote Young Adult adventures including pirate, Western, and spy novels for the next fifteen years. She also worked at the Cleveland Public Library until she retired due to ill health in 1950. Her first s-f novel was *Star Man's Son, 2250 A.D.* (Harcourt, Brace, August 1952). She worked at Gnome Press during the 1950s, coming to specialize in s-f. In 1958 she became a full-time s-f writer, segueing into high fantasy in the 1960s. She was nominated for or won numerous s-f and fantasy awards. Her *Quag Keep* (Atheneum, February 1978) was the first novel with an acknowledged *Dungeons & Dragons*-type plot. She was the first woman to be named a Gandalf Grand Master of Fantasy and a SFWA Grand Master; she was a co-founder of the Swordsmen and Sorcerers' Guild of America (SAGA); and she was the first inductee of the Science Fiction and Fantasy Hall of Fame. Norton moved for her health to Florida in 1966 and to Murfreesboro, Tennessee in 1997, where she died in 2005.

Jody Lynn Nye

Jody Lynn Nye (1957-current) lists her main career activity as "spoiling cats." She lives northwest of Chicago with one of the above and her husband, author and packager Bill Fawcett. She has written over forty books, including *The Ship Who Won* (Baen Books, April 1994) with Anne McCaffrey, eight books with Robert Asprin, (edited) a humorous anthology about mothers, *Don't Forget Your Spacesuit, Dear!* (Baen Books, July 1996), and over 140 short stories. Her latest books are *Rhythm of the Imperium* (Baen Books, December 2015), Book Three in her *View from the Imperium* series, and *Wishing On a Star* (Arc Manor Publishing, November 2015) with Angelina Adams.

Jean Rabe

Jean Rabe (1957-current) tosses tennis balls to her dogs when she isn't writing. When she isn't editing, she tugs on old socks with them. She's working to finish her first murder mystery…she put one of her dogs in it. But she's not new to writing. The author of thirty fantasy and science fiction novels, and about eighty short stories, Jean maintains a website that she's getting better about updating—jeanrabe.com. A former newspaper reporter, she wrote a true crime novel with F. Lee Bailey—*When the Husband is the Suspect*. Among her other novels are the *Dragonlance* series The Stonetellers (*The Rebellion*, August 2007; *Death March*, August 2008; *Goblin Nation*, October 2009) and Dhamon (*Downfall*, May 2000; *Betrayal*, June 2001; *Redemption*, July 2002) from Wizards of the Coast; and the *Finest* trilogy (*The Finest Creation*, November 2004; *The Finest Choice*, September 2005; *The Finest Challenge*, September 2006) from Tor.

She enjoys photography, fantasy football, visiting military museums, and attending writing conventions.

Dusty Rainbolt

Dusty Rainbolt, ACCBC, is the award-winning author of eleven books including the paranormal mystery *Death Under the Crescent Moon* (Yard Dog Press, February 2013), the comedy novel *All the Marbles* (Yard Dog Press, July 2003), and the fantasy series *The Four Redheads of the Apocalypse* (Yard Dog Press, June 2006), written with three other Redheaded authors. She is the editor of *The Mystical Cat* (Sky Warrior Book Publishing, January 2013) which includes "A Spoiled Rotten Cat Lives Here". Dusty's nonfiction books include: *Kittens for Dummies, Cat Wrangling Made Easy: Maintaining Peace & Sanity in Your Multicat Home*, and *Ghost Cats: Human Encounters with Feline Spirits*.

She's worked as a free-lance journalist since the late 1980s, and began specializing in pet journalism in 1995. Dusty's the editor-in-chief of AdoptAShelter.com, a free shop-to-donate website that benefits animal charities. Dusty is past president of the Cat Writers' Association. Dusty's books, columns, reviews and articles have won more than 50 writing awards. In addition to AdoptAShelter.com, she regularly appears on Catster.com and other publications. She has bottle fed over 800 orphan kittens, and rescued more than 700 adults and weaned kittens. She's an associate certified cat behavior consultant and member of International Association of Animal Behavior Consultants.

Kristine Kathryn Rusch

Kristine Kathryn Rusch (1960-current), a *USA Today* bestselling writer, often writes about cats, primarily because she lives with too many cats. (Her husband rescues them routinely.) She has a short story collection called *Five Feline Fancies* (WMG Publishing, August 2012; two fantasies, one s-f, and two mysteries), and cats often show up in her science fiction or in the romance novels she writes under the name Kristine Grayson.

Elizabeth Ann Scarborough

Elizabeth Ann Scarborough (1947-current) has worked for two black cats, Pancho the fuzzy and Cisco the sleek, since October 2002. Both of her feline overlords are now 13 years old and are highly affectionate, still very active, and extremely entitled, as is their hereditary right. They closely attend her writing career, as her computer is located in proximity to the Fancy Feast sack and the food dishes.

James M. Ward

Obviously, James M. Ward was born (1951-current) and has lived a pleasantly long time. He married his high school sweetheart, and has three unusually charming sons; Breck, James, and Theon.

They in turn have given him six startlingly charming grandchildren; Keely, Miriam, Sophia, Preston, Teagan, and Noah (now 18 months old). In that time James wrote the first science fiction role-playing game, *Metamorphosis Alpha*; he wrote the first Apocalypse RPG *Gamma World*, he worked for TSR and did lots of D&D and AD&D things; and designed the best selling *Spellfire* and *Dragon Ball Z* CCGs.

He has written all manner of things: the *Dragon Lairds* board game, the two *Halcyon Blythe* novels, the *My Precious Present* card game; and the RPG supplement *Of Gods & Monsters*. He's currently working with three others at Eldritch Enterprises (eldritchent.com). He reads a lot, he greatly enjoys fencing with a rapier, and he constantly gets beat in board games. Right now he finds himself writing role-playing products for the small company that helps pay his bills. Please check out *77 Lost Worlds* (an Apocalypse RPG), the *Epsion* kickstarter by Goodman Games, and *Monty's Hauls Tower of Doom* generic RPG adventure.

Lawrence Watt-Evans

Lawrence Watt-Evans (1954-current) has spent most of his life in the company of cats, anywhere from one to fourteen at a time. His current lone feline, Samantha, is on her third writer, having previously lived with George Scithers and John Betancourt. He writes stories for a living, and has done so for some thirty-five years—mostly fantasy, but also science fiction, horror, and whatever else editors will buy. He's probably best known for the Legends of Ethshar, starting with *The Misenchanted Sword* (Del Rey/Ballantine, September 1985) and the Obsidian Chronicles, starting with *Dragon Weather* (Tor, October 1999).

Although a New Englander by birth and upbringing, he now lives in Takoma Park, Maryland, just outside Washington, D.C.

About the Artists

<u>Donryu</u>

Donryu was born in Pensacola, Florida years before the internet was a thing, and moved all over the East Coast before finally settling in Michigan for 15 years. He became interested in drawing at a young age, and was inspired by his older brother, Disney, and various anime.

After graduating high school he made a mad dash for Atlanta, Georgia, where he went to art school majoring in animation and storyboarding. He then apprenticed under an animator where he completed his training.

Donryu has been in the furry fandom since 2000 and has enjoyed every year he's been a part of it.

About the Editor

Fred Patten

Fred Patten (1940-current) joined the Los Angeles Science Fantasy Society in 1960 while in college, and has been an active s-f & fantasy fan ever since. He began writing for and publishing fanzines in 1961 (see http://www.zinewiki.com/Salamander), and has written over a thousand reviews of anthropomorphic literature since 1962, irregularly for s-f fanzines in the 1960s, 1970s, and 1980s; for *Yarf!* from 1990 to 2003, for *Claw & Quill* in 2004-2005, for *Anthro* from 2005 to 2008, for *Renard's Menagerie* in 2008, for *Flayrah* from 2011 to 2014, and for *Dogpatch Press* since 2014. He has written two non-fiction books and edited eight anthologies of furry fiction. He founded the Ursa Major Awards and has been on its administrative Anthropomorphic Literature and Arts Association since 2001. He is a member of the Furry Writers' Guild and the Furry Hall of Fame. He co-founded Japanese anime fandom in 1977, and was awarded the Comic-Con's Inkpot Award in 1980 for helping to introduce anime to America. He writes a weekly column on animation, *Funny Animals and More*, for Jerry Beck's Cartoon Research.

A stroke in 2005 has left him hospitalized, from which he carries on his fan activities via a MacBook Pro laptop.

www.ingramcontent.com/pod-product-compliance
Lightning Source LLC
Chambersburg PA
CBHW071850020726
47502CB00003B/679